PENGUIN BOOKS

My Oedipus Complex and Other Stories

Frank O'Connor was the pseudonym of Michael O'Donovan, who was born at Cork in 1903. Largely self-educated, he began to prepare a collected edition of his works at the age of twelve and later worked as a librarian, translator and journalist. When quite young he learned to speak Irish and saturated himself in Gaelic poetry, music and legend. When he was interned by the Free State Government he took the opportunity to learn several languages, but it was in Irish that he wrote a prize-winning study of Turgenev on his release. 'A.E.' began to publish his poems, stories and translations in the *Irish Statesman*. Meanwhile a local clergyman remarked of him, when he produced plays by Ibsen and Chekhov in Cork, that: 'Mike the moke would go down to posterity at the head of the pagan Dublin muses.' Frank O'Connor lived in Dublin and had an American wife, two sons and two daughters. He published *Guests of the Nation*, his first book, in 1931, and then followed over thirty volumes, largely of short stories, in addition to plays. Frank O'Connor died in 1966.

Julian Barnes is the author of ten novels, two volumes of short stories and three collections of essays. His work has been translated into more than thirty languages, and has won many awards. In 2004 he was made a Commandeur de l'Ordre des Artes et des Lettres.

FRANK O'CONNOR

My Oedipus Complex and Other Stories

With an Introduction by JULIAN BARNES

PENGUIN BOOKS

PENGUIN BOOKS

Published by the Penguin Group
Penguin Books Ltd, 80 Strand, London WC2R ORL, England
Penguin Group (USA) Inc., 375 Hudson Street, New York, New York 10014, USA
Penguin Group (Canada), 90 Eglinton Avenue East, Suite 700, Toronto, Ontario, Canada M4P 2Y3
(a division of Pearson Penguin Canada Inc.)
Penguin Ireland, 25 St Stephen's Green, Dublin 2, Ireland
(a division of Penguin Books Ltd)
Penguin Group (Australia), 250 Camberwell Road, Camberwell, Victoria 3124,
Australia (a division of Pearson Australia Group Pty Ltd)
Penguin Books India Pvt Ltd, 11 Community Centre,
Panchsheel Park, New Delhi – 110 017, India
Penguin Group (NZ), cnr Airborne and Rosedale Roads, Albany,
Auckland 1310, New Zealand (a division of Pearson New Zealand Ltd)
Penguin Books (South Africa) (Pty) Ltd, 24 Sturdee Avenue,
Rosebank 2196, South Africa

Penguin Books Ltd, Registered Offices: 80 Strand, London WC2R ORL, England

www.penguin.com

The texts used in this edition are taken from *Guests of the Nation*, first published by Macmillan 1931,
Bones of Contention, first published by Macmillan 1936, *Crab Apple Jelly*, first published by Macmillan
1944, *The Common Chord*, first published by Macmillan 1947, *Traveller's Samples*, first published by
Macmillan 1951, *The Stories of Frank O'Connor*, first published in the United States by Alfred A. Knopf
1952 and in Great Britain by Hamish Hamilton 1953, *More Stories of Frank O'Connor*, first published by
Alfred A. Knopf 1954, *Domestic Relations*, first published in the United States by Alfred A. Knopf and in
Great Britain by Hamish Hamilton 1957, *Collection Two*, first published by Macmillan 1964, *Collection
Three*, first published by Macmillan 1969, and *The Cornet-Player Who Betrayed Ireland*, first published in
Ireland by Poolbeg 1981

This selection published in Penguin Books 2005
010

Texts copyright © Literary Executors of the Estate of Frank O'Connor, 1931, 1933, 1936, 1940, 1942,
1944, 1945, 1947, 1950, 1951, 1952, 1954, 1955, 1956, 1957, 1959, 1964, 1966

Introduction and selection copyright © Julian Barnes, 2005
All rights reserved

The moral right of the author and introducer has been asserted

Set in 10/12.5pt Monotype Dante
Typeset by Rowland Phototypesetting Ltd, Bury St Edmunds, Suffolk
Printed in England by Clays Ltd, St Ives plc

ISBN-13: 978-0-141-18787-7

www.greenpenguin.co.uk

ALWAYS LEARNING   **PEARSON**

Contents

Introduction by Julian Barnes   vii
A Note on the Selection   xiv

The Genius   1
My Oedipus Complex   12
First Confession   23
The Study of History   31
The Man of the World   41
Guests of the Nation   49
Machine-Gun Corps in Action   61
Soirée Chez une Belle Jeune Fille   75
Jumbo's Wife   88
The Cornet-Player Who Betrayed Ireland   102
There is a Lone House   111
News for the Church   131
The Mad Lomasneys   139
Uprooted   164
The Majesty of the Law   183
The Luceys   192
After Fourteen Years   208
Peasants   213
The Bridal Night   221

Contents

A Thing of Nothing 228

Michael's Wife 243

A Bachelor's Story 259

Fish for Friday 272

A Story by Maupassant 284

In the Train 294

The Corkerys 308

Old-Age Pensioners 322

The Long Road to Ummera 330

The Wreath 339

The Mass Island 351

Introduction

I first came to Frank O'Connor by way of a possessive pronoun. The fiction shelves of a secondhand bookshop in Dublin proposed an antique orange Penguin: author's name in white, title in black, no strident capitals on the spine, and the cover taken up with what was in those days a come-on – a blurry author photo. It was not this, or the distantly familiar name, that made me buy it (the original 3/6d now having become six euros), but the title: *My Oedipus Complex and Other Stories*. It was the slyly inviting 'My' that did it. A lesser writer might have settled for 'The', and the book would have stayed on its shelf.

Since his death in 1966, a respectful forgettingness has settled over Frank O'Connor. Indeed, he is now better remembered – and more in print – in the United States than in either Britain or Ireland itself. Why should this have come about? Perhaps because in his large output – of novels, stories, plays, essays, travel books, biography, poetry and translations from the Irish – there is not one particular title to which his name is indelibly attached. Perhaps because his finest work is in the short story, a medium more vulnerable over time. Perhaps because he doesn't require academic explication; in which he resembles some of the writers he most revered – Maupassant, Chekhov, Turgenev. Perhaps because he spent many years away in America, where his best work first appeared: the *New Yorker* ran fifty-one of his stories in a two-decade-long association beginning in 1945. Perhaps because he could be as harsh about the land of his birth as other Irish writers: it was 'a country ruled by fools and blackguards', where life was 'emptiness and horror' – though a country to which he returned, in 1961, for the last five years of his life. Even cumulatively, these reasons seem insufficient.

He was born Michael O'Donovan in Cork in 1903, a demographic rarity at that time: both a late child and an only child. His mother, Mary, had been born in 1865, a date she long concealed from her son; she was an orphan who channelled into him her social and cultural ambitions. His father, Michael, was an old soldier proud of his two pensions from the British Army, a bandsman and navvy, given to powerful drinking bouts which blighted family life. Frank was a self-admitted mother's boy and sissy, who deep into adulthood fought his father for possession of the woman of the house. He left school at fourteen, and worked on the railways as a clerk in the flourishing misdirected-goods department. At fifteen he started doing 'odd jobs', as he put it, for the IRA; but proved a 'wretchedly bad soldier', and was interned by the Irish Free State for a year in 1922–3. Upon release he became a librarian, teacher, translator and man of the theatre, first in Cork then Dublin, rising to become director of the Abbey Theatre. After retiring from that post in 1939, he lived from his writing, with the help of teaching stints at American universities.

Much of his early life, up to and including internment, finds its way into his stories; his later life less (or less obviously) so. His first volume of autobiography, *An Only Child*, is full of brief anecdotes and asides which are recognizably the germ of later stories: how he drank his father's pint; how he decided he was a changeling; how he determined to murder his embarrassing grandmother; how he sought to apply the English public-school ethic in an Irish trades school. Each is, however, only the germ: the final story has less to do with its authenticity of origin, everything to do with the manner of its development. William Maxwell, who was O'Connor's editor at the *New Yorker* and thereby his great friend, said that Frank, despite being an only child, 'behaved as if he were the oldest of a large family of boys and girls'. Such a transforming instinct is a good start for a fiction writer.

So is listening carefully – which may come in many forms, from a child's eavesdropping upwards. In 1959, Maxwell received a letter from one of his magazine's readers asking when to expect a new story from another of the Irish writers he published, Maeve Brennan. He showed the letter to Brennan, who judged its tone (or the request itself) impertinent, and concocted a fantastical reply purporting to come from Maxwell himself. The editor is terribly sorry to have to inform the reader that 'our poor Miss Brennan' has died – indeed, she shot herself ('in the back with the aid of a small handmirror') at the foot of the main altar of St Patrick's Cathedral on Shrove Tuesday. The letter continues: 'Frank O'Connor was where he usually is in the afternoons, sitting in a confession box pretending to be a priest and giving penance to some old woman and he heard the shot and he ran out . . .' Brennan is making fun of her fellow-countryman and his subject-matter; but also of the writer's love of hearing other people's innermost secrets – which he, unlike the priest, will subsequently betray.

O'Connor himself put the point a different way. In *An Only Child* he describes himself as 'a natural collaborationist'. By which he means that, 'Like Dolan's ass, I went a bit of the way with everybody.' An initial biddability followed, at a certain point, by an instinctive intransigence. When he was an internee, Republican prisoners across Ireland were called out on hunger strike against the Free State; O'Connor was one of only three among the thousand prisoners in his camp who both voted and spoke against the decision. The writer has a similar stance, and duty: a bit of the way, but no further; join with others, inhabit their lives at will, but remain mulishly yourself.

Imaginative sympathy, and then, in rendering the lives of others, a furious – and, to some, infuriating – perfectionism. William Maxwell, who knew writers well, said that, 'If there is an alarming object in this world it is a writer delighted with something he has just written. There is no worse sign.' O'Connor almost never gave such a sign. Though he liked to write a quick first draft – obeying Maupassant's injunction to 'Get black on white' – everything thereafter was itchy dissatisfaction and constant revision. His story 'The Little Mother' exists in seventeen versions, published and unpublished; sometimes the count rose as high as fifty drafts. A story might eventually appear in a magazine, but that would not be the end of revisions. Then it might be published in volume form, and still O'Connor would go on tinkering. Finally it might be Selected or Collected, yet there was always further work to be done. All for the sake of what Maxwell, writing about his friend, called 'The happiness of getting it down right.'

Yeats, an admired and loved – if tricky – colleague at the Abbey Theatre, who encouraged O'Connor and published two volumes of his translations from the Irish, said famously – perhaps too famously – that 'O'Connor is doing for Ireland what Chekhov did for Russia.' This was promotionally useful, as such statements tend to be (Richard Ellmann called him 'Flaubert among the bogs', which maybe doesn't work as well), but only true in part. Evidence of O'Connor's love for Chekhov can be adduced from his edition of the writer, which Maxwell inherited and described: 'So lived with – turned down corners, turned down sides of pages, coffee stains, whiskey stains, and perhaps tears.' But the Irishman also knew the dangers of emulation: 'He's inimitable,' he said of Chekhov to his *Paris Review* interviewer, 'a person to read and admire and worship – but never, never, never to imitate.' If seeking Russian connections, we might do better proposing a triangulation consisting of Gorky (O'Connor once described himself as 'an aspiring young writer who wanted to know Ireland as Gorky had known Russia'), Isaak Babel ('the man who has influenced me most') and Turgenev ('my hero among writers'). O'Connor's first published work, written as an internee, was a prize-winning essay in Irish about Turgenev.

And even if we allow that some kind of Chekhovian or Russian mapping is going on, the Irishman's case has an additional complication. Yes, he described without parallel a certain Ireland – provincial, priest-dominated, impoverished, hard-drinking, secretive, generous, collusive – at a certain time: after independence but before modernization or prosperity or (a key factor in numerous stories) contraception. His stories both look and are profoundly Irish in character and setting (there are occasional excursions among the Irish living in England). Yet they are by no means all Irish in origin. Some writers seek to prove their universality – or, at least, their appetite and diversity – by setting their work in different places and times. O'Connor did the opposite. English or American life might provide a story, an anecdote, a potentially useful scrap, but if he came to write it, he would quite deliberately repatriate it to Ireland. In 1955 he was living in Annapolis, and discovered three impeccably 'Irish' stories among local Annapolitans, including 'The Man of the World'. The reasons for such transportation are partly defensive – stick with the voice, and voices, that you know and can render best – but also more high-minded: the external details of a story may vary, but its inner truth is universal. O'Connor liked to cite the story of Lord Edward Fitzgerald meeting an old (American) Indian woman and being told that as far as she was concerned, humanity was 'all one Indian'.

He was to a large degree that paradoxical thing, an oral prose writer. His stories aim for your ear rather than your eye; they depend upon the sense of 'an actual man, talking' – one whose first task is to settle, even lull you (thus sometimes provoking the delusion that an easy, even sentimental, ride lies ahead). In this type of writing, verisimilitude of tone and psychological truth matter more than a flamboyant comparison or a self-advertising phrase. There is the narrative voice, and, within it, the voices: variations and modulations of speech are central to the representation of character. In this, O'Connor's fiction is consonant with his own nature: 'If I remember somebody, for instance, that I was very fond of, I don't remember what he or she looked like, but I can absolutely take off the voices.'

Maxwell judged his friend capable of 'marvellous descriptions' but regretted that they 'didn't interest him'. The *New Yorker* editor would ask what a particular room, or house, in a story looked like, and O'Connor might admit that he didn't really know; though he might ruefully agree to put up a few walls and doors if that was what the customer wanted. On Maxwell's part, this was the reaction of an editor dutifully worrying about his magazine's less imaginative readers; but it was also the response of a practising novelist to a short-story writer. The novelist historically pays more attention to fixtures and fittings than does the creator of the more compacted and poetic form. As O'Connor put it, the novel depends on creating a sense of continuing life, whereas the short story need merely suggest such continuance.

On one occasion, when Maxwell was locationally baffled, O'Connor sent him a couple of sketches to explain his story, marked with helpful annotations like 'Window', 'Door', 'Hallway', 'Table', 'Father' and 'Son'. But this story – about a child ashamed of his parents – survives, fifty years on, not because of any decorative infill, but because of its narrative structure and psychological truth, because O'Connor remembered and understood the full peculiarity and relentlessness of children. He knew that 'Children . . . see only one side of any question and because of their powerlessness see it with hysterical clarity.' Hysterical clarity: in this respect the child is father to the writer. The adult may learn to view others with more tolerance, tenderness and wisdom; but the writer must retain the child's absolutism of eye, whether writing about childhood itself, or war, or marriage, or solitude, about the life of a tramp or the life of a priest.

The child's-eye view. O'Connor describes in *An Only Child* how as a small boy he had a great taste for sitting on roofs. 'I was always very fond of heights, and afterwards it struck me that reading was only another form of height, and a more perilous one. It was a way of looking beyond your back yard into the neighbours'.' This rooftop reader is an additional father to the writer: first you watch the lives of others, later you imagine them.

O'Connor was to exploit this remembrance of height and reading in one of his best stories about childhood, 'The Man of the World', in which two boys, eager for the secrets of adult life, spy on a neighbouring house from a darkened attic. The child as spy as reader as peeping tom as writer.

O'Connor was a most untheoretical writer whose favourite lines from *Faust* were: 'Grey, my dear friend, is all your theory, and green the golden tree of Life.' Nevertheless, like many another literary practitioner who spends time in academe, he ended up with a theory of the short story. This he codified in *The Lonely Voice*, a study of the form which has since become a textbook in American writing schools. 'There is in the short story at its most characteristic,' he proposes, 'something we do not often find in the novel – an intense awareness of human loneliness.' The story deals especially with 'submerged population groups', which helps explain its strength in America, where such groups abound. They contain the form's characteristic personnel: 'outlawed figures wandering about the fringes of society'.

How far would Dolan's ass go with this theory? It's certainly true that many of O'Connor's characters have sadness and loneliness at their centre; but this often seems to make them typical, rather than atypical, of the society to which they belong – one the writer himself described as 'potty, lonely'. Take O'Connor's priests, for example. These are rarely of the gentle, twinkly sort; they tend to be clever, manipulative, fierce, worldly, temptable and despairingly consumed by the life they have chosen. In this they are also analogues of the writer. As O'Connor put it,

The attraction of the religious life for the story-teller is overpowering. It is the attraction of a sort of life lived, or seeking to be lived, by standards other than those of this world, one which, in fact, resembles that of the artist. The good priest, like the good artist, needs human rewards, but no human reward can ever satisfy him.

But if the priest feels an unassuageable loneliness, this hardly makes him an 'outlawed figure' on the 'fringes of society'. Priests were central to Irish society at the time O'Connor was describing. And quite a few others among his cast list might be surprised to discover that their maker considered them submerged and marginalized. Perhaps those priests are not so much outlawed as self-outlawed; and what O'Connor unfailingly locates is the loneliness at the heart of those who are regarded by others, and even by themselves, as normal, assimilated members of society.

Sometimes the writer doesn't know best. Or, at least, someone else may know best as well. As Maxwell affectionately put it in the course of one editorial disagreement, 'Of course you are right about the story, and I am too.' Sometimes the quest for perfection can lead to over-revision; a writer may know his work too well, and find looseness in what was naturalness. Thus O'Connor turned against most of the stories in his first collection, *Guests of the Nation* (1931), on the grounds that they were 'extravagant' and insufficiently revised. He excluded all of them from his first selected, and allowed only one into his second. This seems to me too harsh a judgement; these early stories – many about the Civil War – are an essential part of his work. Here are times of wrenching national division and military chaos described with the verve of a young writer and participant. The older man might have controlled them more, but then the older man might also have filtered out some of the verve.

O'Connor's tireless revisionism sprang from the mania and the quandary at the heart of writing: how to find the balance between life's shapelessness and artistic form, between naturalness and control. In his finest work, this balance is effortlessly achieved (because effortfully achieved). His second wife Harriet O'Donovan Sheehy once described a revealing tic of her husband's: 'There was almost nothing in the world Michael coveted more than someone else's pen or pencil and I often found several sharp pencils and a little metal pencil sharpener in his pajama pockets.' Such is the writer's nature: one who will look down from his rooftop into your back yard, then go part of the way with you, then hear your confession, and then steal your pencil. The contents of a pajama pocket are a give-away: about the writer's covetousness; also about the writer's constant readiness.

Julian Barnes

A Note on the Selection

O'Connor published six volumes of stories in his lifetime: *Guests of the Nation* (1931), *Bones of Contention* (1936), *Crab Apple Jelly* (1944), *The Common Chord* (1947), *Traveller's Samples* (1951) and *Domestic Relations* (1957). He also chose *The Stories of Frank O'Connor* (1952), followed by *More Stories* (1954), which he later reworked as *Collection Two* (1964). After his death his widow, Harriet O'Donovan Sheehy, published *Collection Three* (1969) and *The Cornet-Player Who Betrayed Ireland* (1981). I have chosen thirty stories from the hundred and fifty or so these books contain. O'Connor was very attentive to the ordering of his stories within each volume; I have followed his lead, preferring a kind of overall narrative to the hazards of chronological order. So the book begins with stories about childhood; then war; then peace and adulthood; then age and death. This is not, however, intended to make the contents seem more autobiographical than they are.

O'Connor's letters to and from William Maxwell were published as *The Happiness of Getting It Down Right*, edited by Michael Steinman (Alfred A. Knopf, 1996).

The Genius

1

Some kids are cissies by nature but I was a cissy by conviction. Mother
had told me about geniuses; I wanted to be one, and I could see for myself
that fighting, as well as being sinful, was dangerous. The kids round the
Barrack where I lived were always fighting. Mother said they were savages,
that I needed proper friends, and that once I was old enough to go to
school I would meet them.

My way, when someone wanted to fight and I could not get away, was
to climb on the nearest wall and argue like hell in a shrill voice about Our
Blessed Lord and good manners. This was a way of attracting attention,
and it usually worked because the enemy, having stared incredulously
at me for several minutes, wondering if he would have time to hammer
my head on the pavement before someone came out to him, yelled something like 'blooming cissy' and went away in disgust. I didn't like being
called a cissy but I preferred it to fighting. I felt very like one of those poor
mongrels who slunk through our neighbourhood and took to their heels
when anyone came near them, and I always tried to make friends with
them.

I toyed with games, and enjoyed kicking a ball gently before me along
the pavement till I discovered that any boy who joined me grew violent
and started to shoulder me out of the way. I preferred little girls because
they didn't fight so much, but otherwise I found them insipid and lacking
in any solid basis of information. The only women I cared for were
grown-ups, and my most intimate friend was an old washerwoman called
Miss Cooney who had been in the lunatic asylum and was very religious.
It was she who had told me all about dogs. She would run a mile after

anyone she saw hurting an animal, and even went to the police about them, but the police knew she was mad and paid no attention.

She was a sad-looking woman with grey hair, high cheekbones and toothless gums. While she ironed, I would sit for hours in the hot, steaming, damp kitchen, turning over the pages of her religious books. She was fond of me too, and told me she was sure I would be a priest. I agreed that I might be a bishop, but she didn't seem to think so highly of bishops. I told her there were so many other things I might be that I couldn't make up my mind, but she only smiled at this. Miss Cooney thought there was only one thing a genius could be and that was a priest.

On the whole I thought an explorer was what I would be. Our house was in a square between two roads, one terraced above the other, and I could leave home, follow the upper road for a mile past the Barrack, turn left on any of the intervening roads and lanes, and return almost without leaving the pavement. It was astonishing what valuable information you could pick up on a trip like that. When I came home I wrote down my adventures in a book called *The Voyages of Johnson Martin*, 'with many Maps and Illustrations, Irishtown University Press, 3s. 6d. nett'. I was also compiling *The Irishtown University Song Book for Use in Schools and Institutions by Johnson Martin*, which had the words and music of my favourite songs. I could not read music yet but I copied it from anything that came handy, preferring staff to solfa because it looked better on the page. But I still wasn't sure what I would be. All I knew was that I intended to be famous and have a statue put up to me near that of Father Matthew, in Patrick Street. Father Matthew was called the Apostle of Temperance, but I didn't think much of temperance. So far our town hadn't a proper genius and I intended to supply the deficiency.

But my work continued to bring home to me the great gaps in my knowledge. Mother understood my difficulty and worried herself endlessly finding answers to my questions, but neither she nor Miss Cooney had a great store of the sort of information I needed, and Father was more a hindrance than a help. He was talkative enough about subjects that interested himself but they did not greatly interest me. 'Ballybeg,' he would say brightly. 'Market town. Population 648. Nearest station, Rathkeale.' He was also forthcoming enough about other things, but later, Mother would take me aside and explain that he was only joking again. This made me mad, because I never knew when he was joking and when he wasn't.

I can see now, of course, that he didn't really like me. It was not the poor man's fault. He had never expected to be the father of a genius and it filled him with forebodings. He looked round him at all his contemporaries who had normal, bloodthirsty, illiterate children, and shuddered at the thought that I would never be good for anything but being a genius. To give him his due, it wasn't himself he worried about, but there had never been anything like it in the family before and he dreaded the shame of it. He would come in from the front door with his cap over his eyes and his hands in his trouser pockets and stare moodily at me while I sat at the kitchen table, surrounded by papers, producing fresh maps and illustrations for my book of voyages, or copying the music of 'The Minstrel Boy'.

'Why can't you go out and play with the Horgans?' he would ask wheedlingly, trying to make it sound attractive.

'I don't like the Horgans, Daddy,' I would reply politely.

'But what's wrong with them?' he would ask testily. 'They're fine manly young fellows.'

'They're always fighting, Daddy.'

'And what harm is fighting? Can't you fight them back?'

'I don't like fighting, Daddy, thank you,' I would say, still with perfect politeness.

'The dear knows, the child is right,' Mother would say, coming to my defence. 'I don't know what sort those children are.'

'Ah, you have him as bad as yourself,' Father would snort, and stalk to the front door again, to scald his heart with thoughts of the nice natural son he might have had if only he hadn't married the wrong woman. Granny had always said Mother was the wrong woman for him and now she was being proved right.

She was being proved so right that the poor man couldn't keep his eyes off me, waiting for the insanity to break out in me. One of the things he didn't like was my Opera House. The Opera House was a cardboard box I had mounted on two chairs in the dark hallway. It had a proscenium cut in it, and I had painted some back-drops of mountain and sea, with wings that represented trees and rocks. The characters were pictures cut out, mounted and coloured, and moved on bits of stick. It was lit with candles, for which I had made coloured screens, greased so that they were transparent, and I made up operas from story-books and bits of songs. I was singing a passionate duet for two of the characters while twiddling the

3

screens to produce the effect of moonlight when one of the screens caught fire and everything went up in a mass of flames. I screamed and Father came out to stamp out the blaze, and he cursed me till even Mother lost her temper with him and told him he was worse than six children, after which he wouldn't speak to her for a week.

Another time I was so impressed with a lame teacher I knew that I decided to have a lame leg myself, and there was hell in the home for days because Mother had no difficulty at all in seeing that my foot was already out of shape while Father only looked at it and sniffed contemptuously. I was furious with him, and Mother decided he wasn't much better than a monster. They quarrelled for days over that until it became quite an embarrassment to me because, though I was bored stiff with limping, I felt I should be letting her down by getting better. When I went down the Square, lurching from side to side, Father stood at the gate, looking after me with a malicious knowing smile, and when I had discarded my limp, the way he mocked Mother was positively disgusting.

2

As I say, they squabbled endlessly about what I should be told. Father was for telling me nothing.

'But, Mick,' Mother would say earnestly, 'the child must learn.'

'He'll learn soon enough when he goes to school,' he snarled. 'Why do you be always at him, putting ideas into his head? Isn't he bad enough? I'd sooner the boy would grow up a bit natural.'

But either Mother didn't like children to be natural or she thought I was natural enough as I was. Women, of course, don't object to geniuses half as much as men do. I suppose they find them a relief.

Now one of the things I wanted badly to know was where babies came from, but this was something that no one seemed to be able to explain to me. When I asked Mother she got upset and talked about birds and flowers, and I decided that if she had ever known she must have forgotten it and was ashamed to say so. Miss Cooney only smiled wistfully when I asked her and said, 'You'll know all about it soon enough, child.'

'But, Miss Cooney,' I said with great dignity, 'I have to know now. It's for my work, you see.'

'Keep your innocence while you can, child,' she said in the same tone. 'Soon enough the world will rob you of it, and once 'tis gone 'tis gone for ever.'

But whatever the world wanted to rob me of, it was welcome to it from my point of view, if only I could get a few facts to work on. I appealed to Father and he told me that babies were dropped out of aeroplanes and if you caught one you could keep it. 'By parachute?' I asked, but he only looked pained and said, 'Oh, no, you don't want to begin by spoiling them.' Afterwards, Mother took me aside again and explained that he was only joking. I went quite dotty with rage and told her that one of these days he would go too far with his jokes.

All the same, it was a great worry to Mother. It wasn't every mother who had a genius for a son, and she dreaded that she might be wronging me. She suggested timidly to Father that he should tell me something about it and he danced with rage. I heard them because I was supposed to be playing with the Opera House upstairs at the time. He said she was going out of her mind, and that she was driving me out of my mind at the same time. She was very upset because she had considerable respect for his judgement.

At the same time when it was a matter of duty she could be very, very obstinate. It was a heavy responsibility, and she disliked it intensely – a deeply pious woman who never mentioned the subject at all to anybody if she could avoid it – but it had to be done. She took an awful long time over it – it was a summer day, and we were sitting on the bank of a stream in the Glen – but at last I managed to detach the fact that mummies had an engine in their tummies and daddies had a starting-handle that made it work, and once it started it went on until it made a baby. That certainly explained an awful lot of things I had not understood up to this – for instance, why fathers were necessary and why Mother had buffers on her chest while Father had none. It made her almost as interesting as a locomotive, and for days I went round deploring my own rotten luck that I wasn't a girl and couldn't have an engine and buffers of my own instead of a measly old starting-handle like Father.

Soon afterwards I went to school and disliked it intensely. I was too small to be moved up to the big boys and the other 'infants' were still at the stage of spelling 'cat' and 'dog'. I tried to tell the old teacher about my work, but she only smiled and said, 'Hush, Larry!' I hated being told to hush. Father was always saying it to me.

One day I was standing at the playground gate, feeling very lonely and dissatisfied, when a tall girl from the Senior Girls' school spoke to me. She was a girl with a plump, dark face and black pigtails.

'What's your name, little boy?' she asked.

I told her.

'Is this your first time at school?' she asked.

'Yes.'

'And do you like it?'

'No, I hate it,' I replied gravely. 'The children can't spell and the old woman talks too much.'

Then I talked myself for a change and she listened attentively while I told her about myself, my voyages, my books and the time of the trains from all the city stations. As she seemed so interested I told her I would meet her after school and tell her some more.

I was as good as my word. When I had eaten my lunch, instead of going on further voyages I went back to the Girls' School and waited for her to come out. She seemed pleased to see me because she took my hand and brought me home with her. She lived up Gardiner's Hill, a steep, demure suburban road with trees that overhung the walls at either side. She lived in a small house on top of the hill and was one of a family of three girls. Her little brother, John Joe, had been killed the previous year by a car. 'Look at what I brought home with me!' she said when we went into the kitchen, and her mother, a tall, thin woman, made a great fuss of me and wanted me to have my dinner with Una. That was the girl's name. I didn't take anything, but while she ate I sat by the range and told her mother about myself as well. She seemed to like it as much as Una, and when dinner was over Una took me out in the fields behind the house for a walk.

When I went home at tea-time, Mother was delighted.

'Ah,' she said, 'I knew you wouldn't be long making nice friends at school. It's about time for you, the dear knows.'

I felt much the same about it, and every fine day at three I waited for Una outside the school. When it rained and Mother would not let me out I was miserable.

One day while I was waiting for her there were two senior girls outside the gate.

'Your girl isn't out yet, Larry,' said one with a giggle.

'And do you mean to tell me Larry has a girl?' the other asked with a shocked air.

'Oh, yes,' said the first. 'Una Dwyer is Larry's girl. He goes with Una, don't you, Larry?'

I replied politely that I did, but in fact I was seriously alarmed. I had not realized that Una would be considered my girl. It had never happened to me before, and I had not understood that my waiting for her would be regarded in such a grave light. Now, I think the girls were probably right anyhow, for that is always the way it has happened to me. A woman has only to shut up and let me talk long enough for me to fall head and ears in love with her. But then I did not recognize the symptoms. All I knew was that going with somebody meant you intended to marry them. I had always planned on marrying Mother; now it seemed as if I was expected to marry someone else, and I wasn't sure if I should like it or if, like football, it would prove to be one of those games that two people could not play without pushing.

A couple of weeks later I went to a party at Una's house. By this time it was almost as much mine as theirs. All the girls liked me and Mrs Dwyer talked to me by the hour. I saw nothing peculiar about this except a proper appreciation of geniuses. Una had warned me that I should be expected to sing, so I was ready for the occasion. I sang the Gregorian *Credo*, and some of the little girls laughed, but Mrs Dwyer only looked at me fondly.

'I suppose you'll be a priest when you grow up, Larry?' she asked.

'No, Mrs Dwyer,' I replied firmly. 'As a matter of fact, I intend to be a composer. Priests can't marry, you see, and I want to get married.'

That seemed to surprise her quite a bit. I was quite prepared to continue discussing my plans for the future, but all the children talked together. I was used to planning discussions so that they went on for a long time, but I found that whenever I began one in the Dwyers', it was immediately interrupted so that I found it hard to concentrate. Besides, all the children shouted, and Mrs Dwyer, for all her gentleness, shouted with them and at them. At first, I was somewhat alarmed, but I soon saw that they meant no particular harm, and when the party ended I was jumping up and down on the sofa, shrieking louder than anyone while Una, in hysterics of giggling, encouraged me. She seemed to think I was the funniest thing ever.

It was a moonlit November night, and lights were burning in the little cottages along the road when Una brought me home. On the road outside she stopped uncertainly and said, 'This is where little John Joe was killed.'

There was nothing remarkable about the spot, and I saw no chance of acquiring any useful information.

'Was it a Ford or a Morris?' I asked, more out of politeness than anything else.

'I don't know,' she replied with smouldering anger. 'It was Donegan's old car. They can never look where they're going, the old shows!'

'Our Lord probably wanted him,' I said perfunctorily.

'I dare say He did,' Una replied, though she showed no particular conviction. 'That old fool, Donegan – I could kill him whenever I think of it.'

'You should get your mother to make you another,' I suggested helpfully.

'Make me a what?' Una exclaimed in consternation.

'Make you another brother,' I repeated earnestly. 'It's quite easy, really. She has an engine in her tummy, and all your daddy has to do is to start it with his starting-handle.'

'Cripes!' Una said, and clapped her hand over her mouth in an explosion of giggles. 'Imagine me telling her that!'

'But it's true, Una,' I said obstinately. 'It only takes nine months. She could make you another little brother by next summer.'

'Oh, Jay!' exclaimed Una in another fit of giggles. 'Who told you all that?'

'Mummy did. Didn't your mother tell you?'

'Oh, she says you buy them from Nurse Daly,' said Una, and began to giggle again.

'I wouldn't really believe that,' I said with as much dignity as I could muster.

But the truth was I felt I had made a fool of myself again. I realized now that I had never been convinced by Mother's explanation. It was too simple. If there was anything that woman could get wrong she did so without fail. And it upset me, because for the first time I found myself wanting to make a really good impression. The Dwyers had managed to convince me that whatever else I wanted to be I did not want to be a priest. I didn't even want to be an explorer, a career which would take me away for long periods from my wife and family. I was prepared to be a composer and nothing but a composer.

That night in bed I sounded Mother on the subject of marriage. I tried to be tactful because it had always been agreed between us that I should marry her and I did not wish her to see that my feelings had changed.

'Mummy,' I asked, 'if a gentleman asks a lady to marry him, what does he say?'

'Oh,' she replied shortly, 'some of them say a lot. They say more than they mean.'

She was so irritable that I guessed she had divined my secret and I felt really sorry for her.

'If a gentleman said, "Excuse me, will you marry me?" would that be all right?' I persisted.

'Ah, well, he'd have to tell her first that he was fond of her,' said Mother who, no matter what she felt, could never bring herself to deceive me on any major issue.

But about the other matter I saw that it was hopeless to ask her any more. For days I made the most pertinacious inquiries at school and received some startling information. One boy had actually come floating down on a snowflake, wearing a bright blue dress, but to his chagrin and mine, the dress had been given away to a poor child in the North Main Street. I grieved long and deeply over this wanton destruction of evidence. The balance of opinion favoured Mrs Dwyer's solution, but of the theory of engines and starting-handles no one in the school had ever heard. That theory might have been all right when Mother was a girl but it was now definitely out of fashion.

And because of it I had been exposed to ridicule before the family whose good opinion I valued most. It was hard enough to keep up my dignity with a girl who was doing algebra while I hadn't got beyond long division without falling into childish errors that made her laugh. That is another thing I still cannot stand, being made fun of by women. Once they begin on it they never stop. Once when we were going up Gardiner's Hill together after school she stopped to look at a baby in a pram. The baby grinned at her and she gave him her finger to suck. He waved his fists and sucked like mad, and she went off into giggles again.

'I suppose that was another engine?' she said.

Four times at least she mentioned my silliness, twice in front of other girls and each time, though I pretended to ignore it, I was pierced to the heart. It made me determined not to be exposed again. Once Mother asked

9

Una and her younger sister, Joan, to tea, and all the time I was in an agony of self-consciousness, dreading what she would say next. I felt that a woman who had said such things about babies was capable of anything. Then the talk turned on the death of little John Joe, and it all flowed back into my mind on a wave of mortification. I made two efforts to change the conversation, but Mother returned to it. She was full of pity for the Dwyers, full of sympathy for the little boy and had almost reduced herself to tears. Finally I got up and ordered Una and Joan to play with me. Then Mother got angry.

'For goodness' sake, Larry, let the children finish their tea!' she snapped.

'It's all right, Mrs Delaney,' Una said good-naturedly. 'I'll go with him.'

'Nonsense, Una!' Mother said sharply. 'Finish your tea and go on with what you were saying. It's a wonder to me your poor mother didn't go out of her mind. How can they let people like that drive cars?'

At this I set up a loud wail. At any moment now I felt she was going to get on to babies and advise Una about what her mother ought to do.

'Will you behave yourself, Larry!' Mother said in a quivering voice. 'Oh what's come over you in the past few weeks? You used to have such nice manners, and now look at you! A little corner boy! I'm ashamed of you!'

How could she know what had come over me? How could she realize that I was imagining the family circle in the Dwyers' house and Una, between fits of laughter, describing my old-fashioned mother who still talked about babies coming out of people's stomachs? It must have been real love, for I have never known true love in which I wasn't ashamed of Mother.

And she knew it and was hurt. I still enjoyed going home with Una in the afternoons and while she ate her dinner, I sat at the piano and pretended to play my own compositions, but whenever she called at our house for me I grabbed her by the hand and tried to drag her away so that she and Mother shouldn't start talking.

'Ah, I'm disgusted with you,' Mother said one day. 'One would think you were ashamed of me in front of that little girl. I'll engage she doesn't treat her mother like that.'

Then one day I was waiting for Una at the school gate as usual. Another boy was waiting there as well – one of the seniors. When he heard the screams of the school breaking up he strolled away and stationed himself at the foot of the hill by the crossroads. Then Una herself came rushing out in her wide-brimmed felt hat, swinging her satchel, and approached me with a conspiratorial air.

'Oh, Larry, guess what's happened!' she whispered. 'I can't bring you home with me today. I'll come down and see you during the week though. Will that do?'

'Yes, thank you,' I said in a dead cold voice. Even at the most tragic moment of my life I could be nothing but polite. I watched her scamper down the hill to where the big boy was waiting. He looked over his shoulder with a grin, and then the two of them went off together.

Instead of following them I went back up the hill alone and stood leaning over the quarry wall, looking at the roadway and the valley of the city beneath me. I knew this was the end. I was too young to marry Una. I didn't know where babies came from and I didn't understand algebra. The fellow she had gone home with probably knew everything about both. I was full of gloom and revengeful thoughts. I, who had considered it sinful and dangerous to fight, was now regretting that I hadn't gone after him to batter his teeth in and jump on his face. It wouldn't even have mattered to me that I was too young and weak and that he would have done all the battering. I saw that love was a game that two people couldn't play at without pushing, just like football.

I went home and, without saying a word, took out the work I had been neglecting so long. That too seemed to have lost its appeal. Moodily I ruled five lines and began to trace the difficult sign of the treble clef.

'Didn't you see Una, Larry?' Mother asked in surprise, looking up from her sewing.

'No, Mummy,' I said, too full for speech.

'Wisha, 'twasn't a falling-out ye had?' she asked in dismay, coming towards me. I put my head on my hands and sobbed. 'Wisha, never mind, childeen!' she murmured, running her hand through my hair. 'She was a bit old for you. You reminded her of her little brother that was killed, of course – that was why. You'll soon make new friends, take my word for it.'

But I did not believe her. That evening there was no comfort for me. My great work meant nothing to me and I knew it was all I would ever have. For all the difference it made I might as well become a priest. I felt it was a poor, sad, lonesome thing being nothing but a genius.

My Oedipus Complex

Father was in the army all through the war – the First War, I mean – so, up to the age of five, I never saw much of him, and what I saw did not worry me. Sometimes I woke and there was a big figure in khaki peering down at me in the candlelight. Sometimes in the early morning I heard the slamming of the front door and the clatter of nailed boots down the cobbles of the lane. These were Father's entrances and exits. Like Santa Claus he came and went mysteriously.

In fact, I rather liked his visits, though it was an uncomfortable squeeze between Mother and him when I got into the big bed in the early morning. He smoked, which gave him a pleasant musty smell, and shaved, an operation of astounding interest. Each time he left a trail of souvenirs – model tanks and Gurkha knives with handles made of bullet cases, and German helmets and cap badges and button-sticks, and all sorts of military equipment – carefully stowed away in a long box on top of the wardrobe, in case they ever came in handy. There was a bit of the magpie about Father; he expected everything to come in handy. When his back was turned, Mother let me get a chair and rummage through his treasures. She didn't seem to think so highly of them as he did.

The war was the most peaceful period of my life. The window of my attic faced south-east. My Mother had curtained it, but that had small effect. I always woke with the first light and, with all the responsibilities of the previous day melted, feeling myself rather like the sun, ready to illumine and rejoice. Life never seemed so simple and clear and full of possibilities as then. I put my feet out from under the clothes – I called them Mrs Left and Mrs Right – and invented dramatic situations for them in which they discussed the problems of the day. At least Mrs Right did; she was very demonstrative, but I hadn't the same control of Mrs Left, so she mostly contented herself with nodding agreement.

They discussed what Mother and I should do during the day, what Santa Claus should give a fellow for Christmas, and what steps should be taken to brighten the home. There was that little matter of the baby, for instance. Mother and I could never agree about that. Ours was the only house in the terrace without a new baby, and Mother said we couldn't afford one till Father came back from the war because they cost seventeen and six. That showed how simple she was. The Geneys up the road had a baby, and everyone knew they couldn't afford seventeen and six. It was probably a cheap baby, and Mother wanted something really good, but I felt she was too exclusive. The Geneys' baby would have done us fine.

Having settled my plans for the day, I got up, put a chair under the attic window, and lifted the frame high enough to stick out my head. The window overlooked the front gardens of the terrace behind ours, and beyond these it looked over a deep valley to the tall, red-brick houses terraced up the opposite hillside, which were all still in shadow, while those at our side of the valley were all lit up, though with long strange shadows that made them seem unfamiliar; rigid and painted.

After that I went into Mother's room and climbed into the big bed. She woke and I began to tell her of my schemes. By this time, though I never seem to have noticed it, I was petrified in my nightshirt, and I thawed as I talked until, the last frost melted, I fell asleep beside her and woke again only when I heard her below in the kitchen, making the breakfast.

After breakfast we went into town; heard Mass at St Augustine's and said a prayer for Father, and did the shopping. If the afternoon was fine we either went for a walk in the country or a visit to Mother's great friend in the convent, Mother St Dominic. Mother had them all praying for Father, and every night, going to bed, I asked God to send him back safe from the war to us. Little, indeed, did I know what I was praying for!

One morning I got into the big bed, and there, sure enough, was Father in his usual Santa Claus manner, but later, instead of uniform, he put on his best blue suit, and Mother was as pleased as anything. I saw nothing to be pleased about, because, out of uniform, Father was altogether less interesting, but she only beamed, and explained that our prayers had been answered, and off we went to Mass to thank God for having brought Father safely home.

The irony of it! That very day when he came in to dinner he took off his boots and put on his slippers, donned the dirty old cap he wore about the house to save him from colds, crossed his legs, and began to talk gravely to Mother, who looked anxious. Naturally, I disliked her looking anxious, because it destroyed her good looks, so I interrupted him.

'Just a moment, Larry!' she said gently.

This was only what she said when we had boring visitors, so I attached no importance to it and went on talking.

'Do be quiet, Larry!' she said impatiently. 'Don't you hear me talking to Daddy?'

This was the first time I had heard those ominous words, 'talking to Daddy', and I couldn't help feeling that if this was how God answered prayers, he couldn't listen to them very attentively.

'Why are you talking to Daddy?' I asked with as great a show of indifference as I could muster.

'Because Daddy and I have business to discuss. Now don't interrupt again!'

In the afternoon, at Mother's request, Father took me for a walk. This time we went into town instead of out to the country, and I thought at first, in my usual optimistic way, that it might be an improvement. It was nothing of the sort. Father and I had quite different notions of a walk in town. He had no proper interest in trams, ships, and horses, and the only thing that seemed to divert him was talking to fellows as old as himself. When I wanted to stop he simply went on, dragging me behind him by the hand; when he wanted to stop I had no alternative but to do the same. I noticed that it seemed to be a sign that he wanted to stop for a long time whenever he leaned against a wall. The second time I saw him do it I got wild. He seemed to be settling himself forever. I pulled him by the coat and trousers, but, unlike Mother who, if you were too persistent, got into a wax and said: 'Larry, if you don't behave yourself, I'll give you a good slap,' Father had an extraordinary capacity for amiable inattention. I sized him up and wondered would I cry, but he seemed to be too remote to be annoyed even by that. Really, it was like going for a walk with a mountain! He either ignored the wrenching and pummelling entirely, or else glanced down with a grin of amusement from his peak. I had never met anyone so absorbed in himself as he seemed.

At tea-time, 'talking to Daddy' began again, complicated this time by the fact that he had an evening paper, and every few minutes he put it down and told Mother something new out of it. I felt this was foul play. Man for man, I was prepared to compete with him any time for Mother's attention, but when he had it all made up for him by other people it left me no chance. Several times I tried to change the subject without success.

'You must be quiet while Daddy is reading, Larry,' Mother said impatiently.

It was clear that she either genuinely liked talking to Father better than talking to me, or else that he had some terrible hold on her which made her afraid to admit the truth.

'Mummy,' I said that night when she was tucking me up, 'do you think if I prayed hard God would send Daddy back to the war?'

She seemed to think about that for a moment.

'No, dear,' she said with a smile. 'I don't think he would.'

'Why wouldn't he, Mummy?'

'Because there isn't a war any longer, dear.'

'But, Mummy, couldn't God make another war, if He liked?'

'He wouldn't like to, dear. It's not God who makes wars, but bad people.'

'Oh!' I said.

I was disappointed about that. I began to think that God wasn't quite what he was cracked up to be.

Next morning I woke at my usual hour, feeling like a bottle of champagne. I put out my feet and invented a long conversation in which Mrs Right talked of the trouble she had with her own father till she put him in the Home. I didn't quite know what the Home was but it sounded the right place for Father. Then I got my chair and stuck my head out of the attic window. Dawn was just breaking, with a guilty air that made me feel I had caught it in the act. My head bursting with stories and schemes, I stumbled in next door, and in the half-darkness scrambled into the big bed. There was no room at Mother's side so I had to get between her and Father. For the time being I had forgotten about him, and for several minutes I sat bolt upright, racking my brains to know what I could do with him. He was taking up more than his fair share of the bed, and I couldn't get comfortable, so I gave him several kicks that made him grunt and stretch. He made room all right, though. Mother waked and felt for me. I settled back comfortably in the warmth of the bed with my thumb in my mouth.

'Mummy!' I hummed, loudly and contentedly.

'Sssh! dear,' she whispered. 'Don't wake Daddy!'

This was a new development, which threatened to be even more serious than 'talking to Daddy'. Life without my early-morning conferences was unthinkable.

'Why?' I asked severely.

'Because poor Daddy is tired.'

This seemed to me a quite inadequate reason, and I was sickened by the sentimentality of her 'poor Daddy'. I never liked that sort of gush; it always struck me as insincere.

'Oh!' I said lightly. Then in my most winning tone: 'Do you know where I want to go with you today, Mummy?'

'No, dear,' she sighed.

'I want to go down the Glen and fish for thornybacks with my new net, and then I want to go out to the Fox and Hounds, and –'

'Don't-wake-Daddy!' she hissed angrily, clapping her hand across my mouth.

But it was too late. He was awake, or nearly so. He grunted and reached for the matches. Then he stared incredulously at his watch.

'Like a cup of tea, dear?' asked Mother in a meek, hushed voice I had never heard her use before. It sounded almost as though she were afraid.

'Tea?' he exclaimed indignantly. 'Do you know what the time is?'

'And after that I want to go up the Rathcooney Road,' I said loudly, afraid I'd forget something in all those interruptions.

'Go to sleep at once, Larry!' she said sharply.

I began to snivel. I couldn't concentrate, the way that pair went on, and smothering my early-morning schemes was like burying a family from the cradle.

Father said nothing, but lit his pipe and sucked it, looking out into the shadows without minding Mother or me. I knew he was mad. Every time I made a remark Mother hushed me irritably. I was mortified. I felt it wasn't fair; there was even something sinister in it. Every time I had pointed out to her the waste of making two beds when we could both sleep in one, she had told me it was healthier like that, and now here was this man, this stranger, sleeping with her without the least regard for her health!

He got up early and made tea, but though he brought Mother a cup he brought none for me.

'Mummy,' I shouted, 'I want a cup of tea, too.'

'Yes, dear,' she said patiently. 'You can drink from Mummy's saucer.'

That settled it. Either Father or I would have to leave the house. I didn't want to drink from Mother's saucer; I wanted to be treated as an equal in my own home, so, just to spite her, I drank it all and left none for her. She took that quietly, too.

But that night when she was putting me to bed she said gently:

'Larry, I want you to promise me something.'

'What is it?' I asked.

'Not to come in and disturb poor Daddy in the morning. Promise?'

'Poor Daddy' again! I was becoming suspicious of everything involving that quite impossible man.

'Why?' I asked.

'Because poor Daddy is worried and tired and he doesn't sleep well.'

'Why doesn't he, Mummy?'

'Well, you know, don't you, that while he was at the war Mummy got the pennies from the Post Office?'

'From Miss MacCarthy?'

'That's right. But now, you see, Miss MacCarthy hasn't any more pennies, so Daddy must go out and find us some. You know what would happen if he couldn't?'

'No,' I said, 'tell us.'

'Well, I think we might have to go out and beg for them like the poor old woman on Fridays. We wouldn't like that, would we?'

'No,' I agreed. 'We wouldn't.'

'So you'll promise not to come in and wake him?'

'Promise.'

Mind you, I meant that. I knew pennies were a serious matter, and I was all against having to go out and beg like the old woman on Fridays. Mother laid out all my toys in a complete ring round the bed so that, whatever way I got out, I was bound to fall over one of them.

When I woke I remembered my promise all right. I got up and sat on the floor and played – for hours, it seemed to me. Then I got my chair and looked out the attic window for more hours. I wished it was time for Father to wake; I wished someone would make me a cup of tea. I didn't feel in the least like the sun; instead, I was bored and so very, very cold! I simply longed for the warmth and depth of the big featherbed.

At last I could stand it no longer. I went into the next room. As there was still no room at Mother's side I climbed over her and she woke with a start.

'Larry,' she whispered, gripping my arm very tightly, 'what did you promise?'

'But I did, Mummy,' I wailed, caught in the very act. 'I was quiet for ever so long.'

'Oh, dear, and you're perished!' she said sadly, feeling me all over. 'Now, if I let you stay will you promise not to talk?'

'But I want to talk, Mummy,' I wailed.

'That has nothing to do with it,' she said with a firmness that was new to me. 'Daddy wants to sleep. Now, do you understand that?'

I understood it only too well. I wanted to talk, he wanted to sleep – whose house was it, anyway?

'Mummy,' I said with equal firmness, 'I think it would be healthier for Daddy to sleep in his own bed.'

That seemed to stagger her, because she said nothing for a while.

'Now, once for all,' she went on, 'you're to be perfectly quiet or go back to your own bed. Which is it to be?'

The injustice of it got me down. I had convicted her out of her own mouth of inconsistency and unreasonableness, and she hadn't even attempted to reply. Full of spite, I gave Father a kick, which she didn't notice but which made him grunt and open his eyes in alarm.

'What time is it?' he asked in a panic-stricken voice, not looking at Mother but at the door, as if he saw someone there.

'It's early yet,' she replied soothingly. 'It's only the child. Go to sleep again. . . . Now, Larry,' she added, getting out of bed, 'you've wakened Daddy and you must go back.'

This time, for all her quiet air, I knew she meant it, and knew that my principal rights and privileges were as good as lost unless I asserted them at once. As she lifted me, I gave a screech, enough to wake the dead, not to mind Father. He groaned.

'That damn child! Doesn't he ever sleep?'

'It's only a habit, dear,' she said quietly, though I could see she was vexed.

'Well, it's time he got out of it,' shouted Father, beginning to heave in the bed. He suddenly gathered all the bedclothes about him, turned to the wall, and then looked back over his shoulder with nothing showing only two small, spiteful, dark eyes. The man looked very wicked.

To open the bedroom door, Mother had to let me down, and I broke free and dashed for the farthest corner, screeching. Father sat bolt upright in bed.

'Shut up, you little puppy!' he said in a choking voice.

I was so astonished that I stopped screeching. Never, never had anyone spoken to me in that tone before. I looked at him incredulously and saw his face convulsed with rage. It was only then that I fully realized how God had codded me, listening to my prayers for the safe return of this monster.

'Shut up, you!' I bawled, beside myself.

'What's that you said?' shouted Father, making a wild leap out of the bed.

'Mick, Mick!' cried Mother. 'Don't you see the child isn't used to you?'

'I see he's better fed than taught,' snarled Father, waving his arms wildly. 'He wants his bottom smacked.'

All his previous shouting was as nothing to these obscene words referring to my person. They really made my blood boil.

'Smack your own!' I screamed hysterically. 'Smack your own! Shut up! Shut up!'

At this he lost his patience and let fly at me. He did it with the lack of conviction you'd expect of a man under Mother's horrified eyes, and it ended up as a mere tap, but the sheer indignity of being struck at all by a stranger, a total stranger who had cajoled his way back from the war into our big bed as a result of my innocent intercession, made me completely dotty. I shrieked and shrieked, and danced in my bare feet, and Father, looking awkward and hairy in nothing but a short grey army shirt, glared down at me like a mountain out for murder. I think it must have been then that I realized he was jealous too. And there stood Mother in her nightdress, looking as if her heart was broken between us. I hoped she felt as she looked. It seemed to me that she deserved it all.

From that morning out my life was a hell. Father and I were enemies, open and avowed. We conducted a series of skirmishes against one another, he trying to steal my time with Mother and I his. When she was sitting on my bed, telling me a story, he took to looking for some pair of old boots which he alleged he had left behind him at the beginning of the war. While he talked to Mother I played loudly with my toys to show my total lack of concern. He created a terrible scene one evening when he came in from work and found me at his box, playing with his regimental badges, Gurkha knives, and button-sticks. Mother got up and took the box from me.

'You mustn't play with Daddy's toys unless he lets you, Larry,' she said severely. 'Daddy doesn't play with yours.'

For some reason Father looked at her as if she had struck him and then turned away with a scowl.

'Those are not toys,' he growled, taking down the box again to see had I lifted anything. 'Some of those curios are very rare and valuable.'

But as time went on I saw more and more how he managed to alienate Mother and me. What made it worse was that I couldn't grasp his method or see what attraction he had for Mother. In every possible way he was less winning than I. He had a common accent and made noises at his tea. I thought for a while that it might be the newspapers she was interested in, so I made up bits of news of my own to read to her. Then I thought it might be the smoking, which I personally thought attractive, and took his pipes and went round the house dribbling into them till he caught me. I even made noises at my tea, but Mother only told me I was disgusting. It all seemed to hinge round that unhealthy habit of sleeping together, so I made a point of dropping into their bedroom and nosing round, talking to myself, so that they wouldn't know I was watching them, but they were never up to anything that I could see. In the end it beat me. It seemed to depend on being grown-up and giving people rings, and I realized I'd have to wait.

But at the same time I wanted him to see that I was only waiting, not giving up the fight. One evening when he was being particularly obnoxious, chattering away well above my head, I let him have it.

'Mummy,' I said, 'do you know what I'm going to do when I grow up?'

'No, dear,' she replied. 'What?'

'I'm going to marry you,' I said quietly.

Father gave a great guffaw out of him, but he didn't take me in. I knew it must only be pretence. And Mother, in spite of everything, was pleased. I felt she was probably relieved to know that one day Father's hold on her would be broken.

'Won't that be nice?' she said with a smile.

'It'll be very nice,' I said confidently. 'Because we're going to have lots and lots of babies.'

'That's right, dear,' she said placidly. 'I think we'll have one soon, and then you'll have plenty of company.'

I was no end pleased about that because it showed that in spite of the way she gave in to Father she still considered my wishes. Besides, it would put the Geneys in their place.

It didn't turn out like that, though. To begin with, she was very preoccupied – I supposed about where she would get the seventeen and six – and though Father took to staying out late in the evenings it did me no particular good. She stopped taking me for walks, became as touchy as blazes, and smacked me for nothing at all. Sometimes I wished I'd never mentioned the confounded baby – I seemed to have a genius for bringing calamity on myself.

And calamity it was! Sonny arrived in the most appalling hullabaloo – even that much he couldn't do without a fuss – and from the first moment I disliked him. He was a difficult child – so far as I was concerned he was always difficult – and demanded far too much attention. Mother was simply silly about him, and couldn't see when he was only showing off. As company he was worse than useless. He slept all day, and I had to go round the house on tiptoe to avoid waking him. It wasn't any longer a question of not waking Father. The slogan now was 'Don't-wake-Sonny!' I couldn't understand why the child wouldn't sleep at the proper time, so whenever Mother's back was turned I woke him. Sometimes to keep him awake I pinched him as well. Mother caught me at it one day and gave me a most unmerciful flaking.

One evening, when Father was coming in from work, I was playing trains in the front garden. I let on not to notice him; instead, I pretended to be talking to myself, and said in a loud voice: 'If another bloody baby comes into this house, I'm going out.'

Father stopped dead and looked at me over his shoulder.

'What's that you said?' he asked sternly.

'I was only talking to myself,' I replied, trying to conceal my panic. 'It's private.'

He turned and went in without a word. Mind you, I intended it as a solemn warning, but its effect was quite different. Father started being quite nice to me. I could understand that, of course. Mother was quite sickening about Sonny. Even at mealtimes she'd get up and gawk at him in the cradle with an idiotic smile, and tell Father to do the same. He was always polite about it, but he looked so puzzled you could see he didn't know what she was talking about. He complained of the way Sonny cried at night, but she only got cross and said that Sonny never cried except when there was something up with him – which was a flaming lie, because Sonny never had anything up with him, and only cried for attention. It was really painful to see how simple-minded she was. Father wasn't attractive, but he had a fine intelligence. He saw through Sonny, and now he knew that I saw through him as well.

One night I woke with a start. There was someone beside me in the bed. For one wild moment I felt sure it must be Mother, having come to her senses and left Father for good, but then I heard Sonny in convulsions in the next room, and Mother saying: 'There! There! There!' and I knew it wasn't she. It was Father. He was lying beside me, wide awake, breathing hard and apparently as mad as hell.

After a while it came to me what he was mad about. It was his turn now. After turning me out of the big bed, he had been turned out himself. Mother had no consideration now for anyone but that poisonous pup, Sonny. I couldn't help feeling sorry for Father. I had been through it all myself, and even at that age I was magnanimous. I began to stroke him down and say: 'There! There!' He wasn't exactly responsive.

'Aren't you asleep either?' he snarled.

'Ah, come on and put your arm around us, can't you?' I said, and he did, in a sort of way. Gingerly, I suppose, is how you'd describe it. He was very bony but better than nothing.

At Christmas he went out of his way to buy me a really nice model railway.

First Confession

All the trouble began when my grandfather died and my grandmother – my father's mother – came to live with us. Relations in the one house are a strain at the best of times, but, to make matters worse, my grandmother was a real old countrywoman and quite unsuited to the life in town. She had a fat, wrinkled old face, and, to Mother's great indignation, went round the house in bare feet – the boots had her crippled, she said. For dinner she had a jug of porter and a pot of potatoes with – sometimes – a bit of salt fish, and she poured out the potatoes on the table and ate them slowly, with great relish, using her fingers by way of a fork.

Now, girls are supposed to be fastidious, but I was the one who suffered most from this. Nora, my sister, just sucked up to the old woman for the penny she got every Friday out of the old-age pension; a thing I could not do. I was too honest, that was my trouble; and when I was playing with Bill Connell, the sergeant-major's son, and saw my grandmother steering up the path with the jug of porter sticking out from beneath her shawl, I was mortified. I made excuses not to let him come into the house, because I could never be sure what she would be up to when we went in.

When Mother was at work and my grandmother made the dinner I wouldn't touch it. Nora once tried to make me, but I hid under the table from her and took the bread-knife with me for protection. Nora let on to be very indignant (she wasn't, of course, but she knew Mother saw through her, so she sided with Gran) and came after me. I lashed out at her with the bread-knife, and after that she left me alone. I stayed there till Mother came in from work and made my dinner, but when Father came in later Nora said in a shocked voice: 'Oh, Dadda, do you know what Jackie did at dinner-time?' Then, of course, it all came out; Father gave me a flaking; Mother interfered, and for days after that he didn't speak to me and Mother barely spoke to Nora. And all because of that old woman! God knows, I was heart-scalded.

Then, to crown my misfortunes, I had to make my first confession and communion. It was an old woman called Ryan who prepared us for these. She was about the one age with Gran; she was well-do-to, lived in a big house on Montenotte, wore a black cloak and bonnet, and came every day to school at three o'clock when we should have been going home, and talked to us of hell. She may have mentioned the other place as well, but that could only have been by accident, for hell had the first place in her heart.

She lit a candle, took out a new half-crown, and offered it to the first boy who would hold one finger – only one finger! – in the flame for five minutes by the school clock. Being always very ambitious I was tempted to volunteer, but I thought it might look greedy. Then she asked were we afraid of holding one finger – only one finger! – in a little candle flame for five minutes and not afraid of burning all over in roasting hot furnaces for all eternity. 'All eternity! Just think of that! A whole lifetime goes by and it's nothing, not even a drop in the ocean of your sufferings.' The woman was really interesting about hell, but my attention was all fixed on the half-crown. At the end of the lesson she put it back in her purse. It was a great disappointment; a religious woman like that, you wouldn't think she'd bother about a thing like a half-crown.

Another day she said she knew a priest who woke one night to find a fellow he didn't recognize leaning over the end of his bed. The priest was a bit frightened – naturally enough – but he asked the fellow what he wanted, and the fellow said in a deep, husky voice that he wanted to go to confession. The priest said it was an awkward time and wouldn't it do in the morning, but the fellow said that last time he went to confession, there was one sin he kept back, being ashamed to mention it, and now it was always on his mind. Then the priest knew it was a bad case, because the fellow was after making a bad confession and committing a mortal sin. He got up to dress, and just then the cock crew in the yard outside, and – lo and behold! – when the priest looked round there was no sign of the fellow, only a smell of burning timber, and when the priest looked at his bed didn't he see the print of two hands burned in it? That was because the fellow had made a bad confession. This story made a shocking impression on me.

But the worst of all was when she showed us how to examine our conscience. Did we take the name of the Lord, our God, in vain? Did we honour our father and our mother? (I asked her did this include grand-mothers and she said it did.) Did we love our neighbours as ourselves? Did we covet our neighbour's goods? (I thought of the way I felt about the penny that Nora got every Friday.) I decided that, between one thing and another, I must have broken the whole ten commandments, all on account of that old woman, and so far as I could see, so long as she remained in the house I had no hope of ever doing anything else.

I was scared to death of confession. The day the whole class went I let on to have a toothache, hoping my absence wouldn't be noticed; but at three o'clock, just as I was feeling safe, along comes a chap with a message from Mrs Ryan that I was to go to confession myself on Saturday and be at the chapel for communion with the rest. To make it worse, Mother couldn't come with me and sent Nora instead.

Now, that girl had ways of tormenting me that Mother never knew of. She held my hand as we went down the hill, smiling sadly and saying how sorry she was for me, as if she were bringing me to the hospital for an operation.

'Oh, God help us!' she moaned. 'Isn't it a terrible pity you weren't a good boy? Oh, Jackie, my heart bleeds for you! How will you ever think of all your sins? Don't forget you have to tell him about the time you kicked Gran on the shin.'

'Lemme go!' I said, trying to drag myself free of her. 'I don't want to go to confession at all.'

'But sure, you'll have to go to confession, Jackie,' she replied in the same regretful tone. 'Sure, if you didn't, the parish priest would be up to the house, looking for you. 'Tisn't, God knows, that I'm not sorry for you. Do you remember the time you tried to kill me with the bread-knife under the table? And the language you used to me? I don't know what he'll do with you at all, Jackie. He might have to send you up to the bishop.'

I remember thinking bitterly that she didn't know the half of what I had to tell – if I told it. I knew I couldn't tell it, and understood perfectly why the fellow in Mrs Ryan's story made a bad confession; it seemed to me a great shame that people wouldn't stop criticizing him. I remember that steep hill down to the church, and the sunlit hillsides beyond the valley of the river, which I saw in the gaps between the houses like Adam's last glimpse of Paradise.

Then, when she had manoeuvred me down the long flight of steps to the chapel yard, Nora suddenly changed her tone. She became the raging malicious devil she really was.

'There you are!' she said with a yelp of triumph, hurling me through the church door. 'And I hope he'll give you the penitential psalms, you dirty little caffler.'

I knew then I was lost, given up to eternal justice. The door with the coloured-glass panels swung shut behind me, the sunlight went out and gave place to deep shadow, and the wind whistled outside so that the silence within seemed to crackle like ice under my feet. Nora sat in front of me by the confession box. There were a couple of old women ahead of her, and then a miserable-looking poor devil came and wedged me in at the other side, so that I couldn't escape even if I had the courage. He joined his hands and rolled his eyes in the direction of the roof, muttering aspirations in an anguished tone, and I wondered had he a grandmother too. Only a grandmother could account for a fellow behaving in that heart-broken way, but he was better off than I, for he at least could go and confess his sins; while I would make a bad confession and then die in the night and be continually coming back and burning people's furniture.

Nora's turn came, and I heard the sound of something slamming, and then her voice as if butter wouldn't melt in her mouth, and then another slam, and out she came. God, the hypocrisy of women! Her eyes were lowered, her head was bowed, and her hands were joined very low down on her stomach, and she walked up the aisle to the side altar looking like a saint. You never saw such an exhibition of devotion; and I remembered the devilish malice with which she had tormented me all the way from our door, and wondered were all religious people like that, really. It was my turn now. With the fear of damnation in my soul I went in, and the confessional door closed of itself behind me.

It was pitch-dark and I couldn't see priest or anything else. Then I really began to be frightened. In the darkness it was a matter between God and me, and He had all the odds. He knew what my intentions were before I even started; I had no chance. All I had ever been told about confession got mixed up in my mind, and I knelt to one wall and said: 'Bless me, father, for I have sinned; this is my first confession.' I waited for a few minutes, but nothing happened, so I tried it on the other wall. Nothing happened there either. He had me spotted all right.

It must have been then that I noticed the shelf at about one height with my head. It was really a place for grown-up people to rest their elbows, but in my distracted state I thought it was probably the place you were supposed to kneel. Of course, it was on the high side and not very deep, but I was always good at climbing and managed to get up all right. Staying up was the trouble. There was room only for my knees, and nothing you could get a grip on but a sort of wooden moulding a bit above it. I held on to the moulding and repeated the words a little louder, and this time something happened all right. A slide was slammed back; a little light entered the box, and a man's voice said: 'Who's there?'

' 'Tis me, father,' I said for fear he mightn't see me and go away again. I couldn't see him at all. The place the voice came from was under the moulding, about level with my knees, so I took a good grip of the mould-ing and swung myself down till I saw the astonished face of a young priest looking up at me. He had to put his head on one side to see me, and I had to put mine on one side to see him, so we were more or less talking to one another upside-down. It struck me as a queer way of hearing confessions, but I didn't feel it my place to criticize.

'Bless me, father, for I have sinned; this is my first confession,' I rattled off all in one breath, and swung myself down the least shade more to make it easier for him.

'What are you doing up there?' he shouted in an angry voice; and the strain the politeness was putting on my hold of the moulding, and the shock of being addressed in such an uncivil tone, were too much for me. I lost my grip, tumbled, and hit the door an unmerciful wallop before I found myself flat on my back in the middle of the aisle. The people who had been waiting stood up with their mouths open. The priest opened the door of the middle box and came out, pushing his biretta back from his forehead; he looked something terrible. Then Nora came scampering down the aisle.

'Oh, you dirty little caffler!' she said. 'I might have known you'd do it. I might have known you'd disgrace me. I can't leave you out of my sight for one minute.'

Before I could even get to my feet to defend myself she bent down and gave me a clip across the ear. This reminded me that I was so stunned I had even forgotten to cry, so that people might think I wasn't hurt at all, when in fact I was probably maimed for life. I gave a roar out of me.

'What's all this about?' the priest hissed, getting angrier than ever and pushing Nora off me. 'How dare you hit the child like that, you little vixen?'

'But I can't do my penance with him, father,' Nora cried, cocking an outraged eye up at him.

'Well, go and do it, or I'll give you some more to do,' he said, giving me a hand up. 'Was it coming to confession you were, my poor man?' he asked me.

' 'Twas, father,' said I with a sob.

'Oh,' he said respectfully, 'a big hefty fellow like you must have terrible sins. Is this your first?'

' 'Tis, father,' said I.

'Worse and worse,' he said gloomily. 'The crimes of a lifetime. I don't know will I get rid of you at all today. You'd better wait now till I'm finished with these old ones. You can see by the looks of them they haven't much to tell.'

'I will, father,' I said with something approaching joy.

The relief of it was really enormous. Nora stuck out her tongue at me from behind his back, but I couldn't even be bothered retorting. I knew from the very moment that man opened his mouth that he was intelligent above the ordinary. When I had time to think, I saw how right I was. It only stood to reason that a fellow confessing after seven years would have more to tell than people that went every week. The crimes of a lifetime, exactly as he said. It was only what he expected, and the rest was the cackle of old women and girls with their talk of hell, the bishop, and the penitential psalms. That was all they knew. I started to make my examination of conscience, and barring the one bad business of my grandmother it didn't seem so bad.

The next time, the priest steered me into the confession box himself and left the shutter back the way I could see him get in and sit down at the further side of the grille from me.

'Well, now,' he said, 'what do they call you?'

'Jackie, father,' said I.

'And what's a-trouble to you, Jackie?'

'Father,' I said, feeling I might as well get it over while I had him in good humour, 'I had it all arranged to kill my grandmother.'

He seemed a bit shaken by that, all right, because he said nothing for quite a while.

'My goodness,' he said at last, 'that'd be a shocking thing to do. What put that into your head?'

'Father,' I said, feeling very sorry for myself, 'she's an awful woman.'

'Is she?' he asked. 'What way is she awful?'

'She takes porter, father,' I said, knowing well from the way Mother talked of it that this was a mortal sin, and hoping it would make the priest take a more favourable view of my case.

'Oh, my!' he said, and I could see he was impressed.

'And snuff, father,' said I.

'That's a bad case, sure enough, Jackie,' he said.

'And she goes round in her bare feet, father,' I went on in a rush of self-pity, 'and she know I don't like her, and she gives pennies to Nora and none to me, and my da sides with her and flakes me, and one night I was so heart-scalded I made up my mind I'd have to kill her.'

'And what would you do with the body?' he asked with great interest.

'I was thinking I could chop that up and carry it away in a barrow I have,' I said.

'Begor, Jackie,' he said, 'do you know you're a terrible child?'

'I know, father,' I said, for I was just thinking the same thing myself. 'I tried to kill Nora too with a bread-knife under the table, only I missed her.'

'Is that the little girl that was beating you just now?' he asked.

' 'Tis, father.'

'Someone will go for her with a bread-knife one day, and he won't miss her,' he said rather cryptically. 'You must have great courage. Between ourselves, there's a lot of people I'd like to do the same to but I'd never have the nerve. Hanging is an awful death.'

'Is it, father?' I asked with the deepest interest – I was always very keen on hanging. 'Did you ever see a fellow hanged?'

'Dozens of them,' he said solemnly. 'And they all died roaring.'

'Jay!' I said.

'Oh, a horrible death!' he said with great satisfaction. 'Lots of the fellows I saw killed their grandmothers too, but they all said 'twas never worth it.'

He had me there for a full ten minutes talking, and then walked out the chapel yard with me. I was genuinely sorry to part with him, because he was the most entertaining character I'd ever met in the religious line. Outside, after the shadow of the church, the sunlight was like the roaring of waves on a beach; it dazzled me; and when the frozen silence melted and I heard the screech of trams on the road my heart soared. I knew now I wouldn't die in the night and come back, leaving marks on my mother's furniture. It would be a great worry to her, and the poor soul had enough.

Nora was sitting on the railing, waiting for me, and she put on a very sour puss when she saw the priest with me. She was mad jealous because a priest had never come out of the church with her.

'Well,' she asked coldly, after he left me, 'what did he give you?'

'Three Hail Marys,' I said.

'Three Hail Marys,' she repeated incredulously. 'You mustn't have told him anything.'

'I told him everything,' I said confidently.

'About Gran and all?'

'About Gran and all.'

(All she wanted was to be able to go home and say I'd made a bad confession.)

'Did you tell him you went for me with the bread-knife?' she asked with a frown.

'I did to be sure.'

'And he only gave you three Hail Marys?'

'That's all.'

She slowly got down from the railing with a baffled air. Clearly, this was beyond her. As we mounted the steps back to the main road she looked at me suspiciously.

'What are you sucking?' she asked.

'Bullseyes.'

'Was it the priest gave them to you?'

' 'Twas.'

'Lord God,' she wailed bitterly, 'some people have all the luck! 'Tis no advantage to anybody trying to be good. I might just as well be a sinner like you.'

The Study of History

The discovery of where babies came from filled my life with excitement and interest. Not in the way it's generally supposed to of course. Oh, no! I never seem to have done anything like a natural child in a standard textbook. I merely discovered the fascination of history. Up to this I had lived in a country of my own that had no history, and accepted my parents' marriage as an event ordained from the creation; now, when I considered it in this new, scientific way, I began to see it merely as one of the turning-points of history; one of those apparently trivial events that are little more than accidents, but have the effect of changing the destiny of humanity. I had not heard of Pascal, but I would have approved his remark about what would have happened if Cleopatra's nose had been a bit longer.

It immediately changed my view of my parents. Up to this they had been principles, not characters, like a chain of mountains guarding a green horizon. Suddenly a little shaft of light, emerging from behind a cloud, struck them, and the whole mass broke up into peaks, valleys, and foothills; you could even see whitewashed farmhouses and fields where people worked in the evening light, a whole world of interior perspective. Mother's past was the richer subject for study. It was extraordinary the variety of people and settings that woman had in her background. She had been an orphan, a parlourmaid, a companion, a traveller; and had been proposed to by a plasterer's apprentice, a French chef who had taught her to make superb coffee, and a rich elderly shopkeeper in Sunday's Well. Because I liked to feel myself different, I thought a great deal about the chef and the advantages of being a Frenchman, but the shopkeeper was an even more vivid figure in my imagination because he had married someone else and died soon after – of disappointment, I had no doubt – leaving a large fortune. The fortune was to me what Cleopatra's nose was to Pascal; the ultimate proof that things might have been different.

'How much was Mr Riordan's fortune, Mummy?' I asked thoughtfully.

'Ah, they said he left eleven thousand,' Mother replied doubtfully, 'but you couldn't believe everything people say.'

That was exactly what I could do. I was not prepared to minimize a fortune that I might so easily have inherited.

'And weren't you ever sorry for poor Mr Riordan?' I asked severely.

'Ah, why would I be sorry, child?' she asked with a shrug. 'Sure, what use would money be where there was no liking?'

That, of course, was not what I meant at all. My heart was full of pity for poor Mr Riordan who had tried to be my father; but, even on the low level at which Mother discussed it, money would have been of great use to me. I was not so fond of Father as to think he was worth eleven thousand pounds, a hard sum to visualize but more than twenty-seven times greater than the largest salary I had ever heard of – that of a Member of Parliament. One of the discoveries I was making at the time was that Mother was not only rather hard-hearted but very impractical as well.

But Father was the real surprise. He was a brooding, worried man who seemed to have no proper appreciation of me, and was always want-ing me to go out and play or go upstairs and read, but the historical approach changed him like a character in a fairy-tale. 'Now let's talk about the ladies Daddy nearly married,' I would say; and he would stop what-ever he was doing and give a great guffaw. 'Oh, ho, ho!' he would say, slapping his knee and looking slyly at Mother, 'you could write a book about them.' Even his face changed at such moments. He would look young and extraordinarily mischievous. Mother, on the other hand, would grow black.

'You could,' she would say, looking into the fire. 'Daisies!'

'"The handsomest man that walks Cork!"' Father would quote with a wink at me. 'That's what one of them called me.'

'Yes,' Mother would say, scowling. 'May Cadogan!'

'The very girl!' Father would cry in astonishment. 'How did I forget her name? A beautiful girl! 'Pon my word, a most remarkable girl! And still is, I hear.'

'She should be,' Mother would say in disgust. 'With six of them!'

'Oh, now, she'd be the one that could look after them! A fine head that girl had.'

'She had. I suppose she ties them to a lamp-post while she goes in to drink and gossip.'

That was one of the peculiar things about history. Father and Mother both loved to talk about it but in different ways. She would only talk about it when we were together somewhere, in the park or down the Glen, and even then it was very hard to make her stick to the facts, because her whole face would light up and she would begin to talk about donkey-carriages or concerts in the kitchen, or oil-lamps, and though nowadays I would probably value it for atmosphere, in those days it sometimes drove me mad with impatience. Father, on the other hand, never minded talking about it in front of her, and it made her angry. Particularly when he mentioned May Cadogan. He knew this perfectly well and he would wink at me and make me laugh outright, though I had no idea of why I laughed, and anyway, my sympathy was all with her.

'But, Daddy,' I would say, presuming on his high spirits, 'if you liked Miss Cadogan so much why didn't you marry her?'

At this, to my great delight, he would let on to be filled with doubt and distress. He would put his hands in his trousers pockets and stride to the door leading into the hallway.

'That was a delicate matter,' he would say, without looking at me. 'You see, I had your poor mother to think of.'

'I was a great trouble to you,' Mother would say, in a blaze.

'Poor May said it to me herself,' he would go on as though he had not heard her, 'and the tears pouring down her cheeks. "Mick," she said, "that girl with the brown hair will bring me to an untimely grave."'

'She could talk of hair!' Mother would hiss. 'With her carroty mop!'

'Never did I suffer the way I suffered then, between the two of them,' Father would say with deep emotion as he returned to his chair by the window.

'Oh, 'tis a pity about ye!' Mother would cry in an exasperated tone and suddenly get up and go into the front room with her book to escape his teasing. Every word that man said she took literally. Father would give a great guffaw of delight, his hands on his knees and his eyes on the ceiling and wink at me again. I would laugh with him of course, and then grow wretched because I hated Mother's sitting alone in the front room.

I would go in and find her in her wicker-chair by the window in the dusk, the book open on her knee, looking out at the Square. She would always have regained her composure when she spoke to me, but I would have an uncanny feeling of unrest in her and stroke her and talk to her soothingly as if we had changed places and I were the adult and she the child.

But if I was excited by what history meant to them, I was even more excited by what it meant to me. My potentialities were double theirs. Through Mother I might have been a French boy called Laurence Armady or a rich boy from Sunday's Well called Laurence Riordan. Through Father I might, while still remaining a Delaney, have been one of the six children of the mysterious and beautiful Miss Cadogan. I was fascinated by the problem of who I would have been if I hadn't been me, and, even more, by the problem of whether or not I would have known that there was anything wrong with the arrangement. Naturally I tended to regard Laurence Delaney as the person I was intended to be, and so I could not help wondering whether as Laurence Riordan I would not have been aware of Laurence Delaney as a real gap in my make-up.

I remember that one afternoon after school I walked by myself all the way up to Sunday's Well which I now regarded as something like a second home. I stood for a while at the garden gate of the house where Mother had been working when she was proposed to by Mr Riordan, and then went and studied the shop itself. It had clearly seen better days, and the cartons and advertisements in the window were dusty and sagging. It wasn't like one of the big stores in Patrick Street, but at the same time, in size and fittings it was well above the level of a village shop. I regretted that Mr Riordan was dead because I would like to have seen him for myself instead of relying on Mother's impressions which seemed to me to be biased. Since he had, more or less, died of grief on Mother's account, I conceived of him as a really nice man; lent him the countenance and manner of an old gentleman who always spoke to me when he met me on the road, and felt I could have become really attached to him as a father. I could imagine it all: Mother reading in the parlour while she waited for me to come home up Sunday's Well in a school cap and blazer, like the boys from the Grammar School, and with an expensive leather satchel instead of the old cloth school-bag I carried over my shoulder. I could see myself walking slowly and with a certain distinction, lingering at gateways and looking down at the river; and later I would go out to tea in one of the big houses with long gardens sloping to the water, and maybe row a boat on the river along with a girl in a pink frock. I wondered only whether I would have any awareness of the National School boy with the cloth school-bag who jammed his head between the bars of a gate and thought of me. It was a queer, lonesome feeling that all but reduced me to tears.

But the place that had the greatest attraction of all for me was the Douglas Road where Father's friend, Miss Cadogan, lived, only now she wasn't Miss Cadogan but Mrs O'Brien. Naturally, nobody called Mrs O'Brien could be as attractive to the imagination as a French chef and an elderly shopkeeper with eleven thousand pounds, but she had a physical reality that the other pair lacked. As I went regularly to the library at Parnell Bridge, I frequently found myself wandering up the road in the direction of Douglas and always stopped in front of the long row of houses where she lived. There were high steps up to them, and in the evening the sunlight fell brightly on the house-fronts till they looked like a screen. One evening as I watched a gang of boys playing ball in the street outside, curiosity overcame me. I spoke to one of them. Having been always a child of solemn and unnatural politeness, I probably scared the wits out of him.

'I wonder if you could tell me which house Mrs O'Brien lives in, please?' I asked.

'Hi, Gussie!' he yelled to another boy. 'This fellow wants to know where your old one lives.'

This was more than I had bargained for. Then a thin, good-looking boy of about my own age detached himself from the group and came up to me with his fists clenched. I was feeling distinctly panicky, but all the same I studied him closely. After all, he was the boy I might have been.

'What do you want to know for?' he asked suspiciously.

Again, this was something I had not anticipated.

'My father was a great friend of your mother,' I explained carefully, but, so far as he was concerned, I might as well have been talking a foreign language. It was clear that Gussie O'Brien had no sense of history.

'What's that?' he asked incredulously.

At this point we were interrupted by a woman I had noticed earlier, talking to another over the railing between the two steep gardens. She was a small, untidy-looking woman who occasionally rocked the pram in an absent-minded way as though she only remembered it at intervals.

'What is it, Gussie?' she cried, raising herself on tiptoe to see us better.

'I don't really want to disturb your mother, thank you,' I said, in something like hysterics, but Gussie anticipated me, actually pointing me out to her in a manner I had been brought up to regard as rude.

'This fellow wants you,' he bawled.

'I don't really,' I murmured, feeling that now I was in for it. She skipped down the high flight of steps to the gate with a laughing, puzzled air, her eyes in slits and her right hand arranging her hair at the back. It was not carroty as Mother described it, though it had red lights when the sun caught it.

'What is it, little boy?' she asked coaxingly, bending forward.

'I didn't really want anything, thank you,' I said in terror. 'It was just that my daddy said you lived up here, and, as I was changing my book at the library I thought I'd come up and inquire. You can see,' I added, showing her the book as proof, 'that I've only just been to the library.'

'But who is your daddy, little boy?' she asked, her grey eyes still in long, laughing slits. 'What's your name?'

'My name is Delaney,' I said, 'Larry Delaney.'

'Not *Mike* Delaney's boy?' she exclaimed wonderingly. 'Well, for God's sake! Sure, I should have known it from that big head of yours.' She passed her hand down the back of my head and laughed. 'If you'd only get your hair cut I wouldn't be long recognizing you. You wouldn't think I'd know the feel of your old fellow's head, would you?' she added roguishly.

'No, Mrs O'Brien,' I replied meekly.

'Why, then indeed I do, and more along with it,' she added in the same saucy tone though the meaning of what she said was not clear to me. 'Ah, come in and give us a good look at you! That's my eldest, Gussie, you were talking to,' she added, taking my hand. Gussie trailed behind us for a purpose I only recognized later.

'Ma-a-a-a, who's dat fella with you?' yelled a fat little girl who had been playing hop-scotch on the pavement.

'That's Larry Delaney,' her mother sang over her shoulder. I don't know what it was about that woman but there was something about her high spirits that made her more like a regiment than a woman. You felt that everyone should fall into step behind her. 'Mick Delaney's son from

Barrackton. I nearly married his old fellow once. Did he ever tell you that, Larry?' she added slyly. She made sudden swift transitions from brilliance to intimacy that I found attractive.

'Yes, Mrs O'Brien, he did,' I replied, trying to sound as roguish as she, and she went off into a delighted laugh, tossing her red head.

'Ah, look at that now! How well the old divil didn't forget me! You can tell him I didn't forget him either. And if I married him, I'd be your mother now. Wouldn't that be a queer old three and fourpence? How would you like me for a mother, Larry?'

'Very much, thank you,' I said complacently.

'Ah, go on with you, you would not,' she exclaimed, but she was pleased all the same. She struck me as the sort of woman it would be easy enough to please. 'Your old fellow always said it: your mother was a *most* superior woman, and you're a *most* superior child. Ah, and I'm not too bad myself either,' she added with a laugh and a shrug, wrinkling up her merry little face.

In the kitchen she cut me a slice of bread, smothered it with jam, and gave me a big mug of milk. 'Will you have some, Gussie?' she asked in a sharp voice as if she knew only too well what the answer would be. 'Aideen,' she said to the horrible little girl who had followed us in, 'aren't you fat and ugly enough without making a pig of yourself? Murder the Loaf we call her,' she added smilingly to me. 'You're a polite little boy, Larry, but damn the politeness you'd have if you had to deal with them. Is the book for your mother?'

'Oh, no, Mrs O'Brien,' I replied. 'It's my own.'

'You mean you can read a big book like that?' she asked incredulously, taking it from my hands and measuring the length of it with a puzzled air.

'Oh, yes, I can.'

'I don't believe you,' she said mockingly. 'Go on and prove it!'

There was nothing I asked better than to prove it. I felt that as a performer I had never got my due, so I stood in the middle of the kitchen, cleared my throat and began with great feeling to enunciate one of those horribly involved opening paragraphs you found in children's books of the time. 'On a fine evening in spring, as the setting sun was beginning to gild the blue peaks with its lambent rays, a rider, recognizable as a student by certain niceties of attire, was slowly, and perhaps regretfully making his way . . .' It was the sort of opening sentence I loved.

'I declare to God!' Mrs O'Brien interrupted in astonishment. 'And that fellow there is one age with you, and he can't spell house. How well you wouldn't be down at the library, you caubogue you! . . . That's enough now, Larry,' she added hastily as I made ready to entertain them further.

'Who wants to read that blooming old stuff?' Gussie said contemptuously.

Later, he took me upstairs to show me his air rifle and model aeroplanes. Every detail of the room is still clear to me: the view into the back garden with its jungle of wild plants where Gussie had pitched his tent (a bad site for a tent as I patiently explained to him, owing to the danger from wild beasts); the three cots still unmade, the scribbles on the walls, and Mrs O'Brien's voice from the kitchen calling to Aideen to see what was wrong with the baby who was screaming his head off from the pram outside the front door. Gussie, in particular, fascinated me. He was spoiled, clever, casual; good-looking, with his mother's small clean features; gay and calculating. I saw that when I left and his mother gave me sixpence. Naturally I refused it politely, but she thrust it into my trousers pocket, and Gussie dragged at her skirt, noisily demanding something for himself.

'If you give him a tanner you ought to give me a tanner,' he yelled.

'I'll tan you,' she said laughingly.

'Well, give us a lop anyway,' he begged, and she did give him a penny to take his face off her, as she said herself, and after that he followed me down the street and suggested we should go to the shop and buy sweets. I was simple-minded, but I wasn't an out-and-out fool, and I knew that if I went to a sweet-shop with Gussie I should end up with no sixpence and very few sweets. So I told him I could not buy sweets without Mother's permission, at which he gave me up altogether as a cissy or worse.

It had been an exhausting afternoon but a very instructive one. In the twilight I went back slowly over the bridges, a little regretful for that fast-moving, colourful household, but with a new appreciation of my own home. When I went in the lamp was lit over the fireplace and Father was at his tea.

'What kept you, child?' Mother asked with an anxious air, and suddenly I felt slightly guilty, and I played it as I usually did whenever I was at fault in a loud, demonstrative, grown-up way. I stood in the middle of the kitchen with my cap in my hand and pointed it first at one, then at the other.

'You wouldn't believe who I met!' I said dramatically.

'Wisha, who, child?' Mother asked.

'Miss Cadogan,' I said, placing my cap squarely on a chair and turning on them both again. 'Miss May Cadogan. Mrs O'Brien as she is now.'

'Mrs O'Brien?' Father exclaimed, putting down his cup. 'But where did you meet Mrs O'Brien?'

'I said you wouldn't believe it. It was near the library. I was talking to some fellows, and what do you think but one of them was Gussie O'Brien, Mrs O'Brien's son. And he took me home with him, and his mother gave me bread and jam, and she gave me THIS.' I produced the sixpence with a real flourish.

'Well, I'm blowed!' Father gasped, and first he looked at me, and then he looked at Mother and burst into a loud guffaw.

'And she said to tell you she remembers you too, and that she sent her love.'

'Oh, by the jumping bell of Athlone!' Father crowed and clapped his hands on his knees. I could see he believed the story I had told and was delighted with it, and I could see too that Mother did not believe it and that she was not in the least delighted. That, of course, was the trouble with Mother. Though she would do anything to help me with an intellectual problem, she never seemed to understand the need for experiment. She never opened her mouth while Father cross-questioned me, shaking his head in wonder and storing it up to tell the men in the factory. What pleased him most was Mrs O'Brien's remembering the shape of his head, and later, while Mother was out of the kitchen, I caught him looking in the mirror and stroking the back of his head.

But I knew too that for the first time I had managed to produce in Mother the unrest that Father could produce, and I felt wretched and guilty and didn't know why. That was an aspect of history I only studied later.

That night I was really able to indulge my passion. At last I had the material to work with. I saw myself as Gussie O'Brien, standing in the bedroom, looking down at my tent in the garden, and Aideen as my sister, and Mrs O'Brien as my mother and, like Pascal, I re-created history. I remembered Mrs O'Brien's laughter, her scolding and the way she stroked my head. I knew she was kind – casually kind – and hot-tempered, and recognized that in dealing with her I must somehow be a different sort of person. Being good at reading would never satisfy her. She would almost compel you to be as Gussie was; flattering, impertinent, and exacting. Though I couldn't have expressed it in those terms, she was the sort of woman who would compel you to flirt with her.

Then, when I had had enough, I deliberately soothed myself as I did whenever I had scared myself by pretending that there was a burglar in the house or a wild animal trying to get in the attic window. I just crossed my hands on my chest, looked up at the window and said to myself: 'It is not like that. I am not Gussie O'Brien. I am Larry Delaney, and my mother is Mary Delaney, and we live in Number 8 Wellington Square. Tomorrow I'll go to school at the Cross, and first there will be prayers, and then arithmetic and after that composition.'

For the first time the charm did not work. I had ceased to be Gussie all right, but somehow I had not become myself again, not any self that I knew. It was as though my own identity was a sort of sack I had to live in, and I had deliberately worked my way out of it, and now I couldn't get back again because I had grown too big for it. I practised every trick I knew to reassure myself. I tried to play a counting game; then I prayed, but even the prayer seemed different as though it didn't belong to me at all. I was away in the middle of empty space, divorced from my mother and home and everything permanent and familiar. Suddenly I found myself sobbing. The door opened and Mother came in in her nightdress, shivering, her hair over her face.

'You're not sleeping, child,' she said in a wan and complaining voice.

I snivelled, and she put her hand on my forehead.

'You're hot,' she said. 'What ails you?'

I could not tell her of the nightmare in which I was lost. Instead, I took her hand, and gradually the terror retreated, and I became myself again, shrank into my little skin of identity, and left infinity and all its anguish behind.

'Mummy,' I said, 'I promise I never wanted anyone but you.'

The Man of the World

When I was a kid there were no such things as holidays for me and my likes, and I have no feeling of grievance about it because, in the way of kids, I simply invented them, which was much more satisfactory. One year, my summer holiday was a couple of nights I spent at the house of a friend called Jimmy Leary, who lived at the other side of the road from us. His parents sometimes went away for a couple of days to visit a sick relative in Bantry, and he was given permission to have a friend in to keep him company. I took my holiday with the greatest seriousness, insisted on the loan of Father's old travelling bag and dragged it myself down our lane past the neighbours standing at their doors.

'Are you off somewhere, Larry?' asked one.

'Yes, Mrs Rooney,' I said with great pride. 'Off for my holidays to the Learys'.'

'Wisha, aren't you very lucky?' she said with amusement.

'Lucky' seemed an absurd description of my good fortune. The Learys' house was a big one with a high flight of steps up to the front door, which was always kept shut. They had a piano in the front room, a pair of binoculars on a table near the window, and a toilet on the stairs that seemed to me to be the last word in elegance and immodesty. We brought the binoculars up to the bedroom with us. From the window you could see the whole road up and down, from the quarry at its foot with the tiny houses perched on top of it to the open fields at the other end, where the last gas-lamp rose against the sky. Each morning I was up with the first light, leaning out the window in my nightshirt and watching through the glasses all the mysterious figures you never saw from our lane: policemen, railwaymen, and farmers on their way to market.

I admired Jimmy almost as much as I admired his house, and for much the same reasons. He was a year older than I, was well-mannered and well-dressed, and would not associate with most of the kids on the road at all. He had a way when any of them joined us of resting against a wall with his hands in his trousers pockets and listening to them with a sort of well-bred smile, a knowing smile, that seemed to me the height of elegance. And it was not that he was a softy, because he was an excellent boxer and wrestler and could easily have held his own with them any time, but he did not wish to. He was superior to them. He was – there is only one word that still describes it for me – sophisticated.

I attributed his sophistication to the piano, the binoculars, and the indoor john, and felt that if only I had the same advantages I could have been sophisticated, too. I knew I wasn't, because I was always being deceived by the world of appearances. I would take a sudden violent liking to some boy, and when I went to his house my admiration would spread to his parents and sisters, and I would think how wonderful it must be to have such a home; but when I told Jimmy he would smile in that knowing way of his and say quietly: 'I believe they had the bailiffs in a few weeks ago,' and, even though I didn't know what bailiffs were, bang would go the whole world of appearances, and I would realize that once again I had been deceived.

It was the same with fellows and girls. Seeing some bigger chap we knew walking out with a girl for the first time, Jimmy would say casually: 'He'd better mind himself: that one is dynamite.' And, even though I knew as little of girls who were dynamite as I did of bailiffs, his tone would be sufficient to indicate that I had been taken in by sweet voices and broad-brimmed hats, gaslight and evening smells from gardens.

Forty years later I can still measure the extent of my obsession, for, though my own handwriting is almost illegible, I sometimes find myself scribbling idly on a pad in a small, stiff, perfectly legible hand that I recognize with amusement as a reasonably good forgery of Jimmy's. My admiration still lies there somewhere, a fossil in my memory, but Jimmy's knowing smile is something I have never managed to acquire.

And it all goes back to my curiosity about fellows and girls. As I say, I only imagined things about them, but Jimmy knew. I was excluded from knowledge by the world of appearances that blinded and deafened me with emotion. The least thing could excite or depress me: the trees in the morning when I went to early Mass, the stained-glass windows in the church, the blue hilly streets at evening with the green flare of the gas-lamps, the smells of cooking and perfume – even the smell of a cigarette packet that I had picked up from the gutter and crushed to my nose – all kept me at this side of the world of appearances, while Jimmy, by right of birth or breeding, was always at the other. I wanted him to tell me what it was like, but he didn't seem to be able.

Then one evening he was listening to me talk while he leant against the pillar of his gate, his pale neat hair framing his pale, good-humoured face. My excitability seemed to rouse in him a mixture of amusement and pity.

'Why don't you come over some night the family is away and I'll show you a few things?' he asked lightly.

'What'll you show me, Jimmy?' I asked eagerly.

'Noticed the new couple that's come to live next door?' he asked with a nod in the direction of the house above his own.

'No,' I admitted in disappointment. It wasn't only that I never knew anything but I never noticed anything either. And when he described the new family that was lodging there, I realized with chagrin that I didn't even know Mrs MacCarthy, who owned the house.

'Oh, they're just a newly married couple,' he said. 'They don't know that they can be seen from our house.'

'But how, Jimmy?'

'Don't look up now,' he said with a dreamy smile while his eyes strayed over my shoulder in the direction of the lane. 'Wait till you're going away. Their end wall is only a couple of feet from ours. You can see right into the bedroom from our attic.'

'And what do they do, Jimmy?'

'Oh,' he said with a pleasant laugh, 'everything. You really should come.'

'You bet I'll come,' I said, trying to sound tougher than I felt. It wasn't that I saw anything wrong in it. It was rather that, for all my desire to become like Jimmy, I was afraid of what it might do to me.

But it wasn't enough for me to get behind the world of appearances. I had to study the appearances themselves, and for three evenings I stood under the gas-lamp at the foot of our lane, across the road from the MacCarthys', till I had identified the new lodgers. The husband was the first I spotted, because he came from his work at a regular hour. He was tall, with stiff jet-black hair and a big black guardsman's moustache that somehow failed to conceal the youthfulness and ingenuousness of his face, which was long and lean. Usually, he came accompanied by an older man, and stood chatting for a few minutes outside his door – a black-coated, bowler-hatted figure who made large, sweeping gestures with his evening paper and sometimes doubled up in an explosion of loud laughter.

On the third evening I saw his wife – for she had obviously been waiting for him, looking from behind the parlour curtains, and when she saw him she scurried down the steps to join in the conversation. She had thrown an old jacket about her shoulders and stood there, her arms folded as though to protect herself further from the cold wind that blew down the hill from the open country, while her husband rested one hand fondly on her shoulder.

For the first time, I began to feel qualms about what I proposed to do. It was one thing to do it to people you didn't know or care about, but, for me, even to recognize people was to adopt an emotional attitude towards them, and my attitude to this pair was already one of approval. They looked like people who might approve of me, too. That night I remained awake, thinking out the terms of an anonymous letter that would put them on their guard, till I had worked myself up into a fever of eloquence and indignation.

But I knew only too well that they would recognize the villain of the letter and that the villain would recognize me, so I did not write it. Instead, I gave way to fits of anger and moodiness against my parents. Yet even these were unreal, because on Saturday night when Mother made a parcel of my nightshirt – I had now become sufficiently self-conscious not to take a bag – I nearly broke down. There was something about my own house that night that upset me all over again. Father, with his cap over his eyes, was sitting under the wall-lamp, reading the paper, and Mother, a shawl about her shoulders, was crouched over the fire from her little wickerwork chair, listening; and I realized that they, too, were part of the world of appearances I was planning to destroy, and as I said good-night I almost felt that I was saying goodbye to them as well.

But once inside Jimmy's house I did not care so much. It always had that effect on me, of blowing me up to twice the size, as though I were expanding to greet the piano, the binoculars, and the indoor toilet. I tried to pick out a tune on the piano with one hand, and Jimmy, having listened with amusement for some time, sat down and played it himself as I felt it should be played, and this, too, seemed to be part of his superiority.

'I suppose we'd better put in an appearance of going to bed,' he said disdainfully. 'Someone across the road might notice and tell. *They're* in town, so I don't suppose they'll be back till late.'

We had a glass of milk in the kitchen, went upstairs, undressed, and lay down, though we put our overcoats beside the bed. Jimmy had a packet of sweets but insisted on keeping them till later. 'We may need these before we're done,' he said with his knowing smile, and again I admired his orderliness and restraint. We talked in bed for a quarter of an hour; then put out the light, got up again, donned our overcoats and socks, and tiptoed upstairs to the attic. Jimmy led the way with an electric torch. He was a fellow who thought of everything. The attic had been arranged for our vigil. Two trunks had been drawn up to the little window to act as seats, and there were even cushions on them. Looking out, you could at first see nothing but an expanse of blank wall topped with chimney stacks, but gradually you could make out the outline of a single window, eight or ten feet below. Jimmy sat beside me and opened his packet of sweets, which he laid between us.

'Of course, we could have stayed in bed till we heard them come in,' he whispered. 'Usually you can hear them at the front door, but they might have come in quietly or we might have fallen asleep. It's always best to make sure.'

'But why don't they draw the blind?' I asked as my heart began to beat uncomfortably.

'Because there isn't a blind,' he said with a quiet chuckle. 'Old Mrs MacCarthy never had one, and she's not going to put one in for lodgers who may be gone tomorrow. People like that never rest till they get a house of their own.'

I envied him his nonchalance as he sat back with his legs crossed, sucking a sweet just as though he were waiting in the cinema for the show to begin. I was scared by the darkness and the mystery, and by the sounds that came to us from the road with such extraordinary clarity. Besides, of course, it wasn't my house and I didn't feel at home there. At any moment I expected the front door to open and his parents to come in and catch us.

We must have been waiting for half an hour before we heard voices in the roadway, the sound of a key in the latch and, then, of a door opening and closing softly. Jimmy reached out and touched my arm lightly. 'This is probably our pair,' he whispered. 'We'd better not speak any more in case they might hear us.' I nodded, wishing I had never come. At that moment a faint light became visible in the great expanse of black wall, a faint, yellow stairlight that was just sufficient to silhouette the window frame beneath us. Suddenly the whole room lit up. The man I had seen in the street stood by the doorway, his hand still on the switch. I could see it all plainly now, an ordinary small, suburban bedroom with flowery wallpaper, a coloured picture of the Sacred Heart over the double bed with the big brass knobs, a wardrobe, and a dressing-table.

The man stood there till the woman came in, removing her hat in a single wide gesture and tossing it from her into a corner of the room. He still stood by the door, taking off his tie. Then he struggled with the collar, his head raised and his face set in an agonized expression. His wife kicked off her shoes, sat on a chair by the bed, and began to take off her stockings. All the time she seemed to be talking because her head was raised, looking at him, though you couldn't hear a word she said. I glanced at Jimmy. The light from the window below softly illumined his face as he sucked with tranquil enjoyment.

The woman rose as her husband sat on the bed with his back to us and began to take off his shoes and socks in the same slow, agonized way. At one point he held up his left foot and looked at it with what might have been concern. His wife looked at it, too, for a moment and then swung half-way round as she unbuttoned her skirt. She undressed in swift, jerky movements, twisting and turning and apparently talking all the time. At one moment she looked into the mirror on the dressing-table and touched her cheek lightly. She crouched as she took off her slip, and then pulled her nightdress over her head and finished her undressing beneath it. As she removed her underclothes she seemed to throw them anywhere at all, and I had a strong impression that there was something haphazard and disorderly about her. Her husband was different. Everything he removed seemed to be removed in order and then put carefully where he could find it most readily in the morning. I watched him take out his watch, look at it carefully, wind it, and then hang it neatly over the bed.

Then, to my surprise, she knelt by the bed, facing towards the window, glanced up at the picture of the Sacred Heart, made a large hasty Sign of the Cross, and, covering her face with her hands, buried her head in the bedclothes. I looked at Jimmy in dismay, but he did not seem to be embarrassed by the sight. The husband, his folded trousers in his hand, moved about the room slowly and carefully, as though he did not wish to disturb his wife's devotions, and when he pulled on the trousers of his pyjamas he turned away. After that he put on his pyjama jacket, buttoned it carefully, and knelt beside her. He, too, glanced respectfully at the picture and crossed himself slowly and reverently, but he did not bury his face and head as she had done. He knelt upright with nothing of the abandonment suggested by her pose, and with an expression that combined reverence and self-respect. It was the expression of an employee who, while admitting that he might have a few little weaknesses like the rest of the staff, prided himself on having deserved well of the management. Women, his slightly complacent air seemed to indicate, had to adopt these emotional attitudes, but he spoke to God as one man to another. He finished his prayers before his wife; again he crossed himself slowly, rose, and climbed into bed, glancing again at his watch as he did so.

Several minutes passed before she put her hands out before her on the bed, blessed herself in her wide, sweeping way, and rose. She crossed the room in a swift movement that almost escaped me, and next moment the light went out – it was as if the window through which we had watched the scene had disappeared with it by magic, till nothing was left but a blank black wall mounting to the chimney pots.

Jimmy rose slowly and pointed the way out to me with his flashlight. When we got downstairs we put on the bedroom light, and I saw on his face the virtuous and sophisticated air of a collector who has shown you all his treasures in the best possible light. Faced with that look, I could not bring myself to mention the woman at prayer, though I felt her image would be impressed on my memory till the day I died. I could not have explained to him how at that moment everything had changed for me, how, beyond us watching the young married couple from ambush, I had felt someone else watching us, so that at once we ceased to be the observers and became the observed. And the observed in such a humiliating position that nothing I could imagine our victims doing would have been so degrading.

I wanted to pray myself but found I couldn't. Instead, I lay in bed in the darkness, covering my eyes with my hand, and I think that even then I knew that I should never be sophisticated like Jimmy, never be able to put on a knowing smile, because always beyond the world of appearances I would see only eternity watching.

'Sometimes, of course, it's better than that,' Jimmy's drowsy voice said from the darkness. 'You shouldn't judge it by tonight.'

Guests of the Nation

1

At dusk the big Englishman, Belcher, would shift his long legs out of the ashes and say, 'Well, chums, what about it?' and Noble or myself would say, 'All right, chum' (for we had picked up some of their curious expressions), and the little Englishman, Hawkins, would light the lamp and bring out the cards. Sometimes Jeremiah Donovan would come up and supervise the game, and get excited over Hawkins's cards, which he always played badly, and shout at him as if he was one of our own, 'Ah, you divil, why didn't you play the tray?'

But ordinarily Jeremiah was a sober and contented poor devil like the big Englishman, Belcher, and was looked up to only because he was a fair hand at documents, though he was slow even with them. He wore a small cloth hat and big gaiters over his long pants, and you seldom saw him with his hands out of his pockets. He reddened when you talked to him, tilting from toe to heel and back, and looking down all the time at his big farmer's feet. Noble and myself used to make fun of his broad accent, because we were both from the town.

I could not at the time see the point of myself and Noble guarding Belcher and Hawkins at all, for it was my belief that you could have planted that pair down anywhere from this to Claregalway and they'd have taken root there like a native weed. I never in my short experience saw two men take to the country as they did.

They were passed on to us by the Second Battalion when the search for them became too hot, and Noble and myself, being young, took them over with a natural feeling of responsibility, but Hawkins made us look like fools when he showed that he knew the country better than we did.

'You're the bloke they call Bonaparte,' he says to me. 'Mary Brigid O'Connell told me to ask what you'd done with the pair of her brother's socks you borrowed.'

For it seemed, as they explained it, that the Second had little evenings, and some of the girls of the neighbourhood turned up, and, seeing they were such decent chaps, our fellows could not leave the two Englishmen out. Hawkins learned to dance 'The Walls of Limerick', 'The Siege of Ennis' and 'The Waves of Tory' as well as any of them, though he could not return the compliment, because our lads at that time did not dance foreign dances on principle.

So whatever privileges Belcher and Hawkins had with the Second they just took naturally with us, and after the first couple of days we gave up all pretence of keeping an eye on them. Not that they could have got far, because they had accents you could cut with a knife, and wore khaki tunics and overcoats with civilian pants and boots, but I believe myself they never had any idea of escaping and were quite content to be where they were.

It was a treat to see how Belcher got off with the old woman in the house where we were staying. She was a great warrant to scold, and cranky even with us, but before ever she had a chance of giving our guests, as I may call them, a lick of her tongue, Belcher had made her his friend for life. She was breaking sticks, and Belcher, who had not been more than ten minutes in the house, jumped up and went over to her.

'Allow me, madam,' he said, smiling his queer little smile. 'Please allow me,' and he took the hatchet from her. She was too surprised to speak, and after that, Belcher would be at her heels, carrying a bucket, a basket or a load of turf. As Noble said, he got into looking before she leapt, and hot water, or any little thing she wanted, Belcher would have ready for her. For such a huge man (and though I am five foot ten myself I had to look up at him) he had an uncommon lack of speech. It took us a little while to get used to him, walking in and out like a ghost, without speaking. Especially because Hawkins talked enough for a platoon it was strange to hear Belcher with his toes in the ashes come out with a solitary 'Excuse me, chum,' or 'That's right, chum.' His one and only passion was cards, and he was a remarkably good card player. He could have skinned myself and Noble, but whatever we lost to him, Hawkins lost to us, and Hawkins only played with the money Belcher gave him.

Hawkins lost to us because he had too much old gab, and we probably lost to Belcher for the same reason. Hawkins and Noble argued about religion into the early hours of the morning, and Hawkins worried the life out of Noble, who had a brother a priest, with a string of questions that would puzzle a cardinal. Even in treating of holy subjects, Hawkins had a deplorable tongue. I never met a man who could mix such a variety of cursing and bad language into any argument. He was a terrible man, and a fright to argue. He never did a stroke of work, and when he had no one else to argue with, he got stuck in the old woman.

He met his match in her, for when he tried to get her to complain profanely of the drought she gave him a great come-down by blaming it entirely on Jupiter Pluvius (a deity neither Hawkins nor I had ever heard of, though Noble said that among the pagans it was believed that he had something to do with the rain). Another day he was swearing at the capitalists for starting the German war when the old lady laid down her iron, puckered up her little crab's mouth and said: 'Mr Hawkins, you can say what you like about the war, and think you'll deceive me because I'm only a simple poor countrywoman, but I know what started the war. It was the Italian Count that stole the heathen divinity out of the temple in Japan. Believe me, Mr Hawkins, nothing but sorrow and want can follow people who disturb the hidden powers.'

A queer old girl, all right.

2

One evening we had our tea and Hawkins lit the lamp and we all sat into cards. Jeremiah Donovan came in too, and sat and watched us for a while, and it suddenly struck me that he had no great love for the two Englishmen. It came as a surprise to me because I had noticed nothing of it before.

Late in the evening a really terrible argument blew up between Hawkins and Noble about capitalists and priests and love of country.

'The capitalists pay the priests to tell you about the next world so that you won't notice what the bastards are up to in this,' said Hawkins.

'Nonsense, man!' said Noble, losing his temper. 'Before ever a capitalist was thought of people believed in the next world.'

Hawkins stood up as though he was preaching.

'Oh, they did, did they?' he said with a sneer. 'They believed all the things you believe – isn't that what you mean? And you believe God created Adam, and Adam created Shem, and Shem created Jehoshophat. You believe all that silly old fairy-tale about Eve and Eden and the apple. Well listen to me, chum! If you're entitled to a silly belief like that, I'm entitled to my own silly belief – which is that the first thing your God created was a bleeding capitalist, with morality and Rolls-Royce complete. Am I right, chum?' he says to Belcher.

'You're right, chum,' says Belcher with a smile, and he got up from the table to stretch his long legs into the fire and stroke his moustache. So, seeing that Jeremiah Donovan was going, and that there was no knowing when the argument about religion would be over, I went out with him. We strolled down to the village together, and then he stopped, blushing and mumbling, and said I should be behind, keeping guard. I didn't like the tone he took with me, and anyway I was bored with life in the cottage, so I replied by asking what the hell we wanted to guard them for at all.

He looked at me in surprise and said: 'I thought you knew we were keeping them as hostages.'

'Hostages?' I said.

'The enemy have prisoners belonging to us, and now they're talking of shooting them,' he said. 'If they shoot our prisoners, we'll shoot theirs.'

'Shoot Belcher and Hawkins?' I said.

'What else did you think we were keeping them for?' he said.

'Wasn't it very unforeseen of you not to warn Noble and myself of that in the beginning?' I said.

'How was it?' he said. 'You might have known that much.'

'We could not know it, Jeremiah Donovan,' I said. 'How could we when they were on our hands so long?'

'The enemy have our prisoners as long and longer,' he said.

'That's not the same thing at all,' said I.

'What difference is there?' said he.

I couldn't tell him, because I knew he wouldn't understand. If it was only an old dog that you had to take to the vet's, you'd try and not get too fond of him, but Jeremiah Donovan was not a man who would ever be in danger of that.

'And when is this to be decided?' I said.

'We might hear tonight,' he said. 'Or tomorrow or the next day at latest.

So if it's only hanging round that's a trouble to you, you'll be free soon enough.'

It was not the hanging round that was a trouble to me at all by this time. I had worse things to worry about. When I got back to the cottage the argument was still on. Hawkins was holding forth in his best style, maintaining that there was no next world, and Noble saying that there was; but I could see that Hawkins had had the best of it.

'Do you know what, chum?' he was saying with a saucy smile. 'I think you're just as big a bleeding unbeliever as I am. You say you believe in the next world, and you know just as much about the next world as I do, which is sweet damn-all. What's heaven? You don't know. Where's heaven? You don't know. You know sweet damn-all! I ask you again, do they wear wings?'

'Very well, then,' said Noble. 'They do. Is that enough for you? They do wear wings.'

'Where do they get them then? Who makes them? Have they a factory for wings? Have they a sort of store where you hand in your chit and take your bleeding wings?'

'You're an impossible man to argue with,' said Noble. 'Now, listen to me – ' And they were off again.

It was long after midnight when we locked up and went to bed. As I blew out the candle I told Noble. He took it very quietly. When we'd been in bed about an hour he asked if I thought we should tell the Englishmen. I didn't, because I doubted if the English would shoot our men. Even if they did, the Brigade officers, who were always up and down to the Second Battalion and knew the Englishmen well, would hardly want to see them plugged. 'I think so too,' said Noble. 'It would be great cruelty to put the wind up them now.'

'It was very unforeseen of Jeremiah Donovan, anyhow,' said I.

It was next morning that we found it so hard to face Belcher and Hawkins. We went about the house all day, scarcely saying a word. Belcher didn't seem to notice; he was stretched into the ashes as usual, with his usual look of waiting in quietness for something unforeseen to happen, but Hawkins noticed it and put it down to Noble's being beaten in the argument of the night before.

'Why can't you take the discussion in the proper spirit?' he said severely. 'You and your Adam and Eve! I'm a Communist, that's what I am.

53

Communist or Anarchist, it all comes to much the same thing.' And he went round the house, muttering when the fit took him: 'Adam and Eve! Adam and Eve! Nothing better to do with their time than pick bleeding apples!'

3

I don't know how we got through that day, but I was very glad when it was over, the tea things were cleared away, and Belcher said in his peaceable way: 'Well, chums, what about it?' We sat round the table and Hawkins took out the cards, and just then I heard Jeremiah Donovan's footsteps on the path and a dark presentiment crossed my mind. I rose from the table and caught him before he reached the door.

'What do you want?' I asked.

'I want those two soldier friends of yours,' he said, getting red.

'Is that the way, Jeremiah Donovan?' I asked.

'That's the way. There were four of our lads shot this morning, one of them a boy of sixteen.'

'That's bad,' I said.

At that moment Noble followed me out, and the three of us walked down the path together, talking in whispers. Feeney, the local intelligence officer, was standing by the gate.

'What are you going to do about it?' I asked Jeremiah Donovan.

'I want you and Noble to get them out; tell them they're being shifted again; that'll be the quietest way.'

'Leave me out of that,' said Noble under his breath.

Jeremiah Donovan looked at him hard.

'All right,' he says. 'You and Feeney get a few tools from the shed and dig a hole by the far end of the bog. Bonaparte and myself will be after you. Don't let anyone see you with the tools. I wouldn't like it to go beyond ourselves.'

We saw Feeney and Noble go round to the shed and went in ourselves. I left Jeremiah Donovan to do the explanations. He told them that he had orders to send them back to the Second Battalion. Hawkins let out a mouthful of curses, and you could see that though Belcher didn't say anything, he was a bit upset too. The old woman was for having them stay in spite of us, and she didn't stop advising them until Jeremiah Donovan lost his temper and turned on her. He had a nasty temper, I noticed. It was pitch-dark in the cottage by this time, but no one thought of lighting the lamp, and in the darkness the two Englishmen fetched their topcoats and said good-bye to the old woman.

'Just as a man makes a home of a bleeding place, some bastard at headquarters thinks you're too cushy and shunts you off,' said Hawkins, shaking her hand.

'A thousand thanks, madam,' said Belcher. 'A thousand thanks for everything' – as though he'd made it up.

We went round to the back of the house and down towards the bog. It was only then that Jeremiah Donovan told them. He was shaking with excitement.

'There were four of our fellows shot in Cork this morning and now you're to be shot as a reprisal.'

'What are you talking about?' snaps Hawkins. 'It's bad enough being mucked about as we are without having to put up with your funny jokes.'

'It isn't a joke,' says Donovan. 'I'm sorry, Hawkins, but it's true,' and begins on the usual rigmarole about duty and how unpleasant it is. I never noticed that people who talk a lot about duty find it much of a trouble to them.

'Oh, cut it out!' said Hawkins.

'Ask Bonaparte,' said Donovan, seeing that Hawkins wasn't taking him seriously. 'Isn't it true, Bonaparte?'

'It is,' I said, and Hawkins stopped.

'Ah, for Christ's sake, chum!'

'I mean it, chum,' I said.

'You don't sound as if you meant it.'

'If he doesn't mean it, I do,' said Donovan, working himself up.

'What have you against me, Jeremiah Donovan?'

'I never said I had anything against you. But why did your people take out four of your prisoners and shoot them in cold blood?'

He took Hawkins by the arm and dragged him on, but it was impossible to make him understand that we were in earnest. I had the Smith and Wesson in my pocket and I kept fingering it and wondering what I'd do if they put up a fight for it or ran, and wishing to God they'd do one or the other. I knew if they did run for it, that I'd never fire on them. Hawkins wanted to know was Noble in it, and when we said yes, he asked us why Noble wanted to plug him. Why did any of us want to plug him? What had he done to us? Weren't we all chums? Didn't we understand him and didn't he understand us? Did we imagine for an instant that he'd shoot us for all the so-and-so officers in the so-and-so British Army?

By this time we'd reached the bog, and I was so sick I couldn't even answer him. We walked along the edge of it in the darkness, and every now and then Hawkins would call a halt and begin all over again, as if he was wound up, about our being chums, and I knew that nothing but the sight of the grave would convince him that we had to do it. And all the time I was hoping that something would happen; that they'd run for it or that Noble would take over the responsibility from me. I had the feeling that it was worse on Noble than on me.

4

At last we saw the lantern in the distance and made towards it. Noble was carrying it, and Feeney was standing somewhere in the darkness behind him, and the picture of them so still and silent in the bogland brought it home to me that we were in earnest, and banished the last bit of hope I had.

Belcher, on recognizing Noble, said: 'Hallo, chum,' in his quiet way, but Hawkins flew at him at once, and the argument began all over again, only this time Noble had nothing to say for himself and stood with his head down, holding the lantern between his legs.

It was Jeremiah Donovan who did the answering. For the twentieth time, as though it was haunting his mind, Hawkins asked if anybody thought he'd shoot Noble.

'Yes, you would,' said Jeremiah Donovan.

'No, I wouldn't, damn you!'

'You would, because you'd know you'd be shot for not doing it.'

'I wouldn't, not if I was to be shot twenty times over. I wouldn't shoot a pal. And Belcher wouldn't – isn't that right, Belcher?'

'That's right chum,' Belcher said, but more by way of answering the question than of joining in the argument. Belcher sounded as though whatever unforeseen thing he'd always been waiting for had come at last.

'Anyway, who says Noble would be shot if I wasn't? What do you think I'd do if I was in his place, out in the middle of a blasted bog?'

'What would you do?' asked Donovan.

'I'd go with him wherever he was going, of course. Share my last bob with him and stick by him through thick and thin. No one can ever say of me that I let down a pal.'

'We had enough of this,' said Jeremiah Donovan, cocking his revolver. 'Is there any message you want to send?'

'No, there isn't.'

'Do you want to say your prayers?'

Hawkins came out with a cold-blooded remark that even shocked me and turned on Noble again.

'Listen to me, Noble,' he said. 'You and me are chums. You can't come over to my side, so I'll come over to your side. That show you I mean what I say? Give me a rifle and I'll go along with you and the other lads.'

Nobody answered him. We knew that was no way out.

'Hear what I'm saying?' he said. 'I'm through with it. I'm a deserter or anything else you like. I don't believe in your stuff, but it's no worse than mine. That satisfy you?'

Noble raised his head, but Donovan began to speak and he lowered it again without replying.

'For the last time, have you any messages to send?' said Donovan in a cold, excited sort of voice.

'Shut up, Donovan! You don't understand me, but these lads do. They're not the sort to make a pal and kill a pal. They're not the tools of any capitalist.'

I alone of the crowd saw Donovan raise his Webley to the back of Hawkins's neck, and as he did so I shut my eyes and tried to pray. Hawkins had begun to say something else when Donovan fired, and as I opened my eyes at the bang, I saw Hawkins stagger at the knees and lie out flat at Noble's feet, slowly and as quiet as a kid falling asleep, with the lantern-light on his lean legs and bright farmer's boots. We all stood very still, watching him settle out in the last agony.

Then Belcher took out a handkerchief and began to tie it about his own eyes (in our excitement we'd forgotten to do the same for Hawkins), and, seeing it wasn't big enough, turned and asked for the loan of mine. I gave it to him and he knotted the two together and pointed with his foot at Hawkins.

'He's not quite dead,' he said. 'Better give him another.'

Sure enough, Hawkins's left knee was beginning to rise. I bent down and put my gun to his head; then, recollecting myself, I got up again. Belcher understood what was in my mind.

'Give him his first,' he said. 'I don't mind. Poor bastard, we don't know what's happening to him now.'

I knelt and fired. By this time I didn't seem to know what I was doing. Belcher, who was fumbling a bit awkwardly with the handkerchiefs, came out with a laugh as he heard the shot. It was the first time I had heard him laugh and it sent a shudder down my back; it sounded so unnatural.

'Poor bugger!' he said quietly. 'And last night he was so curious about it all. It's very queer, chums, I always think. Now he knows as much about it as they'll ever let him know, and last night he was all in the dark.'

Donovan helped him to tie the handkerchiefs about his eyes. 'Thanks, chum,' he said. Donovan asked if there were any messages he wanted sent.

'No, chum,' he said. 'Not for me. If any of you would like to write to Hawkins's mother, you'll find a letter from her in his pocket. He and his mother were great chums. But my missus left me eight years ago. Went away with another fellow and took the kid with her. I like the feeling of a home, as you may have noticed, but I couldn't start another again after that.'

It was an extraordinary thing, but in those few minutes Belcher said more than in all the weeks before. It was just as if the sound of the shot had started a flood of talk in him and he could go on the whole night like that, quite happily, talking about himself. We stood around like fools now that he couldn't see us any longer. Donovan looked at Noble, and Noble shook his head. Then Donovan raised his Webley, and at that moment Belcher gave his queer laugh again. He may have thought we were talking about him, or perhaps he noticed the same thing I'd noticed and couldn't understand it.

'Excuse me, chums,' he said. 'I feel I'm talking the hell of a lot, and so silly, about my being so handy about a house and things like that. But this thing came on me suddenly. You'll forgive me, I'm sure.'

'You don't want to say a prayer?' asked Donovan.

'No, chum,' he said. 'I don't think it would help. I'm ready, and you boys want to get it over.'

'You understand that we're only doing our duty?' said Donovan.

Belcher's head was raised like a blind man's, so that you could only see his chin and the top of his nose in the lantern-light.

'I never could make out what duty was myself,' he said. 'I think you're all good lads, if that's what you mean. I'm not complaining.'

Noble, just as if he couldn't bear any more of it, raised his fist at Donovan, and in a flash Donovan raised his gun and fired. The big man went over like a sack of meal, and this time there was no need of a second shot.

I don't remember much about the burying, but that it was worse than all the rest because we had to carry them to the grave. It was all mad lonely with nothing but a patch of lantern-light between ourselves and the dark, and birds hooting and screeching all round, disturbed by the guns. Noble went through Hawkins's belongings to find the letter from his mother, and then joined his hands together. He did the same with Belcher. Then, when we'd filled in the grave, we separated from Jeremiah Donovan and Feeney and took our tools back to the shed. All the way we didn't speak a word. The kitchen was dark and cold as we'd left it, and the old woman was sitting over the hearth, saying her beads. We walked past her into the room, and Noble struck a match to light the lamp. She rose quietly and came to the doorway with all her cantankerousness gone.

'What did ye do with them?' she asked in a whisper, and Noble started so that the match went out in his hand.

'What's that?' he asked without turning round.

'I heard ye,' she said.

'What did you hear?' asked Noble.

'I heard ye. Do ye think I didn't hear ye, putting the spade back in the houseen?'

Noble struck another match and this time the lamp lit for him.

'Was that what ye did to them?' she asked.

Then, by God, in the very doorway, she fell on her knees and began praying, and after looking at her for a minute or two Noble did the same by the fireplace. I pushed my way out past her and left them at it. I stood at the door, watching the stars and listening to the shrieking of the birds dying out over the bogs. It is so strange what you feel at times like that

that you can't describe it. Noble says he saw everything ten times the size, as though there were nothing in the whole world but that little patch of bog with the two Englishmen stiffening into it, but with me it was as if the patch of bog where the Englishmen were was a million miles away, and even Noble and the old woman, mumbling behind me, and the birds and the bloody stars were all far away, and I was somehow very small and very lost and lonely like a child astray in the snow. And anything that happened to me afterwards, I never felt the same about again.

Machine-Gun Corps in Action

When Sean Nelson and I were looking for a quiet spot in the hills for the brigade printing press we thought of Kilvara, one of the quietest of all the mountain hamlets we knew. And as we drove down the narrow road into it, we heard the most ferocious devil's fusilade of machine-gun fire we had heard since the troubles began.

Nelson slipped the safety-catch of his rifle and I held the car at a crawl. Not that we could see anything or anybody. The firing was as heavy as ever, but no bullet seemed to come near us, and for miles around the vast, bleak, ever-changing screen of hillside with its few specks of cottages was as empty as before.

We seemed to be in the very heart of the invisible battle when suddenly the firing ceased and a little ragged figure – looking, oh, so unspectacular against that background of eternal fortitude – detached itself from behind a hillock, dusted its knees, shouldered a strange-looking machine-gun, and came towards us. It hailed us and signalled us to stop. I pulled up the car, and Nelson lowered his rifle significantly. The little ragged figure looked harmless enough, God knows, and we both had the shyness of unprofessional soldiers.

What we saw was a wild, very under-sized cityman, dressed in an outworn check suit, a pair of musical-comedy tramp's brogues, and a cap which did no more than half conceal his shock of dirty yellow hair. As he came towards us he produced the butt-end of a cigarette, hung it from one corner of his mouth, struck a match upon his boot-sole without pausing in his stride, and carelessly flicked the light across his lips. Then, as he accosted us, he let out a long grey stream of smoke through his nostrils.

'Comrades,' he said companionably. 'Direct me to Jo Kenefick's column, eh? Doing much fighting your end of the line? I'm all the way from Waterford, pure Cork otherwise.'

'Yeh?' we asked in astonishment, though not at the second clause of his statement, of the truth of which his accent left no room for doubt. He knew as much.

'Sure,' he replied, 'sure, sir. You have a look at my boots. All the way without as much as a lift. Couldn't risk that with the baby. Been doing a bit of practice now to keep my hand in.'

'It sounded quite professional to me,' said Nelson mildly.

'Ah!' The little man shook his head. 'Amateur, amateur, but I must keep the old hand in. A beauty though, isn't she? All I've left in the world now.'

He lovingly smoothed off some imaginary rust from his gun, which I took to be of foreign make. I bent out of the car to examine it, but he stepped back.

'No, no. Don't come near her. She's a touchy dame. Guess how much I paid for her? Two pounds. The greatest bargain ever. Two pounds! I heard the Tommy offering it to my wife. By way of a joke, you know. So I said, "You lend me two pounds, old girl, and I'll buy her." Nearly died when she heard I wanted to buy a machine-gun. "Buy a machine-gun – *a machine-gun* – what use would a machine-gun be to her? Wouldn't a mangle be more in her line?" So I said, "Cheerio, old girl, don't get so huffy, a mangle may be a useful article, but it isn't much fun, and anyway, this round is on me." And I rose the money off an old Jew in the Marsh. So help me, God, amen. Wasn't I right?'

'And where are you off to now?' asked Nelson.

'You gentlemen will tell me that, I hope. Jo Kenefick's column, that's where I'm going. Know Tom Casey? No? Well, I served under Tom. He'll tell you all about me, soldier.'

We directed him to Jo's column, which we had left in a village a few miles down the valley.

'You gentlemen wouldn't have an old bob about you, I suppose?' he asked dreamily, and seeing the answer in our eyes hurried on with, 'No, no, of course you wouldn't. Where would you get it? Hard times with us all these days. . . . Or a cigarette? I'm down to my last butt as you may see.'

Out of sheer pity we gave him three of the seven we had between us, and, in acknowledgment of the kindness, he showed us how he could wag both ears in imitation of a dog. It struck me that it was not the first time he had fallen on evil days. Then with a cheerful good-bye he left us, and we sat in the car watching his game, sprightly, dilapidated figure disappear over the mountains on its way to the column. After that we drove into Kilvara.

At the schoolmaster's house we stopped to examine the old school which had been indicated as a likely headquarters for our press. There Nelson set himself to win round the schoolmaster's daughter, a fine, tall, red-haired girl, who looked at us with open hostility. He succeeded so well that she invited us in to tea; but with the tea we had to win over the schoolmaster himself and his second daughter, a much more difficult job. Neither Nelson nor I could fathom what lay beneath their hostility; the family seemed to have no interest in politics outside the court and society column of the daily press; and it was not until the old teacher asked with a snarl whether we had heard firing as we came up that we began to see bottom.

'Ah,' said Nelson laughing, 'you're finished with the tramp.'

'Are we, I wonder?' asked the teacher grimly.

'That man,' said Nelson, 'was the funniest thing I've seen for months.'

'Funny?' exclaimed the younger daughter flaring up. 'I'm glad you think it fun!'

'Well, what did he do to you, anyhow?' asked Nelson irritably. Nelson was touchy about what he called the *bourgeoisie*.

'Do you know,' she asked angrily, 'when my dad said he had no room for him here with two girls in the house, your "funny" friend took his trench mortar, and put it on a sort of camera stand in front of the hall door, and threatened to blow us all into eternity?'

'The little rat!' said Nelson. 'And he actually wanted to stay here?'

'Wanted to stay?' said the daughters together. 'Wanted to stay! Did he stay for a fortnight and the gun mounted all night on the chair beside his bed?'

'Holy Lord God!' said Nelson profanely, 'and we without as much as a good pea-shooter on the armoured car!'

After this the story expanded to an almost incredible extent, for not alone did it concern Kilvara, but other places where the tramp's activities had already become the stuff of legend.

'He'll behave himself when Jo Kenefick gets him,' said Nelson grimly.

'I tell you what, girls,' he went on, 'come back with us in the car and tell Jo Kenefick the story as you told it now.'

At this the girls blushed and giggled, but at last they agreed, and proceeded to ready themselves for the journey, the old schoolmaster meanwhile becoming more and more polite and even going to the trouble of explaining to us the half-dozen different reasons why we could *not* win the war.

I have no intention of describing the journey to Coolenagh and back under an autumn moon – though I can picture it very clearly: mountains and pools and misty, desolate ribbons of mountain road – for that is the story of how we almost retrieved the reputation of the Irish Republican Army in the little hamlet of Kilvara; but what I should like to describe is Jo Kenefick's face when we (that is to say Sean and I, for we judged it unwise to lay Jo open to temptation) told the tale of the tramp's misdeeds.

'Mercy of God!' said Jo, 'Ye nabbed him and let him go again?'

'But didn't he arrive yet?' asked Nelson.

'Arrive?' asked Jo. 'Arrive where, tell me?'

'Here, of course.'

'Here?' asked Jo with a sour scowl. 'And I looking for him this fortnight to massacree him!'

'Damn!' said Nelson, seeing light.

'It was great negligence in ye to let him go,' said Jo severely. 'And I wouldn't mind at all but ye let the gun go too. Do you know I have seventy-five thousand rounds of that stuff in the dump, and he have the only gun in Ireland that will shoot it?'

'He said he bought it for two pounds,' said I.

'He did,' replied Jo. 'He did. And my Q.M. came an hour after and bid fifty. It was an Italian gun not inventoried at all, and it was never looked for in the evacuation. Where did ye find him?'

We told him the exact spot in which we had last seen the gunner.

'Be damn!' said Jo, 'I'll send out a patrol on motor-bikes to catch him. That armoured car isn't much use to me without a gun.'

But when we returned from our joy-ride at two o'clock the following morning – leaving, I hope, two happy maidens in the hills behind – the patrols were back without gunner or gun.

2

Three days later the gunner turned up – between two stalwart country boys with cocked Webleys. He was very downcast, and having explained to Jo Kenefick how he had been sent out of his way by two men answering to our description, he added, a moment after we had made our appearance, that he had been caught in a storm on the hills.

The same night it was decided to make amends for our previous inaction by attacking the nearest town, and that no later than the following morning. The men were hurriedly called together and the plans explained to them. The town was garrisoned by about forty soldiers and the armoured car, driven by me and manned by the tramp, was to prepare the way for the attack.

At dawn I stood in my overalls by the door of the armoured car and lectured the tramp. He was extremely nervous, and tapped the body at every point, looking for what he called leaks. I explained, as clearly as I could to a man who paid no attention to me, that his principal danger would be from inside, and showed him that my revolver was fully loaded to cope with emergencies.

We pulled out of the village and passed little groups of armed men converging on the town. I had to drive slowly, principally because it was impossible to get much speed out of the car, which was far too heavy for its chassis, and needed skilful negotiation, but partly because the lumbering old truck refused to work on reverse and, to avoid occasional detours of a few miles, I had to be careful to get my turns right.

Jo Kenefick, Sean Nelson and some others were waiting for us outside the town and gave us a few necessary directions; then we closed all apertures except that for the machine-gun and the shielded slit through which I watched the road immediately in front of me, and gave the old bus her head downhill. She slowed down of her own accord as we entered a level street the surface of which was far worse than any I had ever seen. As we drew near the spot where I thought the barrack should be I heard the tramp mumble something; I looked back and saw him fiercely sighting his gun; then the most deafening jumble of noise I have ever heard in my life began.

'Slow! Slow!' the tramp shouted, and I held her in as we lumbered down the main street, letting her rip again as we took a side-street that brought us back to the centre of the town. I knew that the enemy was in occupation of some half-dozen houses. Beyond this I knew nothing of what went on about me. The tramp shouted directions which I followed without question. 'Slow!' he cried when we were passing some occupied post, and two or three times he exclaimed that he had 'got' somebody. This was none of my business. I had enough to do at the wheel.

Besides I was almost deaf from the shooting and the chugging and jumbling of the old bus (all concentrated and magnified within that little steel box until it sounded like the day of judgment and the anger of the Lord) and suffocated by the fumes of petrol and oil that filled it. This went on, as I afterwards calculated, for at least two hours and a half. I could not tell what was happening between our men and the regulars, but I guessed that Kenefick would have bagged some of the supplies we needed under cover of our fire.

Suddenly, in the midst of a terrific burst of firing from the tramp, the engine kicked. My heart stood still. The old bus went on smoothly for a little while, and then, in the middle of the main street, kicked again. I realized that the only hope was to get her out of the town as quickly as possible, and leave the men to escape as best they could. I put her to it, stepping on the gas and praying to her maker. Again she ran smoothly for a few yards and suddenly stopped, not fifty feet from the barrack door as I judged. I let my hands drop from the wheel and sat there in despair. There was no self-starter.

'What's wrong with you, man?' shouted the tramp. 'Start her again, quick.'

'Are any of our men around?' I shouted, indulging a last faint hope.

'How could they be?' yelled the tramp, letting rip an occasional shot. 'Nobody could move in that fire.'

'Then one of us must get out and start her.'

'Get out? Not likely. Stay where you are; you're in no danger.'

'No danger?' I asked bitterly. 'And when they roll a bomb under the car?'

'They'd never think of that!' he said with pathetic consternation.

I pushed open the door that was farthest from the barrack, pushed it just an inch or so in hope that it would not be detected. It occurred to me that with care, with very great care, one might even creep round under cover as far as the starting-handle. I yelled to the tramp to open heavy fire. He did so with a will, and when I banged the steel door back and knelt on the footboard a perfect tornado of machine-gun bullets was whirling madly in wide circles above my head. Inch by inch I crept along the side of the car, my head just level with the footboard. My progress was maddeningly slow, but I reached the front mudguard in safety, and, still bent double, gave the starting-handle a spin. The car started, jumped, and stood still again with a faint sigh, and at that very moment something happened that I shall never forget the longest day I live.

Silence, an unutterable, appalling silence fell about me. For a full minute I was quite unable to guess what had happened; then it occurred to me – a dreadful revelation – that I had become stone-deaf. I did not dare to move, but crouched there with one hand upon the starter and the other upon the gun in my belt. I looked round me; the street with all its shattered window-panes was quite empty and silent with the silence of midnight. I tried to remember what it was one did when one became suddenly deaf.

Then, the simplest of sounds, my hand jolting the starting-handle, roused me to the knowledge that, whatever else had happened, my hearing must be intact. To make certain I jolted the handle again, and again I distinctly heard the creak. But the silence had now become positively sinister. I gave the handle a ferocious spin, the engine started, and I crept back to the door on hands and knees. Still there was no sound. I raised myself slowly; still nothing. I looked into the car and saw to my horror that it was empty of gunner and gun. Then I glanced along the street and round the farthest corner I saw the last rags of my crew flutter triumphantly before they disappeared for good. The crew had gone over to the enemy, and left me to find my way out of the town as best I could.

I sat in among a heap of spent bullet cases, made the doors tight, and drove lamely out of town. Nobody tried to hinder me nor did I see any sign of our men; it was like a town of the dead, with glass littering the pavements and great gaping holes in every shop window.

I drove for half an hour through a deserted countryside until at last I caught up with a small group of men, two of whom were carrying a stretcher. I drove in amongst them and they surrounded the car, furiously waving rifles and bombs. For safety sake I opened the turret and spoke to them through that.

'Where is he?' they yelled, 'where is he?'

'Where's who?'

'Where's the man with the gun? He hit Mike Cronin one in the leg, and if Mike gets him alive . . .' From the stretcher Mike fully confirmed the intention, adding his vivid impressions of us both.

At that moment Jo Kenefick and Nelson pushed their way through the excited crowd, and probably saved me from a bad mauling. But they were almost as unreasonable and excited as the others; Jo in particular, who promptly threatened to have me court-martialed.

'But how could I know?' I yelled down at him. 'I couldn't see but what was before my eyes. And how does Mike Cronin know it was a bullet from the car he stopped?'

'What else could it be?' asked Jo. 'Where did you let that lunatic go?'

'He went over to the Staters while I was starting the car.'

'Staters!' said Kenefick bitterly. 'He went over to the Staters! Listen to him! And the last man evacuated the town at four o'clock this morning.'

I groaned, the whole appalling truth beginning to dawn upon me.

'And the grub?' I asked.

'Grub? Nobody dared to stir from cover with that fool blazing away. And the people will rend us if ever we show our noses there again.'

That was the truest word Jo Kenefick ever spoke. We did *not* dare to show our noses in the town again, and this time Nelson and I could be of no use as peacemakers.

3

A fortnight later and Jo Kenefick could talk about the affair; if he were pushed to extremity he could even laugh at it, but as his laughter always preceded a bitter little lecture to me about the necessity for foresight and caution, I preferred him in philosophic mood, as when he said:

'Now, you think you have a man when you haven't him at all. There aren't any odds high enough again' a man doing a thing you don't expect him to do. Take that tramp of yours for instance. That man never done a stroke of work in his life. His wife have a little old-clothes shop on the quays. She's a dealing woman – with a tidy stocking, I'd say. She kep' him in 'baccy an' buns an' beer. He never had one solitary thing to worry him. And all of a sudden, lo and behold ye! he wants to be a soldier.

Not an ordinary soldier either, mind you, but a free lance; brigadier and bomba'dier, horse, foot and artillery all at once! What's the odds again' that, I ask you? And which of ye will give me odds on what he's going to do next? Will you?'

'I will not,' said Nelson.

'Nor will I,' said myself.

'There you are,' said Jo. 'My belief is you can't be certain of anything in human nature. As for that skew-eyed machine-gun man of yours, well, there's nothing on heaven or earth I'd put apast him.'

Some hours later Jo's capacity for receiving shocks was put to the test. A mountainy man appeared to complain that the tramp was at his old tricks again. This time it was in connection with a squabble about land; there was a second marriage, a young widow, a large family, and a disputed will in it, but of the rights and wrongs of these affairs no outsider can ever judge. They begin in what is to him a dim and distant past; somebody dies and the survivors dispute over his property; somebody calls somebody else a name; six months later somebody's window is smashed; years after somebody's fences are broken down; the infection spreads to the whole parish; the school is boycotted; there is a riot in the nearest town on fair day; and then, quite casually, some unfortunate wretch who seems to have had nothing to do with the dispute is found in a ditch with a portion of his skull blown away.

Not that we gathered anything as lucid or complete from the slob of a mountainy man who talked to us at such length. All he could tell us was that his cousin's house had been machine-gunned, and that, in the opinion of the parish, was carrying the matter too far. Nor did we want to know more. Jo Kenefick was on his feet calling for men when Sean Nelson stopped him.

'Leave it to us, Jo, leave it to us! Remember we've an account to square with him.'

'I'm remembering that,' said Jo slowly. 'And I'm remembering too he got away from ye twice.'

'All the more reason he won't get away a third time.'

'If I leave him to ye,' said Jo, 'will ye swear to me to bring him back here, dead or alive, with his machine-gun?'

'Dead or alive,' nodded Sean.

'And more dead than alive?' said Jo with his heavy humour.

'Oh, more dead than alive!' said Sean.

And so it was that we three, Sean, myself, and the mountainy man set out from the village that evening.

Three-quarters of an hour of jolting and steady climbing and we came to a little valley set between three hills; a stream flowing down the length of it and a few houses set distantly upon the lower slopes. The mountainy man pointed out a comfortable farmhouse backed by a wall of elm-trees as our destination. He refused to come with us, nor indeed did we ask for his company.

The door of the little farmhouse was open, and we walked straight into the kitchen. A young woman was sitting by an open hearth in the twilight, and she rose to greet us.

' 'Morrow, ma'am,' said Nelson.

'Good morrow and welcome,' she said.

'A man we're looking for, ma'am, a man with a machine-gun, I'm told he's staying here?'

'He is, faith,' she said. 'But he's out at this minute. Won't you sit down and wait for him?'

We sat down. She lifted the kettle on to a hook above the fire and blew on the red turves until they gathered to a flame. It was easy to see that Nelson, the emotional firebrand of the brigade, was impressed. She was a young woman; not an out-and-out beauty, certainly, but good-tempered and kind. Her hair was cut straight across her brow and short at the poll. She was tall, limber and rough, with a lazy, swinging, impudent stride.

'We've been looking for the same man this long time,' said Nelson. 'We've had a good many complaints of him, ma'am, and now he's caused more crossness here, we heard.'

'If that's all you came about,' she said pertly, 'you might have found something better to do.'

'That's for us to say,' said Nelson sharply.

'Clever boy!' she replied with an impudent pretence of surprise, and I saw by the way she set her tongue against her lower lip that Nelson had approached her in the wrong way.

'That man,' I said, 'accidentally shot one of our fellows, and we're afraid something else will happen.'

At this she laughed, a quiet, bubbling, girlish laugh that surprised and delighted me.

'It will,' she said gaily, 'something will happen unless you take that gun from him.'

Her attitude had changed completely. Laughing still she told us how the tramp had arrived at her house one night, wet to the skin, and carrying his gun wrapped up in oilcloth. He had heard how her husband's people had been annoying her, had heard something about herself as well and come fired with a sort of quixotic enthusiasm to protect her. On the very night of his arrival he had begun his career as knight-errant by gunning the house of one of the responsible parties, and only her persuasion had discouraged him from doing them further mischief. Three times a day he paraded the boundaries of her farm to make sure that all was well, and at night he would rise and see that the cattle were safely in their stalls and that fences and gates were standing. It was all very idyllic, all very amusing; and as there is little sentiment or chivalry in an Irish countryside there was no doubt that the young widow liked it, and appreciated with a sort of motherly regard the tramp's unnecessary attentions. But Nelson soon made it clear that all this would have to cease. Nelson liked being a little bit officious and did it very well. Her face fell as she listened to him.

'Of course,' he added loftily, 'you won't have any more annoyance. We'll settle that for you, and a great deal better than anyone else could. I'll come back tomorrow and see you straight.'

A few moments later the tramp himself came in; it was amazing how his face changed when he saw us sitting there. Nelson was as solemn as a judge, but for the life of me I could not resist laughing. This encouraged the tramp, who began to laugh, too, as though it were all a very good joke and would go no further. Nelson looked at me severely.

'I see nothing to laugh about,' he said; and to the tramp: 'Be ready to travel back with us inside the next five minutes.'

'Let him have his tea,' said the woman of the house roughly.

'I protest,' said the tramp.

'It's no use protesting,' said Nelson, 'if you don't choose to come you know what the consequences will be.'

'What will they be?' asked the tramp, beginning to grow pale.

'I was ordered to bring you back dead or alive, and dead or alive I'll bring you!'

'There!' said the young woman, putting a teapot on the table. 'Have your tea first, and start shooting after. Will I light the lamp?'

'There's no need,' said Nelson, 'I can shoot quite well in the dark.'

'Aren't you very clever?' she replied.

They glared at one another, and then Nelson pushed over his chair. We took our tea in silence, but after about five minutes the tramp, who had obviously been summoning up his courage, put down his knife with a bang.

'Gentlemen,' he said solemnly. 'I protest. I refuse to return with you. I'm a free citizen of this country and nobody has any rights over me. I warn you I'll resist.'

'Resist away,' growled Nelson into his teacup.

There was silence again. We went on with our tea. Then the latch of the door was lifted and a tall, worn woman dressed in a long black shawl appeared. She stood at the door for a moment, and a very softly-breathed 'So there you are, my man,' warned us whom we were dealing with.

'Maggie! Maggie!' said the tramp. 'Is it you?'

'The same,' she whispered, still in the same hushed, contented voice.

'How did you get here?' he asked.

'I'm searching for you these three days,' she replied soothingly. 'I've a car at the door. Are you ready to come back with me?'

'I – I – I'm sorry, Maggie, but I can't.'

'Och aye, me poor man, and why can't you?' The hush in her voice, even to my ears, was awe-inspiring, but he plunged recklessly into it.

'I'm to go back with these gentlemen, Maggie. By order –'

'Order? Order?' she shrieked, standing to her full height and tossing the shawl back from one shoulder. 'Let me see the order that can take my husband away from me without my will and consent! Let me see the one that's going to do it!'

She threw herself into the middle of the kitchen, the shawl half-flung across one arm, like a toreador going into action. Nelson, without so much as a glance at her, shook his head at the table.

'I'm not taking him against your wishes, ma'am – far be it from me! I'd be the last to try and separate ye. Only I must ask you to take him home with you out of this immediately.'

'Oh! I'll take him home!' she said with a nod of satisfaction. 'Lave that to me.' And with a terrifying shout she turned on the tramp. 'On with your hat, James!'

The poor man stumbled to his feet, looking distractedly at Nelson and me.

'Anything with you?' she rapped out.

'Only me gun.'

'Fetch it along.'

Now Nelson was on his feet protesting.

'No, he can't take that with him.'

'Who's to stop him?'

'I will.'

'Fetch it along, James!'

'And I say he won't fetch it along.' Now it was Nelson who was excited and the woman who was calm.

'There's nobody can interfere with a wife's rights over her husband – and her husband's property.'

'I'll shoot your husband and then I'll show you what I can do with his property,' said Nelson, producing his Webley and laying it beside him on the table.

'What did you give for it?' she asked the tramp.

'Two pounds,' he muttered.

'Give it to you for ten!' she said coolly to Nelson.

'I'll see you damned first,' said Nelson.

'Fetch it along, James,' she said, with an impudent smile.

'There's a car outside waiting to take him somewhere he'll never come back from,' said Nelson. 'I'm warning you not to rouse me.'

'Five so,' she said.

'Go along to hell out of this,' he shouted, 'you and your husband!'

'I'm waiting for me own,' she said.

'You'll get your two pounds,' he said, breathing through his nose.

'Five,' she said, without turning a hair.

'Two!' he bellowed.

'Five!'

'Get along with you now!' he said.

'I rely on your word as an officer and a gentleman,' she shouted suddenly. 'And if you fail me, I'll folly you to the gates of hell. Go on, James,' she said, and without another word the strange pair went out the door.

The young widow rose slowly and watched them through a lifted curtain go down the pathway to the road where a car was waiting for them.

'Well?' she said, turning to me with a sad little smile.

'Well?' said I.

'Well?' said Nelson. 'Somebody's got to stay here and clear up this mess.'

'Somebody had better go and break the news to Jo Kenefick,' said I.

'I can't drive a car,' remarked Nelson significantly.

'It wouldn't be the only thing you can't do,' said the young widow viciously.

Nelson pretended not to hear her.

'You can explain to him how things stand here, and tell him I can't be back until tomorrow.'

'Not before then?' she put in sarcastically.

'I suppose you'll tell me you haven't room for me?' he asked angrily.

'Oh, there's always a spare cowshed if the mountains aren't wide enough,' she retorted.

So I took the hint, and musing upon the contrariness of men and the inhuman persuadableness of motors, I took my machine-gun and drove off through the hills as dark was coming on.

Soirée Chez une Belle Jeune Fille

This was Helen Joyce's first experience as courier.

On Tuesday morning one of the other girls passed her a note. The class was half asleep, the old professor was half asleep, and as always when he was drowsy his lecture grew more and more unintelligible. She looked at the slip of paper. 'Call at the Western before 5 and say you've come about a room to let. Bring your bicycle. *Destroy this.*' Conspiratorial methods – there was no reason why the message could not have been given verbally. 'And may we not say,' old Turner asked querulously, 'or perhaps it is too serious a thing to say – though Burke – or it may be Newman – I have forgotten which – remarks (though he qualifies the remark – and let me add in passing that whatever we may think – and think we must – though of course within certain limits . . .)'. The day was cloudy and warm; the lecture hall was suffocating, and a girl beside her was lazily sketching Turner who looked for all the world like an old magician or mediaeval alchemist with his long, skinny arms, flowing gown and white beard.

She called at the Western. Its real name was The Western Milk and Butter Emporium, and it was a little dairy in the slums kept by a cripple and his wife. Besides being used as a dairy and a political rendezvous it was also a brothel of sorts, but this she did not learn until long after. Low, dark, cobwebby, with blackened rafters that seemed to absorb whatever light came through the little doorway, it gave her a creepy feeling, 'a hospital feeling', as she said herself. She looked about her at the case of eggs, the two shining churns of milk, and the half-dozen butter boxes, and wondered who in heaven's name the customers might be.

The cripple led her into a little back room, half kitchen, half bedroom, that was if anything lower and darker and cobwebbier than the shop; it was below the street level and was unfurnished except for a bed, a kitchen table, and two chairs. Here he produced the dispatch, and gave her directions as to how it was to be delivered. She paid more attention to his appearance than to his instructions. Somehow she had not imagined revolutionaries of his sort. He was low-sized almost to dwarfishness; his voice was a woman's voice, and his eyes, screwed-up close to her own, were distorted by convex spectacles tied with twine. He spoke quickly and clearly but with the accent of a half-educated man; she guessed that he read a great many newspapers, and probably had a brother or cousin in America who sent him supplies. At last he left her, sniggering, 'to dispose of de dispatches as she tought best', but before she hid the tiny manilla envelope in her clothes she took care to bolt the door behind him.

Then she cycled off. The streets were slobbery and greasy. It was one of those uncertain southern days when the sky lifts and lowers, lifts and lowers, endlessly. But if the city streets were greasy the country roads were far worse. Walking, she was ankle-deep in mud, and when she stepped in a pothole she had to drag her foot away as though it belonged to someone else. Rain came on in spells and then there was nothing for it but to take shelter under some bush or tree. When it cleared from where she stood she saw it hanging in wait for her on top of the next hill, or above the river, or trailing in a sort of cottony mist along the blue-grey fences. And finally, when a ray of light did break through the dishevelled, dribbling clouds, it was a silvery cold light that made the ploughed lands purple like heather.

For four miles she met nothing upon the road but a wain of hay that swayed clumsily to and fro before her like the sodden hinder-parts of some great unwieldy animal. After that two more miles and not a soul. Civil war was having its effect. Then came a pony and trap driven by an old priest, and again desolation as she cycled into a tantalizingly beautiful sunset that dripped with liquid red and gold. By this time she was so wet that she could enjoy it without thinking of what was to come. She was tired and happy and full of high spirits. At last she was doing the work she had always longed to do, not her own work but Ireland's. The old stuffy, proprietary world she had been reared in was somewhere far away behind her; before her was a world of youth and comradeship and adventure.

She looked with wonder at the flat valley road in front. Along it two parallel lines of potholes were overflowing with the momentary glory of the setting sun. It sank, and in the fresh sky above it, grey-green like a pigeon's breast, a wet star flickered out and shone as brightly as a white flower in dew-drenched grass. Then a blob of rain splashed upon her bare hand. Another fell, and still another, and in a moment a brown mist sank like a weighted curtain across the glowing west. The bell on her handle-bars, jogged by the potholes, tinkled, and she shivered, clinging to her bicycle.

In a little while she was pushing it up the miry boreen of a farmhouse to which she had been directed. Here her trip should have ended, but, in fact, it did nothing of the sort. There was no one to be seen but an old woman who leaned over her half-door; a very difficult and discreet old woman in a crimson shawl that made a bright patch in the greyness of evening. First, she affected not to hear what Helen said; then she admitted that some men had been there, but where they had gone to or when she had no idea. She doubted if they were any but boys from the next parish. She did not know when they would return, if they returned at all. In fact, she knew nothing of them, had never seen them, and was relying entirely on hearsay.

Helen was almost giving up in despair when the man of the house, a tall, bony, good-natured lad, drove up the boreen in a country cart. 'The boys,' he said, 'were wesht beyant the hill in Crowley's, where all the boys wint, and likely they wouldn't be back before midnight. There was only Mike Redmond and Tom Jordan in it; the resht of the column got shcattered during the day.'

A gaunt figure under the gloom of the trees, he shook rain from the peak of his cap with long sweeps of his arm and smiled. Her heart warmed to him. He offered to lead her to Crowley's, and pushed her bicycle for her as they went down the lane together. 'It was surprising,' he said, 'that no wan had told her of Crowley's; it was a famous shpot,' and he thought 'everywan knew of it'.

Crowley's was what he called 'a good mile off', which meant something less than two, and it was still raining. But she found him good company, and inquisitive, as ready to listen as to talk; and soon she was hearing about his brothers in America, and his efforts to learn Irish, and the way he had hidden four rifles when the Black and Tans were coming up the boreen. She said goodbye to him with regret, and went up the avenue to Crowley's alone. It was a comfortable modern house with two broad bay windows that cast an amber glow out into the garden and on to the golden leaves of a laurel that stood before the door.

She knocked and a young woman answered, standing between her and the hall light, while she, half-blinded, asked for Michael Redmond. All at once the young woman pounced upon her and pulled her inside the door.

'Helen!' she gasped. 'Helen Joyce as I'm alive!'

Helen looked at her with astonishment and suddenly remembered the girl with the doll-like features and fair, fluffy hair who held her by the arms. Eric Nolan, the college high-brow, had called her the Darling because she resembled the heroine of some Russian story, and the name had stuck, at least among those who, with Helen and her friends, disliked her. She was not pretty; neither was she intelligent: so the girls said, but the boys replied that she was so feminine! Her eyes were weak and narrowed into slits when she was observing somebody, and when she smiled her lower lip got tucked away behind a pair of high teeth. And as she helped Helen to remove her wet coat and gaiters the latter remembered a habit of hers that had become a college joke, the habit of pulling younger girls aside and asking if there wasn't something wrong with her lip. Not that there ever was, but it provided the Darling with an excuse to pull a long face, and say with a sigh, 'Harry bit me, dear. Whatever am I to do with that boy?' She was so feminine!

She showed Helen into the drawing-room. There were two men inside and they rose to greet her. She handed her dispatch to Michael Redmond, who merely glanced at the contents and put it in his coat pocket. 'There was no answer?' she asked in consternation. 'Not at all,' he replied with a shrug of his shoulders and offered her instead several letters to post. She looked incredulously at him, perilously close to tears.

She was actually sniffing as she followed the Darling upstairs. It was her first experience of headquarters work and already it was too much. She had come all this way and must go back again that night; yet it appeared as if the dispatch she had carried was of no importance to anyone and might as well have been left over until morning, if, indeed, it was worth carrying at all. She did not want to stay for tea and meet Michael Redmond again, but stay she must. Anything was better than facing out immediately, cold and hungry, into the darkness and rain.

She changed her stockings and put on a pair of slippers. When she came downstairs again the room seemed enchantingly cosy. There were thick rugs, a good fire, and a table laid for tea.

She knew Redmond by sight. The other man, Jordan, she had known when she was fifteen or sixteen and went to Gaelic League dances. He used to come in full uniform, fresh from a parade, or after fighting began, in green breeches with leather gaiters, the very cut of a fine soldier. The girls all raved about him.

He looked no older now than he had looked then, and was still essentially the same suave, spectacular young man with the long studious face, the thin-lipped mouth and the dark, smouldering eyes. He was as fiery, as quick in speech, as ever. Eric Nolan had called him The Hero of All Dreams (a nickname which was considered to be in bad taste and had not stuck). In real life the Hero of All Dreams had a little plumbing business in a poor quarter of the city, was married, and had fathered seven children of whom three only were alive.

Michael Redmond, the more urbane and conventional of the two, was genuinely a Don Juan of sorts. He looked rather like an ape with his low, deeply-rounded forehead and retreating chin, his thick lips and short nose. He had small, good-humoured eyes and the most complacent expression Helen had ever seen upon a man. It was a caricature of self-satisfaction. About his forehead and eyes and mouth the skin had contracted into scores of little wrinkles, and each wrinkle seemed to be saying, 'Look! *I* am experience.' His hair was wiry with the alertness of the man's whole nature; it was cut close and going grey in patches. Clearly, he was no longer young. But he exuded enthusiasms, and talked in sharp, quick spurts that were like the crackling of a machine-gun.

Helen found herself rather liking him.

Jordan had been describing their experiences of the day and for Helen's benefit he went back to the beginning. While she was sleeping in her warm bed (he seemed to grudge her the bed) they were being roused out of a cold and comfortless barn in the mountains between Dunmanway and Gugan by word of a column that was conducting a house-to-house search for them. And as they crept out of the barn in the mist of dawn, their feet numbed with cold, they saw troops gathering in the village below with lorries and an armoured car.

Michael Redmond snatched at the tale and swept it forward. As they were making off they had been attacked and forced to take cover behind the heaps of turf that were laid out in rows along the side of the hill. It was only the grouping of the soldiers in the village street that had saved them. (He rubbed his hands gleefully as he said it.) Ten minutes of rapid fire into that tightly-packed mass and it had scattered helter-skelter, leaving three casualties behind. Long before it had time to reform in anything like fighting order they had made their escape. And they had been marching all day.

So being in the neighbourhood, added Jordan slyly, they had called on the Crowleys. Oh, of course, they had called! exclaimed Redmond unaware of any sarcastic intent on his companion's part. May would never have forgiven them if they hadn't. And he smiled at her with a carefully prepared, unctuous smile that showed a pair of gold-stopped teeth and spread slowly to the corners of his mouth while his face contracted into a hundred wrinkles.

'Oh, everyone drops in here,' tinkled the Darling as she flitted about the room. 'Mother calls our house "No Man's Land". Last week we had – let me see – we had seven here, three republicans and four Free Staters.'

'Not all together, I hope?' asked Jordan with a sneer.

'Well, not altogether. But what do you think of this? Vincent Kelly – you know Vincent, Helen, the commanding officer in M— – came in one evening about three weeks ago, and who was sitting by the fire but Tom Keogh, all dressed up in riding-breeches and gaiters, on his way to the column!'

'No?'

'Yes, I tell you. The funniest thing you ever saw!'

'And what happened?' asked Helen breathlessly.

'Well, I introduced them. "Commandant Kelly, *Mr Burke*," and Vincent held out his fist like a little gentleman, and said, "How do you do, *Mr Burke*?" And after ten minutes Tommy gave in and said with his best Sunday morning smile, "So sorry I must go, Commandant," and they solemnly shook hands again – just as though they wouldn't have liked to cut one another's throats instead!'

'But do you mean to say –?' Helen was incredulous. 'Do you really mean to say you don't bang the door in these people's faces?'

'Who do you mean?' asked the Darling with equal consternation. 'Is it Tommy Keogh and Vincent Kelly?'

'No, no. But Free State soldiers?'

'God, no!'

'You don't?'

'Not at all. I've known Vincent Kelly since he was that high. Why the devil *should* I bang the door in his face? I remember when he and Tommy were as thick as thieves, when Vincent wouldn't go to a dance unless Tommy went too. Tomorrow they'll be as thick again – unless they shoot one another in the meantime. . . . And you think I'm going to quarrel with one about the other?'

'Certainly not,' said Michael Redmond with dignity. 'No one expects impossibilities.'

'Of course not,' echoed Jordan, his voice tinged with the same elaborate irony. Obviously he was enjoying Helen's discomfiture.

'But what a ridiculous idea!' gasped the Darling as she poured out tea.

'Well, I don't understand it,' Helen added weakly.

Whatever explanation she might have received was anticipated by a startling incident. They had noticed no previous sound before the front gate clanged open with a scream of hinges, and they heard the chug-chug of a car turning in from the road. The two men started up. Jordan's hand flew to his hip-pocket.

'Don't be silly!' said the Darling. 'As for you,' she added resentfully to Jordan, 'you seem to have a passion for showing that you pack a gun.'

His hand fell back to his side.

'Nobody's going to raid us. Besides, if they were, do you really think they'd drive up to the door like that?'

The car stopped running and she went out into the hall. Her reasoning seemed sound, and the two men sat down again, Jordan on the edge of his chair with his hands between his knees. They looked abashed, but did not take their eyes from the door.

There was a murmur of voices in the hall; the door opened and again Jordan as if instinctively drew back his arm. In the doorway stood a tall young man in the uniform of the Regular Army.

'Don't be afraid, children,' sang the Darling's voice from behind him. 'You all know one another. You know Doctor Considine, Helen? – Doctor Considine, Miss Helen Joyce. . . . Rebels all, Bill! Have a cup of tea.'

The newcomer bowed stiffly, sat down close to the door and accepted in silence the cup of tea which May Crowley handed him. He had a narrow head with blond hair, cropped very close, and an incipient fair moustache.

He was restless, almost irritable, and coughed and crossed and recrossed his legs without ceasing, as though he wished himself anywhere but in their company. The other two men showed hardly less constraint, and in the conversation, such as it was there was a suggestion that everybody had forgotten everybody else's name. The Darling prattled on, but her prattling had no effect and scarcely raised a smile. Even turning on the gramophone did not help to dissipate the general gloom. Considine looked positively penitential.

Suddenly, putting his cup on the table and pushing it decisively away from him, he said without looking round:

'I suppose neither of you fellows would care to come into town with me?'

A mystified silence followed his question.

'I'd be glad of somebody's company,' he added with a sigh.

'But Helen is going back to town, Bill,' said the Darling with astonishment.

'I doubt if she'd care to come back with me,' Considine muttered with rapidly increasing gloom.

'Why shouldn't she? I thought you'd never met before tonight?'

The doctor ignored the insinuation, and turning to Redmond he went on almost appealingly.

'I'd take it as a personal favour.'

'Very sorry,' replied Redmond from behind a suspicious smile. 'I'm afraid it's impossible.'

'What about you?' This to Jordan.

Jordan shook his head.

'Nothing to be afraid of, of course. I'd guarantee to bring you there and back safely.'

Jordan looked at Redmond, who avoided the silent question, and once again, but with less decision, he made a gesture of refusal.

'But what in Heaven's name do you want him for?' asked the Darling. 'It will take you three-quarters of an hour at most to get home. Less if you cross the blown-up bridge. At your age you're not afraid of travelling alone, surely?'

'I'm not alone,' said the doctor.

'Not alone?' three voices asked in unison.

'No. There's a stiff in the car.'

Fully aware of the dramatic quality of his announcement he rose in gloomy meditation, crossed to the window and spun up the blind, as though to assure himself that the 'stiff' was still there. The others looked at one another in stupefaction.

'And how did *you* come by the stiff?' asked the Darling at last.

'A fight outside Dunmanway this morning. He got it through the chest.'

His audience looked at one another again. There was a faint gleam of satisfaction in Michael Redmond's eyes that seemed to say, 'There! What did I tell you?' The doctor sat down and lit a cigarette before he resumed.

'He was all right when we left B—. At least I was certain he'd be all right if only we could operate at once. There was no ambulance – there never is in this bloody army – so I dumped him into the car and drove off for Cork. We had to go slow. The roads were bad, and I was afraid the jolting might be too much for him. I swear to God I couldn't have driven more carefully!'

He took out a handkerchief and wiped the sweat from his face.

'We talked a bit at first. He spoke very intelligently. He was a nice boy, about nineteen. Then I noticed he was sleepy as I thought, nodding and only answering now and again, but I paid no heed to that. It was only to be expected. It was getting dark, too, at the time, and I had to keep my eyes on the road. Then, as I was passing the cross a half-mile back, I got nervous. I can't describe it – it was a sort of eerie feeling. It may have been the trees; trees affect me like that. Or the mist – I don't know. I called back to him and he didn't answer, so I stopped the car and switched on a torch I have (here he fumbled in his pockets, produced the lamp, and switched it on in evidence). Then I saw his tunic was saturated with blood. The poor devil was stone dead.

'So I'm in a bit of a hole,' he added irrelevantly.

They sat still, and for the first time Helen heard the pock-pock of the rain against the window like the faint creak of a loose board.

'I thought there might be someone here who'd come into town with me. I don't like facing in alone. I'm not ashamed to admit that.'

He was watching Jordan out of the corner of his eye. So were the others, for at the same moment all seemed to become aware of his presence. He seemed to project an aura of emotional disturbance.

'Well,' he began hesitantly, seeing their eyes on him, 'what can I do?' He gave a shrug that said the very opposite of what his face was saying.

'I'll admit I'd like to help you. I don't want to see another man in a hole but – when the thing's impossible?'

'I'd bring you back tomorrow night.'

'Of course. . . .' Jordan hovered upon the brink of an avowal. 'There's another reason. The wife and kiddies. I haven't seen them now for close on three months.'

'You'll be absolutely safe,' said the doctor with growing emphasis. 'Absolutely. I can guarantee that. If necessary I can even speak for the Commanding Officer. Isn't that enough for you?'

Jordan looked at Redmond and Redmond looked back with a shrug that seemed to say, 'Do as you please.' Jordan was alone, and knew it, and his face grew redder and redder as he looked from one to another. A helpless silence fell upon them all, so complete that Helen was positively startled by the doctor's voice saying, almost with satisfaction:

'Plenty of time, you know. It's only seven o'clock.'

She looked at her watch and rose with a little gasp of dismay. At the same moment Jordan too sprang up.

'I may as well chance it,' he said with brazen nonchalance, his hands locked behind his head and a faint smile playing about the corners of his mouth. 'A married man needs a little relaxation now and then.'

'Certainly,' said Michael Redmond.

Though there was no sarcasm in the voice Jordan looked up as though he had been struck.

'You people know nothing about it,' he said sharply, and wounded vanity triumphed over his assumed nonchalance. 'Wait until you're married! Perhaps you'll see things differently then. Wait until you've children of your own.'

He glanced angrily at the girls.

Considine waved a vague, disparaging hand.

'Why, it's the most natural thing in the world,' he said, imparting a sort of general scientific absolution to the sentiment implied. 'The most natural thing in the world.'

The others said nothing. The two girls went upstairs, and while Helen changed back into her shoes and gaiters May Crowley sat on the bed beside her, and a look of utter disgust settled upon her vapid mouth.

'Honest to God,' she said petulantly, 'wouldn't he give you the sick, himself and his wife? Why doesn't he stay at home with her altogether?

It's revolting! He should be kept with a column for five years at a time. He's been carrying on for years like that, skipping back like a kid to a jampot, and his poor drag of a wife suffering for him. There she is every twelve months trotting out in that old fur coat of hers – the same old fur coat she got when they were married – and she has to face police and soldiers night after night in that condition! If they raid his house at all they raid it twice a week to keep her company. Because he's such a great soldier! Soldier my eye! If they only knew! But it is revolting, isn't it, Helen?'

'I suppose it is,' replied Helen weakly.

'Of course it is. . . . Michael Redmond is more in my line,' she went on as she stood before the mirror and added a dab of powder to her nose. 'He's a man of the world if you understand me, the sort of man who can talk to a woman. I think I prefer him to any of them, with the exception of Vincent Kelly. . . . Now Vincent is a gentleman if you like. I'm sure you'd love him if only you knew him better. . . . But Jordan! Ugh! Thanks be to God, Bill Considine is taking him out of this. When he looks at you it's as though he was guessing how many children you'd have. He's a breeder, my dear, that's what he is, a breeder!'

Helen did not reply. She was thinking of the dead boy outside in the car.

'Helen, child,' the Darling went on inconsequentially, 'you'd better stop the night.'

'No, really,' said Helen, 'I must get home.'

'I suppose you must.' The Darling looked at her out of indifferent, half-shut eyes. 'Michael is a sweet man! . . . It's the way they hold you, isn't it, dear? I mean, don't you know immediately a man puts his arm round you what his character is like?'

When they came downstairs the others were waiting in a group under the hall-lamp; Considine in his uniform cap and great coat; Jordan looking more than ever like a hero of romance in trench-coat and soft hat, his muddy gaiters showing beneath the ragged edges of his coat.

Michael Redmond opened the door, and they felt the breath of the cold, wet night outside, without a star, and saw the great balloon-like laurel bush in the centre of the avenue, catching the golden beams from doorway and window, and reflecting them from its wet leaves. The car was standing beside it out of range of the light. Helen stood behind for a moment while the others approached it, then, fascinated, she followed them. Considine produced his electric torch, and a beam from it shot through the light rain into the darkness of the car. There was nothing to be seen.

Startled, the Darling and Jordan stepped back, and the little group remained for a few seconds looking where the grey light played upon the car's dark hood. Then the doctor laughed, a slight, nervous laugh, and his hand went to the catch of the door. It shot open with a click and something slid out, and hung suspended a few inches above the footboard. It was a man's head, the face upturned, the long, dark hair brushing the footboard of the car, the eyes staring back at them, bright but cold. The face was the face of a boy, but the open mouth, streaked with blood, made it seem like the face of an old man. There was a brown stain across the right cheek, as though the boy had drawn his sleeve across it when the haemorrhage began.

No one said anything; all were too fascinated to speak. Then Michael Redmond's hand went out and, catching the doctor's wrist, forced the light quietly away. It went out, and Redmond lifted the body and thrust it back on the seat.

'Now,' he said, and the pompousness seemed to have gone from his voice. 'You'd better start, doctor.'

'What about you, Miss Joyce?' asked Considine.

'I'm cycling in,' she said.

'We can pace you, of course. The roads are bad, and we shouldn't be able to go fast anyhow.'

'Never mind,' said Redmond roughly. 'It won't take her long to get home.'

Helen liked him more than ever.

He lit her bicycle lamp, and, with a hurried good-bye, she cycled down the avenue. She had gone the best part of half her way before the car caught up on her. Mentally she thanked Michael Redmond for the delay – 'man of the world, man of the world', she thought. The car slowed down, and Jordan shouted something which she did not catch and did not reply to. It went on again, and his voice lingered in her ears, faintly repulsive.

The tail-light of the car (the red glass had gone and there was only a white blob leaping along the road) disappeared round a corner, and left her to the wet waste night and the gloom of the trees. Already the rain was beginning to clear; soon there would be a fine spell, with stars perhaps, but the road was full of potholes, and she could almost feel the mud that rose in the lamplight on each side of her front wheel, and spattered her gaiters and coat. And still the voice of Jordan lingered in her ears, and from the depths of her memory rose a bit of a poem that she had heard old Turner quote in college. Had he said that it was one of the finest in the English language? It would be like old Turner to say that. Fat lot he knew about it anyway! But it haunted her mind.

> So the two brothers with their murdered man
> Rode past fair Florence . . .

Jumbo's Wife

1

When he had taken his breakfast, silently as his way was after a drunk, he lifted the latch and went out without a word. She heard his feet tramp down the flagged laneway, waking iron echoes, and, outraged, shook her fist after him; then she pulled off the old red flannel petticoat and black shawl she was wearing, and crept back into the hollow of the bed. But not to sleep. She went over and over in her mind the shame of last night's bout, felt at her lip where he had split it with a blow, and recalled how she had fled into the roadway screaming for help and been brought back by Pa Kenefick, the brother of the murdered boy. Somehow that had sobered Jumbo. Since Michael, the elder of the Kenefick brothers, had been taken out and killed by the police, the people looked up to Pa rather as they looked up to the priest, but more passionately, more devotedly. She remembered how even Jumbo, the great swollen insolent Jumbo, had crouched back into the darkness when he saw that slip of a lad walk in before her. 'Stand away from me,' he had said, but not threateningly. 'It was a shame,' Pa had retorted, 'a confounded shame for a drunken elephant of a man to beat his poor decent wife like that,' but Jumbo had said nothing, only 'Let her be, boy, let her be! Go away from me now and I'll quieten down.' 'You'd better quieten down,' Pa had said, 'or you'll answer for it to me, you great bully you,' and he had kicked about the floor the pieces of the delft that Jumbo in his drunken frenzy had shattered one by one against the wall. 'I tell you I won't lay a finger on her,' Jumbo had said, and sure enough, when Pa Kenefick had gone, Jumbo was a quiet man.

But it was the sight of the brother of the boy that had been murdered rather than the beating she had had or the despair at seeing her little share of delft smashed on her, that brought home to Jumbo's wife her own utter humiliation. She had often thought before that she would run away from Jumbo, even, in her wild way, that she would do for him, but never before had she seen so clearly what a wreck he had made of her life. The sight of Pa had reminded her that she was no common trollop but a decent girl; he had said it, 'your decent poor wife', that was what Pa had said, and it was true; she was a decent poor woman. Didn't the world know how often she had pulled the little home together on her blackguard of a husband, the man who had 'listed in the army under a false name so as to rob her of the separation money, the man who would keep a job only as long as it pleased him, and send her out then to work in the nurseries, picking fruit for a shilling a day?

She was so caught up into her own bitter reflections that when she glanced round suddenly and saw the picture that had been the ostensible cause of Jumbo's fury awry, the glass smashed in it, and the bright colours stained with tea, her lip fell, and she began to moan softly to herself. It was a beautiful piece – that was how she described it – a beautiful, massive piece of a big, big castle, all towers, on a rock, and mountains and snow behind. Four shillings and sixpence it had cost her in the Coal Quay market. Jumbo would spend three times that on a drunk; ay, three times and five times that Jumbo would spend, and for all, he had smashed every cup and plate and dish in the house on her poor little picture – because it was extravagance, he said.

She heard the postman's loud double knock, and the child beside her woke and sat up. She heard a letter being slipped under the door. Little Johnny heard it too. He climbed down the side of the bed, pattered across the floor in his nightshirt and brought it to her. A letter with the On-His-Majesty's-Service stamp; it was Jumbo's pension that he drew every quarter. She slipped it under her pillow with a fresh burst of rage. It would keep. She would hold on to it until he gave her his week's wages on Friday. Yes, she would make him hand over every penny of it even if he killed her after. She had done it before, and would do it again.

Little Johnny began to cry that he wanted his breakfast, and she rose, sighing, and dressed. Over the fire as she boiled the kettle she meditated again on her wrongs, and was startled when she found the child actually between her legs holding out the long envelope to the flames, trying to boil the kettle with it. She snatched it wildly from his hand and gave him a vicious slap across the face that set him howling. She stood turning the letter over and over in her hand curiously, and then started as she remembered that it wasn't until another month that Jumbo's pension fell due. She counted the weeks; no, that was right, but what had them sending out Jumbo's pension a month before it was due?

When the kettle boiled she made the tea, poured it out into two tin ponnies, and sat into table with the big letter propped up before her as though she was trying to read its secrets through the manilla covering. But she was no closer to solving the mystery when her breakfast of bread and tea was done, and, sudden resolution coming to her, she held the envelope over the spout of the kettle and slowly steamed its fastening away. She drew out the flimsy note inside and opened it upon the table. It was an order, a money order, but not the sort they sent to Jumbo. The writing on it meant little to her, but what did mean a great deal were the careful figures, a two and a five that filled one corner. A two and a five and a sprawling sign before them; this was not for Jumbo – or was it? All sorts of suspicions began to form in her mind, and with them a feeling of pleasurable excitement.

She thought of Pa Kenefick. Pa was a good scholar and the proper man to see about a thing like this. And Pa had been good to her. Pa would feel she was doing the right thing in showing him this mysterious paper, even if it meant nothing but a change in the way they paid Jumbo's pension; it would show how much she looked up to him.

She threw her old black shawl quickly about her shoulders and grabbed at the child's hand. She went down the low arched laneway where they lived – Melancholy Lane, it was called – and up the road to the Keneficks'. She knocked at their door, and Mrs Kenefick, whose son had been dragged to his death from that door, answered it. She looked surprised when she saw the other woman, and only then Jumbo's wife realized how early it was. She asked excitedly for Pa. He wasn't at home, his mother said, and she didn't know when he would be home, if he came at all. When she saw how crestfallen her visitor looked at this, she asked politely if she couldn't send a message, for women like Jumbo's wife frequently brought information that was of use to the volunteers. No, no, the other woman said earnestly, it was for Pa's ears, for Pa's ears alone, and it couldn't wait. Mrs Kenefick asked her into the parlour, where the picture of the murdered

boy, Michael, in his Volunteer uniform hung. It was dangerous for any of
the company to stay at home, she said, the police knew the ins and outs
of the district too well; there was the death of Michael unaccounted for,
and a dozen or more arrests, all within a month or two. But she had never
before seen Jumbo's wife in such a state and wondered what was the best
thing for her to do. It was her daughter who decided it by telling where
Pa was to be found, and immediately the excited woman raced off up the
hill towards the open country.

She knocked at the door of a little farmhouse off the main road, and
when the door was opened she saw Pa himself, in shirt-sleeves, filling out
a basin of hot water to shave. His first words showed that he thought it
was Jumbo who had been at her again, but, without answering him,
intensely conscious of herself and of the impression she wished to create,
she held the envelope out at arm's length. He took it, looked at the address
for a moment, and then pulled out the flimsy slip. She saw his brows bent
above it, then his lips tightened. He raised his head and called, 'Jim, Liam,
come down! Come down a minute!' The tone in which he said it delighted
her as much as the rush of footsteps upstairs. Two men descended a ladder
to the kitchen, and Pa held out the slip. 'Look at this!' he said. They looked
at it, for a long time it seemed to her, turning it round and round and
examining the postmark on the envelope. She began to speak rapidly. 'Mr
Kenefick will tell you, gentlemen, Mr Kenefick will tell you, the life he
leads me. I was never one for regulating me own, gentlemen, but I say
before me God this minute, hell will never be full till they have him
roasting there. A little pitcher I bought, gentlemen, a massive little piece –
Mr Kenefick will tell you – I paid four and sixpence for it – he said I was
extravagant. Let me remark he'd spend three times, ay, and six times, as
much on filling his own gut as I'd spend upon me home and child. Look
at me, gentlemen, look at me lip where he hit me – Mr Kenefick will tell
you – I was in gores of blood.' 'Listen now, ma'am,' one of the men
interrupted suavely, 'we're very grateful to you for showing us this letter.
It's something we wanted to know this long time, ma'am. And now like a
good woman will you go back home and not open your mouth to a soul
about it, and, if himself ask you anything, say there did ne'er a letter come?'
Of course, she said, she would do whatever they told her. She was in their
hands. Didn't Mr Kenefick come in, like the lovely young man he was,
and save her from the hands of that dancing hangman Jumbo? And wasn't

she sorry for his mother, poor little 'oman, and her fine son taken away on her? Weren't they all crazy about her?

The three men had to push her out the door, saying that she had squared her account with Jumbo at last.

2

At noon with the basket of food under her arm, and the child plodding along beside her, she made her way through the northern slums to a factory on the outskirts of the city. There, sitting on the grass beside a little stream – her usual station – she waited for Jumbo. He came just as the siren blew, sat down beside her on the grass, and, without as much as fine day, began to unpack the food in the little basket. Already she was frightened and unhappy; she dreaded what Jumbo would do if ever he found out about the letter, and find out he must. People said he wouldn't last long on her, balloon and all as he was. Some said his heart was weak, and others that he was bloated out with dropsy and would die in great agony at any minute. But those who said that hadn't felt the weight of Jumbo's hand.

She sat in the warm sun, watching the child dabble his fingers in the little stream, and all the bitterness melted away within her. She had had a hard two days of it, and now she felt Almighty God might well have pity on her, and leave her a week or even a fortnight of quiet, until she pulled her little home together again. Jumbo ate placidly and contentedly; she knew by this his drinking bout was almost over. At last he pulled his cap well down over his eyes and lay back with his wide red face to the sun. She watched him, her hands upon her lap. He looked for all the world like a huge, fat, sulky child. He lay like that without stirring for some time; then he stretched out his legs, and rolled over and over and over downhill through the grass. He grunted with pleasure, and sat up blinking drowsily at her from the edge of the cinder path. She put her hand in her pocket. 'Jim, will I give you the price of an ounce of 'baccy?' He stared up at her for a moment. 'There did ne'er a letter come for me?' he asked, and her heart sank. 'No, Jim,' she said feebly, 'what letter was it you were expecting?' 'Never mind, you. Here, give us a couple of lob for a wet!' She counted him out six coppers and he stood up to go.

All the evening she worried herself about Pa Kenefick and his friends – though to be sure they were good-natured, friendly boys. She was glad when Jumbo came in at tea-time; the great bulk of him stretched out in the corner gave her a feeling of security. He was almost in good humour again, and talked a little, telling her to shut up when her tongue wagged too much, or sourly abusing the 'bummers' who had soaked him the evening before. She had cleared away the supper things when a motor-car drove up the road and stopped at the end of Melancholy Lane. Her heart misgave her. She ran to the door and looked out; there were two men coming up the lane, one of them wearing a mask; when they saw her they broke into a trot. 'Merciful Jesus!' she screamed, and rushed in, banging and bolting the door behind her. Jumbo stood up slowly. 'What is it?' he asked. 'That letter.' 'What letter?' 'I showed it to Pa Kenefick, that letter from the barrack.' The blue veins rose on Jumbo's forehead as though they would burst. He could barely speak but rushed to the fireplace and swept the poker above her head. 'If it's the last thing I ever do I'll have your sacred life!' he said in a hoarse whisper. 'Let me alone! Let me alone!' she shrieked. 'They're at the door!' She leaned her back against the door, and felt against her spine the lurch of a man's shoulder. Jumbo heard it; he watched her with narrowed, despairing eyes, and then beckoned her towards the back door. She went on before him on tiptoe and opened the door quietly for him. 'Quick,' he said, 'name of Jasus, lift me up this.' This was the back wall, which was fully twice his own height but had footholes by which he could clamber up. She held his feet in them, and puffing and growling, he scrambled painfully up, inch by inch, until his head was almost level with the top of the wall; then with a gigantic effort he slowly raised his huge body and laid it flat upon the spiny top. 'Keep them back, you!' he said. 'Here,' she called softly up to him, 'take this,' and he bent down and caught the poker.

It was dark in the little kitchen. She crept to the door and listened, holding her breath. There was no sound. She was consumed with anxiety and impatience. Suddenly little Johnny sat up and began to howl. She grasped the key and turned it in the lock once; there was no sound; at last she opened the door slowly. There was no one to be seen in the lane. Night was setting in – maybe he would dodge them yet. She locked the screaming child in behind her and hurried down to the archway.

The motor-car was standing where it had stopped and a man was leaning over the wheel smoking a cigarette. He looked up and smiled at her. 'Didn't they get him yet?' he asked, 'No,' she said mechanically. 'Ah, cripes!' he swore, 'with the help of God they'll give him an awful end when they ketch him.' She stood there looking up and down the road in the terrible stillness: there were lamps lighting behind every window but not a soul appeared. At last a strange young man in a trench-coat rushed down the lane towards them. 'Watch out there,' he cried. 'He's after giving us the slip. Guard this lane and the one below, don't shoot unless you can get him.' He doubled down the road and up the next laneway.

The young man in the car topped his cigarette carefully, put the butt-end in his waistcoat pocket and crossed to the other side of the road. He leaned nonchalantly against the wall and drew a heavy revolver. She crossed too and stood beside him. An old lamplighter came up one of the lanes from the city and went past them to the next gas-lamp, his torch upon his shoulder. 'He's a brute of a man,' the driver said consolingly, 'sure, I couldn't but hit him in the dark itself. But it's a shame now they wouldn't have a gas-lamp at that end of the lane, huh!' The old lamp-lighter disappeared up the road, leaving two or three pale specks of light behind him.

They stood looking at the laneways each end of a little row of cottages, not speaking a word. Suddenly the young man drew himself up stiffly against the wall and raised his left hand towards the fading sky. 'See that?' he said gleefully. Beyond the row of cottages a figure rose slowly against a chimney-pot; they could barely see it in the twilight, but she could not doubt who it was. The man spat upon the barrel of his gun and raised it upon his crooked elbow; then the dark figure leaped out as it were upon the air and disappeared among the shadows of the houses. 'Jasus!' the young man swore softly, 'wasn't that a great pity?' She came to her senses in a flash. 'Jumbo!' she shrieked, 'me poor Jumbo! He's kilt, he's kilt!' and began to weep and clap her hands. The man looked at her in comical bewilderment. 'Well, well!' he said, 'to think of that! And are you his widda, ma'am?' 'God melt and wither you!' she screamed and rushed away towards the spot where Jumbo's figure had disappeared.

At the top of the lane a young man with a revolver drove her back. 'Is he kilt?' she cried. 'Too well you know he's not kilt,' the young man replied savagely. Another wearing a mask came out of a cottage and said 'He's dished us again. Don't stir from this. I'm going round to Samson's

Lane.' 'How did he manage it?' the first man asked. 'Over the roofs. This place is a network, and the people won't stir a finger to help us.'

For hours that duel in the darkness went on, silently, without a shot being fired. What mercy the people of the lanes showed to Jumbo was a mercy they had never denied to any hunted thing. His distracted wife went back to the road. Leaving the driver standing alone by his car she tramped up and down staring up every tiny laneway. It did not enter her head to run for assistance. On the opposite side of the road another network of lanes, all steep-sloping, like the others, or stepped in cobbles, went down into the heart of the city. These were Jumbo's only hope of escape, and that was why she watched there, glancing now and then at the maze of lights beneath her.

Ten o'clock rang out from Shandon – shivering, she counted the chimes. Then down one of the lanes from the north she heard a heavy clatter of ironshod feet. Clatter, clatter, clatter; the feet drew nearer, and she heard other, lighter, feet pattering swiftly behind. A dark figure emerged through an archway, running with frantic speed. She rushed out into the middle of the road to meet it, sweeping her shawl out on either side of her head like a dancer's sash. 'Jumbo, me lovely Jumbo!' she screamed. 'Out of me way, y'ould crow!' the wild quarry panted, flying past.

She heard him take the first flight of steps in the southern laneway at a bound. A young man dashed out of the archway a moment after and gave a hasty look around him. Then he ran towards her and she stepped out into the lane to block his passage. Without swerving he rushed into her at full speed, sweeping her off her feet, but she drew the wide black shawl about his head as they fell and rolled together down the narrow sloping passage. They were at the top of the steps and he still struggled frantically to free himself from the filthy enveloping shawl. They rolled from step to step, to the bottom, he throttling her and cursing furiously at her strength; she still holding the shawl tight about his head and shoulders. Then the others came and dragged him off, leaving her choking and writhing upon the ground.

But by this time Jumbo was well beyond their reach.

3

Next morning she walked dazedly about the town, stopping every policeman she met and asking for Jumbo. At the military barrack on the hill they
told her she would find him in one of the city police barracks. She explained
to the young English officer who spoke to her about Pa Kenefick, and how
he could be captured, and for her pains was listened to in wide-eyed
disgust. But what she could not understand in the young officer's attitude
to her, Jumbo, sitting over the fire in the barrack day-room, had already
been made to understand, and she was shocked to see him so pale, so
sullen, so broken. And this while she was panting with pride at his escape!
He did not even fly at her as she had feared he would, nor indeed abuse
her at all. He merely looked up and said with the bitterness of utter
resignation, 'There's the one that brought me down!' An old soldier, he
was cut to the heart that the military would not take him in, but had
handed him over to the police for protection. 'I'm no use to them now,'
he said, 'and there's me thanks for all I done. They'd as soon see me out
of the way; they'd as soon see the poor old crature that served them out
of the way.' 'It was all Pa Kenefick's doings,' his wife put in frantically, 'it
was no one else done it. Not that my poor slob of a man ever did him or
his any harm. . . .' At this the policemen round her chuckled and Jumbo
angrily bade her be silent. 'But I told the officer of the swaddies where he
was to be found,' she went on unheeding. 'What was that?' the policemen
asked eagerly, and she told them of how she had found Pa Kenefick in the
little cottage up the hill.

Every day she went to see Jumbo. When the weather was fine they sat
in the little garden behind the barrack, for it was only at dusk that Jumbo
could venture out and then only with military or police patrols. There
were very few on the road who would speak to her now, for on the night
after Jumbo's escape the little cottage where Pa Kenefick had stayed had
been raided and smashed up by masked policemen. Of course, Pa and his
friends were gone. She hated the neighbours, and dug into her mind with
the fear of what might happen to Jumbo was the desire to be quit of Pa
Kenefick. Only then, she felt in her blind headlong way, would Jumbo be
safe. And what divil's notion took her to show him the letter? She'd swing
for Pa, she said, sizing up to the policemen.

And Jumbo grew worse and worse. His face had turned from brick-red to grey. He complained always of pain and spent whole days in bed. She had heard that there was a cure for his illness in red flannel, and had made him a nightshirt of red flannel in which he looked more than ever like a ghost, his hair grey, his face quite colourless, his fat paws growing skinny under the wide crimson sleeves. He applied for admission to the military hospital, which was within the area protected by the troops, and the request was met with a curt refusal. That broke his courage. To the military for whom he had risked his life he was only an informer, a common informer, to be left to the mercy of their enemy when his services were no longer of value. The policemen sympathized with him, for they too were despised by the 'swaddies' as makers of trouble, but they could do nothing for him. And when he went out walking under cover of darkness with two policemen for an escort the people turned and laughed at him. He heard them, and returned to the barrack consumed with a rage that expressed itself in long fits of utter silence or sudden murderous outbursts.

She came in one summer evening when the fit was on him, to find him struggling in the dayroom with three of the policemen. They were trying to wrest a loaded carbine from his hands. He wanted blood, he shouted, blood, and by Christ they wouldn't stop him. They wouldn't, they wouldn't, he repeated, sending one of them flying against the hearth. He'd finish a few of the devils that were twitting him before he was plugged himself. He'd shoot everyone, man, woman, and child that came in his way. His frenzy was terrifying and the three policemen were swung this way and that, to right and left, as the struggle swept from wall to door and back. Then suddenly he collapsed and lay unconscious upon the floor. When they brought him round with whiskey he looked from one to the other, and drearily, with terrible anguish, he cursed all the powers about him, God, the King, the republicans, Ireland, and the country he had served.

'Kimberley, Pietermaritzburg, Bethlem, Bloemfontein,' he moaned. 'Ah, you thing, many's the hard day I put down for you! Devil's cure to me for a crazy man! Devil's cure to me, I say! With me cane and me busby and me scarlet coat – 'twas aisy you beguiled me! . . . The curse of God on you! . . . Tell them to pay me passage, d'you hear me? Tell them to pay me passage and I'll go out to Inja and fight the blacks for you!'

It was easy to see whom he was talking to.

'Go the road resigned, Jim,' his wife counselled timidly from above his head. Seeing him like this she could already believe him dying.

'I will not. . . . I will not go the road resigned.'

'. . . to His blessed and holy Will,' she babbled.

Lifting his two fists from the ground he thumped upon his chest like a drum.

' ''Tisn't sickness that ails me, but a broken heart,' he cried. 'Tell them to pay me passage! Ah, why didn't I stay with the lovely men we buried there, not to end me days as a public show . . . They put the croolety of the world from them young, the creatures, they put the croolety of the world from them young!'

The soldiers had again refused to admit him to the military hospital. Now the police had grown tired of him, and on their faces he saw relief, relief that they would soon be shut of him, when he entered some hospital in the city, where everyone would know him, and sooner or later his enemies would reach him. He no longer left the barrack. Disease had changed that face of his already; the only hope left to him now was to change it still further. He grew a beard.

And all this time his wife lay in wait for Pa Kenefick. Long hours on end she watched for him over her half-door. Twice she saw him pass by the laneway, and each time snatched her shawl and rushed down to the barrack, but by the time a car of plain-clothes men drove up to the Kenefick's door Pa was gone. Then he ceased to come home at all, and she watched the movements of his sister and mother. She even trained little Johnny to follow them, but the child was too young and too easily outdistanced. When she came down the road in the direction of the city, all the women standing at their doors would walk in and shut them in her face.

One day the policeman on duty at the barrack door told her gruffly that Jumbo was gone. He was in hospital somewhere; she would be told where if he was in any danger. And she knew by the tone in which he said it that the soldiers had not taken Jumbo in; that somewhere he was at the mercy of his changed appearance and assumed name, unless, as was likely, he was already too far gone to make it worth the 'rebels'' while to shoot him. Now that she could no longer see him there was a great emptiness in her life, an emptiness that she filled only with brooding and hatred. Everything within her had turned to bitterness against Pa Kenefick, the boy who had been the cause of it all, to whom she had foolishly shown the letter and who had brought the 'dirty Shinners' down on her, who alone had cause to strike at Jumbo now that he was a sick and helpless man.

'God, give me strength!' she prayed. 'I'll sober him. O God, I'll put him in a quiet habitation!'

She worked mechanically about the house. A neighbour's averted face or the closing of a door in her path brought her to such a pitch of fury that she swept out into the road, her shawl stretched out behind her head, and tore up and down, screaming like a madwoman; sometimes leaping into the air with an obscene gesture; sometimes kneeling in the roadway and cursing those that had affronted her; sometimes tapping out a few dance steps, a skip to right and a skip to left, just to rouse herself. 'I'm a bird alone!' she shrieked, 'a bird alone and the hawks about me! Good man, clever man, handsome man, I'm a bird alone!' And 'That they might rot and wither, root and branch, son and daughter, born and unborn; that every plague and pestilence might end them and theirs; that they might be called in their sins' – this was what she prayed in the traditional formula, and the neighbours closed their doors softly and crossed themselves. For a week or more she was like a woman possessed.

4

Then one day when she was standing by the archway she saw Pa Kenefick and another man come down the road. She stood back without being seen, and waited until they had gone by before she emerged and followed them. It was no easy thing to do upon the long open street that led to the quays, but she pulled her shawl well down over her eyes, and drew up her shoulders so that at a distance she might look like an old woman. She reached the foot of the hill without being observed, and after that, to follow them through the crowded, narrow side-streets of the city where every second woman wore a shawl was comparatively easy. But they walked so fast it was hard to keep up with them, and several times she had to take short-cuts that they did not know of, thus losing sight of them for the time being. Already they had crossed the bridge, and she was growing mystified; this was unfamiliar country and, besides, the pace was beginning to tell on her. They had been walking now for a good two miles and she knew that they would soon outdistance her. And all the time she had seen neither policeman nor soldier.

Gasping she stood and leaned against a wall, drawing the shawl down about her shoulders for a breath of air. 'Tell me, ma'am,' she asked of a passer-by, 'where do this road go to?' 'This is the Mallow Road, ma'am,' the other said, and since Jumbo's wife made no reply she asked was it any place she wanted. 'No, indeed,' Jumbo's wife answered without conviction. The other lowered her voice and asked sympathetically, 'Is it the hospital you're looking for, poor woman?' Jumbo's wife stood for a moment until the question sank in. 'The hospital?' she whispered. 'The hospital? Merciful God Almighty!' Then she came to her senses. 'Stop them!' she screamed, rushing out into the roadway, 'stop them! Murder! Murder! Stop them!'

The two men who by this time were far ahead heard the shout and looked back. Then one of them stepped out into the middle of the road and signalled to a passing car. They leaped in and the car drove off. A little crowd had gathered upon the path, but when they understood what the woman's screams signified they melted silently away. Only the woman to whom she had first spoken remained. 'Come with me, ma'am,' she said. ' 'Tis only as you might say a step from this.'

A tram left them at the hospital gate and Jumbo's wife and the other woman rushed in. She asked for Jumbo Geany, but the porter looked at her blankly and asked what ward she was looking for. 'There were two men here a minute ago,' she said frantically, 'where are they gone to?' 'Ah,' he said, 'now I have you! They're gone over to St George's Ward. . . .'

In St George's Ward at that moment two or three nuns and a nurse surrounded the house doctor, a tall young man who was saying excitedly, 'I couldn't stop them, couldn't stop them! I told them he was at his last gasp, but they wouldn't believe me!' 'He was lying there,' said the nurse pointing to an empty bed, 'when that woman came in with the basket, a sort of dealing woman she was. When she saw him she looked hard at him and then went across and drew back the bedclothes. "Is it yourself is there, Jumbo?" says she, and, poor man, he starts up in bed and says out loud-like "You won't give me away? Promise me you won't give me away." So she laughs and says, "A pity you didn't think of that when you gave Mike Kenefick the gun, Jumbo!" After she went away he wanted to get up and go home. I seen by his looks he was dying and I sent for the priest and Doctor Connolly, and he got wake-like, and that pair came in, asking for a stretcher, and – ' The nurse began to bawl.

Just then Jumbo's wife appeared, a distracted, terrified figure, the shawl drawn back from her brows, the hair falling about her face. 'Jumbo Geany?' she asked. 'You're too late,' said the young doctor harshly, 'they've taken him away.' 'No, come back, come back!' he shouted as she rushed towards the window that opened on to the garden at the back of the hospital, 'You can't go out there!' But she wriggled from his grasp, leaving her old black shawl in his hands. Alone she ran across the little garden, to where another building jutted out and obscured the view of the walls. As she did so three shots rang out in rapid succession. She heard a gate slam; it was the little wicket gate on to another road; beside it was a stretcher with a man's body lying on it. She flung herself screaming upon the body, not heeding the little streams of blood that flowed from beneath the armpit and the head. It was Jumbo, clad only in a nightshirt and bearded beyond recognition. His long, skinny legs were naked, and his toes had not ceased to twitch. For each of the three shots there was a tiny wound, two over the heart and one in the temple, and pinned to the cheap flannelette nightshirt was a little typed slip that read.

SPY.

They had squared her account with Jumbo at last.

The Cornet-Player Who Betrayed Ireland

At this hour of my life I don't profess to remember what we inhabitants of Blarney Lane were patriotic about: all I remember is that we were very patriotic, that our main principles were something called 'Conciliation and Consent', and that our great national leader, William O'Brien, once referred to us as 'The Old Guard'. Myself and other kids of the Old Guard used to parade the street with tin cans and toy trumpets, singing 'We'll hang Johnnie Redmond on a sour apple tree.' (John Redmond, I need hardly say, was the leader of the other side.)

Unfortunately, our neighbourhood was bounded to the south by a long ugly street leading uphill to the cathedral, and the lanes off it were infested with the most wretched specimens of humanity who took the Redmondite side for whatever could be got from it in the way of drink. My personal view at the time was that the Redmondite faction was maintained by a conspiracy of publicans and brewers. It always saddened me, coming through this street on my way from school, and seeing the poor misguided children, barefoot and in rags, parading with tin cans and toy trumpets and singing 'We'll hang William O'Brien on a sour apple tree.' It left me with very little hope for Ireland.

Of course, my father was a strong supporter of 'Conciliation and Consent'. The parish priest who had come to solicit his vote for Redmond had told him he would go straight to Hell, but my father had replied quite respectfully that if Mr O'Brien was an agent of the devil, as Father Murphy said, he would go gladly.

I admired my father as a rock of principle. As well as being a house-painter (a regrettable trade which left him for six months 'under the ivy', as we called it), he was a musician. He had been a bandsman in the British Army, played the cornet extremely well, and had been a member of the

Irishtown Brass and Reed Band from its foundation. At home we had two big pictures of the band after each of its most famous contests, in Belfast and Dublin. It was after the Dublin contest when Irishtown emerged as the premier brass band that there occurred an unrecorded episode in operatic history. In those days the best band in the city was always invited to perform in the Soldiers' Chorus scene in Gounod's *Faust*. Of course, they were encored to the echo, and then, ignoring conductor and everything else, they burst into a selection from Moore's Irish Melodies. I am glad my father didn't live to see the day of pipers' bands. Even fife and drum bands he looked on as primitive.

As he had great hopes of turning me into a musician too he frequently brought me with him to practices and promenades. Irishtown was a very poor quarter of the city, a channel of mean houses between breweries and builders' yards with the terraced hillsides high above it on either side, and nothing but the white Restoration spire of Shandon breaking the skyline. You came to a little footbridge over the narrow stream; on one side of it was a red-brick chapel, and when we arrived there were usually some of the bandsmen sitting on the bridge, spitting back over their shoulders into the stream. The bandroom was over an undertaker's shop at the other side of the street. It was a long, dark, barn-like erection overlooking the bridge and decorated with group photos of the band. At this hour of a Sunday morning it was always full of groans, squeaks and bumps.

Then at last came the moment I loved so much. Out in the sunlight, with the bridge filled with staring pedestrians, the band formed up. Dickie Ryan, the bandmaster's son, and myself took our places at either side of the big drummer, Joe Shinkwin. Joe peered over his big drum to right and left to see if all were in place and ready; he raised his right arm and gave the drum three solemn flakes: then, after the third thump the whole narrow channel of the street filled with a roaring torrent of drums and brass, the mere physical impact of which hit me in the belly. Screaming girls in shawls tore along the pavements calling out to the bandsmen, but nothing shook the soldierly solemnity of the men with their eyes almost crossed on the music before them. I've heard Toscanini conduct Beethoven, but compared with Irishtown playing 'Marching Through Georgia' on a Sunday morning it was only like Mozart in a girls' school. The mean little houses, quivering with the shock, gave it back to us: the terraced hillsides that shut out the sky gave it back to us; the interested faces of passers-by in their Sunday clothes from the pavements were like mirrors reflecting the glory of the music. When the band stopped and again you could hear the gapped sound of feet, and people running and chattering, it was like a parachute jump into commonplace.

Sometimes we boarded the paddle-steamer and set up our music stands in some little field by the sea, which all day echoed of Moore's Melodies, Rossini and Gilbert and Sullivan: sometimes we took a train into the country to play at some sports meeting. Whatever it was, I loved it, though I never got a dinner: I was fed on lemonade, biscuits and sweets, and, as my father spent most of the intervals in the pub, I was sometimes half mad with boredom.

One summer day we were playing at a fête in the grounds of Blarney Castle, and, as usual, the band departed to the pub and Dickie Ryan and myself were left behind, ostensibly to take care of the instruments. A certain hanger-on of the band, one John P., who to my knowledge was never called anything else, was lying on the grass, chewing a straw and shading his eyes from the light with the back of his hand. Dickie and I took a side drum each and began to march about with them. All at once Dickie began to sing to his own accompaniment. 'We'll hang William O'Brien on a sour apple tree.' I was so astonished that I stopped drumming and listened to him. For a moment or two I thought he must be mocking the poor uneducated children of the lanes round Shandon Street. Then I suddenly realized that he meant it. Without hesitation I began to rattle my side drum even louder and shouted 'We'll hang Johnnie Redmond on a sour apple tree.' John P. at once started up and gave me an angry glare. 'Stop that now, little boy!' he said threateningly. It was quite plain that he meant me, not Dickie Ryan.

I was completely flabbergasted. It was bad enough hearing the band-master's son singing a traitorous song, but then to be told to shut up by a fellow who wasn't even a bandsman; merely a hanger-on who looked after the music stands and carried the big drum in return for free drinks! I realized that I was among enemies. I quietly put aside the drum and went to find my father. I knew that he could have no idea what was going on behind his back in the band.

I found him at the back of the pub, sitting on a barrel and holding forth to a couple of young bandsmen.

'Now, "Brian Boru's March",' he was saying with one finger raised, 'that's a beautiful march. I heard the Irish Guards do that on Salisbury Plain, and they had the English fellows' eyes popping out. "Paddy," one of them says to me (they all call you Paddy) "wot's the name of the shouting march?" but somehow we don't get the same fire into it at all. Now, listen, and I'll show you how that should go!'

'Dadda,' I said in a whisper, pulling him by the sleeve, 'do you know what Dickie Ryan was singing?'

'Hold on a minute now,' he said, beaming at me affectionately. 'I just want to illustrate a little point.'

'But, dadda,' I went on determinedly, 'he was singing "We'll hang William O'Brien from a sour apple tree."'

'Hah, hah, hah,' laughed my father, and it struck me that he hadn't fully appreciated the implications of what I had said.

'Frank,' he added, 'get a bottle of lemonade for the little fellow.'

'But, dadda,' I said despairingly, 'when I sang "We'll hang Johnnie Redmond", John P. told me to shut up.'

'Now, now,' said my father with sudden testiness, 'that's not a nice song to be singing.'

This was a stunning blow. The anthem of 'Conciliation and Consent' – not a nice song to be singing!

'But, dadda,' I wailed, 'aren't we *for* William O'Brien?'

'Yes, yes, yes,' he replied, as if I were goading him, 'but everyone to his own opinion. Now drink your lemonade and run out and play like a good boy.'

I drank my lemonade all right, but I went out not to play but to brood. There was but one fit place for that. I went to the shell of the castle; climbed the stair to the tower and leaning over the battlements watching the landscape like bunting all round me I thought of the heroes who had stood here, defying the might of England. Everyone to his own opinion! What would they have thought of a statement like that? It was the first time that I realized the awful strain of weakness and the lack of strong principle in my father, and understood that the old bandroom by the bridge was in the heart of enemy country and that all round me were enemies of Ireland like Dickie Ryan and John P.

It wasn't until months after that I realized how many these were. It was Sunday morning, but when we reached the bandroom there was no one on the bridge. Upstairs the room was almost full. A big man wearing a bowler hat and a flower in his buttonhole was standing before the fireplace. He had a red face with weak, red-rimmed eyes and a dark moustache. My father, who seemed as surprised as I was, slipped quietly into a seat behind the door and lifted me on to his knee.

'Well, boys,' the big man said in a deep husky voice, 'I suppose ye have a good notion what I'm here for. Ye know that next Saturday night Mr Redmond is arriving in the city, and I have the honour of being Chairman of the Reception Committee.'

'Well, Alderman Doyle,' said the bandmaster doubtfully, 'you know the way we feel about Mr Redmond, most of us anyway.'

'I do, Tim, I do,' said the Alderman evenly as it gradually dawned on me that the man I was listening to was the Arch-Traitor, locally known as Scabby Doyle, the builder whose vile orations my father always read aloud to my mother with chagrined comments on Doyle's past history. 'But feeling isn't enough, Tim. Fair Lane Band will be there of course. Water-grasshill will be there. The Butter Exchange will be there. What will the backers of this band, the gentlemen who helped it through so many difficult days, say if we don't put in an appearance?'

'Well, ye see, Alderman,' said Ryan nervously, 'we have our own little difficulties.'

'I know that, Tim,' said Doyle. 'We all have our difficulties in troubled times like these, but we have to face them like men in the interests of the country. What difficulties have you?'

'Well, that's hard to describe, Alderman,' said the bandmaster.

'No, Tim,' said my father quietly, raising and putting me down from his knee, ''tis easy enough to describe. I'm the difficulty, and I know it.'

'Now, Mick,' protested the bandmaster, 'there's nothing personal about it. We're all old friends in this band.'

'We are, Tim,' agreed my father. 'And before ever it was heard of, you and me gave this bandroom its first coat of paint. But every man is entitled to his principles, and I don't want to stand in your light.'

'You see how it is, Mr Doyle,' said the bandmaster appealingly. 'We had others in the band that were of Mick Twomey's persuasion, but they left us to join O'Brienite bands. Mick didn't, nor we didn't want him to leave us.'

'Nor don't,' said a mournful voice, and I turned and saw a tall, gaunt, spectacled young man sitting on the window sill. 'I had three men,' said my father earnestly, holding up three fingers in illustration of the fact, 'three men up at the house on different occasions to get me to join other bands. I'm not boasting. Tim Ryan knows who they were.'

'I do, I do,' said the bandmaster.

'And I wouldn't,' said my father passionately. 'I'm not boasting, but you can't deny it: there isn't another band in Ireland to touch ours.'

'Nor a cornet-player in Ireland to touch Mick Twomey,' chimed in the gaunt young man, rising to his feet. 'And I'm not saying that to coddle or cock him up.'

'You're not, you're not,' said the bandmaster. 'No one can deny he's a musician.'

'And listen here to me, boys,' said the gaunt young man, with a wild wave of his arm, 'don't leave us be led astray by anyone. What were we before we had the old band? Nobody. We were no better than the poor devils that sit on that bridge outside all day, spitting into the river. Whatever we do, leave us be all agreed. What backers had we when we started, only what we could collect ourselves outside the chapel gates on Sunday, and hard enough to get permission for that itself? I'm as good a party man as anyone here, but what I say is, music is above politics . . . Alderman Doyle,' he begged, 'tell Mr Redmond whatever he'll do not to break up our little band on us.'

'Jim Ralegh,' said the Alderman, with his red-rimmed eyes growing moist, 'I'd sooner put my hand in the fire than injure this band. I know what ye are, a band of brothers . . . Mick,' he boomed at my father, 'will you desert it in its hour of trial?'

'Ah,' said my father testily, 'is it the way you want me to play against William O'Brien?'

'Play against William O'Brien,' echoed the Alderman. 'No one is asking you to play *against* anyone. As Jim Ralegh here says, music is above politics. What we're asking you to do is to play *for* something: for the band, for the sake of unity. You know what'll happen if the backers withdraw? Can't you pocket your pride and make this sacrifice in the interest of the band?'

My father stood for a few moments, hesitating. I prayed that for once he might see the true light; that he might show this group of misguided men the faith that was in him. Instead he nodded curtly, said 'Very well, I'll play,' and sat down again. The rascally Alderman said a few humbugging words in his praise which didn't take me in. I don't think they even took my father in, for all the way home he never addressed a word to me. I saw then that his conscience was at him. He knew that by supporting the band in the unprincipled step it was taking he was showing himself a traitor to Ireland and our great leader, William O'Brien.

Afterwards, whenever Irishtown played at Redmondite demonstrations, my father accompanied them, but the moment the speeches began he retreated to the edge of the crowd, rather like a pious Catholic compelled to attend a heretical religious service, and stood against the wall with his hands in his pockets, passing slighting and witty comments on the speakers to any O'Brienites he might meet. But he had lost all dignity in my eyes. Even his gibes at Scabby Doyle seemed to me false, and I longed to say to him. 'If that's what you believe, why don't you show it?' Even the seaside lost its attraction when at any moment the beautiful daughter of a decent O'Brienite family might point to me and say: 'There is the son of the cornet-player who betrayed Ireland.'

Then one Sunday we went to play at some idolatrous function in a seaside town called Bantry. While the meeting was on my father and the rest of the band retired to the pub and I with them. Even by my presence in the Square I wasn't prepared to countenance the proceedings. I was looking idly out of the window when I suddenly heard a roar of cheering and people began to scatter in all directions. I was mystified until someone outside started to shout, 'Come on, boys! The O'Brienites are trying to break up the meeting.' The bandsmen rushed for the door. I would have done the same but my father looked hastily over his shoulder and warned me to stay where I was. He was talking to a young clarinet-player of serious appearance.

'Now,' he went on, raising his voice to drown the uproar outside. 'Teddy the Lamb was the finest clarinet-player in the whole British Army.'

There was a fresh storm of cheering, and wild with excitement I saw the patriots begin to drive a deep wedge of whirling sticks through the heart of the enemy, cutting them into two fighting camps.

'Excuse me, Mick,' said the clarinet-player, going white, 'I'll go and see what's up.'

'Now, whatever is up,' my father said appealingly, 'you can't do anything about it.'

'I'm not going to have it said I stopped behind while my friends were fighting for their lives,' said the young fellow hotly.

'There's no one fighting for their lives at all,' said my father irascibly, grabbing him by the arm. 'You have something else to think about. Man alive, you're a musician, not a bloody infantryman.'

'I'd sooner be that than a bloody turncoat, anyway,' said the young fellow, dragging himself off and making for the door.

'Thanks, Phil,' my father called after him in a voice of a man who had to speak before he has collected his wits. 'I well deserved that from you. I well deserved that from all of ye.' He took out his pipe and put it back into his pocket again. Then he joined me at the window and for a few moments he looked unseeingly at the milling crowd outside. 'Come on,' he said shortly.

Though the couples were wrestling in the very gutters no one accosted us on our way up the street; otherwise I feel murder might have been committed. We went to the house of some cousins and had tea, and when we reached the railway station my father led me to a compartment near the engine; not the carriage reserved for the band. Though we had ten minutes to wait it wasn't until just before the whistle went that Tim Ryan, the bandmaster, spotted us through the window.

'Mick!' he shouted in astonishment. 'Where the hell were you? I had men out all over the town looking for you? Is it anything wrong?'

'Nothing, Tim,' replied my father, leaning out of the window to him. 'I wanted to be alone, that's all.'

'But we'll see you at the other end?' bawled Tim as the train began to move.

'I don't know will you,' replied my father grimly. 'I think ye saw too much of me.'

When the band formed up outside the station we stood on the pavement and watched them. He had a tight hold of my hand. First Tim Ryan and then Jim Ralegh came rushing over to him. With an intensity of hatred I watched those enemies of Ireland again bait their traps for my father, but now I knew they would bait them in vain.

'No, no Tim,' said my father, shaking his head, 'I went too far before for the sake of the band, and I paid dear for it. None of my family was ever called a turncoat before today, Tim.'

'Ah, it is a young fool like that?' bawled Jim Ralegh with tears in his wild eyes. 'What need a man like you care about him?'

'A man have his pride, Jim,' said my father gloomily.

'He have,' cried Ralegh despairingly, 'and a fat lot any of us has to be proud of. The band was all we ever had, and if that goes the whole thing goes. For the love of the Almighty God, Mick Twomey, come back with us to the bandroom anyway.'

'No, no, no,' shouted my father angrily. 'I tell you after today I'm finished with music.'

'Music is finished with us you mean,' bawled Jim. 'The curse of God on the day we ever heard of Redmond or O'Brien! We were happy men before it . . . All right, lads,' he cried, turning away with a wild and whirling motion of his arm. 'Mick Twomey is done with us. Ye can go on without him.'

And again I heard the three solemn thumps on the big drum, and again the street was flooded with a roaring torrent of music, and though it no longer played for me, my heart rose to it and the tears came from my eyes. Still holding my hand, my father followed on the pavement. They were playing 'Brian Boru's March', his old favourite. We followed them through the ill-lit town and as they turned down the side-street to the bridge, my father stood on the kerb and looked after them as though he wished to impress every detail on his memory. It was only when the music stopped and the silence returned to the narrow channel of the street that we resumed our lonely way homeward.

There is a Lone House

The woman stood at the foot of the lane, her right hand resting on the gate, her left fumbling at the neck of her blouse. Her face was lined, particularly about mouth and forehead; it was a face that rarely smiled, but was soft for all that, and plump and warm. She was quite grey. From a distance, this made her seem old; close at hand it had precisely the opposite effect, and tended to emphasize sharply what youthfulness still lingered in her, so that one thought of her as having suffered terribly at some time in the past.

The man came down the road, whistling a reel, the crisp, sprinkled notes of which were like the dripping of water in a cistern. She could hear his footsteps from a long way off, keeping irregular time to the elfin music, and drew aside a whitethorn bush by the gateway to watch him from cover. Apparently satisfied by her inspection, she kicked away the stone that held the gate in place, and, as he drew level with her, stepped out into the roadway. When he saw her he stopped, bringing down his ash plant with a twirl, but she did not look up.

'Morrow, ma'am,' he cried jovially.

Then she did look up, and a helpless blush that completely and utterly belied the apparent calculation of her previous behaviour flowed over her features, giving them a sudden, startling freshness. 'Good morrow and good luck,' she answered in a low voice.

'Is it far to Ballysheery, ma'am?'

' 'Tis seven miles.'

'Seven Irish, ma'am?'

'Seven English.'

'That's better.'

She drew her tongue across her lips to moisten them. The man was young. He was decently dressed, but flaunted a rough, devil-may-care expression. He wore no hat, and his dark hair was all a tangle. You were struck by the length of his face, darkened by hot June suns; the high-boned nose jutting out rather too far, the irregular, discoloured teeth, the thick cracked lips, the blue eyes so far apart under his narrow, bony forehead that they seemed to sink back into the temples. A craggy face with high cheekbones, all hills and hollows, it was rendered extraordinarily mobile by the unexpected shadows that caught it here and there as the pale eyes drew it restlessly about. She judged him to be about twenty-six or -seven.

'You seemed to be belting it out fine enough.'

'How's that, ma'am?'

'I heard you whistling.'

'That's to encourage the feet, ma'am. . . . You'll pardon my asking, is there any place around a man would get a cup of tea, ma'am?'

'There's no one would grudge you that, surely.'

Another would have detected the almost girlish timidity of the answer, but not he. He appeared both puzzled and disappointed.

'I'll go a bit farther so,' he said stiffly.

'What hurry is on you?'

' 'Tis my feet gets cramped.'

'If you come with me you can rest them a while.'

'God increase you, ma'am,' he replied.

They went up the boreen together. The house was on top of a hill, and behind it rose the mountainside, studded with rocks. There were trees about it, and in front a long garden with a hedge of fuchsia, at one side of which ran a stream. There were four or five apple trees, and beside the kitchen garden were a few flower beds with a profusion of tall snapdragon, yellow, red and white.

She put on the kettle and turned the wheel of the bellows. The kitchen filled with blue turf smoke, and the man sat beside the door, almost invisible behind a brilliant column of dustmotes, whirling spirally in the evening sunlight. But his hands lay on his knees in a pool of light, great brown hands with knuckles like polished stones. Fascinated, she watched them, and as she laid the table she almost touched them for sheer pleasure. His wild eyes, blue as the turf smoke, took in everything about the kitchen with its deal table, chairs and dresser, all scrubbed white; its delft arranged with a sort of pedantic neatness that suggests the old maid.

'This is a fine, fancy place, ma'am,' he said.

' 'Tis a quiet place.'

' 'Tis so. The men are all away?'

'There are no men.'

'Oh!'

'Only a boy that does turns for me.'

'Oh!'

That was all he said before he turned to his meal. He was half-starved, she decided, as she watched him wolf the warm, crumbling bread. He saw her grey eyes fixed on him and laughed brightly.

'I has a great stroke, ma'am.'

'You have, God bless you. I might have boiled you another egg.'

When tea was over he sighed, stretching himself in his chair, and lit his pipe.

'Would you mind if I took off my boots, ma'am?' he asked shyly.

'Why would I? Take them off and welcome.'

'My feet is crucified.'

She bent and took up the boot he removed.

'No wonder. Your boots are in need of mending.'

He laughed at her expressive politeness.

'Mending, ma'am? Did you say mending? They're long past praying for.'

'They are, that's true. I wonder. . . . There's an old pair inside these years and years. They'd be better than the ones you have if they'd fit you.'

She brought them in, good substantial boots but stiff, and a trifle large for him. Not that he was in a state to mind.

'God, but they're grand, ma'am, they're grand! One little patch now, and they'd be as good as new. Better than new, for they're a better boot than I could ever buy in a shop. Wait now! Wait!' With boyish excitement he foraged in his pockets, and from the lining of his coat produced a piece of leather. He held it up with the air of a professional conjurer. 'Watch me now. Are you watching?' The leather fitted over the slight hole and he gave a whoop of joy. She found him last and hammer; he provided tacks from a paper bag in a vest pocket, and set to mending the damage with something like a tradesman's neatness.

'Is that your trade?' she asked curiously.

'One of my trades, ma'am. Cobbler, carpenter, plumber, gardener, thatcher, painter, poet; everything under the sun and moon, and nothing for long. But a cobbler is what I do be most times.'

He walked the kitchen in his new boots with all a child's inconsequent pleasure. There was something childlike about him, she decided, and she liked it. He peered at the battered alarm clock on the smoky heights of the mantelpiece and sighed.

'I'd like to stop here always,' he said wistfully, 'but I suppose I'd better be going.'

'What hurry is on you?'

'Seven miles, ma'am. Two hours. Maybe more. And I have to be in the old doss early if I want to get a place to sleep.'

But he sat down once more and put a match to his pipe.

'Not, mind you, ma'am, that there's many could put me out of a warm corner if I'd a mind to stay in it. No indeed, but unless I had a drop in me I'd never fight for a place. Never. I'm apt to be cross when I'm drunk, but I never hit a man sober yet only once. That was a foxy tinker out of the Ranties, and the Ranties are notorious cross men, ma'am. You see, there was a little blind man, ma'am, trying to sleep, and this Ranty I'm talking about, whenever he saw the blind man dozing, he'd give his beard a tug. So I got that mad I rose up, and without saying as much as "by your leave", I hit him such a terrible blow under the chin the blood hopped out on me in the dark. Yes, ma'am, hopped clean out on me. That was a frightful hard blow.' He looked at her for approval and awe, and saw her, womanlike, draw up her shoulders and shiver. His dramatic sense was satisfied.

It was quite dark when he rose to go. The moon was rising over the hills to the left, far away, and the little stream beside the house sounded very loud in the stillness.

'If there was e'er an old barn or an outhouse,' he said as if to himself.

'There's a bed inside,' she answered. He looked round at her in surprise.

'Ah, I wouldn't ask to stop within,' he exclaimed.

Suddenly her whole manner changed. All the brightness, if brightness it could be called, seemed to drop away from her, leaving her listless, cold and melancholy.

'Oh, please yourself,' she said shortly, as if banishing him from her thoughts. But still he did not go. Instead, he sat down again, and they faced one another across the fireplace, not speaking, for he too had lost his chatter. The kitchen was in darkness except for the dwindling glow of the turf inside its cocoon of grey dust, and the wan nightlight above the half-door. Then he laughed, rubbing his palms between his knees.

'And still you know, I'd ask nothing better,' he added shyly.

'What's that?'

'I'd ask nothing better than to stop.'

'Go or stop as you like.'

'You see,' he went on, ignoring her gathering surprise, 'I'm an honest fellow. I am, on my oath, though maybe you wouldn't think it, with the rough talk I have, and the life I lead. You could leave me alone with a bag of sovereigns, not counting them, and I'd keep them safe for you. And I'm just the same other ways. I'm not a bit forward. They say a dumb priest loses his benefit, and I'm just like that. I'm apt to lose me benefit for want of a bit of daring.'

Then (and this time it was he who was surprised) she laughed, more with relief, he thought, than at anything he had said. She rose and closed the door, lit the lamp and hung up the heavy kettle. He leaned back in his chair with a fresh sigh of pleasure, stretching out his feet to the fire, and in that gesture she caught something of his nostalgia. He settled down gratefully to one of those unexpected benefits which are the bait with which life leads us onward.

When she rose next morning, she was surprised to find him about before her, the fire lit, and the kettle boiling. She saw how much he needed a shave, and filled out a pan of water for him. Then when he began to scrub his face with the soap, she produced a razor, strop and brush. He was enchanted with these, and praised the razor with true lyric fire.

'You can have it,' she said. 'Have them all if they're any use to you.'

'By God, aren't they though,' he exclaimed reverently.

After breakfast he lit his pipe and sat back, enjoying to the full the last moments which politeness would impose upon hospitality.

'I suppose you're anxious to be on your road?' she asked awkwardly. Immediately he reddened.

'I suppose I'm better to,' he replied. He rose and looked out. It was a grey morning and still. The green stretched no farther than the hedge; beyond that lay a silver mist, flushed here and there with rose. 'Though 'tis no anxiety is on me – no anxiety at all,' he added with a touch of bitterness.

'Don't take me up wrong,' she said hastily. 'I'm not trying to hunt you. Stop and have your dinner. You'll be welcome.'

'I chopped a bit of kindling for you,' he replied, looking shyly at her from under lowered lids. 'If there was something else I could be doing, I'd be glad enough to stop, mind you.'

There was. Plenty else to be doing. For instance, there was an outhouse that needed whitewashing, and blithely enough he set about his task, whistling. She came and watched him; went, and came again, standing silently beside him, a strange stiff figure in the bright sunlight, but he had no feeling of supervision. Because he had not finished when dinner was ready he stayed to tea, and even then displayed no hurry to be gone. He sang her some of his poems. There was one about Mallow Races, another about a girl he had been in love with as a boy, 'the most beautiful girl that was ever seen in Kerry since the first day', so he naively told her. It began:

> I praise no princesses or queens or great ladies,
>> Or figures historical noted for style,
> Or beauties of Asia or Mesopotamia,
>> But sweet Annie Bradie, the rose of Dunmoyle.

A sort of confidence had established itself between them. The evening passed quickly in talk and singing – in whistling too, for he was a good whistler, and sometimes performed for dancing: to judge by his own statements he was a great favourite at wakes and weddings and she could understand that.

It was quite dark when they stopped the conversation. Again he made as if to go, and again in her shy, cold way she offered him the chance of staying. He stayed.

For days afterward there seemed to be some spell upon them both. A week passed in excuses and delays, each morning finding him about long before she appeared with some new suggestion, the garden to be weeded, potatoes to be dug, the kitchen to be whitewashed. Neither suggested anything but as it were from hour to hour, yet it did not occur to the man that for her as for him their companionship might be an unexpected benefit.

He did her messages to the village whenever Dan, the 'boy', a sullen, rather stupid, one-eyed old man, was absent, and though she gave no sign that she did not like this, he was always surprised afresh by the faint excitement with which she greeted his return; had it been anyone else one might have called her excitement gaiety, but gay was hardly a word one could apply to her, and the emotion quickly died and gave place to a sullen apathy.

She knew the end must come soon, and it did. One evening he returned from an errand, and told her someone had died in the village. He was slightly shocked by her indifference. She would not go with him to the wake, but she bade himself go if he pleased. He did please. She could see there was an itch for company on him; he was made that way. As he polished his boots he confessed to her that among his other vocations he had tried being a Trappist monk, but stuck it only for a few months. It wasn't bad in summer, but it was the divil and all in winter, and the monks told him there were certain souls like himself the Lord called only for six months of the year (the irony of this completely escaped him).

He promised to be back before midnight, and went off very gay. By this time he had formed his own opinion of the woman. It was not for nothing she lived there alone, not for nothing a visitor never crossed the threshold. He knew she did not go to Mass, yet on Sunday when he came back unexpectedly for his stick, he had seen her, in the bedroom, saying her rosary. Something was wrong, but he could not guess what.

Her mood was anything but gay and the evening seemed to respond to it. It was very silent after the long drought; she could hear the thrush's beak go tip-tap among the stones like a fairy's hammer. It was making for rain. To the north-west the wind had piled up massive archways of purple cloud like a ruined cloister, and through them one's eyes passed on to vistas of feathery cloudlets, violet and gold, packed thick upon one another. A cold wind had sprung up: the trees creaked, and the birds flew by, their wings blown up in a gesture of horror. She stood for a long while looking at the sky, until it faded, chilled by the cold wind. There was something mournful and sinister about it all.

It was quite dark when she went in. She sat over the fire and waited. At half past eleven she put down the kettle and brewed herself tea. She told herself she was not expecting him, but still she waited. At half past twelve she stood at the door and listened for footsteps. The wind had risen, and her mind filled slowly with its childish sobbing and with the harsh gushing of the stream beside the house. Then it began to rain. To herself she gave him until one. At one she relented and gave him another half-hour, and it was two before she quenched the light and went to bed. She had lost him, she decided.

She started when an hour or more later she heard his footsteps up the path. She needed no one to tell her he was alone and drunk: often before she had waited for the footsteps of a drunken old man. But instead of rushing to the door as she would have done long ago, she waited.

He began to moan drowsily to himself. She heard a thud followed by gusty sighing; she knew he had fallen. Everything was quiet for a while. Then there came a bang at the door which echoed through the house like a revolver shot, and something fell on the flagstones outside. Another bang and again silence. She felt no fear, only a coldness in her bowels.

Then the gravel scraped as he staggered to his feet. She glanced at the window. She could see his head outlined against it, his hands against its frame. Suddenly his voice rose in a wail that chilled her blood.

'What will the soul do at the judgement? Ah, what will the soul do? I will say to ye, "Depart from me into everlasting fire that was prepared for the divil and his angels. Depart from me, depart!"'

It was like a scream of pain, but immediately upon it came a low chuckle of malice. The woman's fists clenched beneath the clothes. 'Never again,' she said to herself aloud, 'never again!'

'Do you see me, do you?' he shouted. 'Do you see me?'

'I see you,' she whispered to herself.

'For ye, for ye, I reddened the fire,' went on the man, dropping back into his whine, 'for ye, for ye, I dug the pit. The black bitch on the hill, let ye torment her for me, ye divils. Forever, forever! Gather round, ye divils, gather round, and let me see ye roast the black bitch that killed a man. . . . Do you hear me, do you?'

'I hear you,' she whispered.

'Listen to me!

> 'When the old man was sleeping
>   She rose up from her bed,
> And crept into his lone bedroom
>   And cruelly struck him dead;
> 'Twas with a hammer she done the deed,
>   May god it her repay,
> And then she . . . then she . . .

'How does it go? I have it!

> '*And then she lifted up the body*
> *And hid it in the hay.*'

Suddenly a stone came crashing through the window and a cold blast followed it. 'Never again,' she cried, hammering the bedframe with her fists, 'dear God, never again.' She heard the footsteps stumbling away. She knew he was running. It was like a child's malice and terror.

She rose and stuffed the window with a rag. Day was breaking. When she went back to bed she was chilled and shaken. Despairing of rest, she rose again, lit a candle and blew up the fire.

But even then some unfamiliar feeling was stirring at her heart. She felt she was losing control of herself and was being moved about like a chessman. Sighing, she slipped her feet into heavy shoes, threw an old coat about her shoulders, and went to the door. As she crossed the threshold she stumbled over something. It was a boot; another was lying some little distance away. Something seemed to harden within her. She placed the boots inside the door and closed it. But again came the faint thrill at her heart, so light it might have been a fluttering of untried wings and yet so powerful it shook her from head to foot, so that almost before she had closed the door she opened it again and went out, puzzled and trembling, into a cold noiseless rain. She called the man in an extra-ordinarily gentle voice as though she were afraid of being heard; then she made the circle of the farmhouse, a candle sheltered in the palm of her hand.

He was lying in the outhouse he had been whitewashing. She stood and looked down at him for a moment, her face set in a grim mask of disgust. Then she laid down the candle and lifted him, and at that moment an onlooker would have been conscious of her great physical strength. Half lifting, half guiding him, she steered the man to the door. On the doorstep he stood and said something to her, and immediately, with all her strength, she struck him across the mouth. He staggered and swore at her, but she caught him again and pushed him across the threshold. Then she went back for the candle, undressed him and put him to bed.

It was bright morning when she had done.

*

That day he lay on in bed, and came into the kitchen about two o'clock looking sheepish and sullen. He was wearing his own ragged boots.

'I'm going now,' he said stiffly.

'Please yourself,' she answered coolly. 'Maybe you'd be better.'

He seemed to expect something more, and because she said nothing he felt himself being put subtly in the wrong. This was not so surprising, because even she was impressed by her own nonchalance that seemed to have come suddenly to her from nowhere.

'Well?' he asked, and his look seemed to say, 'Women are the divil and all!' one could read him like a book.

'Well?'

'Have you nothing to say for yourself?'

'Have you nothing to say for yourself?' she retorted. 'I had enough of your blackguarding last night. You won't stop another hour in this house unless you behave yourself, mark me well, you won't.'

He grew very red.

'That's strange,' he answered sulkily.

'What's strange?'

'The likes of you saying that to me.'

'Take it or leave it. And if you don't like it, there's the door.'

Still he lingered. She knew now she had him at her mercy, and the nonchalance dropped from her.

'Aren't you a queer woman?' he commented, lighting his pipe. 'One'd think you wouldn't have the face to talk like that to an honest man. Have you no shame?'

'Listen to who's talking of shame,' she answered bitterly. 'A pity you didn't see yourself last night, lying in your dirt like an old cow. And you call yourself a man. How ready you were with your stones!'

'It was the shock,' he said sullenly.

'It was no shock. It was drink.'

'It was the shock I tell you. I was left an orphan with no one to tell me the badness of the world.'

'I was left an orphan too. And I don't go round crying about the badness of the world.'

'Oh, Christ, don't remind me what you were. 'Tis only myself, the poor fool, wouldn't know, and all the old chat I had about the man I drew blood from, as if I was a terrible fellow entirely. I might have known to see a handsome woman living lonely that she wouldn't be that way only no man in Ireland would look at the side of the road she walked on.'

He did not see how the simple flattery of his last words went through her, quickening her with pleasure; he noticed only the savage retort she gave him, for the sense of his own guilt was growing stronger in him at every moment. Her silence was in part the cause of that; her explanation would have been his triumph. That at least was how he had imagined it. He had not been prepared for this silence which drew him like a magnet. He could not decide to go, yet his fear of her would not allow him to remain. The day passed like that. When twilight came she looked across at him and asked:

'Are you going or stopping?'

'I'm stopping, if you please,' he answered meekly.

'Well, I'm going to bed. One sleepless night is enough for me.'

And she went, leaving him alone in the kitchen. Had she delayed until darkness fell, he would have found it impossible to remain, but there was no suspicion of this in her mind. She understood only that people might hate her; that they might fear her never entered her thoughts.

An hour or so later she looked for the candle and remembered that she had left it in his room. She rose and knocked at his door. There was no answer. She knocked again. Then she pushed in the door and called him. She was alarmed. The bed was empty. She laid her hand to the candle (it was lying still where she had left it, on the dresser beside the door) but as she did so she heard his voice, husky and terrified.

'Keep away from me! Keep away from me, I tell you!'

She could discern his figure now. He was standing in a corner, his little white shirt half way up his thighs, his hand grasping something, she did not see what. It was some little while before the explanation dawned on her, and with it came a sudden feeling of desolation within her.

'What ails you?' she asked gently. 'I was only looking for the candle.'

'Don't come near me!' he cried.

She lit the candle, and as he saw her there, her face as he had never seen it before, stricken with pain, his fear died away. A moment later she was gone, and the back door slammed behind her. It was only then he realized what his insane fear had brought him to, and the obsession of his own guilt returned with a terrible clarity. He walked up and down the little room in desperation.

Half an hour later he went to her room. The candle was burning on a chair beside the bed. She lifted herself on the pillow and looked at him with strangely clear eyes.

'What is it?' she asked.

'I'm sorry,' he answered. 'I shouldn't be here at all. I'm sorry. I'm queer. I'll go in the morning and I won't trouble you any more.'

'Never mind,' she said, and held out her hand to him. He came closer and took it timidly. 'You wouldn't know.'

'God pity me,' he said. 'I was distracted. You know I was distracted. You were so good to me, and that's the way I paid you out. But I was going out of my mind. I couldn't sleep.'

'Sure you couldn't.' She drew him down to her until his head was resting on the pillow, and made him lie beside her.

'I couldn't, I couldn't,' he said into her ear. 'I wint raving mad. And I thought whin you came into the room –'

'I know, I know.'

'I did, whatever came over me.'

'I know.' He realized that she was shivering all over.

She drew back the clothes for him. He was eager to explain, to tell her about himself, his youth, the death of his father and mother, his poverty, his religious difficulties, his poetry. What was wrong with him was, he was wild; could stick at no trade, could never keep away from drink.

'You were wild yourself,' he said.

'Fifteen years ago. I'm tame now in earnest.'

'Tell me about it,' he said eagerly, 'talk to me, can't you? Tell me he was bad. Tell me he was a cruel old uncle to you. Tell me he beat you. He used to lock you up for days, usedn't he, to keep you away from boys? He must have been bad or you'd never had done what you did, and you only a girl.'

But still she said nothing. Bright day was in the room when he fell asleep, and for a long while she lay, her elbow on the pillow, her hand covering her left breast, while she looked at him. His mouth was wide open, his irregular teeth showed in a faint smile. Their shyness had created a sort of enchantment about them, and she watched over his sleep with something like ecstasy, ecstasy which disappeared when he woke, to find her, the same hard quiet woman he knew.

After that she ceased making his bed in the small room, and he slept with her. Not that it made any difference to their relations. Between them after those few hours of understanding persisted a fierce, unbroken shyness, the shyness of lonely souls. If it rasped the nerves of either, there was no open sign of it, unless a curiously irritable tenderness revealed anything of their thoughts. She was forever finding things done for her; there was no longer any question of his going, and he worked from morning until late night with an energy and intelligence that surprised her. But she knew he felt the lack of company, and one evening she went out to him as he worked in the garden.

'Why don't you go down to the village now?' she asked.

'Ah, what would I be doing there?' But it was clear that it had been on his mind at that very moment.

'You might drop in for a drink and a chat.'

'I might do that,' he agreed.

'And why don't you?'

'Me? I'd be ashamed.'

'Ashamed? Ashamed of what? There's no one will say anything to you. And if they do, what are you, after all, but a working man?'

It was clear that this excuse had not occurred to him, but it would also have been clear to anyone else that she would have thought poorly of such as gave it credit. So he got his coat and went.

It was late when he came in, and she saw he had drunk more than his share. His face was flushed and he laughed too easily. For two days past a bottle of whiskey had been standing on the dresser (what a change for her!) but if he had noticed it he had made no sign. Now he went directly to it and poured himself out a glass.

'You found it,' she said with a hint of bitterness.

'What's that?'

'You found it, I say.'

'Of course I did. Have a drop yourself.'

'No.'

'Do. Just a drop.'

'I don't want it.'

He crossed to her, stood behind her chair for a moment; then he bent over and kissed her. She had been expecting it, but on the instant she revolted.

'Don't do that again,' she said appealingly, wiping her mouth.

'You don't mind me, do you?' he sniggered, still standing behind her.

'I do. I mind it when you're drunk.'

'Well, here's health.'

'Don't drink any more of that.'

'Here's health.'

'Good health.'

'Take a drop yourself, do.'

'No, I tell you,' she answered angrily.

'By God, you must.'

He threw one arm about her neck and deliberately spilt the whiskey between her breasts. She sprang up and threw him away from her. Whatever had been in her mind was now forgotten in her loathing.

'Bad luck to you!' she cried savagely.

'I'm sorry,' he said quickly. 'I didn't mean it.' Already he was growing afraid.

'You didn't mean it,' she retorted mockingly. 'Who taught you to do it then? Was it Jimmie Dick? What sort of woman do you think I am, you fool? You sit all night in a public-house talking of me, and when you come back you try to make me out as loose and dirty as your talk.'

'Who said I was talking of you?'

'I say it.'

'Then you're wrong.'

'I'm not wrong. Don't I know you, you poor sheep? You sat there, letting them make you out a great fellow, because they thought you were like themselves and thought I was a bitch, and you never as much as opened your mouth to give them the lie. You sat there and gaped and bragged. That's what you are.'

'That's not true.'

'And then you come strutting back, stuffed with drink, and think I'll let you make love to me, so that you can have something to talk about in the public-house.'

Her eyes were bright with tears of rage. She had forgotten that something like this was what she knew would happen when she made him go to the village, so little of our imagination can we bear to see made real. He sank into a chair, and put his head between his hands in sulky dignity. She lit the candle and went off to bed.

She fell asleep and woke to hear him stirring in the kitchen. She rose and flung open the door. He was still sitting where she had seen him last.

'Aren't you going to bed at all tonight?' she asked.

'I'm sorry if I disturbed you,' he replied. The drunkenness had gone, and he did look both sorry and miserable. 'I'll go now.'

'You'd better. Do you see the time?'

'Are you still cross? I'm sorry, God knows I am.'

'Never mind.'

' 'Twas all true.'

'What was true?' She had already forgotten.

'What you said. They were talking about you, and I listened.'

'Oh, that.'

'Only you were too hard on me.'

'Maybe I was.'

She took a step forward. He wondered if she had understood what he was saying at all.

'I was fond of you all right.'

'Yes,' she said.

'You know I was.'

'Yes.'

She was like a woman in a dream. She had the same empty feeling within her, the same sense of being pushed about like a chessman, as on the first night when she carried him in. He put his arm about her and kissed her. She shivered and clung to him, life suddenly beginning to stir within her.

One day, some weeks later, he told her he was going back home on a visit; there were cousins he wished to see; something or other; she was not surprised. She had seen the restlessness on him for some time past and had no particular belief in the cousins. She set about preparing a parcel of food for him, and in this little attention there was something womanly that touched him.

'I'll be back soon,' he said, and meant it. He could be moved easily enough in this fashion, and she saw through him. It was dull being the lover of a woman like herself; he would be best married to a lively girl of eighteen or so, a girl he could go visiting with and take pride in.

'You're always welcome,' she said. 'The house is your own.'

As he went down the boreen he was saying to himself 'She'll be lost! She'll be lost!' but he would have spared his pity if he had seen how she took it.

Her mood shifted from busy to idle. At one hour she was working in the garden, singing, at another she sat in the sun, motionless and silent for a long, long time. As weeks went by and the year drifted into a rainy autumn, an astonishing change took place in her, slowly, almost imperceptibly. It seemed a physical rather than a spiritual change. Line by line her features divested themselves of strain, and her body seemed to fall into easier, more graceful curves. It would not be untrue to say she scarcely thought of the man, unless it was with some slight relief to find herself alone again. Her thoughts were all contracted within herself.

One autumn evening he came back. For days she had been expecting him; quite suddenly she had realized that he would return, that everything was not over between them, and very placidly accepted the fact.

He seemed to have grown older and maturer in his short absence; one felt it less in his words than in his manner. There was decision in it. She saw that he was rapidly growing into a deferred manhood, and was secretly proud of the change. He had a great fund of stories about his wanderings (never a word of the mythical cousins); and while she prepared his supper, she listened to him, smiling faintly, almost as if she were not listening at all. He was as hungry now as the first evening she met him, but everything was easier between them; he was glad to be there and she to have him.

'Are you pleased I came?' he asked.

'You know I'm pleased.'

'Were you thinking I wouldn't come?'

'At first I thought you wouldn't. You hadn't it in your mind to come back. But afterward I knew you would.'

'A man would want to mind what he thinks about a woman like you,' he grumbled good-humouredly. 'Are you a witch?'

'How would I be a witch?' Her smile was attractive.

'Are you?' He gripped her playfully by the arm.

'I am not and well you know it.'

'I have me strong doubts of you. Maybe you'll say now you know what happened? Will you? Did you ever hear of a man dreaming three times of a crock of gold? Well, that's what happened me. I dreamt three times of you. What sign is that?'

'A sign you were drinking too much.'

' 'Tis not. I know what sign it is.'

He drew his chair up beside her own, and put his arm about her. Then he drew her face round to his and kissed her. At that moment she could feel very clearly the change in him. His hand crept about her neck and down her breast, releasing the warm smell of her body.

'That's enough love-making,' she said. She rose quickly and shook off his arm. A strange happy smile like a newly-open flower lingered where he had kissed her. 'I'm tired. Your bed is made in there.'

'My bed?'

She nodded.

'You're only joking me. You are, you divil, you're only joking.'

His arms out, he followed her, laughing like a lad of sixteen. He caught at her, but she forced him off again. His face altered suddenly, became sullen and spiteful.

'What is it?'

'Nothing.'

' 'Tis a change for you.'

' 'Tis.'

'And for why?'

'For no why. Isn't it enough for you to know it?'

'Is it because I wint away?'

'Maybe.'

'Is it?'

'I don't know whether 'tis or no.'

'And didn't I come back as I said I would?'

'You did. When it suited you.'

'The divil is in ye all,' he said crossly.

Later he returned to the attack; he was quieter and more persuasive; there was more of the man in him, but she seemed armed at every point. He experienced an acute sense of frustration. He had felt growing in him this new, lusty manhood, and returned with the intention of dominating her, only to find she too had grown, and still outstripped him. He lay awake for a long time, thinking it out, but when he rose next morning the barrier between them seemed to have disappeared. As ever she was dutiful, unobtrusive; by day at any rate she was all he would have her to be. Even when he kissed her she responded; of his hold on her he had no doubt, but he seemed incapable of taking advantage of it.

That night when he went to bed he began to think again of it, and rage grew in him until it banished all hope of sleep. He rose and went into her room.

'How long is this going to last?' he asked thickly.

'What?'

'This. How long more are you going to keep me out?'

'Maybe always,' she said softly, as if conjuring up the prospect.

'Always?'

'Maybe.'

'Always? And what in hell do you mean by it? You lure me into it, and then throw me away like an old boot.'

'Did I lure you into it?'

'You did. Oh, you fooled me right enough at the time, but I've been thinking about it since. 'Twas no chance brought you on the road the first day I passed.'

'Maybe I did,' she admitted. She was stirred again by the quickness of his growth. 'If I did you had nothing to complain of.'

'Haven't I now?'

'Now is different.'

'Why? Because I wint away?'

'Because you didn't think me good enough for you.'

'That's a lie. You said that before, and you know 'tis a lie.'

'Then show it.'

He sat on the bed and put his face close to hers.

'You know I can't.'

'Yes.'

'You know I can't.'

'What hinders you?'

'For a start, I have no money. Neither have you.'

'There's money enough.'

'Where would it come from?'

'Never you mind where 'twould come from. 'Tis there.'

He looked at her hard.

'You planned it well,' he said at last. 'They said he was a miser . . . Oh, Christ, I can't marry you!'

'The divil send you better meat than mutton,' she retorted coarsely.

He sat on the edge of the bed, his big hand caressing her cheek and bare shoulder.

'Why don't you tell the truth?' she asked. 'You have no respect for me.'

'Why do you keep on saying that?'

'Because 'tis true.' In a different voice she added: 'Nor I hadn't for myself till you went away. Take me now or leave me. . . . Stop that, you fool!'

'Listen to me –'

'Stop that then! I'm tame now, but I'm not tame enough for that.'

Even in the darkness she could feel that she had awakened his old dread of her; she put her arms about his head, drew him down to her, and whispered in his ear.

'Now do you understand?' she said.

A few days later he got out the cart and harnessed the pony. They drove into the town three miles away. As they passed through the village people came to their doors to look after them. They left the cart a little outside the town, and, following country practice, separated to meet again on the priest's doorstep. The priest was at home, and he listened incredulously to the man's story.

'You know I'll have to write to your parish priest first,' he said severely.

'I know,' said the man. 'You'll find and see he have nothing against me.'

The priest was shaken.

'And this woman has told you everything?'

'She told me nothing. But I know.'

'About her uncle?'

'About her uncle,' repeated the man.

'And you're satisfied to marry her, knowing that?'

'I'm satisfied.'

'It's all very strange,' said the priest wearily. 'You know,' he added to the woman, 'Almighty God has been very merciful to you. I hope you are conscious of all He in His infinite mercy has done for you, who deserve it so little.'

'I am. From this out I'll go to Mass regularly.'

'I hope,' he repeated emphatically, 'you are fully conscious of it. If I thought there was any lightness in you, if I thought for an instant that you wouldn't make a good wife to this man, my conscience wouldn't allow me to marry you. Do you understand that?'

'Never fear,' she said, without lifting her eyes, 'I'll make him a good wife. And he knows it.'

The man nodded. 'I know it,' he said.

The priest was impressed by the solemn way in which she spoke. She was aware that the strength which had upheld her till now was passing from her to the young man at her side; the future would be his.

From the priest's they went to the doctor's. He saw her slip on a ring before they entered. He sat in the room while the doctor examined her. When she had dressed again her eyes were shining. The strength was passing from her, and she was not sorry to see it pass. She laid a sovereign on the table.

'Oho,' exclaimed the doctor, 'how did you come by this?' The man started and the woman smiled.

'I earned it hard,' she answered.

The doctor took the coin to the window and examined it.

'By Jove,' he said, 'it's not often I see one of these.'

'Maybe you'll see more of them,' she said with a gay laugh. He looked at her from under his eyes and laughed too; her brightness had a strange other-world attraction.

'Maybe I will,' he replied. 'In a few months time, eh? Sorry I can't give you change in your own coin. Ah, well! Good luck, anyway. And call me in as often as you please.'

News for the Church

When Father Cassidy drew back the shutter of the confessional he was a little surprised at the appearance of the girl at the other side of the grille. It was dark in the box but he could see she was young, of medium height and build, with a face that was full of animation and charm. What struck him most was the long pale slightly freckled cheeks, pinned high up behind the grey-blue eyes, giving them a curiously oriental slant.

She wasn't a girl from the town, for he knew most of these by sight and many of them by something more, being notoriously an easy-going confessor. The other priests said that one of these days he'd give up hearing confessions altogether on the ground that there was no such thing as sin and that even if there was it didn't matter. This was part and parcel of his exceedingly angular character, for though he was kind enough to individual sinners, his mind was full of obscure abstract hatreds. He hated English; he hated the Irish government, and he particularly hated the middle classes, though so far as anyone knew none of them had ever done him the least bit of harm. He was a heavybuilt man, slow-moving and slow-thinking with no neck and a Punchinello chin, a sour wine-coloured face, pouting crimson lips, and small blue hot-tempered eyes.

'Well, my child,' he grunted in a slow and mournful voice that sounded for all the world as if he had pebbles in his mouth, 'how long is it since your last confession?'

'A week, father,' she replied in a clear firm voice. It surprised him a little, for though she didn't look like one of the tough shots, neither did she look like the sort of girl who goes to confession every week. But with women you could never tell. They were all contrary, saints and sinners.

'And what sins did you commit since then?' he asked encouragingly.

'I told lies, father.'

'Anything else?'

'I used bad language, father.'

'I'm surprised at you,' he said with mock seriousness. 'An educated girl with the whole of the English language at your disposal! What sort of bad language?'

'I used the Holy Name, father.'

'Ach,' he said with a frown, 'you ought to know better than that. There's no great harm in damning and blasting but blasphemy is a different thing. To tell you the truth,' he added, being a man of great natural honesty, 'there isn't much harm in using the Holy Name either. Most of the time there's no intentional blasphemy but at the same time it coarsens the character. It's all the little temptations we don't indulge in that give us true refinement. Anything else?'

'I was tight, father.'

'Hm,' he grunted. This was rather more the sort of girl he had imagined her to be; plenty of devilment but no real badness. He liked her bold and candid manner. There was no hedging or false modesty about her as about most of his women penitents. 'When you say you were "tight" do you mean you were just merry or what?'

'Well, I mean I passed out,' she replied candidly with a shrug.

'I don't call that "tight," you know,' he said sternly. 'I call that beastly drunk. Are you often tight?'

'I'm a teacher in a convent school so I don't get much chance,' she replied ruefully.

'In a convent school?' he echoed with new interest. Convent schools and nuns were another of his phobias; he said they were turning the women of the country into imbeciles. 'Are you on holidays now?'

'Yes. I'm on my way home.'

'You don't live here then?'

'No, down the country.'

'And is it the convent that drives you to drink?' he asked with an air of unshakable gravity.

'Well,' she replied archly, 'you know what nuns are.'

'I do,' he agreed in a mournful voice while he smiled at her through the grille. 'Do you drink with your parents' knowledge?' he added anxiously.

'Oh, yes. Mummy is dead but Daddy doesn't mind. He lets us take a drink with him.'

'Does he do that on principle or because he's afraid of you?' the priest asked dryly.

'Ah, I suppose a little of both,' she answered gaily, responding to his queer dry humour. It wasn't often that women did, and he began to like this one a lot.

'Is your mother long dead?' he asked sympathetically.

'Seven years,' she replied, and he realized that she couldn't have been much more than a child at the time and had grown up without a mother's advice and care. Having worshipped his own mother, he was always sorry for people like that.

'Mind you,' he said paternally, his hands joined on his fat belly, 'I don't want you to think there's any harm in a drop of drink. I take it myself. But I wouldn't make a habit of it if I were you. You see, it's all very well for old jossers like me that have the worst of their temptations behind them, but yours are all ahead and drink is a thing that grows on you. You need never be afraid of going wrong if you remember that your mother may be watching you from heaven.'

'Thanks, father,' she said, and he saw at once that his gruff appeal had touched some deep and genuine spring of feeling in her. 'I'll cut it out altogether.'

'You know, I think I would,' he said gravely, letting his eyes rest on her for a moment. 'You're an intelligent girl. You can get all the excitement you want out of life without that. What else?'

'I had bad thoughts, father.'

'Ach,' he said regretfully, 'we all have them. Did you indulge them?'

'Yes, father.'

'Have you a boy?'

'Not a regular: just a couple of fellows hanging round.'

'Ah, that's worse than none at all,' he said crossly. 'You ought to have a boy of your own. I know there's old cranks that will tell you different, but sure, that's plain foolishness. Those things are only fancies, and the best cure for them is something real. Anything else?'

There was a moment's hesitation before she replied but it was enough to prepare him for what was coming.

'I had carnal intercourse with a man, father,' she said quietly and deliberately.

'You what?' he cried, turning on her incredulously. 'You had carnal intercourse with a man? At your age?'

'I know,' she said with a look of distress. 'It's awful.'

'It is awful,' he replied slowly and solemnly. 'And how often did it take place?'

'Once, father – I mean twice, but on the same occasion.'

'Was it a married man?' he asked, frowning.

'No, father, single. At least I think he was single,' she added with sudden doubt.

'You had carnal intercourse with a man,' he said accusingly, 'and you don't know if he was married or single!'

'I assumed he was single,' she said with real distress. 'He was the last time I met him but, of course, that was five years ago.'

'Five years ago? But you must have been only a child then.'

'That's all, of course,' she admitted. 'He was courting my sister, Kate, but she wouldn't have him. She was running round with her present husband at the time and she only kept him on a string for amusement. I knew that and I hated her because he was always so nice to me. He was the only one that came to the house who treated me like a grown-up. But I was only fourteen, and I suppose he thought I was too young for him.'

'And were you?' Father Cassidy asked ironically. For some reason he had the idea that this young lady had no proper idea of the enormity of her sin and he didn't like it.

'I suppose so,' she replied modestly. 'But I used to feel awful, being sent up to bed and leaving him downstairs with Kate when I knew she didn't care for him. And then when I met him again the whole thing came back. I sort of went all soft inside. It's never the same with another fellow as it is with the first fellow you fall for. It's exactly as if he had some sort of hold over you.'

'If you were fourteen at the time,' said Father Cassidy, setting aside the obvious invitation to discuss the power of first love, 'you're only nineteen now.'

'That's all.'

'And do you know,' he went on broodingly, 'that unless you can break yourself of this terrible vice once for all it'll go on like that till you're fifty?'

'I suppose so,' she said doubtfully, but he saw that she didn't suppose anything of the kind.

'You suppose so!' he snorted angrily. 'I'm telling you so. And what's more,' he went on, speaking with all the earnestness at his command, 'it won't be just one man but dozens of men, and it won't be decent men but whatever low-class pups you can find who'll take advantage of you – the same horrible, mortal sin, week in week out till you're an old woman.'

'Ah, still, I don't know,' she said eagerly, hunching her shoulders ingratiatingly, 'I think people do it as much from curiosity as anything else.'

'Curiosity?' he repeated in bewilderment.

'Ah, you know what I mean,' she said with a touch of impatience. 'People make such a mystery of it!'

'And what do you think they should do?' he asked ironically. 'Publish it in the papers?'

'Well, God knows, 'twould be better than the way some of them go on,' she said in a rush. 'Take my sister, Kate, for instance. I admit she's a couple of years older than me and she brought me up and all the rest of it, but in spite of that we were always good friends. She showed me her love letters and I showed her mine. I mean, we discussed things as equals, but ever since that girl got married you'd hardly recognize her. She talks to no one only other married women, and they get in a huddle in a corner and whisper, whisper, whisper, and the moment you come into the room they begin to talk about the weather, exactly as if you were a blooming kid! I mean you can't help feeling 'tis something extraordinary.'

'Don't you try and tell me anything about immorality,' said Father Cassidy angrily. 'I know all about it already. It may begin as curiosity but it ends as debauchery. There's no vice you could think of that gets a grip on you quicker and degrades you worse, and don't you make any mistake about it, young woman! Did this man say anything about marrying you?'

'I don't think so,' she replied thoughtfully, 'but of course that doesn't mean anything. He's an airy, light-hearted sort of fellow and it mightn't occur to him.'

'I never supposed it would,' said Father Cassidy grimly. 'Is he in a position to marry?'

'I suppose he must be since he wanted to marry Kate,' she replied with fading interest.

'And is your father the sort of man that can be trusted to talk to him?'

'Daddy?' she exclaimed aghast. 'But I don't want Daddy brought into it.'

'What you want, young woman,' said Father Cassidy with sudden exasperation, 'is beside the point. Are you prepared to talk to this man yourself?'

'I suppose so,' she said with a wondering smile. 'But about what?'

'About what?' repeated the priest angrily. 'About the little matter he so conveniently overlooked, of course.'

'You mean ask him to marry me?' she cried incredulously. 'But I don't want to marry him.'

Father Cassidy paused for a moment and looked at her anxiously through the grille. It was growing dark inside the church, and for one horrible moment he had the feeling that somebody was playing an elaborate and most tasteless joke on him.

'Do you mind telling me,' he inquired politely, 'am I mad or are you?'

'But I mean it, father,' she said eagerly. 'It's all over and done with now. It's something I used to dream about, and it was grand, but you can't do a thing like that a second time.'

'You can't what?' he asked sternly.

'I mean, I suppose you can, really,' she said, waving her piously joined hands at him as if she were handcuffed, 'but you can't get back the magic of it. Terry is light-hearted and good-natured, but I couldn't live with him. He's completely irresponsible.'

'And what do you think you are?' cried Father Cassidy, at the end of his patience. 'Have you thought of all the dangers you're running, girl? If you have a child who'll give you work? If you have to leave this country to earn a living what's going to become of you? I tell you it's your bounden duty to marry this man if he can be got to marry you – which, let me tell you,' he added with a toss of his great head, 'I very much doubt.'

'To tell you the truth I doubt it myself,' she replied with a shrug that fully expressed her feelings about Terry and nearly drove Father Cassidy insane. He looked at her for a moment or two and then an incredible idea began to dawn on his bothered old brain. He sighed and covered his face with his hand.

'Tell me,' he asked in a far-away voice, 'when did this take place?'

'Last night, father,' she said gently, almost as if she were glad to see him come to his senses again.

'My God,' he thought despairingly, 'I was right!'

'In town, was it?' he went on.

'Yes, father. We met on the train coming down.'

'And where is he now?'

'He went home this morning, father.'

'Why didn't you do the same?'

'I don't know, father,' she replied doubtfully as though the question had now only struck herself for the first time.

'Why didn't you go home this morning?' he repeated angrily. 'What were you doing round town all day?'

'I suppose I was walking,' she replied uncertainly.

'And of course you didn't tell anyone?'

'I hadn't anyone to tell,' she said plaintively. 'Anyway,' she added with a shrug, 'it's not the sort of thing you can tell people.'

'No, of course,' said Father Cassidy. 'Only a priest,' he added grimly to himself. He saw now how he had been taken in. This little trollop, wandering about town in a daze of bliss, had to tell someone her secret, and he, a good-natured old fool of sixty, had allowed her to use him as a confidant. A philosopher of sixty letting Eve, aged nineteen, tell him all about the apple! He could never live it down.

Then the fighting blood of the Cassidys began to warm in him. Oh, couldn't he, though? He had never tasted the apple himself, but he knew a few things about apples in general and that apple in particular that little Miss Eve wouldn't learn in a whole lifetime of apple-eating. Theory might have its drawbacks but there were times when it was better than practice. 'All right, my lass,' he thought grimly, 'we'll see which of us knows most!'

In a casual tone he began to ask her questions. They were rather intimate questions, such as a doctor or priest may ask, and, feeling broadminded and worldly-wise in her new experience, she answered courageously and straightforwardly, trying to suppress all signs of her embarrassment. It emerged only once or twice, in a brief pause before she replied. He stole a furtive look at her to see how she was taking it, and once more he couldn't withhold his admiration. But she couldn't keep it up. First she grew uncomfortable and then alarmed, frowning and shaking herself in her clothes as if something were biting her. He grew graver and more personal. She didn't see his purpose; she only saw that he was stripping off veil after veil of romance, leaving her with nothing but a cold, sordid, cynical adventure like a bit of greasy meat on a plate.

'And what did he do next?' he asked.

'Ah,' she said in disgust, 'I didn't notice.'

'You didn't notice!' he repeated ironically.

'But does it make any difference?' she burst out despairingly, trying to pull the few shreds of illusion she had left more tightly about her.

'I presume you thought so when you came to confess it,' he replied sternly.

'But you're making it sound so beastly!' she wailed.

'And wasn't it?' he whispered, bending closer, lips pursed and brows raised. He had her now, he knew.

'Ah, it wasn't, father,' she said earnestly. 'Honest to God it wasn't. At least at the time I didn't think it was.'

'No,' he said grimly, 'you thought it was a nice little story to run and tell your sister. You won't be in such a hurry to tell her now. Say an Act of Contrition.'

She said it.

'And for your penance say three Our Fathers and three Hail Marys.'

He knew that was hitting below the belt, but he couldn't resist the parting shot of a penance such as he might have given a child. He knew it would rankle in that fanciful little head of hers when all his other warnings were forgotten. Then he drew the shutter and didn't open the farther one. There was a noisy woman behind, groaning in an excess of contrition. The mere volume of sound told him it was drink. He felt he needed a breath of fresh air.

He went down the aisle creakily on his heavy policeman's-feet and in the dusk walked up and down the path before the presbytery, head bowed, hands behind his back. He saw the girl come out and descend the steps under the massive fluted columns of the portico, a tiny, limp, dejected figure. As she reached the pavement she pulled herself together with a jaunty twitch of her shoulders and then collapsed again. The city lights went on and made globes of coloured light in the mist. As he returned to the church he suddenly began to chuckle, a fat good-natured chuckle, and as he passed the statue of St Anne, patron of marriageable girls, he almost found himself giving her a wink.

The Mad Lomasneys

1

Ned Lowry and Rita Lomasney had, one might say, been lovers from childhood. The first time they had met was when he was fourteen and she a year or two younger. It was on the North Mall on a Saturday afternoon, and she was sitting on a bench by the river under the trees; a tall, bony string of a girl with a long, obstinate jaw. Ned was a studious-looking young fellow in a blue and white college cap – thin, pale and spectacled. As he passed he looked at her owlishly, and she gave him back an impudent stare. This upset him – he had no experience of girls – so he blushed and raised his cap. At this she seemed to relent.

'Hallo,' she said experimentally.

'Good afternoon,' he replied with a pale, prissy smile.

'Where are you off to?' she asked.

'Oh, just up the Dyke for a walk.'

'Sit down,' she said in a sharp voice, laying her hand on the bench beside her, and he did as he was told. It was a summer evening, and the white quay walls and tall, crazy, claret-coloured tenements under a blue and white sky were reflected in the lazy water, which wrinkled only at the edges and seemed like a painted carpet.

'It's very pleasant here,' he said complacently.

'Is it?' she asked with a truculence that startled him. 'I don't see anything very pleasant about it.'

'Oh, it's very nice and quiet,' he said in mild surprise as he raised his fair eyebrows and looked up and down the Mall. 'My name is Lowry,' he added politely.

'Are ye the ones that have the jeweller's shop on the Parade?' she asked.

'That's right,' he replied with modest pride.

'We have a clock we got from ye,' she said. ' 'Tisn't much good of an old clock either,' she added with quiet malice.

'You should bring it back to the shop,' he said with concern. 'It probably needs overhauling.'

'I'm going down the river in a boat with a couple of fellows,' she said, going off at a tangent. 'Will you come?'

'Couldn't,' he said with a smile.

'Why not?'

'I'm only left go up the Dyke for a walk,' he replied complacently. 'On Saturdays I go to Confession at St Peter and Paul's; then I go up the Dyke and come back the Western Road. Sometimes you see very good cricket matches. Do you like cricket?'

'A lot of old sissies pucking a ball!' she said shortly. 'I do not.'

'I like it,' he said firmly. 'I go up there every Saturday when it's fine. Of course, I'm not supposed to talk to anyone,' he added with mild amusement at his own audacity.

'Why not?'

'My mother doesn't like me to.'

'Why doesn't she?'

'She comes of an awfully good family,' he answered mildly, and but for his gentle smile she might have thought he was deliberately insulting her. 'You see,' he went on gravely in his thin, pleasant voice, ticking things off on his fingers and then glancing at each finger individually as he ticked it off – a tidy sort of boy – 'there are three main branches of the Hourigan family: the Neddy Neds, the Neddy Jerrys, and the Neddy Thomases. The Neddy Neds are the Hayfield Hourigans. They are the oldest branch. My mother is a Hayfield Hourigan, and she'd have been a rich woman only for her father backing a bill for a Neddy Jerry. He defaulted and ran away to Australia,' he concluded with a contemptuous sniff.

'Cripes!' said the girl. 'And had she to pay?'

'She had. But of course,' he went on with as close as he ever seemed likely to get to a burst of real enthusiasm, 'my grandfather was a very well-behaved man. When he was eating his dinner the boys from the National School in Bantry used to be brought up to watch him, he had such beautiful table manners. Once he caught my uncle eating cabbage with a knife, and he struck him with a poker. They had to put four stitches in him after,' he added with a joyous chuckle.

'Cripes!' said the girl again. 'What did he do that for?'

'To teach him manners,' Ned said earnestly.

'That's a queer way to teach him manners. He must have been dotty.'

'Oh, I wouldn't say that,' Ned said, a bit ruffled. Everything this girl said seemed to come as a shock to him. 'But that's why my mother won't let us mix with other children. On the other hand, we read a good deal. Are you fond of reading, Miss – I didn't catch the name.'

'You weren't told it,' she said quietly, showing her claws. 'But, if you want to know, it's Rita Lomasney.'

'Do you read much, Miss Lomasney?'

'I couldn't be bothered.'

'I read everything,' he said enthusiastically. 'And as well as that, I'm learning the violin from Miss Maude on the Parade. Of course, it's very difficult, because it's all classical music.'

'What's that?'

'*Maritana* is classical music,' he said eagerly. He was a bit of a puzzle to Rita. She had never before met anyone who had such a passion for teaching. 'Were you at *Maritana* in the Opera House, Miss Lomasney?'

'I was never there at all,' she said curtly, humiliated.

'And *Alice Where Art Thou* is classical music,' he added. 'It's harder than plain music. It has signs like this on it' – he began to draw things on the air – 'and when you see the signs, you know it's after turning into a different tune, though it has the same name. Irish music is all the same tune and that's why my mother won't let us learn it.'

'Were you ever at the Opera in Paris?' she asked suddenly.

'No,' said Ned with regret. 'I was never in Paris. Were you?'

'That's where you ought to go,' she said with airy enthusiasm. 'You couldn't hear any operas here. The staircase alone is bigger than the whole Opera House here.'

It seemed as if they were in for a really informative conversation when two fellows came down Wyse's Hill. Rita got up to meet them. Ned looked up at them for a moment and then rose too, lifting his college cap politely.

'Well, good afternoon,' he said cheerfully. 'I enjoyed the talk. I hope we meet again.'

'Some other Saturday,' said Rita with regret. By this time she would readily have gone up the Dyke and even watched cricket with him if he asked her.

'Oh, good evening, old man,' one of the fellows said in an affected English accent, pretending to raise a top hat. 'Do come and see us soon again.'

'Shut up, Foster, or I'll give you a puck in the gob!' Rita said sharply.

'Oh, by the way,' Ned said, returning to hand her a number of the *Gem*, which he took from his jacket pocket, 'you might like to look at this. It's not bad.'

'I'd love to,' she said insincerely, and he smiled and touched his cap again. Then with a polite and almost deferential air he went up to Foster. 'Did you say something?' he asked.

Foster looked as astonished as though a kitten had suddenly got up on his hind legs and challenged him to fight.

'I did not,' he said, and backed away.

'I'm glad,' Ned said, almost purring. 'I was afraid you might be looking for trouble.'

It astonished Rita. 'There's a queer one for you!' she said when Ned had gone. But she was curiously pleased to see that he was no sissy. She didn't like sissies.

2

The Lomasneys lived on Sunday's Well in a small house with a long sloping garden and a fine view of the river and the city. Harry Lomasney, the builder, was a small man who wore grey tweed suits and soft collars several sizes too big for him. He had a ravaged brick-red face with keen blue eyes, and a sandy straggling moustache with one side going up and the other down, and the workmen said you could tell what humour he was in by the side he pulled. He was nicknamed 'Hasty Harry'. 'Great God!' he fumed when his wife was having her first baby. 'Nine months over a little job like that! I'd do it in three weeks if I could get started.'

His wife was tall and matronly and very pious, but her piety never got much in her way. A woman who had survived Hasty would have survived anything. Their eldest daughter, Kitty, was loud-voiced and gay, and had been expelled from school for writing indecent letters to a boy. She had failed to tell the nuns that she had copied the letters out of a French novel and didn't know what they meant. Nellie was placider than her sister and took more after her mother; besides, she didn't read French novels.

Rita was the exception among the girls. She seemed to have no softness, never had a favourite saint or a favourite nun, and said it was soppy. For the same reason she never had flirtations. Her friendship with Ned Lowry was the nearest she got to that, and though Ned came regularly to the house and took her to the pictures every week, her sisters would have found it hard to say if she ever did anything with him she wouldn't do with a girl. There was something tongue-tied, twisted and unhappy in her. She had a curious raw, almost timid smile as though she thought people only intended to hurt her. At home she was reserved, watchful, mocking. She could listen for hours to her mother and sisters without opening her mouth, and then suddenly mystify them by dropping a well-aimed jaw-breaker – about classical music, for instance – before relapsing into sulky silence, as though she had merely drawn back the veil for a moment on depths in herself she would not permit them to explore. This annoyed her sisters, because they knew there weren't any depths; it was all swank.

After taking her degree, she got a job in a convent school in a provincial town in the west of Ireland. She and Ned corresponded, and he even went to see her there. At home he reported that she seemed quite happy.

But it didn't last. A few months later, the Lomasneys were at supper when they heard a car stop; the gate squeaked, and steps came up the long path to the front door. Then came the bell and a cheerful voice from the hall.

'Hallo, Paschal, I suppose ye weren't expecting me?'

' 'Tis never Rita!' said her mother, meaning that it was but shouldn't be.

'As true as God, that one is after getting into trouble,' said Kitty prophetically.

The door opened and Rita slouched in; a long, stringy girl with a dark, glowing face. She kissed her father and mother lightly.

'What happened you at all, child?' her mother asked placidly.

'Nothing,' replied Rita, an octave up the scale. 'I just got the sack.'

'The sack?' said her father, beginning to pull the wrong side of his moustache. 'What did you get the sack for?' Hasty would sack a man three times in a day, but nobody paid any attention.

'Give us a chance to get something to eat first, can't you?' Rita said laughingly. She took off her hat and smiled at herself in the mirror above the mantelpiece. It was a curious smile as though she were amused by what she saw. Then she smoothed back her thick black hair. 'I told Paschal to bring in whatever was going. I'm on the train since ten. The heating was off as usual. I'm frizzled.'

'A wonder you wouldn't send us a wire,' said Mrs Lomasney as Rita sat down and grabbed some bread and butter.

'Hadn't the cash,' said Rita.

'But what happened, Rita?' Kitty asked brightly.

'You'll hear it all in due course. Reverend Mother is bound to write and tell ye how I lost my character.'

'Wisha, what did you do to her, child?' asked her mother with amusement. She had been through all this before, with Hasty and Kitty, and she knew that God was very good and nothing much ever happened.

'Fellow that wanted to marry me,' said Rita. 'He was in his last year at college, and his mother didn't like me, so she got Reverend Mother to give me the push.'

'But what business is it of hers?' asked Nellie.

'None whatever, girl,' said Rita.

But Kitty looked suspiciously at her. Rita wasn't natural: there was something about her that was not in control. After all, this was her first real love affair, and Kitty could not believe that she had gone about it like anyone else.

'Still, you worked pretty fast,' she said.

'You'd have to work fast in that place,' said Rita. 'There was only one possible man in the whole place – the bank clerk. We used to call him "The One". I wasn't there a week when a nun ticked me off for riding on the pillion of his motor-bike.'

'And did you?' Kitty asked innocently.

'Fat chance I got!' said Rita. 'They did that to every teacher to give her the idea that she was well-watched. The unfortunates were scared out of their wits. I only met Tony Donoghue a fortnight ago. He was home with a breakdown.'

'Well, well, well!' said her mother without rancour. 'No wonder his poor mother was upset. A boy that's not left college yet! Couldn't ye wait till he was qualified anyway?'

'Not very well,' said Rita. 'He's going to be a priest.'

Kitty sat back with a superior grin. She had known it all the time. Of course, Rita couldn't do anything like other people. If it hadn't been a priest it would have been a married man or a negro, and Rita would have shown off about it just the same.

'What's that you say?' her father asked, springing to his feet.

'All right, don't blame me!' Rita said hastily, beaming at him. 'It wasn't my fault. He said he didn't want to be a priest. His mother was driving him into it. That's why he had the breakdown.'

'Let me out of this before I have a breakdown myself,' said Hasty. 'I'm the one that should be the priest. If I was I wouldn't be saddled with a mad, distracted family the way I am.'

He stamped out of the room, and the girls laughed. The idea of their father as a priest appealed to them almost as much as the idea of him as a mother. But Mrs Lomasney did not laugh.

'Reverend Mother was perfectly right,' she said severely. 'As if it wasn't hard enough on the poor boys without girls like you throwing temptation in their way. I think you behaved very badly, Rita.'

'All right, if you say so,' Rita said shortly with a boyish shrug, and refused to talk any more about it.

After supper, she said she was tired and went to bed, and her mother and sisters sat on in the front room, discussing the scandal. Someone rang and Nellie opened the door.

'Hallo, Ned,' she said, 'I suppose you came up to congratulate us.'

'Hallo,' Ned said, smiling primly with closed lips. With a sort of automatic movement he took off his overcoat and hat and hung them on the rack. Then he emptied the pockets with the same thoroughness. He had not changed much. He was thin and pale, spectacled and clever, with the same precise and tranquil manner – 'like an old Persian cat', as Nellie said. He read too many books. In the last year or two something seemed to have happened him. He did not go to Mass any longer. Not going to Mass struck all the Lomasneys as too damn clever. 'On what?' he added, having avoided any unnecessary precipitation.

'You didn't know who was here?'

'No,' he said, raising his brows mildly.

'Rita!'

'Oh!' The same tone. It was part of his cleverness not to be surprised at anything. It was as though he regarded any attempt to surprise him as an invasion of his privacy.

'She's after getting the sack for trying to run off with a priest,' said Nellie.

If she thought that would shake him she was badly mistaken. He tossed his head with a silent chuckle and went into the room, adjusting his pinc-nez. For a fellow who was supposed to be in love with her, this was very peculiar behaviour, Nellie thought. He put his hands in his trousers pockets and stood on the hearth with his legs well apart.

'Isn't it awful, Ned?' Mrs Lomasney asked in her deep voice.

'Is it?' Ned purred, smiling.

'With a priest!' cried Nellie.

'Now, he wasn't a priest, Nellie,' Mrs Lomasney said severely. 'Don't be trying to make it worse.'

'Suppose you tell me what happened,' suggested Ned.

'But sure, when we don't know, Ned,' cried Mrs Lomasney. 'You know what that one is like in one of her sulky fits. Maybe she'll tell you. She's up in bed.'

'I may as well try,' said Ned.

Still with his hands in his pockets, he rolled after Mrs Lomasney up the thickly carpeted stairs to Rita's little bedroom at the top of the house. While Mrs Lomasney went in to see that her daughter was decent he paused to look out over the river and the lighted city behind it. Rita, wearing a pink dressing jacket, was lying with one arm under her head. By the bed was a table with a packet of cigarettes she had been using as an ashtray. He smiled and shook his head reprovingly.

'Hallo, Ned,' she said, reaching him a bare arm. 'Give us a kiss. I'm quite kissable now.'

He didn't need to be told that. He was astonished at the change in her. Her whole bony, boyish face seemed to have gone soft and mawkish and to be lit up from inside. He sat on an armchair by the bed, carefully pulling up the bottoms of his trousers, then put his hands in the pockets again and sat back with crossed legs.

'I suppose they're hopping downstairs,' said Rita.

'They seem a little excited,' Ned replied, with bowed head cocked sideways, looking like some wise old bird.

'Wait till they hear the details!' Rita said grimly.

'Are there details?' he asked mildly.

'Masses of them,' said Rita. 'Honest to God, Ned, I used to laugh at the glamour girls in the convent. I never knew you could get like that about a fellow. It's like something busting inside you. Cripes, I'm as soppy as a kid!'

'And what's the fellow like?' Ned asked curiously.

'Tony? How the hell do I know? He's decent enough, I suppose. His mother has a shop in the Main Street. He kissed me one night coming home and I was so furious I cut the socks off him. Next evening, he came round to apologize, and I never got up or asked him to sit down or anything. I suppose I was still mad with him. He said he never slept a wink. "Didn't you?" said I. "It didn't trouble me much." Bloody lies, of course; I was twisting and turning the whole night. "I only did it because I was so fond of you," says he. "Is that what you told the last one, too?" said I. That got him into a wax as well, and he said I was calling him a liar. "And aren't you?" said I. Then I waited for him to hit me, but instead he began to cry, and then I began to cry – imagine me crying, Ned! – and next thing I was sitting on his knee. Talk about the Babes in the Wood. First time he ever had a girl on his knee, he said, and you know how much of it I did.'

There was a discreet knock and Mrs Lomasney smiled benevolently at them round the door.

'I suppose 'tis tea Ned is having?' she asked in her deep voice.

'No, I'm having the tea,' Rita said lightly, throwing him a cigarette. 'Ned says he'd sooner a drop of the hard tack.'

'Oh, isn't that a great change, Ned?' cried Mrs Lomasney.

' 'Tis the shock,' said Rita. 'He didn't think I was that sort of girl.'

'He mustn't know much about girls,' said Mrs Lomasney.

'He's learning now,' said Rita.

When Paschal brought up the tray, Rita poured out tea for Ned and whiskey for herself. He made no comment; things like that were a commonplace in the Lomasney household.

'Anyway,' she went on, pulling at her cigarette, 'he told his old one he wanted to chuck the Church and marry me. There was ructions. The people in the shop at the other side of the street had a son a priest, and she wanted to be as good as them. Away with her up to Reverend Mother, and Reverend Mother sends for me. Did I want to destroy the young man and he on the threshold of a great calling? I told her 'twas his mother wanted to destroy him, and I asked her what sort of a priest did she think Tony would make. Oh, he'd be twice the man, after a sacrifice like that. Honest to God, Ned, the way that woman went on, you'd think she was talking of doctoring an old tom-cat. I think this damn country must be full of female vets. After that, she dropped the Holy Willie stuff and told me his mother was after getting into debt to put him in for the priesthood, and if he chucked it now, she'd never be able to pay it back. Wouldn't they kill you with style?'

'And what did you do then?'

'I went to see his mother, of course.'

'You didn't!'

'I told you I was off my head. I thought I might work it with the personal touch.'

'You don't seem to have been successful.'

'I'd as soon try the personal touch on a traction engine, Ned,' Rita said ruefully. 'That woman was twice my weight. I told her I wanted to marry Tony. "I'm sorry, you can't," she said. "What's to stop me?" says I. "He's gone too far," says she. "If he was gone farther it wouldn't stop me," says I. I told her then what Reverend Mother said about the three hundred pounds and offered to pay it back for her if she let me marry him.'

'And had you the three hundred?' Ned asked in surprise.

'Ah, where would I get three hundred? And she knew it, the old jade! She didn't believe a word I said. I saw Tony afterwards, and he was crying. He said he didn't want to break her heart. I declare to God, Ned, that woman has as much heart as a traction engine.'

'Well, you seem to have done it in style,' said Ned as he put away his teacup.

'That wasn't the half of it. When I heard the difficulties his mother was making, I offered to live with him instead.'

'Live with him!' said Ned. That startled even him.

'Well, go away on holidays with him. Lots of girls do it. I know they do. And, God Almighty, isn't it only natural?'

'And what did he say to that?' Ned asked curiously.

'He was scared stiff.'

'He would be,' said Ned, giving his superior little sniff as he took out a packet of cigarettes.

'Oh, it's all very well for you,' cried Rita, bridling up. 'You may think you're a great fellow, all because you read Tolstoy and don't go to Mass, but you'd be just as scared if a doll offered to go to bed with you.'

'Try me,' he said sedately as he lit her cigarette, but somehow the idea of suggesting such a thing to Ned only made her laugh.

He stayed till quite late, and when he went downstairs Mrs Lomasney and the girls fell on him and dragged him into the sitting-room.

'Well, doctor, how's the patient?' asked Mrs Lomasney.

'Oh, I think the patient is coming round nicely,' said Ned with a smile.

'But would you ever believe it, Ned?' she cried. 'A girl that wouldn't look at the side of the road a fellow was on, unless 'twas to go robbing orchards with him. You'll have another drop of whiskey?'

'I won't.'

'And is that all you're going to tell us?'

'You'll hear it all from herself.'

'We won't.'

'I dare say not,' he said with a hearty chuckle, and went for his coat.

'Wisha, Ned, what will your mother say when she hears it?' asked Mrs Lomasney, and Ned put his nose in the air and gave an exaggerated version of what Mrs Lomasney called 'his Hayfield sniff'.

' "All *quite* mad," ' he said.

'The dear knows, she might be right,' she said with resignation, helping him on with his coat. 'I hope your mother doesn't notice the smell of whiskey from your breath,' she added dryly just to show him that she missed nothing, and then stood at the door, looking up and down, while she waited for him to wave from the gate.

'Ah, with the help of God it might be all for the best,' she said as she closed the door behind him.

'If you think he's going to marry her, you're mistaken,' said Kitty. 'Merciful God, I'd like to see myself telling Bill O'Donnell a thing like that. He'd have my sacred life. That fellow positively enjoys it.'

'Ah, God is good,' her mother said cheerfully, kicking a mat into place. 'Some men might like that.'

3

Ned apparently did, but he was the only one. Within a week, Kitty and Nellie were sick to death of Rita round the house. She was bad enough at the best of times – or so they said – but now she brooded and mooned and quarrelled. Most afternoons she strolled down the Dyke to Ned's little shop, where she sat on the counter, swinging her legs and smoking, while Ned leaned against the window, tinkering with some delicate instrument at the insides of a watch. Nothing seemed to rattle Ned, not even Rita doing what no customer would dare to do. When he finished work he changed his coat and they went out to tea. He sat in a corner at the back of the teashop, pulled up the bottoms of his trousers, and took out a packet of cigarettes and a box of matches, which he placed on the table before him with a look that commanded them to stay there and not get lost. His face was pale and clear and bright, like an evening sky when the last light has drained from it.

'Anything wrong?' he asked one evening when she was moodier than usual.

'Oh, just fed up,' she said, thrusting out her jaw.

'Still fretting?' he asked in surprise.

'Ah, no. I can get over that. It's Kitty and Nellie. They're bitches, Ned; proper bitches. And all because I don't wear my heart on my sleeve. If one of them got dumped by a fellow she'd take two aspirins and go to bed with the other one. They'd have a lovely talk – can't you imagine? "And was it then he said he loved you?" That sort of balls! I can't do it. And it's all because they're not sincere, Ned. They couldn't be sincere.'

'Remember, they have a long start on you,' Ned said.

Is that it?' she asked without interest. 'They think I'm batty. Do you, Ned?'

'Not altogether,' he said with a tight-lipped smile. 'I've no doubt that Mrs Donoghue, if that's her name, thought something of the sort.'

'And wasn't she right?' Rita asked tensely. 'Suppose she'd agreed to take the three hundred quid, wouldn't I be properly shown up? I wake in a sweat whenever I think of it. I'm just a bloody chancer, Ned. Where would I get three hundred quid?'

'Oh, I dare say someone would have lent it to you,' he said with a shrug.

'They would like hell. Would you?'

'Probably,' he said gravely after a moment's thought. 'I think I could raise it.'

'Are you serious?' she whispered earnestly.

'Quite,' he said in the same tone.

'Cripes, you must be very fond of me,' she gasped.

'Looks like it,' said Ned, and this time he laughed with real heartiness; a boy's laugh of sheer delight at her astonishment. Of course, it was just like Rita to regard a lifetime's friendship as sport, and the offer of three hundred pounds as the real thing.

'Would you marry me?' she asked with a frown. 'I'm not proposing to you, mind, only asking,' she added hastily.

'Certainly, whenever you like,' he said, spreading his hands.

'Honest to God?'

'Cut my throat,' he replied, making the schoolboy gesture.

'My God, why didn't you ask me before I went down to that kip? I'd have married you like a shot. Was it the way you weren't keen on me?' she added, wondering if there wasn't really something queer about him, as her sisters said.

'No,' he replied matter-of-factly, drawing himself together like an old clock preparing to strike. 'I think I've been keen on you since the first day I met you.'

'It's easily seen you're a Neddy Ned,' she said. 'I go after mine with a scalping knife.'

'I stalk mine,' he said smugly.

'Cripes, Ned,' she said with real regret, 'I wish you'd told me sooner. I couldn't marry you now.'

'Couldn't you? Why not?'

'Because it wouldn't be fair to you.'

'You think I can't look after myself?'

'I have to look after you now.' She glanced round the restaurant to make sure that no one was listening, and then went on in a dry, dispassionate voice, leaning one elbow wearily on the table. 'I suppose you'll think this is all cod, but it's not. Honest to God, I think you're the finest bloody man I ever met – even though you do think you're an atheist or something,' she interjected maliciously with a characteristic Lomasney flourish in the cause of Faith and Fatherland. 'There's no one in the world I have more respect for. I think I'd nearly cut my throat if I did something you really disapproved of – I don't mean telling lies or going on a skite,' she added hastily. 'That's only gas. I mean something that really shocked you. I think if I was tempted I'd ask myself: "How the hell would I face Lowry afterwards?"'

For a moment she thought from his smile that he was going to cry. Then he squelched the butt of his cigarette on a plate and spoke in an extraordinarily quiet voice.

'That'll do me grand for a beginning,' he said.

'It wouldn't, Ned,' she said sadly. 'That's why I say I have to look after you now. You couldn't understand it unless it happened to yourself and you fell in love with a doll the way I fell in love with Tony. Tony is a scut, and a cowardly scut at that, but I was cracked about him. If he came in here now and asked me to go off to Killarney on a week-end with him, I'd buy a nightdress and a toothbrush and go. And I wouldn't give a damn what you or anybody thought. I might chuck myself in the lake afterwards, but I'd go. Christ, Ned,' she exclaimed, flushing and looking as though she might burst into tears, 'he couldn't come into a room but I went all mushy inside. That's what the real thing is like.'

'Well,' said Ned, apparently not in the least put out – in fact, looking rather pleased with himself, Rita thought – 'I'm in no hurry. In case you get tired of scalping them, the offer will still be open.'

'Thanks, Ned,' she said absent-mindedly, as though she weren't listening.

While he paid the bill, she stood in the porch, doing her face in the big mirror that flanked it, and paying no attention to the crowds who were hurrying homeward through lighted streets. As he emerged from the shop she turned on him suddenly.

'About that matter, Ned,' she said. 'Will you ask me again, or do I have to ask you?'

He just managed to refrain from laughing outright.

'As you like,' he said with quiet amusement. 'Suppose I repeat the proposal every six months.'

'That would be a hell of a time to wait if I changed my mind,' she said with a scowl. 'All right,' she added, taking his arm. 'I know you well enough to ask you. If you don't want me by that time, you can always say so. I won't mind. I'm used to it now.'

4

Ned's proposal came as a considerable support to Rita. It buttressed her self-esteem, which was always in danger of collapsing. She might be ugly and uneducated and a bit of a chancer, but the best man in Cork – the best in Ireland, she sometimes thought – wanted to marry her, even when she had been let down by another man. That was a queer one for her enemies! So while Kitty and Nellie made fun of her, she bided her time, waiting till she could really rock them. Since her childhood she had never given anything away without squeezing the last ounce of theatrical effect from it. She would tell her sisters, but not till she could make them feel properly sick.

It was a pity she didn't because Ned was not the only one. There was also Justin Sullivan, the lawyer, who had once been by way of being engaged to Nellie. He had not become engaged to her because Nellie was as slippery as an eel, and had her cap set all the time at a solicitor called Fahy whom Justin despised with his whole heart and soul as a light-headed, butterfly sort of man. But Justin continued to come to the house. There happened to be no other that suited him half as well, and besides, he knew that sooner or later Nellie would make a mess of her life with Fahy, and his services would be required.

Justin, in fact, was a sticker. He was a good deal older than Rita; a tall, burly man with a broad face, a brow that was rising from baldness as well as brains, and a slow, watchful, ironic air. Like many lawyers he tended to conduct a conversation as though the person he was speaking to were a hostile witness who had to be coaxed into an admission of perjury or bullied into one of mental deficiency.

When Justin began to talk Fahy simply clutched his head and retired to sit on the stairs. 'Can no one shut that fellow up?' he would moan with a martyred air. No one could. The girls shot their little darts at him, but he only brushed them aside. Ned was the only one who could even stand up to him, and when the two of them argued about religion, the room became a desert. Justin, of course, was all for the Church. 'Imagine for a moment that I am Pope,' he would declaim in a throaty, rounded voice that turned easily to pompousness. 'Easiest thing in the world, Justin,' Kitty assured him once. He drank whiskey like water, and the more he drank, the more massive and logical and piously Catholic he became.

But for all his truculent airs he was exceedingly gentle, patient and understanding, and disliked the way her sisters ragged Rita.

'Tell me, Nellie,' he asked one night in his lazy, amiable way, 'do you talk like that to Rita because you like it, or out of a sense of duty?'

'How soft you have it!' cried Nellie. 'We have to live with her. You haven't.'

'That may be my misfortune, Nellie,' said Justin.

'Is that a proposal, Justin?' Kitty asked shrewdly.

'Scarcely, Kitty,' said Justin. 'You're not what I might call a good jury.'

'Better be careful or you'll have her calling on your mother, Justin,' Kitty said maliciously.

'I hope my mother has sufficient sense to realize it would be an honour, Kitty,' Justin said severely.

When he rose to go, Rita accompanied him to the hall.

'Thanks for the moral support, Justin,' she said in a low voice and threw an overcoat over her shoulders to accompany him to the gate. When he opened the door they both stood and gazed round them. It was a moonlit night: the garden, patterned in black and silver sloped to the quiet suburban roadway where the gas-lamps burned with a dim green light. Beyond this gateways shaded by black trees led to flights of steps or steep-sloping avenues behind the moonlit houses on the river's edge.

'God, isn't it lovely?' said Rita.

'Oh, by the way, Rita, that was a proposal,' he said, slipping his arm through hers.

'Janey Mack, they're falling,' she said, and gave his arm a squeeze.

'What are?'

'Proposals. I never knew I was so popular.'

'Why? Have you had others?'

'I had one anyway.'

'And did you accept it?'

'No,' Rita said doubtfully. 'Not quite. At least, I don't think I did.'

'You might consider this one,' Justin said with unusual humility. 'You know, of course, that I was very fond of Nellie. At one time I was very fond of her, indeed. You don't mind that, I hope. It's all over and done with now, and no regrets on either side.'

'No, Justin, of course I don't mind. If I felt like marrying you I wouldn't give it a second thought. But I was very much in love with Tony too, and that's not all over and done with yet.'

'I know that, Rita,' he said gently. 'I know exactly what you feel. We've all been through it.' He might as well have left it there, but, being a lawyer, Justin liked to see his case properly set out. 'That won't last for ever. In a month or two you'll be over it, and then you'll wonder what you saw in that fellow.'

'I don't think so, Justin,' she said with a crooked smile, not altogether displeased to be able to enlighten him about the utter hopelessness of her position. 'I think it will take a great deal longer than that.'

'Well, say six months even,' Justin went on, prepared to yield a point to the defence. 'All I ask is that in one month or six, when you've got over your regrets for this – this amiable young man' (momentarily his voice took on its familiar ironic tone) 'you'll give me a thought. I'm old enough not to make any more mistakes. I know I'm fond of you, and I feel sure I could make a success of my end of it.'

'What you really mean is that I wasn't in love with Tony at all,' Rita said, keeping her temper with the greatest difficulty. 'Isn't that it?'

'Not quite,' Justin replied judiciously. Even if he had had a serenade as well as moonlight and a girl, Justin could not have resisted correcting what he considered a false deduction. 'I've no doubt you were very much attracted by this – this clerical Adonis; this Mr Whatever-his-name-is, or that at any rate you thought you were, which in practice comes to the same thing, but I also know that that sort of thing, though it's painful enough while it lasts, doesn't last very long.'

'You mean yours didn't, Justin,' Rita said tartly. By this time she was flaming.

'I mean mine or anyone else's,' said Justin. 'Because love – the only sort of thing you can really call love – is something that comes with experience. You're probably too young yet to know what the real thing is.'

As Rita had only recently told Ned that he didn't yet know what the real thing was, she found this very hard to stomach.

'How old would you say you'd have to be,' she asked viciously. 'Thirty-five?'

'You'll know soon enough – when it hits you,' said Justin.

'Honest to God, Justin,' she said withdrawing her arm and looking at him furiously, 'I think you're the thickest man I ever met.'

'Good-night, my dear,' said Justin with perfect good humour, and he took the few steps to the gate at a run.

Rita stood gazing after him with folded arms. At the age of twenty to be told that there is anything you don't know about love is like a knife in your heart.

5

Kitty and Nellie persuaded Mrs Lomasney that the best way of distracting Rita's mind was to find her a new job. As a new environment was also supposed to be good for her complaint, Mrs Lomasney wrote to her sister, who was a nun in England, and the sister found her work in a convent there. Rita let on to be indifferent though she complained bitterly enough to Ned.

'But why England?' he asked in surprise.

'Why not?'

'Wouldn't any place nearer do you?'

'I suppose I wouldn't be far enough away.'

'But why not make up your own mind?'

'I'll probably do that too,' she said with a short laugh. 'I'd like to see what's in theirs first though. I might have a surprise for them.'

She certainly had that. She was to leave for England on Friday, and on Wednesday the girls gave a farewell party. Wednesday was the weekly half-holiday, and it rained steadily all day. The girls' friends all turned up. Most of these were men: Bill O'Donnell of the bank, who was engaged to Kitty; Fahy, the solicitor, who was Justin's successful rival for Nellie; Justin himself, who simply could not be kept out of the house by anything short of an injunction, Ned Lowry and a few others. Hasty soon retired with his wife to the dining-room to read the evening paper. He said all his daughters' young men looked exactly alike and he never knew which of them he was talking to.

Bill O'Donnell was acting as barman. He was a big man, bigger even than Justin, with a battered boxer's face and a negro smile that seemed to well up from depths of good humour with life rather than from anything that happened in it. He carried out loud conversations with everyone he poured out a drink for, and his voice overrode every intervening tête-à-tête, and even challenged the piano, on which Nellie was vamping music-hall songs.

'Who's this one for, Rita?' he asked. 'A bottle of Bass for Paddy. Ah, the stout man! Remember the New Year's Night in Bandon, Paddy? Remember how you had to carry me up to the bank in evening dress and jack me up between the two wings of the desk? Kitty, did I ever tell you about that night in Bandon?'

'Once a week for the past five years, Bill,' Kitty sang out cheerfully.

'Nellie,' said Rita. 'I think it's time for Bill to sing his song. "Let Me Like a Soldier Fall", Bill!'

'My one little song!' Bill said with a roar of laughter. 'The only song I know, but I sing it grand. Don't I, Nellie? Don't I sing it fine?'

'Fine!' agreed Nellie, looking up at his big moon-face beaming at her over the piano. 'As the man said to my mother, "Finest bloody soprano I ever heard."'

'He did not, Nellie,' Bill said sadly. 'You're making that up. . . . Silence, please!' he shouted, clapping his hands. 'Ladies and gentlemen, I must apologize. I ought to sing something like Tosti's "Good-bye" but the fact is, ladies and gentlemen, that I don't know Tosti's "Good-bye".'

'Recite it, Bill,' suggested Justin amiably.

'I don't know the words of it either, Justin,' said Bill. 'In fact, I'm not sure if there is any such song, but if there is, I ought to sing it.'

'Why, Bill?' asked Rita innocently. She was wearing a long black dress that threw up the unusual brightness of her dark, bony face. She looked more cheerful than she had looked for months. All the evening it was as though she were laughing to herself at something.

'Because 'twould be only right, Rita,' Bill said with great melancholy, putting his arm round her and drawing her closer. 'You know I'm very fond of you, don't you, Rita?'

'And I'm mad about you, Bill,' Rita said candidly.

'I know that, Rita,' he said mournfully, pulling at his collar as though to give himself air. 'I only wish you weren't going, Rita. This place isn't the same without you. Kitty won't mind my saying that,' he added with a nervous glance at Kitty, who was flirting with Justin on the sofa.

'Are you going to sing your blooming old song or not?' Nellie asked impatiently, running her fingers over the keys.

'I'm going to sing now in one minute, Nellie,' Bill replied ecstatically, stroking Rita fondly under the chin. 'I only want Rita to know we'll miss her.'

'Damn it, Bill,' Rita said, snuggling up to him, 'if you go on like that I won't go at all. Would you sooner I didn't go?'

'I would sooner it, Rita,' he said, stroking her cheeks and eyes. 'You're too good for the fellows there.'

'Oh, go on doing that, Bill,' she said. 'It's gorgeous, and you're making Kitty mad jealous.'

'Kitty isn't jealous,' Bill said mawkishly. 'Kitty is a lovely girl and you're a lovely girl. I hate to see you go, Rita.'

'That settles it, Bill,' she said, pulling herself free of him with a mock-determined air. 'As you feel that way about it, I won't go at all.'

'Won't you though!' said Kitty sweetly.

'Don't worry your head about it, Bill,' said Rita briskly. 'It's all off.'

Justin, who had been quietly getting through large whiskies, looked up lazily.

'Perhaps I should have mentioned that the young lady has just done me the honour of proposing to me, and I've accepted her,' he boomed.

Ned, who had been enjoying the little scene between Bill and Rita, looked at Justin in surprise.

'Bravo! Bravo!' cried Bill, clapping his hands with delight. 'A marriage has been arranged and all the rest of it – what? I must give you a kiss, Rita. Justin, you don't mind if I give Rita a kiss?'

'Not at all, not at all,' said Justin with a lordly wave of the hand. 'Anything that's mine is yours.'

'You're not serious, Justin, are you?' Kitty asked incredulously.

'Oh, I'm serious all right,' said Justin, and then he gave Rita a puzzled look. 'I'm not quite certain whether your sister is. Are you, Rita?'

'What?' Rita asked, as though she were listening to something else.

'Why? Are you trying to give me the push already?' asked Rita with amusement.

'We're much obliged for the information,' Nellie said angrily as she rose from the piano. 'I wonder did you tell Father?'

'Hardly,' said Rita coolly. 'It was only settled an hour ago.'

'Maybe 'twill do with some more settling by the time Father is done with you,' Nellie said furiously. 'The impudence of you! Go in at once and tell him.'

'Keep your hair on, girl,' Rita said with cool malice and then went jauntily out of the room. Kitty and Nellie began to squabble viciously with Justin. They were convinced that the whole scene had been arranged by Rita to make them look ridiculous, and in this they weren't very far out. Justin sat back and began to enjoy the sport. Then Ned struck a match and lit another cigarette, and something about the slow, careful way he did it drew everyone's attention. Just because he was not the sort to make a fuss, anything unusual about him stuck out, and a feeling of awkwardness ensued. Ned was too old a friend for the girls not to feel that way about him.

Rita returned, laughing.

'Consent refused,' she growled, bowing her head and tugging the wrong side of an imaginary moustache.

'What did I tell you?' Nellie said without rancour.

'You don't think it makes any difference?' asked Rita dryly.

'What did he say?' asked Kitty.

'Oh, he hadn't a notion who I was talking about,' Rita said lightly. ' "Justin who?" ' she mimicked. ' "How the hell do you think I can remember all the young scuts ye bring to the house?" '

'Was he mad?' asked Kitty.

'Hopping. The poor man can't even settle down to read his *Echo* without one of his daughters interrupting him to announce her engagement.'

'He didn't call us scuts?' Bill asked in a tone of genuine grief.

'Oh, begor, that was the very word he used, Bill.'

'Did you tell him he was very fond of me the day I gave him the tip for Golden Boy at the Park Races?' asked Justin.

'I did,' said Rita. 'I told him you were the stout block of a fellow with the brown hair that he said had the fine intelligence, and he said he never gave a damn about intelligence. Character was all that mattered. He wanted me to marry the thin fellow with the specs. "Only bloody gentleman that comes to this house." '

'Is it Ned?' asked Nellie.

'Of course. I asked him why he didn't tell me that before and he nearly ate the head off me. "Jesus Christ, girl, don't I feed and clothe ye? Isn't that enough without having to coort for ye as well. Next thing is ye'll be asking me to have a couple of babies for ye." Anyway, Ned,' she added with a crooked, almost malicious smile, 'there's no doubt about who was Pa's favourite.'

Once more the attention was directed on Ned. He put his cigarette down with care and rose, holding out his hand.

'I wish you all the luck in the world, Justin,' he said.

'I know that well, Ned,' boomed Justin, catching Ned's hand. 'And I'd feel the same if it was you.'

'And you, too, Miss Lomasney,' Ned said gaily.

'Thanks, Mr Lowry,' she replied with the same crooked smile.

And they all felt afterwards as though they had been attending a funeral.

6

Justin and Rita married, and Ned, like all the Hayfield Hourigans, behaved in a decorous and sensible manner. He did not take to drink or violence or do any of the things people are expected to do under the circumstances. He gave them an expensive clock as a wedding present, went a couple of times to visit them, permitted Justin to try and convert him back to Catholicism, and took Rita to the pictures when Justin was on circuit. At the same time he began to walk out with an assistant in Halpin's; a gentle, humorous girl with a great mass of jetblack hair, a snub nose and a long, melancholy face. You saw them everywhere together.

He also went regularly to Sunday's Well to see the old couple and Nellie, who wasn't married yet. One evening when he called, Mr and Mrs Lomasney were down at the church, but Rita was there, Justin being again away. It was months since she and Ned had met; she was having a baby and very near her time, and it made her self-conscious and rude. She said it made her feel like a yacht that had been turned into a cargo-boat. Three or four times she said things to Ned that would have maddened anyone else, but he took them in his usual way, without resentment.

'And how's little Miss Bitch?' she asked insolently.

'Little Miss who?' he asked.

'Miss – how the hell can I remember the names of all your dolls? The Spanish-looking one who sells the knickers at Halpin's.'

'Oh, she's very well, thanks.'

'What you might call a prudent marriage,' Rita went on, all on edge.

'How's that?'

'You'll have the ring and the trousseau at cost price.'

'Aren't you very interested in her?' Nellie asked suspiciously.

'I don't give a damn about her,' Rita said contemptuously. 'Would Senorita What's-her-name ever let you stand godfather to my footballer, Ned?'

'Why not?' Ned asked mildly. 'I'd be delighted, of course.'

'You have the devil's own neck to ask him after the way you treated him,' said Nellie.

Nellie was fascinated. She knew that Rita was in one of her emotional states and longed to know what it all meant. Ordinarily Rita would have delighted in thwarting her, but now it was as though she actually wanted an audience.

'What did I do to him?' she asked with interest.

'Codding him along like that for years, and then marrying a man that was twice your age. What sort of conduct is that?'

'Well, how did he expect me to know the difference?'

Ned rose and took out a packet of cigarettes. Like Nellie, he knew that Rita had deliberately staged the scene for some purpose of her own. She was leaning far back in her chair and laughed up at him while she took a cigarette and waited for him to light it.

'Come on, Rita,' he said encouragingly. 'As you've said so much you may as well tell us the rest.'

'What else is there to tell?'

'What had you against me,' he said, growing pale.

'Who said I had anything against you?'

'Didn't you?'

'Not a damn thing. Just that I didn't love you. Didn't I tell you distinctly when you asked me to marry you that I didn't love you? I suppose you thought I didn't mean it?'

He paused for a moment and then raised his eyebrows.

'I did,' he said quietly.

She laughed. Nellie did not laugh.

'The conceit of some people!' Rita said lightly: then, with a change of tone: 'I had nothing against you, Ned. This was the one I had the needle in. Herself and Kitty forcing me into it.'

'Well, the impudence of you!' cried Nellie.

'And isn't it true for me? Weren't you both trying to get me out of the house?'

'We were not,' Nellie replied hotly. 'And even if we were, that has nothing to do with it. We didn't want you to marry Justin if you wanted to marry Ned.'

'I didn't want to marry Ned. I didn't want to marry at all.'

'What made you change your mind, so?'

'Nothing made me change my mind. I didn't care about anyone only Tony, only I didn't want to go to that damn place, and I had no alternative. I had to marry one of them, so I made up my mind that I'd marry the first one that called.'

It was directed to Nellie, but every word was aimed straight at Ned, and Nellie was wise enough to realize it.

'My God, you must have been mad!' she said.

'I felt it,' Rita said with a shrug. 'I sat at the window the whole afternoon, looking out at the rain. Remember that day, Ned?'

He nodded.

'Blame the rain if you want to blame something. I think I half hoped you'd come first. Justin came instead – an old aunt of his was sick and he came to supper. I saw him at the gate and he waved to me with his old brolly. I ran downstairs to open the door for him. "Justin, if you still want to marry me, I'm ready," I said, and I grabbed him by the coat. He gave me a dirty look – you know Justin! "Young woman, there's a time and place for everything," he said, and off with him to the lavatory. Talk about romantic engagements! Damn the old kiss did I get off him, even!'

'I declare to God!' Nellie said in stupefaction. 'You're not natural, Rita.'

'I know,' Rita said, laughing again at her own irresponsibility. 'Cripes, when I knew what I'd done I nearly dropped dead!'

'Oh, so you did come to your senses, for once?' Nellie asked.

'Of course I did. That's the trouble with Justin. He's always right. That fellow knew I wouldn't be married a week before I'd forgotten Tony. And there was I, sure that my life was over and that it was marriage or the river. Women!' she cried, shaking her head in a frenzy. 'God! God! The idiots we make of ourselves about men!'

'And I suppose it was then that you found out you'd married the wrong man?' Nellie asked, but not inquisitively this time. She knew.

'Who said I married the wrong man?' Rita asked hotly.

'It sounds damn like it, Rita,' Nellie said wearily.

'You get things all wrong, Nellie,' Rita said, her teeth on edge again. 'You jump to conclusions too much. If I married the wrong man, I wouldn't be likely to tell you – or Ned either.'

She looked mockingly at Ned, but her look belied her. It was plain enough now why she needed Nellie as audience. It kept her from saying more than she had to say, from saying things that once said, might make her own life unbearable. We all do it. Once let her say 'Ned, I love you', which was all she was saying, and he would have to do something about it, and then everything would fall in ruin about them.

He rose and flicked his cigarette ash into the fire. Then he stood with his back to it, his hands behind his back, his feet spread out on the hearth, exactly as he had stood on that night when he had defended her against her family.

'You mean, if I'd come earlier you'd have married me?' He asked quietly.

'If you'd come earlier, I'd probably be asking Justin to stand godfather to your brat,' said Rita. 'And how do you know but Justin would be walking out the Senorita, Ned?'

'And you wouldn't be quite so interested whether he was or not,' Nellie said, but she didn't say it maliciously. It was only too plain what Rita meant, and Nellie was sorry for her. She had a long lifetime yet to go through. 'Dear God,' she added ingenuously, 'isn't life awful?'

Ned turned and lashed his cigarette savagely into the fire. Rita looked up at him mockingly.

'Go on!' she taunted him. 'Say it, blast you!'

'I couldn't,' he said bitterly.

A month later, he married the Senorita.

Uprooted

Spring had only come and already he was tired to death; tired of the city, tired of his job. He had come up from the country intending to do wonders, but he was as far as ever from that. He would be lucky if he could carry on, be at school each morning at half past nine and satisfy his half-witted principal.

He lodged in a small red-brick house in Rathmines that was kept by a middle-aged brother and sister who had been left a bit of money and thought they would end their days enjoyably in a city. They did not enjoy themselves, regretted their little farm in Kerry, and were glad of Ned Keating because he could talk to them about all the things they remembered and loved.

Keating was a slow, cumbrous young man with dark eyes and a dark cow's-lick that kept tumbling into them. He had a slight stammer and ran his hand through his long limp hair from pure nervousness. He had always been dreamy and serious. Sometimes on market days you saw him standing for an hour in Nolan's shop, turning the pages of a schoolbook. When he could not afford it he put it back with a sigh and went off to find his father in a pub, just raising his eyes to smile at Jack Nolan. After his elder brother Tom had gone for the church he and his father had constant rows. Nothing would do Ned now but to be a teacher. Hadn't he all he wanted now? his father asked. Hadn't he the place to himself? What did he want going teaching? But Ned was stubborn. With an obstinate, almost despairing determination he had fought his way through the training college into a city job. The city was what he had always wanted. And now the city had failed him. In the evenings you could still see him poking round the second-hand bookshops on the quays, but his eyes were already beginning to lose their eagerness.

It had all seemed so clear. But then he had not counted on his own temper. He was popular because of his gentleness, but how many concessions that involved! He was hesitating, good-natured, slow to see guile, slow to contradict. He felt he was constantly underestimating his own powers. He even felt he lacked spontaneity. He did not drink, smoked little, and saw dangers and losses everywhere. He blamed himself for avarice and cowardice. The story he liked best was about the country boy and the letter box. 'Indeed, what a fool you think I am! Put me letther in a pump!'

He was in no danger of putting his letter in a pump or anywhere else for the matter of that. He had only one friend, a nurse in Vincent's Hospital, a wild, light-hearted, light-headed girl. He was very fond of her and supposed that some day when he had money enough he would ask her to marry him; but not yet: and at the same time something that was both shyness and caution kept him from committing himself too far. Sometimes he planned excursions beside the usual weekly walk or visit to the pictures but somehow they seldom came to anything.

He no longer knew why he had come to the city, but it was not for the sake of the bed-sitting room in Rathmines, the oblong of dusty garden outside the window, the trams clanging up and down, the shelf full of second-hand books, or the occasional visit to the pictures. Half humorously, half despairingly, he would sometimes clutch his head in his hands and admit to himself that he had no notion of what he wanted. He would have liked to leave it all and go to Glasgow or New York as a labourer, not because he was romantic, but because he felt that only when he had to work with his hands for a living and was no longer sure of his bed would he find out what all his ideals and emotions meant and where he could fit them into the scheme of his life.

But no sooner did he set out for school next morning, striding slowly along the edge of the canal, watching the trees become green again and the tall claret-coloured houses painted on the quiet surface of the water, than all his fancies took flight. Put his letter in a pump indeed! He would continue to be submissive and draw his salary and wonder how much he could save and when he would be able to buy a little house to bring his girl into; a nice thing to think of on a spring morning: a house of his own and a wife in the bed beside him. And his nature would continue to contract about him, every ideal, every generous impulse another mesh to draw his head down tighter to his knees till in ten years' time it would tie him hand and foot.

2

Tom who was a curate in Wicklow wrote and suggested that they might go home together for the long week-end, and on Saturday morning they set out in Tom's old Ford. It was Easter weather, pearly and cold. They stopped at several pubs on the way and Tom ordered whiskies. Ned was feeling expansive and joined him. He had never quite grown used to his brother, partly because of old days when he felt that Tom was getting the education he should have got, partly because his ordination seemed to have shut him off from the rest of the family, and now it was as though he were trying to surmount it by his boisterous manner and affected *bonhomie*. He was like a man shouting to his comrades across a great distance. He was different from Ned; lighter in colour of hair and skin; fat-headed, fresh-complexioned, deep-voiced, and autocratic; an irascible, humorous, friendly man who was well-liked by those he worked for. Ned, who was shy and all tied up within himself, envied him his way with men in garages and barmaids in hotels.

It was nightfall when they reached home. Their father was in his shirt-sleeves at the gate waiting to greet them, and immediately their mother rushed out as well. The lamp was standing in the window and threw its light as far as the whitewashed gate-posts. Little Brigid, the girl from up the hill who helped their mother now she was growing old, stood in the doorway in half-silhouette. When her eyes caught theirs she bent her head in confusion.

Nothing was changed in the tall, bare, whitewashed kitchen. The harness hung in the same place on the wall, the rosary on the same nail in the fireplace, by the stool where their mother usually sat; table under the window, churn against the back door, stair without banisters mounting straight to the attic door that yawned in the wall – all seemed as unchanging as the sea outside. Their mother sat on the stool, her hands on her knees, a coloured shawl tied tightly about her head, like a gipsy woman with her battered yellow face and loud voice. Their father, fresh-complexioned like Tom, stocky and broken bottomed, gazed out the front door, leaning with one hand on the dresser in the pose of an orator while Brigid wet the tea.

'I said ye'd be late,' their father proclaimed triumphantly, twisting his moustache. 'Didn't I, woman? Didn't I say they'd be late?'

'He did, he did,' their mother assured them. ''Tis true for him.'

'Ah, I knew ye'd be making halts. But damn it, if I wasn't put astray by Thade Lahy's car going east!'

'And was that Thade Lahy's car?' their mother asked in a shocked tone.

'I told ye 'twas Thade Lahy's,' piped Brigid, plopping about in her long frieze gown and bare feet.

'Sure I should know it, woman,' old Tomas said with chagrin. 'He must have gone into town without us noticing him.'

'Oye, and how did he do that?' asked their mother.

'Leave me alone now,' Tomas said despairingly. 'I couldn't tell you, I could not tell you.'

'My goodness, I was sure that was the Master's car,' their mother said wonderingly, pulling distractedly at the tassels of her shawl.

'I'd know the rattle of Thade Lahy's car anywhere,' little Brigid said very proudly and quite unregarded.

It seemed to Ned that he was interrupting a conversation that had been going on since his last visit, and that the road outside and the sea beyond it, and every living thing that passed before them, formed a pantomime that was watched endlessly and passionately from the darkness of the little cottage.

'Wisha, I never asked if ye'd like a drop of something,' their father said with sudden vexation.

'Is it whiskey?' boomed Tom.

'Why? Would you sooner whiskey?'

'Can't you pour it out first and ask us after?' growled Tom.

'The whiskey, is it?'

''Tis not. I didn't come all the ways to this place for what I can get better at home. You'd better have a bottle ready for me to take back.'

'Coleen will have it. Damn it, wasn't it only last night I said to Coleen that you'd likely want a bottle? Some way it struck me you would. Oh, he'll have it, he'll have it.'

'Didn't they catch that string of misery yet?' asked Tom with the cup to his lips.

'Ah, man alive, you'd want to be a greyhound to catch him. God Almighty, hadn't they fifty police after him last November, scouring the mountains from one end to the other and all they caught was a glimpse of the white of his ass. Ah, but the priest preached a terrible sermon against him – by name, Tom, by name!'

'Is old Murphy blowing about it still?' growled Tom.

'Oh, let me alone now!' Tomas threw his hands to heaven and strode to and fro in his excitement, his bucket-bottom wagging. Ned knew to his sorrow that his father could be prudent, silent, and calculating; he knew only too well the cock of the head, the narrowing of the eyes, but, like a child, the old man loved innocent excitement and revelled in scenes of the wildest passion, all about nothing. Like an old actor he turned everything to drama. 'The like of it for abuse was never heard, never heard, never heard! How Coleen could ever raise his head again after it! And where the man got the words from! Tom, my treasure, my son, you'll never have the like.'

'I'd spare my breath to cool my porridge,' Tom replied scornfully. 'I dare say you gave up your own still so?'

'I didn't, Tom, I didn't. The drop I make, 'twould harm no one. Only a drop for Christmas and Easter.'

The lamp was in its own place on the rear wall, and made a circle of brightness on the fresh lime-wash. Their mother was leaning over the fire with joined hands, lost in thought. The front door was open and night thickening outside, the coloured night of the west; and as they ate their father walked to and fro in long ungainly strides, pausing each time at the door to give a glance up and down the road and at the fire to hoist his broken bottom to warm. Ned heard steps come up the road from the west. His father heard them too. He returned to the door and glued his hand to the jamb. Ned covered his eyes with his hands and felt that everything was as it had always been. He could hear the noise of the strand as a background to the voices.

'God be with you, Tomas,' the voice said.

'God and Mary be with you, Teig.' (In Irish they were speaking.) 'What way are you?'

'Well, honour and praise be to God. 'Tis a fine night.'

' 'Tis, 'tis, 'tis so indeed. A grand night, praise be to God.'

'Musha, who is it?' their mother asked, looking round.

' 'Tis young Teig,' their father replied, looking after him.

'Shemus's young Teig?'

' 'Tis, 'tis, 'tis.'

'But where would Shemus's young Teig be going at this hour of night? 'Tisn't to the shop?'

'No, woman, no, no, no. Up to the uncle's I suppose.'

'Is it Ned Willie's?'

'He's sleeping at Ned Willie's,' Brigid chimed in in her high-pitched voice, timid but triumphant. ' 'Tis since the young teacher came to them.'

There was no more to be said. Everything was explained and Ned smiled. The only unfamiliar voice, little Brigid's, seemed the most familiar of all.

3

Tom said first Mass next morning and the household, all but Brigid, went. They drove, and Tomas in high glee sat in front with Tom, waving his hand and shouting greetings at all they met. He was like a boy, so intense was his pleasure. The chapel was perched high above the road. Outside the morning was grey and beyond the windy edge of the cliff was the sea. The wind blew straight in, setting cloaks and petticoats flying.

After dinner as the two boys were returning from a series of visits to the neighbours' houses their father rushed down the road to meet them, shaking them passionately by the hand and asking were they well. When they were seated in the kitchen he opened up the subject of his excitement.

'Well,' he said, 'I arranged a grand little outing for ye tomorrow, thanks be to God,' and to identify further the source of his inspiration he searched at the back of his neck for the peak of his cap and raised it solemnly.

'Musha, what outing are you talking about?' their mother asked angrily.

'I arranged for us to go over the bay to your brother's.'

'And can't you leave the poor boys alone?' she bawled.

'Haven't they only the one day? Isn't it for the rest they came?'

'Even so, even so, even so,' Tomas said with mounting passion. 'Aren't their own cousins to lay eyes on them?'

'I was in Carriganassa for a week last summer,' said Tom.

'Yes, but I wasn't, and Ned wasn't. 'Tis only decent.'

' 'Tisn't decency is worrying you at all but drink,' growled Tom.

'Oh!' gasped his father, fishing for the peak of his cap to swear with, 'that I might be struck dead!'

'Be quiet, you old heathen!' crowed his wife. 'That's the truth, Tom my pulse. Plenty of drink is what he wants where he won't be under my eye. Leave ye stop at home.'

'I can't stop at home, woman,' shouted Tomas. 'Why do you be always picking at me? I must go whether they come or not. I must go, I must go, and that's all there is about it.'

'Why must you?' asked his wife.

'Because I warned Red Pat and Dempsey,' he stormed. 'And the woman from the island is coming as well to see a daughter of hers that's married there. And what's more, I borrowed Cassidy's boat and he lent it at great inconvenience, and 'twould be very bad manners for me to throw his kindness back in his face. I must go.'

'Oh, we may as well all go,' said Tom.

It blew hard all night and Tomas, all anxiety, was out at break of day to watch the whitecaps on the water. While the boys were at breakfast he came in and, leaning his arms on the table with hands joined as though in prayer, he announced in a caressing voice that it was a beautiful day, thank God, a pet day with a moist gentle little bit of a breezheen that would only blow them over. His voice would have put a child to sleep, but his wife continued to nag and scold, and he stumped out again in a fury and sat on the wall with his back to the house and his legs crossed, chewing his pipe. He was dressed in his best clothes, a respectable blue tailcoat and pale frieze trousers with only one patch on the seat. He had turned his cap almost right way round so that the peak covered his right ear.

He was all over the boat like a boy. Dempsey, a haggard, pock-marked, melancholy man with a soprano voice of astounding penetration, took the tiller and Red Patrick the sail. Tomas clambered into the bows and stood there with one knee up, leaning forward like a figurehead. He knew the bay like a book. The island woman was perched on the ballast with her rosary in her hands and her shawl over her eyes to shut out the sight of the waves. The cumbrous old boat took the sail lightly enough and Ned leaned back on his elbows against the side, rejoicing in it all.

'She's laughing,' his father said delightedly when her bows ran white.

'Whose boat is that, Dempsey?' he asked, screwing up his eyes as another brown sail tilted ahead of them.

' 'Tis the island boat,' shrieked Dempsey.

' 'Tis not, Dempsey. 'Tis not indeed, my love. That's not the island boat.'

'Whose boat is it then?'

'It must be some boat from Carriganassa, Dempsey.'

' 'Tis the island boat I tell you.'

'Ah, why will you be contradicting me, Dempsey, my treasure? 'Tis not the island boat. The island boat has a dark-brown sail; 'tis only a month since 'twas tarred, and that's an old tarred sail, and what proves it out and out, Dempsey, the island boat has a patch in the corner.'

He was leaning well over the bows, watching the rocks that fled beneath them, a dark purple. He rested his elbow on his raised knee and looked back at them, his brown face sprinkled with spray and lit from below by the accumulated flickerings of the water. His flesh seemed to dissolve, to become transparent, while his blue eyes shone with extraordinary brilliance. Ned half-closed his eyes and watched sea and sky slowly mount and sink behind the red-brown, sun-filled sail and the poised and eager figure.

'Tom!' shouted his father, and the battered old face peered at them from under the arch of the sail, with which it was almost one in tone, the silvery light filling it with warmth.

'Well?' Tom's voice was an inexpressive boom.

'You were right last night, Tom, my boy. My treasure, my son, you were right. 'Twas for the drink I came.'

'Ah, do you tell me so?' Tom asked ironically.

' 'Twas, 'twas, 'twas,' the old man said regretfully. ' 'Twas for the drink. 'Twas so, my darling. They were always decent people, your mother's people, and 'tis her knowing how decent they are makes her so suspicious. She's a good woman, a fine woman, your poor mother, may the Almighty God bless her and keep her and watch over her.'

'Aaaa-men,' Tom chanted irreverently as his father shook his old cap piously towards the sky.

'But Tom! Are you listening, Tom?'

'Well, what is it now?'

'I had another reason.'

'Had you indeed?' Tom's tone was not encouraging.

'I had, I had, God's truth, I had. God blast the lie I'm telling you, Tom, I had.'

' 'Twas boasting out of the pair of ye,' shrieked Dempsey from the stern, the wind whipping the shrill notes from his lips and scattering them wildly like scraps of paper.

' 'Twas so, Dempsey, 'twas so. You're right, Dempsey. You're always right. The blessing of God on you, Dempsey, for you always had the true word.' Tomas's laughing leprechaun countenance gleamed under the bellying, tilting, chocolate-coloured sail and his powerful voice beat Dempsey's down. 'And would you blame me?'

'The O'Donnells hadn't the beating of them in their own hand,' screamed Dempsey.

'Thanks be to God for all His goodness and mercy,' shouted Tomas, again waving his cap in a gesture of recognition towards the spot where he felt the Almighty might be listening, 'they have not. They have not so, Dempsey. And they have a good hand. The O'Donnells are a good family and an old family and a kind family, but they never had the like of my two sons.'

'And they were stiff enough with you when you came for the daughter,' shrieked Dempsey.

'They were, Dempsey, they were. They were stiff. They were so. You wouldn't blame them, Dempsey. They were an old family and I was nothing only a landless man.' With a fierce gesture the old man pulled his cap still farther over his ear, spat, gave his moustache a tug, and leaned at a still more precarious angle over the bow, his blue eyes dancing with triumph. 'But I had the gumption, Dempsey. I had the gumption, my love.'

The islands slipped past; the gulf of water narrowed and grew calmer, and white cottages could be seen scattered under the tall ungainly church. It was a wild and rugged coast, the tide was full, and they had to pull in as best they could among the rocks. Red Patrick leaped lightly ashore to draw in the boat. The others stepped after him into several inches of water and Red Patrick, himself precariously poised, held them from slipping. Rather shamefastly, Ned and Tom took off their shoes.

'Don't do that!' shrieked their father. 'We'll carry ye up. Mother of God, yeer poor feet!'

'Will you shut your old gob?' Tom said angrily.

They halted for a moment at the stile outside Caherag... had a red beard and a broad, smiling face. Then they went on t... who had two houses, modern and old, separated by a yard. In... Uncle Maurice and his family and in the other Maurice's marrie... Sean. Ned and Tom remained with Sean and his wife. Tom and he we... old friends. When he spoke he rarely looked at Tom, merely giving him a sidelong glance that just reached to his chin and then dropped his eyes with a peculiar timid smile. ' 'Twas,' Ned heard him say, and then: 'He did,' and after that: 'Hardly.' Shuvaun was tall, nervous and matronly. She clung to their hands with an excess of eagerness as though she couldn't bear to let them go, uttering ejaculations of tenderness, delight, astonishment, pity, and admiration. Her speech was full of diminutives: 'childeen', 'handeen', 'boateen'. Three young children scrambled about the floor with a preoccupation scarcely broken by the strangers. Shuvaun picked her way through them, filling the kettle and cutting the bread, and then, as though afraid of neglecting Tom, she clutched his hand again. Her feverish concentration gave an impression that its very intensity bewildered her and made it impossible for her to understand one word they said. In three days' time it would all begin to drop into place in her mind and then she would begin quoting them.

Young Niall O'Donnell came in with his girl; one of the Deignans from up the hill. She was plump and pert; she had been in service in town. Niall was a well-built boy with a soft, wild-eyed, sensuous face and a deep mellow voice of great power. While they were having a cup of tea in the parlour where the three or four family photos were skyed, Ned saw the two of them again through the back window. They were standing on the high ground behind the house with the spring sky behind them and the light in their faces. Niall was asking her something but she, more interested in the sitting-room window, only shook her head.

'Ye only just missed yeer father,' said their Uncle Maurice when they went across to the other house for dinner. Maurice was a tightlipped little man with a high bald forehead and a snappy voice. 'He went off to Owney Pat's only this minute.'

'The devil!' said Tom. 'I knew he was out to dodge me. Did you give him whiskey?'

'What the hell else could I give him?' snapped Maurice. 'Do you think 'twas tea the old coot was looking for?'

Tom took the place of honour at the table. He was the favourite. Through the doorway into the bedroom could be seen a big canopy bed and on the whiteness of a raised pillow a skeleton face in a halo of smoke-blue hair surmounted with what looked suspiciously like a mauve tea-cosy. Sometimes the white head would begin to stir and everyone fell silent while Niall, the old man's pet, translated the scarcely audible whisper. Sometimes Niall would go in with his stiff ungainly swagger and repeat one of Tom's jokes in his drawling, powerful bass. The hens stepped daintily about their feet, poking officious heads between them, and rushing out the door with a wild flutter and shriek when one of the girls hooshed them. Something timeless, patriarchal, and restful about it made Ned notice everything. It was as though he had never seen his mother's house before.

'Tell me,' Tom boomed with mock concern, leaning over confidentially to his uncle and looking under his brows at young Niall, 'speaking as a clergyman and for the good of the family and so on, is that son of yours coorting Delia Deignan?'

'Why? Was the young blackguard along with her again?' snapped Maurice in amusement.

'Of course I might be mistaken,' Tom said doubtfully.

'You wouldn't know a Deignan, to be sure,' Sean said dryly.

'Isn't any of them married yet?' asked Tom.

'No, by damn, no,' said Maurice. 'Isn't it a wonder?'

'Because,' Tom went on in the same solemn voice, 'I want someone to look after this young brother of mine. Dublin is a wild sort of place and full of temptations. Ye wouldn't know a decent little girl I could ask?'

'Cait! Cait!' they all shouted, Niall's deep voice loudest of all.

'Now all the same, Delia looks a smart little piece,' said Tom.

'No, Cait! Cait! Delia isn't the same since she went to town. She has notions of herself. Leave him marry Cait!'

Niall rose gleefully and shambled in to the old man. With a gamesome eye on the company Tom whispered:

'Is she a quiet sort of girl? I wouldn't like Ned to get anyone rough.'

'She is, she is,' they said, 'a grand girl!'

Sean rose quietly and went to the door with his head bowed.

'God knows, if anyone knows he should know and all the times he manhandled her.'

Tom sat bolt upright with mock indignation while the table rocked. Niall shouted the joke into his grandfather's ear. The mauve tea-cosy shook; it was the only indication of the old man's amusement.

4

The Deignans' house was on top of a hill high over the road and commanded a view of the countryside for miles. The two brothers with Sean and the O'Donnell girls reached it by a long winding boreen that threaded its way uncertainly through little grey rocky fields and walls of unmortared stone which rose against the sky along the edges of the hill like lacework. On their way they met another procession coming down the hill. It was headed by their father and the island woman, arm in arm, and behind came two locals with Dempsey and Red Patrick. All the party except the island woman were well advanced in liquor. That was plain when their father rushed forward to shake them all by the hand and ask them how they were. He said that divil such honourable and kindly people as the people of Carriganassa were to be found in the whole world, and of these there was no one a patch on the O'Donnells; kings and sons of kings as you could see from one look at them. He had only one more call to pay and promised to be at Caheragh's within a quarter of an hour.

They looked over the Deignans' half-door. The kitchen was empty. The girls began to titter. They knew the Deignans must have watched them coming from Maurice's door. The kitchen was a beautiful room; woodwork and furniture, homemade and shapely, were painted a bright red-brown and the painted dresser shone with pretty ware. They entered and looked about them. Nothing was to be heard but the tick of the cheap alarm clock on the dresser. One of the girls began to giggle hysterically. Sean raised his voice.

'Are ye in or are ye out, bad cess to ye!'

For a moment there was no reply. Then a quick step sounded in the attic and a girl descended the stairs at a run, drawing a black knitted shawl tighter about her shoulders. She was perhaps twenty-eight or thirty, with a narrow face, sharp like a ferret's, and blue nervous eyes. She entered the kitchen awkwardly sideways, giving the customary greetings but without looking at anyone.

'A hundred welcomes. . . . How are ye? . . . 'Tis a fine day.'

The O'Donnell girls giggled again. Nora Deignan looked at them in astonishment, biting nervously at the tassel of her shawl. She had tiny sharp white teeth.

'What is it, aru?' she asked.

'Musha, will you stop your old cimeens,' boomed Tom, 'and tell us where's Cait from you? You don't think 'twas to see your ugly puss that we came up here?'

'Cait!' Nora called in a low voice.

'What is it?' another voice replied from upstairs.

'Damn well you know what it is,' bellowed Tom, 'and you cross-eyed expecting us since morning. Will you come down out of that or will I go up and fetch you?'

There was the same hasty step and a second girl descended the stairs. It was only later that Ned was able to realize how beautiful she was. She had the same narrow pointed face as her sister, the same slight features sharpened by a sort of animal instinct, the same blue eyes with their startled brightness; but all seemed to have been differently composed, and her complexion had a transparency as though her whole nature were shining through it. 'Child of Light, thy limbs are burning through the veil which seems to hide them,' Ned found himself murmuring. She came on them in the same hostile way, blushing furiously. Tom's eyes rested on her; soft, bleary, emotional eyes incredibly unlike her own.

'Have you nothing to say to me, Cait?' he boomed, and Ned thought his very voice was soft and clouded.

'Oh, a hundred welcomes.' Her blue eyes rested for a moment on him with what seemed a fierce candour and penetration and went past him to the open door. Outside a soft rain was beginning to fall; heavy clouds crushed down the grey landscape, which grew clearer as it merged into one common plane; the little grey bumpy fields with the walls of grey unmortared stone that drifted hither and over across them like blown sand, the whitewashed farmhouses lost to the sun sinking back into the brown-grey hillsides.

'Nothing else, my child?' he growled, pursing his lips.

'How are you?'

'The politeness is suffocating you. Where's Delia?'

'Here I am,' said Delia from the doorway immediately behind him. In her furtive way she had slunk round the house. Her bland impertinence raised a laugh.

'The reason we called,' said Tom, clearing his throat, 'is this young brother of mine that's looking for a wife.'

Everyone laughed again. Ned knew the oftener a joke was repeated the better they liked it, but for him this particular joke was beginning to wear thin.

'Leave him take me,' said Delia with an arch look at Ned who smiled and gazed at the floor.

'Be quiet, you slut!' said Tom. 'There are your two sisters before you.'

'Even so, I want to go to Dublin. . . . Would you treat me to lemonade, mister?' she asked Ned with her impudent smile. 'This is a rotten hole. I'd go to America if they left me.'

'America won't be complete without you,' said Tom. 'Now, don't let me hurry ye, ladies, but my old fellow will be waiting for us in Johnny Kit's.'

'Well go along with you,' said Nora, and the three girls took down three black shawls from inside the door. Some tension seemed to have gone out of the air. They laughed and joked between themselves.

'Ye'll get wet,' said Sean to the two brothers.

'Cait will make room for me under her shawl,' said Tom.

'Indeed I will not,' she cried, starting back with a laugh.

'Very shy you're getting,' said Sean with a good-natured grin.

' 'Tisn't that at all but she'd sooner the young man,' said Delia.

'What's strange is wonderful,' said Nora.

Biting her lip with her tiny front teeth, Cait looked angrily at her sisters and Sean, and then began to laugh. She glanced at Ned and smilingly held out her shawl in invitation, though at the same moment angry blushes chased one another across her forehead like squalls across the surface of a lake. The rain was a mild, persistent drizzle and a strong wind was blowing. Everything had darkened and grown lonely and, with his head in the blinding folds of the shawl, which reeked of turf-smoke, Ned felt as if he had dropped out of Time's pocket.

They waited in Caheragh's kitchen. The bearded old man sat in one chimney corner and a little bare-legged boy in the other. The dim blue light poured down the wide chimney on their heads in a shower with the delicacy of light on old china, picking out surfaces one rarely saw; and between them the fire burned a bright orange in the great whitewashed hearth with the black, swinging bars and pothook. Outside the rain fell softly, almost soundlessly, beyond the half-door. Delia, her black shawl trailing from her shoulders, leaned over it, acting the part of watcher as in a Greek play. Their father's fifteen minutes had strung themselves out to an hour and two little barefooted boys had already been sent to hunt him down.

'Where are they now, Delia?' one of the O'Donnells would ask.

'Crossing the fields from Patsy Kit's.'

'He wasn't there so.'

'He wouldn't be,' the old man said. 'They'll likely go on to Ned Kit's now.'

'That's where they're making for,' said Delia. 'Up the hill at the far side of the fort.'

'They'll find him there,' the old man said confidently.

Ned felt as though he were still blanketed by the folds of the turf-reeking shawl. Something seemed to have descended on him that filled him with passion and loneliness. He could scarcely take his eyes off Cait. She and Nora sat on the form against the back wall, a composition in black and white, the black shawl drawn tight under the chin, the cowl of it breaking the curve of her dark hair, her shadow on the gleaming wall behind. She did not speak except to answer some question of Tom's about her brother, but sometimes Ned caught her looking at him with naked eyes. Then she smiled swiftly and secretly and turned her eyes again to the door, sinking back into pensiveness. Pensiveness or vacancy? he wondered. While he gazed at her face with the animal instinctiveness of its over-delicate features it seemed like a mirror in which he saw again the falling rain, the rocks and hills and angry sea.

The first announced by Delia was Red Patrick. After him came the island woman. Each had last seen his father in a different place. Ned chuckled at a sudden vision of his father, eager and impassioned and aflame with drink, stumping with his broken bottom across endless fields through pouring rain with a growing procession behind him. Dempsey was the last to come. He doubted if Tomas would be in a condition to take the boat at all.

'What matter, aru?' said Delia across her shoulder. 'We can find room for the young man.'

'And where would we put him?' gaped Nora.

'He can have Cait's bed,' Delia said innocently.

'Oye, and where would Cait sleep?' Nora asked and then skitted and covered her face with her shawl. Delia scoffed. The men laughed and Cait, biting her lip furiously, looked at the floor. Again Ned caught her eyes on him and again she laughed and turned away.

Tomas burst in unexpected on them all like a sea-wind that scattered them before him. He wrung Tom's hand and asked him how he was. He did the same to Ned. Ned replied gravely that he was very well.

In God's holy name,' cried his father, waving his arms like a windmill, 'what are ye all waiting for?'

The tide had fallen. Tomas grabbed an oar and pushed the boat on to a rock. Then he raised the sail and collapsed under it and had to be extricated from its drenching folds, glauming and swearing at Cassidy's old boat. A little group stood on a naked rock against a grey background of drifting rain. For a long time Ned continued to wave back to the black shawl that was lifted to him. An extraordinary feeling of exultation and loss enveloped him. Huddled up in his overcoat he sat with Dempsey in the stern, not speaking.

'It was a grand day,' his father declared, swinging himself to and fro, tugging at his Viking moustache, dragging the peak of his cap farther over his ear. His gestures betrayed a certain lack of rhythmical cohesion; they began and ended abruptly. 'Dempsey, my darling, wasn't it a grand day?'

' 'Twas a grand day for you,' shrieked Dempsey as if his throat would burst.

' 'Twas, my treasure, 'twas a beautiful day. I got an honourable reception and my sons got an honourable reception.'

By this time he was flat on his belly, one leg completely over the edge of the boat. He reached back a clammy hand to his sons.

' 'Twas the best day I ever had,' he said. 'I got porter and I got whiskey and I got poteen. I did so, Tom, my calf. Ned, my brightness, I went to seven houses and in every house I got seven drinks and with every drink I got seven welcomes. And your mother's people are a hand of trumps. It was no slight they put on me at all even if I was nothing but a landless man. No slight, Tom. No slight at all.'

Darkness had fallen, the rain had cleared, the stars came out of a pitch-black sky under which the little tossing, nosing boat seemed lost beyond measure. In all the waste of water nothing could be heard but the splash of the boat's sides and their father's voice raised in tipsy song.

The evening was fair and the sunlight was yellow,
   I halted, beholding a maiden bright
Coming to me by the edge of the mountain,
   Her cheeks had a berry-bright rosy light.

5

Ned was the first to wake. He struck a match and lit the candle. It was time for them to be stirring. It was just after dawn, and at half past nine he must be in his old place in the schoolroom before the rows of pinched little city-faces. He lit a cigarette and closed his eyes. The lurch of the boat was still in his blood, the face of Cait Deignan in his mind, and as if from far away he heard a line of the wild love-song his father had been singing: 'And we'll drive the geese at the fall of night.'

He heard his brother mumble something and nudged him. Tom looked big and fat and vulnerable with his fair head rolled sideways and his heavy mouth dribbling on to the sleeve of his pyjamas. Ned slipped quietly out of bed, put on his trousers, and went to the window. He drew the curtains and let in the thin cold daylight. The bay was just visible and perfectly still. Tom began to mumble again in a frightened voice and Ned shook him. He started out of his sleep with a cry of fear, grabbing at the bedclothes. He looked first at Ned, then at the candle and drowsily rubbed his eyes.

'Did you hear it too?' he asked.

'Did I hear what?' asked Ned with a smile.

'In the room,' said Tom.

'There was nothing in the room,' replied Ned. 'You were ramaishing so I woke you up.'

'Was I? What was I saying?'

'You were telling no secrets,' said Ned with a quiet laugh.

'Hell!' Tom said in disgust and stretched out his arm for a cigarette. He lit it at the candle flame, his drowsy red face puckered and distraught. 'I slept rotten.'

'Oye!' Ned said quietly, raising his eyebrows. It wasn't often Tom spoke in that tone. He sat on the edge of the bed, joined his hands, and leaned forward, looking at Tom with wide gentle eyes.

'Is there anything wrong?' he asked.

'Plenty.'

'You're not in trouble?' Ned asked without raising his voice.

'Not that sort of trouble. The trouble is in myself.'

Ned gave him a look of intense sympathy and understanding. The soft emotional brown eyes were searching him for a judgement. Ned had never felt less like judging him.

'Ay,' he said gently and vaguely, his eyes wandering to the other side of the room while his voice took on its accustomed stammer, 'the trouble is always in ourselves. If we were contented in ourselves the other things wouldn't matter. I suppose we must only leave it to time. Time settles everything.'

'Time will settle nothing for me,' Tom said despairingly. 'You have something to look forward to. I have nothing. It's the loneliness of my job that kills you. Even to talk about it would be a relief but there's no one you can talk to. People come to you with their troubles but there's no one you can go to with your own.'

Again the challenging glare in the brown eyes and Ned realized with infinite compassion that for years Tom had been living in the same state of suspicion and fear, a man being hunted down by his own nature; and that for years to come he would continue to live in this way, and perhaps never be caught again as he was now.

'A pity you came down here,' stammered Ned flatly. 'A pity we went to Carriganassa. 'Twould be better for both of us if we went somewhere else.'

'Why don't you marry her, Ned?' Tom asked earnestly.

'Who?' asked Ned.

'Cait.'

'Yesterday,' said Ned with the shy smile he wore when he confessed something, 'I nearly wished I could.'

'But you can, man,' Tom said eagerly, sitting upon his elbow. Like all men with frustration in their hearts he was full of schemes for others. 'You could marry her and get a school down here. That's what I'd do if I was in your place.'

'No,' Ned said gravely. 'We made our choice a long time ago. We can't go back on it now.'

Then with his hands in his trouser pockets and his head bowed he went out to the kitchen. His mother, the coloured shawl about her head, was blowing the fire. The bedroom door was open and he could see his father in shirt-sleeves kneeling beside the bed, his face raised reverently towards a holy picture, his braces hanging down behind. He unbolted the half-door, went through the garden and out on to the road. There was a magical light on every thing. A boy on a horse rose suddenly against the sky, a startling picture. Through the apple-green light over Carriganassa ran long streaks of crimson, so still they might have been enamelled. Magic, magic, magic! He saw it as in a children's picture-book with all its colours intolerably bright; something he had outgrown and could never return to, while the world he aspired to was as remote and intangible as it had seemed even in the despair of youth.

It seemed as if only now for the first time was he leaving home; for the first time and forever saying good-bye to it all.

The Majesty of the Law

Old Dan Bride was breaking brosna for the fire when he heard a step on the path. He paused, a bundle of saplings on his knee.

Dan had looked after his mother while the life was in her, and after her death no other woman had crossed his threshold. Signs on it, his house had that look. Almost everything in it he had made with his own hands in his own way. The seats of the chairs were only slices of log, rough and round and thick as the saw had left them, and with the rings still plainly visible through the grime and polish that coarse trouser-bottoms had in the course of long years imparted. Into these Dan had rammed stout knotted ash-boughs that served alike for legs and back. The deal table, bought in a shop, was an inheritance from his mother and a great pride and joy to him though it rocked whenever he touched it. On the wall, unglazed and fly-spotted, hung in mysterious isolation a Marcus Stone print, and beside the door was a calendar with a picture of a racehorse. Over the door hung a gun, old but good, and in excellent condition, and before the fire was stretched an old setter who raised his head expectantly whenever Dan rose or even stirred.

He raised it now as the steps came nearer and when Dan, laying down the bundle of saplings, cleaned his hands thoughtfully on the seat of his trousers, he gave a loud bark, but this expressed no more than a desire to show off his own watchfulness. He was half human and knew people thought he was old and past his prime.

A man's shadow fell across the oblong of dusty light thrown over the half-door before Dan looked round.

'Are you alone, Dan?' asked an apologetic voice.

'Oh, come in, come in, sergeant, come in and welcome,' exclaimed the old man, hurrying on rather uncertain feet to the door which the tall policeman opened and pushed in. He stood there, half in sunlight, half in shadow, and seeing him so, you would have realized how dark the interior of the house really was. One side of his red face was turned so as to catch the light, and behind it an ash tree raised its boughs of airy green against the sky. Green fields, broken here and there by clumps of red-brown rock, flowed downhill, and beyond them, stretched all across the horizon, was the sea, flooded and almost transparent with light. The sergeant's face was fat and fresh, the old man's face, emerging from the twilight of the kitchen, had the colour of wind and sun, while the features had been so shaped by the struggle with time and the elements that they might as easily have been found impressed upon the surface of a rock.

'Begor, Dan,' said the sergeant, ' 'tis younger you're getting.'

'Middling I am, sergeant, middling,' agreed the old man in a voice which seemed to accept the remark as a compliment of which politeness would not allow him to take too much advantage. 'No complaints.'

'Begor, 'tis as well because no one would believe them. And the old dog doesn't look a day older.'

The dog gave a low growl as though to show the sergeant that he would remember this unmannerly reference to his age, but indeed he growled every time he was mentioned, under the impression that people had nothing but ill to say of him.

'And how's yourself, sergeant?'

'Well, now, like the most of us, Dan, neither too good nor too bad. We have our own little worries, but, thanks be to God, we have our compensations.'

'And the wife and family?'

'Good, praise be to God, good. They were away from me for a month, the lot of them, at the mother-in-law's place in Clare.'

'In Clare, do you tell me?'

'In Clare. I had a fine quiet time.'

The old man looked about him and then retired to the bedroom, from which he returned a moment later with an old shirt. With this he solemnly wiped the seat and back of the log-chair nearest the fire.

'Sit down now, sergeant. You must be tired after the journey. 'Tis a long old road. How did you come?'

'Teigue Leary gave me the lift. Wisha now, Dan, don't be putting yourself out. I won't be stopping. I promised them I'd be back inside an hour.'

'What hurry is on you?' asked Dan. 'Look, your foot was only on the path when I made up the fire.'

'Arrah, Dan, you're not making tea for me?'

'I am not making it for you, indeed; I'm making it for myself, and I'll take it very bad of you if you won't have a cup.'

'Dan, Dan, that I mightn't stir, but 'tisn't an hour since I had it at the barracks!'

'Ah, whisht, now, whisht! Whisht, will you! I have something here to give you an appetite.'

The old man swung the heavy kettle on to the chain over the open fire, and the dog sat up, shaking his ears with an expression of the deepest interest. The policeman unbuttoned his tunic, opened his belt, took a pipe and a plug of tobacco from his breast pocket, and, crossing his legs in an easy posture, began to cut the tobacco slowly and carefully with his pocket knife. The old man went to the dresser and took down two handsomely decorated cups, the only cups he had, which, though chipped and handle-less, were used at all only on very rare occasions; for himself he preferred his tea from a basin. Happening to glance into them, he noticed that they bore signs of disuse and had collected a lot of the fine white turf-dust that always circulated in the little smoky cottage. Again he thought of the shirt, and, rolling up his sleeves with a stately gesture, he wiped them inside and out till they shone. Then he bent and opened the cupboard. Inside was a quart bottle of pale liquid, obviously untouched. He removed the cork and smelt the contents, pausing for a moment in the act as though to recollect where exactly he had noticed that particular smoky smell before. Then, reassured, he stood up and poured out with a liberal hand.

'Try that now, sergeant,' he said with quiet pride.

The sergeant, concealing whatever qualms he might have felt at the idea of drinking illegal whiskey, looked carefully into the cup, sniffed, and glanced up at old Dan.

'It looks good,' he commented.

'It should be good,' replied Dan with no mock modesty.

'It tastes good too,' said the sergeant.

'Ah, sha,' said Dan, not wishing to praise his own hospitality in his own house, ''tis of no great excellence.'

'You'd be a good judge, I'd say,' said the sergeant without irony.

'Ever since things became what they are,' said Dan, carefully guarding

himself against a too-direct reference to the peculiarities of the law adminis-
tered by his guest, 'liquor isn't what it used to be.'

'I've heard that remark made before now, Dan,' said the sergeant
thoughtfully. 'I've heard it said by men of wide experience that it used to
be better in the old days.'

'Liquor,' said the old man, 'is a thing that takes time. There was never
a good job done in a hurry.'

' 'Tis an art in itself.'

'Just so.'

'And an art takes time.'

'And knowledge,' added Dan with emphasis. 'Every art has its secrets,
and the secrets of distilling are being lost the way the old songs were lost.
When I was a boy there wasn't a man in the barony but had a hundred
songs in his head, but with people running here, there, and everywhere,
the songs were lost. . . . Ever since things became what they are,' he
repeated on the same guarded note, 'there's so much running about the
secrets are lost.'

'There must have been a power of them.'

'There was. Ask any man today that makes whiskey do he know how
to make it out of heather.'

'And was it made of heather?' asked the policeman.

'It was.'

'You never drank it yourself?'

'I didn't, but I knew old men that did, and they told me that no whiskey
that's made nowadays could compare with it.'

'Musha, Dan, I think sometimes 'twas a great mistake of the law to set
its hand against it.'

Dan shook his head. His eyes answered for him, but it was not in nature
for a man to criticize the occupation of a guest in his own home.

'Maybe so, maybe not,' he said noncommittally.

'But sure, what else have the poor people?'

'Them that makes the laws have their own good reasons.'

'All the same, Dan, all the same, 'tis a hard law.'

The sergeant would not be outdone in generosity. Politeness required
him not to yield to the old man's defence of his superiors and their
mysterious ways.

'It is the secrets I'd be sorry for,' said Dan, summing up. 'Men die and men are born, and where one man drained another will plough, but a secret lost is lost forever.'

'True,' said the sergeant mournfully. 'Lost forever.'

Dan took his cup, rinsed it in a bucket of clear water by the door and cleaned it again with the shirt. Then he placed it carefully at the sergeant's elbow. From the dresser he took a jug of milk and a blue bag containing sugar; this he followed up with a slab of country butter and – a sure sign that he had been expecting a visitor – a round cake of home-made bread, fresh and uncut. The kettle sang and spat and the dog, shaking his ears, barked at it angrily.

'Go away, you brute!' growled Dan, kicking him out of his way.

He made the tea and filled the two cups. The sergeant cut himself a large slice of bread and buttered it thickly.

'It is just like medicines,' said the old man, resuming his theme with the imperturbability of age. 'Every secret there was is lost. And leave no one tell me that a doctor is as good a man as one that had the secrets of old times.'

'How could he be?' asked the sergeant with his mouth full.

'The proof of that was seen when there were doctors and wise people there together.'

'It wasn't to the doctors the people went, I'll engage?'

'It was not. And why?' With a sweeping gesture the old man took in the whole world outside his cabin. 'Out there on the hillsides is the sure cure for every disease. Because it is written' – he tapped the table with his thumb – 'it is written by the poets "wherever you find the disease you will find the cure". But people walk up the hills and down the hills and all they see is flowers. Flowers! As if God Almighty – honour and praise to Him! – had nothing better to do with His time than be to making old flowers!'

'Things no doctor could cure the wise people cured,' agreed the sergeant.

'Ah, musha, 'tis I know it,' said Dan bitterly. 'I know it, not in my mind but in my own four bones.'

'Have you the rheumatics at you still?' the sergeant asked in a shocked tone.

'I have. Ah, if you were alive, Kitty O'Hara, or you, Nora Malley of the Glen, 'tisn't I'd be dreading the mountain wind or the sea wind; 'tisn't I'd be creeping down with my misfortunate red ticket for the blue and pink and yellow dribble-drabble of their ignorant dispensary.'

'Why then indeed,' said the sergeant, 'I'll get you a bottle for that.'

'Ah, there's no bottle ever made will cure it.'

'That's where you're wrong, Dan. Don't talk now till you try it. It cured my own uncle when he was that bad he was shouting for the carpenter to cut the two legs off him with a handsaw.'

'I'd give fifty pounds to get rid of it,' said Dan magniloquently. 'I would and five hundred.'

The sergeant finished his tea in a gulp, blessed himself, and struck a match which he then allowed to go out as he answered some question of the old man. He did the same with a second and third, as though titillating his appetite with delay. Finally he succeeded in getting his pipe alight and the two men pulled round their chairs, placed their toes side by side in the ashes, and in deep puffs, lively bursts of conversation, and long, long silences enjoyed their smoke.

'I hope I'm not keeping you?' said the sergeant, as though struck by the length of his visit.

'Ah, what would you keep me from?'

'Tell me if I am. The last thing I'd like to do is waste another man's time.'

'Begor, you wouldn't waste my time if you stopped all night.'

'I like a little chat myself,' confessed the policeman.

And again they became lost in conversation. The light grew thick and coloured and, wheeling about the kitchen before it disappeared, became tinged with gold; the kitchen itself sank into cool greyness with cold light on the cups and basins and plates of the dresser. From the ash tree a thrush began to sing. The open hearth gathered brightness till its light was a warm, even splash of crimson in the twilight.

Twilight was also descending outside when the sergeant rose to go. He fastened his belt and tunic and carefully brushed his clothes. Then he put on his cap, tilted a little to side and back.

'Well, that was a great talk,' he said.

' 'Tis a pleasure,' said Dan, 'a real pleasure.'

'And I won't forget the bottle for you.'

'Heavy handling from God to you!'

'Good-bye now, Dan.'

'Good-bye, sergeant, and good luck.'

Dan didn't offer to accompany the sergeant beyond the door. He sat in his old place by the fire, took out his pipe once more, blew through it thoughtfully, and just as he leaned forward for a twig to kindle it, heard the steps returning. It was the sergeant. He put his head a little way over the half-door.

'Oh, Dan!' he called softly.

'Ay, sergeant?' replied Dan, looking round, but with one hand still reaching for the twig. He couldn't see the sergeant's face, only hear his voice.

'I suppose you're not thinking of paying that little fine, Dan?'

There was a brief silence. Dan pulled out the lighted twig, rose slowly, and shambled towards the door, stuffing it down in the almost empty bowl of the pipe. He leaned over the half-door while the sergeant with hands in the pockets of his trousers gazed rather in the direction of the laneway, yet taking in a considerable portion of the sea line.

'The way it is with me, sergeant,' replied Dan unemotionally, 'I am not.'

'I was thinking that, Dan; I was thinking you wouldn't.'

There was a long silence during which the voice of the thrush grew shriller and merrier. The sunken sun lit up rafts of purple cloud moored high above the wind.

'In a way,' said the sergeant, 'that was what brought me.'

'I was just thinking so, sergeant, it only struck me and you going out the door.'

'If 'twas only the money, Dan, I'm sure there's many would be glad to oblige you.'

'I know that, sergeant. No, 'tisn't the money so much as giving that fellow the satisfaction of paying. Because he angered me, sergeant.'

The sergeant made no comment on this and another long silence ensued.

'They gave me the warrant,' the sergeant said at last, in a tone which dissociated him from all connexion with such an unneighbourly document.

'Did they so?' exclaimed Dan, as if he was shocked by the thoughtlessness of the authorities.

'So whenever 'twould be convenient for you –'

'Well, now you mention it,' said Dan, by way of throwing out a suggestion for debate, 'I could go with you now.'

'Ah, sha, what do you want going at this hour for?' protested the sergeant with a wave of his hand, dismissing the notion as the tone required.

'Or I could go tomorrow,' added Dan, warming to the issue.

'Would it be suitable for you now?' asked the sergeant, scaling up his voice accordingly.

'But, as a matter of fact,' said the old man emphatically, 'the day that would be most convenient to me would be Friday after dinner, because I have some messages to do in town, and I wouldn't have the journey for nothing.'

'Friday will do grand,' said the sergeant with relief that this delicate matter was now practically disposed of. 'If it doesn't they can damn well wait. You could walk in there yourself when it suits you and tell them I sent you.'

'I'd rather have yourself there, sergeant, if it would be no inconvenience. As it is, I'd feel a bit shy.'

'Why then, you needn't feel shy at all. There's a man from my own parish there, a warder; one Whelan. Ask for him; I'll tell him you're coming, and I'll guarantee when he knows you're a friend of mine he'll make you as comfortable as if you were at home.'

'I'd like that fine,' Dan said with profound satisfaction. 'I'd like to be with friends, sergeant.'

'You will be, never fear. Good-bye again now, Dan. I'll have to hurry.'

'Wait now, wait till I see you to the road.'

Together the two men strolled down the laneway while Dan explained how it was that he, a respectable old man, had had the grave misfortune to open the head of another old man in such a way as to require his removal to hospital, and why it was that he couldn't give the old man in question the satisfaction of paying in cash for an injury brought about through the victim's own unmannerly method of argument.

'You see, sergeant,' Dan said, looking at another little cottage up the hill, 'the way it is, he's there now, and he's looking at us as sure as there's a glimmer of sight in his weak, wandering, watery eyes, and nothing would give him more gratification than for me to pay. But I'll punish him. I'll lie on bare boards for him. I'll suffer for him, sergeant, so that neither he nor any of his children after him will be able to raise their heads for the shame of it.'

On the following Friday he made ready his donkey and butt and set out.

On his way he collected a number of neighbours who wished to bid him farewell. At the top of the hill he stopped to send them back. An old man, sitting in the sunlight, hastily made his way indoors, and a moment later the door of his cottage was quietly closed.

Having shaken all his friends by the hand, Dan lashed the old donkey, shouted: 'Hup there!' and set out alone along the road to prison.

The Luceys

It's extraordinary, the bitterness there can be in a town like ours between two people of the same family. More particularly between two people of the same family. I suppose living more or less in public as we do we are either killed or cured by it, and the same communal sense that will make a man be battered into a reconciliation he doesn't feel gives added importance to whatever quarrel he thinks must not be composed. God knows, most of the time you'd be more sorry for a man like that than anything else.

The Luceys were like that. There were two brothers, Tom and Ben, and there must have been a time when the likeness between them was greater than the difference, but that was long before most of us knew them. Tom was the elder; he came in for the drapery shop. Ben had to have a job made for him on the County Council. This was the first difference and it grew and grew. Both were men of intelligence and education but Tom took it more seriously. As Ben said with a grin, he could damn well afford to with the business behind him.

It was an old-fashioned shop which prided itself on only stocking the best, and though the prices were high and Tom in his irascible opinionated way refused to abate them – he said haggling was degrading! – a lot of farmer's wives would still go nowhere else. Ben listened to his brother's high notions with his eyes twinkling, rather as he read the books which came his way, with profound respect and the feeling that this would all be grand for some other place, but was entirely inapplicable to the affairs of the County Council. God alone would ever be able to disentangle these, and meanwhile the only course open to a prudent man was to keep his mind to himself. If Tom didn't like the way the County Council was run, neither did Ben, but that was the way things were, and it rather amused him to rub it in to his virtuous brother.

Tom and Ben were both married. Tom's boy, Peter, was the great friend of his cousin, Charlie – called 'Charliss' by his Uncle Tom. They were nice boys; Peter a fat, heavy, handsome lad who blushed whenever a stranger spoke to him, and Charles with a broad face that never blushed at anything. The two families were always friendly; the mothers liked to get together over a glass of port wine and discuss the fundamental things that made the Lucey brothers not two inexplicable characters but two aspects of one inexplicable family character; the brothers enjoyed their regular chats about the way the world was going, for intelligent men are rare and each appreciated the other's shrewdness.

Only young Charlie was occasionally mystified by his Uncle Tom; he hated calling for Peter unless he was sure his uncle was out, for otherwise he might be sent into the front room to talk to him. The front room alone was enough to upset any high-spirited lad, with its thick carpet, mahogany sideboard, ornamental clock, and gilt mirror with cupids. The red curtains alone would depress you, and as well as these there was a glass-fronted mahogany bookcase the length of one wall, with books in sets, too big for anyone only a priest to read: *The History of Ireland*, *The History of the Popes*, *The Roman Empire*, *The Life of Johnson*, and *The Cabinet of Literature*. It gave Charlie the same sort of shivers as the priest's front room. His uncle suited it, a small, frail man, dressed in clerical black with a long pinched yellow face, tight lips, a narrow skull going bald up the brow, and a pair of tin specs.

All conversations with his uncle tended to stick in Charlie's mind for the simple but alarming reason that he never understood what the hell they were about, but one conversation in particular haunted him for years as showing the dangerous state of lunacy to which a man could be reduced by reading old books. Charlie was no fool, far from it; but low cunning and the most genuine benevolence were mixed in him in almost equal parts, producing a blend that was not without charm but gave no room for subtlety or irony.

'Good afternoon, Charliss,' said his uncle after Charlie had tied what he called 'the ould pup' to the leg of the hallstand. 'How are you?'

'All right,' Charlie said guardedly. (He hated being called Charliss; it made him sound such a sissy.)

'Take a seat, Charliss,' said his uncle benevolently. 'Peter will be down in a minute.'

'I won't,' said Charlie. 'I'd be afraid of the ould pup.'

'The expression, Charliss,' said his uncle in that rasping little voice of his, 'sounds like a contradiction in terms, but, not being familiar with dogs, I presume 'tis correct.'

'Ah, 'tis,' said Charlie, just to put the old man's mind at rest.

'And how is your father, Charliss?'

'His ould belly is bad again,' said Charlie. 'He'd be all right only the ould belly plays hell with him.'

'I'm sorry to hear it,' his uncle said gravely. 'And tell me, Charliss,' he added, cocking his head on one side like a bird, 'what is he saying about me now?'

This was one of the dirtiest of his Uncle Tom's tricks, assuming that Charlie's father was saying things about him, which to give Ben his due, he usually was. But on the other hand, he was admitted to be one of the smartest men in town, so he was entitled to do so, while everyone without exception appeared to agree that his uncle had a slate loose. Charlie looked at him cautiously, low cunning struggling with benevolence in him, for his uncle though queer was open-handed, and you wouldn't want to offend him. Benevolence won.

'He's saying if you don't mind yourself you'll end up in the poorhouse,' he said with some notion that if only his uncle knew the things people said about him he might mend his ways.

'Your father is right as always, Charliss,' said his uncle, rising and standing on the hearth with his hands behind his back and his little legs well apart. 'Your father is perfectly right. There are two main classes of people, Charliss – those who gravitate towards the poorhouse and those who gravitate towards the jail. . . . Do you know what "gravitate" means, Charliss?'

'I do not,' said Charlie without undue depression. It struck him as being an unlikely sort of word.

' "Gravitate," Charliss, means "tend" or "incline". Don't tell me you don't know what they mean!'

'I don't,' said Charlie.

'Well, do you know what this is?' his uncle asked smilingly as he held up a coin.

'I do,' said Charlie, humouring him as he saw that the conversation was at last getting somewhere. 'A tanner.'

'I am not familiar with the expression, Charliss,' his uncle said tartly and Charlie knew, whatever he'd said out of the way, his uncle was so irritated that he was liable to put the tanner back. 'We'll call it sixpence. Your eyes, I notice, gravitate towards the sixpence' (Charlie was so shocked that his eyes instantly gravitated towards his uncle) 'and in the same way, people gravitate, or turn naturally, towards the jail or poorhouse. Only a small number of either group reach their destination, though – which might be just as well for myself and your father,' he added in a low impressive voice, swaying forward and tightening his lips. 'Do you understand a word I'm saying, Charliss?' he added with a charming smile.

'I do not,' said Charlie.

'Good man! Good man!' his uncle said approvingly. 'I admire an honest and manly spirit in anybody. Don't forget your sixpence, Charliss.'

And as he went off with Peter, Charlie scowled and muttered savagely under his breath: 'Mod! Mod! Mod! The bleddy mon is mod!'

2

When the boys grew up Peter trained for a solicitor while Charlie, one of a large family, followed his father into the County Council. He grew up a very handsome fellow with a square, solemn, dark-skinned face, a thick red lower lip, and a mass of curly black hair. He was reputed to be a great man with greyhounds and girls and about as dependable with one as with the other. His enemies called him 'a crooked bloody bastard' and his father, a shrewd man, noted with alarm that Charlie thought him simple-minded.

The two boys continued the best of friends, though Peter, with an office in Asragh, moved in circles where Charlie felt himself lost; professional men whose status was calculated on their furniture and food and wine. Charlie thought that sort of entertainment a great pity. A man could have all the fun he wanted out of life without wasting his time on expensive and unsatisfactory meals and carrying on polite conversation while you dodged between bloody little tables that were always falling over, but Charlie, who was a modest lad, admired the way Peter never knocked anything over and never said: 'Chrisht!' Wine, coffee-cups, and talk about old books came as easy to him as talk about a dog or a horse.

Charlie was thunderstruck when the news came to him that Peter was in trouble. He heard it first from Mackesy the detective, whom he hailed outside the courthouse. (Charlie was like his father in that; he couldn't let a man go by without a greeting.)

'Hallo, Matt,' he shouted gaily from the courthouse steps. 'Is it myself or my father you're after?'

'I'll let ye off for today,' said Mackesy, making a garden-seat of the crossbar of his bicycle. Then he lowered his voice so that it didn't travel further than Charlie. 'I wouldn't mind having a word with a relative of yours, though.'

'A what, Matt?' Charlie asked, skipping down the steps on the scent of news. (He was like his father in that, too.) You don't mean one of the Luceys is after forgetting himself?'

'Then you didn't hear about Peter?'

'Peter! Peter in trouble! You're not serious, Matt?'

'There's a lot of his clients would be glad if I wasn't, Cha,' Mackesy said grimly. 'I thought you'd know about it as ye were such pals.'

'But we are, man, we are,' Charlie insisted. 'Sure, wasn't I at the dogs with him – when was it? – last Thursday? I never noticed a bloody thing, though, now you mention it, he was lashing pound notes on that Cloonbullogue dog. I told him the Dalys could never train a dog.'

Charlie left Mackesy, his mind in a whirl. He tore through the cashier's office. His father was sitting at his desk, signing paying-orders. He was wearing a grey tweed cap, a grey tweed suit, and a brown cardigan. He was a stocky, powerfully built man with a great expanse of chest, a plump, dark, hairy face, long quizzical eyes that tended to close in slits; hair in his nose, hair in his ears; hair on his high cheekbones that made them like small cabbage-patches.

He made no comment on Charlie's news, but stroked his chin and looked worried. Then Charlie shot out to see his uncle. Quill, the assistant, was serving in the shop and Charlie stumped in behind the counter to the fitting-room. His uncle had been looking out the back, all crumpled up. When Charlie came in he pulled himself erect with fictitious jauntiness. With his old black coat and wrinkled yellow face he had begun to look like an old rabbi.

'What's this I hear about Peter?' began Charlie, who was never one to be ceremonious.

'Bad news travels fast, Charlie,' said his uncle in his dry little voice, clamping his lips so tightly that the wrinkles ran up his cheeks from the corners of his mouth. He was so upset that he forgot even to say 'Charliss'.

'Have you any notion how much it is?' asked Charlie.

'I have not, Charlie,' Tom said bitterly. 'I need hardly say my son did not take me into his confidence about the extent of his robberies.'

'And what are you going to do?'

'What can I do?' The lines of pain belied the harsh little staccato that broke up every sentence into disjointed phrases as if it were a political speech. 'You saw yourself, Charliss, the way I reared that boy. You saw the education I gave him. I gave him the thing I was denied myself, Charliss. I gave him an honourable profession. And now for the first time in my life I am ashamed to show my face in my own shop. What can I do?'

'Ah, now, ah, now, Uncle Tom, we know all that,' Charlie said truculently, 'but that's not going to get us anywhere. What can we do now?'

'Is it true that Peter took money that was entrusted to him?' Tom asked oratorically.

'To be sure he did,' replied Charlie without the thrill of horror which his uncle seemed to expect. 'I do it myself every month, only I put it back.'

'And is it true he ran away from his punishment instead of standing his ground like a man?' asked Tom, paying no attention to him.

'What the hell else would he do?' asked Charlie, who entirely failed to appreciate the spiritual beauty of atonement. 'Begod, if I had two years' hard labour facing me you wouldn't see my heels for dust.'

'I dare say you think I'm old-fashioned, Charliss,' said his uncle, 'but that's not the way I was reared, nor the way my son was reared.'

'And that's where the ferryboat left ye,' snorted Charlie. 'Now that sort of thing may be all very well, Uncle Tom, but 'tis no use taking it to the fair. Peter made some mistake, the way we all make mistakes, but instead of coming to me or some other friend, he lost his nerve and started gambling. Chrisht, didn't I see it happen to better men? You don't know how much it is?'

'No, Charliss, I don't.'

'Do you know where he is, even?'

'His mother knows.'

'I'll talk to my old fellow. We might be able to do something. If the bloody fool might have told me on Thursday instead of backing that Cloonbullogue dog!'

Charlie returned to the office to find his father sitting at his desk with his hands joined and his pipe in his mouth, staring nervously at the door.

'Well?'

'We'll go over to Asragh and talk to Toolan of the Guards ourselves,' said Charlie. 'I want to find out how much he let himself in for. We might even get a look at the books.'

'Can't his father do it?' Ben asked gloomily.

'Do you think he'd understand them?'

'Well, he was always fond of literature,' Ben said shortly.

'God help him,' said Charlie. 'He has enough of it now.'

' 'Tis all his own conceit,' Ben said angrily, striding up and down the office with his hands in his trouser pockets. 'He was always good at criticizing other people. Even when you got in here it was all influence. Of course, he'd never use influence. Now he wants us to use it.'

'That's all very well,' Charlie said reasonably, 'but this is no time for raking up old scores.'

'Who's raking up old scores?' his father shouted angrily.

'That's right,' Charlie said approvingly. 'Would you like me to open the door so that you can be heard all over the office?'

'No one is going to hear me at all,' his father said in a more reasonable tone – Charlie had a way of puncturing him. 'And I'm not raking up any old scores. I'm only saying now what I always said. The boy was ruined.'

'He'll be ruined with a vengeance unless we do something quick,' said Charlie. 'Are you coming to Asragh with me?'

'I am not.'

'Why?'

'Because I don't want to be mixed up in it at all. That's why. I never liked anything to do with money. I saw too much of it. I'm only speaking for your good. A man done out of his money is a mad dog. You won't get any thanks for it, and anything that goes wrong, you'll get the blame.'

Nothing Charlie could say would move his father, and Charlie was shrewd enough to know that everything his father said was right. Tom wasn't to be trusted in the delicate negotiations that would be needed to get Peter out of the hole; the word here, the threat there; all the complicated machinery of family pressure. And alone he knew he was powerless. Despondently he went and told his uncle and Tom received the news with resignation, almost without understanding.

But a week later Ben came back to the office deeply disturbed. He closed the door carefully behind him and leaned across the desk to Charlie, his face drawn. For a moment he couldn't speak.

'What ails you?' Charlie asked with no great warmth.

'Your uncle passed me just now in the Main Street,' whispered his father.

Charlie wasn't greatly put out. All of his life he had been made a party to the little jabs and asides of father and uncle, and he did not realize what it meant to a man like his father, friendly and popular, this public rebuke.

'That so?' he asked without surprise. 'What did you do to him?'

'I thought you might know that,' his father said, looking at him with a troubled air from under the peak of his cap.

'Unless 'twas something you said about Peter?' suggested Charlie.

'It might, it might,' his father agreed doubtfully. 'You didn't – ah – repeat anything I said to you?'

'What a bloody fool you think I am!' Charlie said indignantly. 'And indeed I thought you had more sense. What did you say?'

'Oh, nothing. Nothing only what I said to you,' replied his father and went to the window to look out. He leaned on the sill and then tapped nervously on the frame. He was haunted by all the casual remarks he had made or might have made over a drink with an acquaintance – remarks that were no different from those he and Tom had been passing about one another all their lives. 'I shouldn't have said anything at all, of course, but I had no notion 'twould go back.'

'I'm surprised at my uncle,' said Charlie. 'Usually he cares little enough what anyone says of him.'

But even Charlie, who had moments when he almost understood his peppery little uncle, had no notion of the hopes he had raised and which his more calculating father had dashed. Tom Lucey's mind was in a rut, a rut of complacency, for the idealist too has his complacency and can be aware of it. There are moments when he would be glad to walk through any mud, but he no longer knows the way; he needs to be led; he cannot degrade himself even when he is most ready to do so. Tom was ready to beg favours from a thief. Peter had joined the Air Force under an assumed name, and this was the bitterest blow of all to him, the extinction of the name. He was something of an amateur genealogist, and had managed to convince himself, God knows how, that his family was somehow related to the Gloucestershire Lucys. This was already a sort of death.

The other death didn't take long in coming. Charlie, in the way he had, got wind of it first, and, having sent his father to break the news to Min, he went off himself to tell his uncle. It was a fine spring morning. The shop was empty but for his uncle, standing with his back to the counter studying the shelves.

'Good morning, Charliss,' he crackled over his shoulder. 'What's the best news?'

'Bad, I'm afraid, Uncle Tom,' Charlie replied, leaning across the counter to him.

'Something about Peter, I dare say?' his uncle asked casually, but Charlie noticed how, caught unawares, he had failed to say 'my son', as he had taken to doing.

'Just so.'

'Dead, I suppose?'

'Dead, Uncle Tom.'

'I was expecting something of the sort,' said his uncle. 'May the Almighty God have mercy on his soul! . . . Con!' he called at the back of the shop while he changed his coat. 'You'd better close up the shop. You'll find the crepe on the top shelf and the mourning-cards in my desk.'

'Who is it, Mr Lucey?' asked Con Quill. ' 'Tisn't Peter?'

' 'Tis, Con, 'tis, I'm sorry to say,' and Tom came out briskly with his umbrella over his arm. As they went down the street two people stopped them: the news was already round.

Charlie, who had to see about the arrangements for the funeral, left his uncle outside the house and so had no chance of averting the scene that took place inside. Not that he would have had much chance of doing so. His father had found Min in a state of collapse. Ben was the last man in the world to look after a woman, but he did manage to get her a pillow, put her legs on a chair and cover her with a rug, which was more than Charlie would have given him credit for. Min smelt of brandy. Then Ben strode up and down the darkened room with his hands in his pockets and his cap over his eyes, talking about the horrors of airplane travel. He knew he was no fit company for a woman of sensibility like Min, and he almost welcomed Tom's arrival.

'That's terrible news, Tom,' he said.

'Oh, God help us!' cried Min. 'They said he disgraced us but he didn't disgrace us long.'

'I'd sooner 'twas one of my own, Tom,' Ben said excitedly. 'As God is listening to me I would. I'd still have a couple left, but he was all ye had.'

He held out his hand to Tom. Tom looked at it, then at him, and then deliberately put his own hands behind his back.

'Aren't you going to shake hands with me, Tom?' Ben asked appealingly.

'No, Ben,' Tom said grimly. 'I am not.'

'Oh, Tom Lucey!' moaned Min with her crucified smile. 'Over your son's dead body!'

Ben looked at his brother in chagrin and dropped his hand. For a moment it looked as though he might strike him. He was a volatile, hot-tempered man.

'That wasn't what I expected from you, Tom,' he said, making a mighty effort to control himself.

'Ben,' said his brother, squaring his frail little shoulders, 'you disrespected my son while he was alive. Now that he's dead I'd thank you to leave him alone.'

'I disrespected him?' Ben exclaimed indignantly. 'I did nothing of the sort. I said things I shouldn't have said. I was upset. You know the sort I am. You were upset yourself and I dare say you said things you regret.'

' 'Tisn't alike, Ben,' Tom said in a rasping, opinionated tone. 'I said them because I loved the boy. You said them because you hated him.'

'I hated him?' Ben repeated incredulously. 'Peter? Are you out of your mind?'

'You said he changed his name because it wasn't grand enough for him,' Tom said, clutching the lapels of his coat and stepping from one foot to another. 'Why did you say such a mean, mocking, cowardly thing about the boy when he was in trouble?'

'All right, all right,' snapped Ben. 'I admit I was wrong to say it. There were a lot of things you said about my family, but I'm not throwing them back at you.'

'You said you wouldn't cross the road to help him,' said Tom. Again he primmed up the corners of his mouth and lowered his head. 'And why, Ben? I'll tell you why. Because you were jealous of him.'

'I was jealous of him?' Ben repeated. It seemed to him that he was

talking to a different man, discussing a different life, as though the whole of his nature was being turned inside out.

'You were jealous of him, Ben. You were jealous because he had the upbringing and education your own sons lacked. And I'm not saying that to disparage your sons. Far from it. But you begrudged my son his advantages.'

'Never!' shouted Ben in a fury.

'And I was harsh with him,' Tom said, taking another nervous step forward while his neat waspish little voice grew harder, 'I was harsh with him and you were jealous of him, and when his hour of trouble came he had no one to turn to. Now, Ben, the least you can do is to spare us your commiserations.'

'Oh, wisha, don't mind him, Ben,' moaned Min. 'Sure, everyone knows you never begrudged my poor child anything. The man isn't in his right mind.'

'I know that, Min,' Ben said, trying hard to keep his temper. 'I know he's upset. Only for that he'd never say what he did say – or believe it.'

'We'll see, Ben, we'll see,' said Tom grimly.

3

That was how the row between the Luceys began, and it continued like that for years. Charlie married and had children of his own. He always remained friendly with his uncle and visited him regularly; sat in the stuffy front room with him and listened with frowning gravity to Tom's views, and no more than in his childhood understood what the old man was talking about. All he gathered was that none of the political parties had any principle and the country was in a bad way due to the inroads of the uneducated and ill-bred. Tom looked more and more like a rabbi. As is the way of men of character in provincial towns, he tended more and more to become a collection of mannerisms, a caricature of himself. His academic jokes on his simple customers became more elaborate; so elaborate, in fact, that in time he gave up trying to explain them and was content to be set down as merely queer. In a way it made things easier for Ben; he was able to treat the breach with Tom as another example of his brother's cantankerousness, and spoke of it with amusement and good nature.

Then he fell ill. Charlie's cares were redoubled. Ben was the world's worst patient. He was dying and didn't know it, wouldn't go to hospital, and broke the heart of his wife and daughter. He was awake at six, knocking peremptorily for his cup of tea; then waited impatiently for the paper and the post. 'What the hell is keeping Mick Duggan? That fellow spends half his time gossiping along the road. Half past nine and no post!' After that the day was a blank to him until evening when a couple of County Council chaps dropped in to keep him company and tell him what was afoot in the courthouse. There was nothing in the long low room, plastered with blue and green flowered wallpaper, but a bedside table, a press, and three or four holy pictures, and Ben's mind was not on these but on the world outside – feet passing and repassing on errands which he would never be told about. It broke his heart. He couldn't believe he was as bad as people tried to make out; sometimes it was the doctor he blamed, sometimes the chemist who wasn't careful enough of the bottles and pills he made up – Ben could remember some shocking cases. He lay in bed doing involved calculations about his pension.

Charlie came every evening to sit with him. Though his father didn't say much about Tom, Charlie knew the row was always there in the back of his mind. It left Ben bewildered, a man without bitterness. And Charlie knew he came in for some of the blame. It was the illness all over again: someone must be slipping up somewhere; the right word hadn't been dropped in the right quarter or a wrong one had been dropped instead. Charlie, being so thick with Tom, must somehow be to blame. Ben did not understand the inevitable. One night it came out.

'You weren't at your uncle's?' Ben asked.

'I was,' Charlie said with a nod. 'I dropped in on the way up.'

'He wasn't asking about me?' Ben asked, looking at him out of the corner of his eye.

'Oh, he was,' Charlie said with a shocked air. 'Give the man his due, he always does that. That's one reason I try to drop in every day. He likes to know.'

But he knew this was not the question his father wanted answered. That question was: 'Did you say the right words? Did you make me out the feeble figure you should have made me out, or did you say the wrong thing, letting him know I was better?' These things had to be managed. In Charlie's place Ben would have managed it splendidly.

'He didn't say anything about dropping up?' Ben asked with affected lightness.

'No,' Charlie said with assumed thoughtfulness. 'I don't remember.'

'There's blackness for you!' his father said with sudden bitterness. It came as a shock to Charlie; it was the first time he had heard his father speak like that, from the heart, and he knew the end must be near.

'God knows,' Charlie said, tapping one heel nervously, 'he's a queer man. A queer bloody man!'

'Tell me, Charlie,' his father insisted, 'wouldn't you say it to him? 'Tisn't right and you know 'tisn't right.'

' 'Tisn't,' said Charlie, tearing at his hair, 'but to tell you the God's truth I'd sooner not talk to him.'

'Yes,' his father added in disappointment. 'I see it mightn't do for you.'

Charlie realized that his father was thinking of the shop, which would now come to him. He got up and stood against the fireplace, a fat, handsome, moody man.

'That has nothing to do with it,' he said. 'If he gave me cause I'd throw his bloody old shop in his face in the morning. I don't want anything from him. 'Tis just that I don't seem to be able to talk to him. I'll send Paddy down tonight and let him ask him.'

'Do, do,' his father said with a knowing nod. 'That's the very thing you'll do. And tell Julie to bring me up a drop of whiskey and a couple of glasses. You'll have a drop yourself?'

'I won't.'

'You will, you will. Julie will bring it up.'

Charlie went to his brother's house and asked him to call on Tom and tell him how near the end was. Paddy was a gentle, good-natured boy with something of Charlie's benevolence and none of his guile.

'I will to be sure,' he said. 'But why don't you tell him? Sure, he thinks the world of you.'

'I'll tell you why, Paddy,' Charlie whispered with his hand on his brother's sleeve. 'Because if he refused me I might do him some injury.'

'But you don't think he will?' Paddy asked in bewilderment.

'I don't think at all, Paddy,' Charlie said broodingly. 'I know.'

He knew all right. When he called on his way home the next afternoon his mother and sister were waiting for him, hysterical with excitement.

Paddy had met with a cold refusal. Their hysteria was infectious. He understood now why he had caught people glancing at him curiously in the street. It was being argued out in every pub, what Charlie Lucey ought to do. People couldn't mind their own bloody business. He rapped out an oath at the two women and took the stairs three at a time. His father was lying with his back to the window. The whiskey was still there as Charlie had seen it the previous evening. It tore at his heart more than the sight of his father's despair.

'You're not feeling too good?' he said gruffly.

'I'm not, I'm not,' Ben said, lifting the sheet from his face. 'Paddy didn't bring a reply to that message?' he added questioningly.

'Do you tell me so?' Charlie replied, trying to sound shocked.

'Paddy was always a bad man to send on a message,' his father said despondently, turning himself painfully in the bed, but still not looking at Charlie. 'Of course, he hasn't the sense. Tell me, Charlie,' he added in a feeble voice, 'weren't you there when I was talking about Peter?'

'About Peter?' Charlie exclaimed in surprise.

'You were, you were,' his father insisted, looking at the window. 'Sure, 'twas from you I heard it. You wanted to go to Asragh to look at the books, and I told you if anything went wrong you'd get the blame. Isn't that all I said?'

Charlie had to readjust his mind before he realized that his father had been going over it all again in the long hours of loneliness and pain, trying to see where he had gone wrong. It seemed to make him even more remote. Charlie didn't remember what his father had said; he doubted if his uncle remembered.

'I might have passed some joke about it,' his father said, 'but sure I was always joking him and he was always joking me. What the hell more was there in it?'

'Oh, a chance remark!' agreed Charlie.

'Now, the way I look at that,' his father said, seeking his eyes for the first time, 'someone was out to make mischief. This town is full of people like that. If you went and told him he'd believe you.'

'I will, I will,' Charlie said, sick with disgust. 'I'll see him myself today.'

He left the house, cursing his uncle for a brutal egotist. He felt the growing hysteria of the town concentrating on himself and knew that at last it had got inside him. His sisters and brothers, the people in the little shops along the street, expected him to bring his uncle to book, and failing that, to have done with him. This was the moment when people had to take their side once and for all. And he knew he was only too capable of taking sides.

Min opened the door to him, her red-rimmed eyes dirty with tears and the smell of brandy on her breath. She was near hysterics, too.

'What way is he, Charlie?' she wailed.

'Bad enough, Aunt Min,' he said as he wiped his boots and went past her. 'He won't last the night.'

At the sound of his voice his uncle had opened the sitting-room door and now he came out and drew Charlie in by the hand. Min followed. His uncle didn't release his hand, and betrayed his nervousness only by the way his frail fingers played over Charlie's hand, like a woman's.

'I'm sorry to hear it, Charliss,' he said.

'Sure, of course you are, Uncle Tom,' said Charlie, and at the first words the feeling of hysteria within him dissolved and left only a feeling of immense understanding and pity. 'You know what brought me?'

His uncle dropped his hand.

'I do, Charliss,' he said and drew himself erect. They were neither of them men to beat about the bush.

'You'll come and see the last of him,' Charlie said, not even marking the question.

'Charliss,' Tom said with that queer tightening at the corners of his mouth, 'I was never one to hedge or procrastinate. I will not come.'

He almost hissed the final words. Min broke into a loud wail.

'Talk to him, Charlie, do! I'm sick and tired of it. We can never show our faces in the town again.'

'And I need hardly say, Charliss,' his uncle continued with an air of triumph that was almost evil, 'that that doesn't trouble me.'

'I know,' Charlie said earnestly, still keeping his eyes on the withered old face with the narrow-winged, almost transparent nose. 'And you know that I never interfered between ye. Whatever disagreements ye had, I never took my father's side against you. And 'twasn't for what I might get out of you.'

In his excitement his uncle grinned, a grin that wasn't natural, and that combined in a strange way affection and arrogance, the arrogance of the idealist who doesn't realize how easily he can be fooled.

'I never thought it, boy,' he said, raising his voice. 'Not for an instant. Nor 'twasn't in you.'

'And you know too you did this once before and you regretted it.'

'Bitterly! Bitterly!'

'And you're going to make the same mistake with your brother that you made with your son?'

'I'm not forgetting that either, Charliss,' said Tom. 'It wasn't today nor yesterday I thought of it.'

'And it isn't as if you didn't care for him,' Charlie went on remorselessly. 'It isn't as if you had no heart for him. You know he's lying up there waiting for you. He sent for you last night and you never came. He had the bottle of whiskey and the two glasses by the bed. All he wants is for you to say you forgive him. . . . Jesus Christ, man,' he shouted with all the violence in him roused, 'never mind what you're doing to him. Do you know what you're doing to yourself?'

'I know, Charliss,' his uncle said in a cold, excited voice. 'I know that too. And 'tisn't as you say that I have no heart for him. God knows it isn't that I don't forgive him. I forgave him long years ago for what he said about – one that was very dear to me. But I swore that day, Charliss, that never the longest day I lived would I take your father's hand in friendship, and if God was to strike me dead at this very moment for my presumption I'd say the same. You know me, Charliss,' he added, gripping the lapels of his coat. 'I never broke my word yet to God or man. I won't do it now.'

'Oh, how can you say it?' cried Min. 'Even the wild beasts have more nature.'

'Some other time I'll ask you to forgive me,' added Tom, ignoring her.

'You need never do that, Uncle Tom,' Charlie said with great simplicity and humbleness. ' 'Tis yourself you'll have to forgive.'

At the door he stopped. He had a feeling that if he turned he would see Peter standing behind him. He knew his uncle's barren pride was all he could now offer to the shadow of his son, and that it was his dead cousin who stood between them. For a moment he felt like turning and appealing to Peter. But he was never much given to the supernatural. The real world was trouble enough for him, and he went slowly homeward, praying that he might see the blinds drawn before him.

After Fourteen Years

Nicholas Coleman arrived in B— on a fair day. The narrow streets were crowded with cattle that lurched and lounged dangerously as the drovers goaded them out of the way of passing cars. The air was charged with smells and dust and noise. Jobbers swung their sticks and shouted at one another across the street; shopkeepers displayed their wares and haggled with customers on the high pavements; shrill-voiced women sold apples, cigarettes and lemonade about the statue of the Maid of Erin in the market-place, and jovial burly farmers with shrewd ascetic faces under their Spanish hats jostled him as they passed.

He was glad when he succeeded in getting his business done and could leave the town for a while. It unnerved him. Above the roofs one could see always the clear grey-green of a hill that rose sharply above them and seemed as if at any moment it might fall and crush them. The sea road was better. There were carts on that too, and creels passed full of squealing animals; but at least one had the great bay with its many islands and its zone of violet hills through which sunlight and shadow circulated ceaselessly, without effort, like the flowing of water. The surface of the bay was very calm, and it seemed as if a rain of sunlight were pelting upon a bright flagstone and being tossed back again in a faint glittering spray, so that when one looked at it for long it dazzled the eye. Three or four fishing smacks and a little railway steamer with a bright red funnel were all that the bay held.

He had his dinner over an old shop in the market-place, but he was so nervous that he ate little. The farmers and jobbers tried to press him into conversation, but he had nothing to say; they talked of prices and crops, the Government and the County Council, about all of which he knew next to nothing. Eventually they let him be, much to his relief.

After dinner he climbed the hill that led out of town. The traffic had grown less: he climbed, and as the town sank back against the growing circle of the bay it seemed a quiet place enough, too quiet perhaps. He felt something like awe as he went up the trim gravel path to the convent. 'At seven,' he thought, 'the train will take me back to the city. At ten I shall be walking through Patrick Street on my way home. Tomorrow I shall be back at my old stool in the office. I shall never see this place again, never!'

But in spite of this, and partly because of it, his heart beat faster when the lay sister showed him into the bare parlour, with its crucifix, its polished floor, its wide-open windows that let in a current of cool air.

And at last *she* came; a slim figure in black with starched white facings. He scarcely looked at her, but took her hand, smiling, embarrassed and silent. She too was ill at ease.

They sat together on a garden seat from which he saw again the town and the bay, even more quite now. He heard nothing of its noise but the desolate screech of a train as it entered the station. Her eyes took it all in dispassionately, and now and again he glanced shyly up at her fine profile. That had not changed, and he wondered whether he had altered as little as she. Perhaps he hadn't, perhaps for her at least he was still the same as he had always been. Yet – there was a change in her! Her face had lost something; perhaps it was intensity; it no longer suggested the wildness and tenderness that he knew was in her. She looked happier and stronger.

'And Kate?' she asked after they had talked for a little while. 'How is she?'

'Oh, Kate is very well. They have a nice house in Passage – you know Tom has a school there. It's just over the river – the house, I mean; sometimes I go down to them on a Sunday evening for tea. . . . They have five children now; the eldest is sixteen.'

'Yes, of course – Marie. Why, she was called after me! She's my godchild.'

'Yes, yes, fancy I'd forgotten! You were always with Kate in those days.'

'I'd love to see Marie. She has written to me for my feastday ever since she was nine.'

'Has she? I didn't know. They don't talk to me about it.'

A faint flush mounted her cheek; for a moment she was silent, and if he had looked at her he would have seen a sudden look of doubt and pain in her eyes. But he did not look up, and she continued.

'Kate writes to me off and on too – but you know Kate! It was from her

I heard of your mother's death. That must have been a terrible blow to you.'

'Yes, it was very sudden. I was the only one with her when it came.'

'We had Mass for her here. How did she die? Was she –?'

'She died hard. She didn't want to leave me.'

'Oh!'

Her lips moved silently for a little.

'I've never forgotten her. She was so gentle, so – so unobtrusive, and Fair Hill used to be such a happy place then, before Kate married, when there were only the three of ourselves. . . . Do you remember, I used to go without my dinner to come up after school? . . . And so the house is gone?'

'Yes, the house is gone.'

'And Jennifer? The parrot?'

'Jennifer died long ago. She choked herself with an apple.'

'And Jasper?'

'Jasper too. An Alsatian killed him. I have another now, a sheepdog, a great lazy fellow. He's made friends with the Kerry Blue next door and the Kerry Blue comes with us and catches rabbits for him. He's fond of rabbits, but he's so big, so big and lazy!'

'You're in lodgings. Why didn't you go to live with Kate and Tom? You know they'd have been glad to have you.'

'Why should I? They were married; they had children at the time; they needed the house for themselves. . . . Besides, you know what I am. I'm a simple fellow, I'm not a bit clever, I don't read books or papers. At dinner the cattle-jobbers were trying to get me talking politics, and honest, I didn't know what they were at! What would Tom and his friends from the University have thought of a stupid creature like me?'

'No, you spent all your time in the country. I remember you getting up at five and going out with the dogs, around White's Cross and back through Ballyvolane. Do you still do that?'

'Yes, every fine morning and most Sundays. But I had to give up the birds when mother died.'

'Ah, the birds! What a pity! I remember them too, and how beautifully they sang.' She laughed happily, without constraint. 'The other girls envied me so much because you were always giving me birds' eggs, and I swapped them for other things, and I came back to you crying, pretending I'd lost them. . . . I don't think you ever guessed what a cheat I was. . . . Ah, well! And you're still in the factory.'

'Still in the factory! . . . You were right, you see. Do you remember you said I'd stick there until I grew grey hairs. You used to be angry with me then, and that worried me, and I'd give a spurt or two – No, no, I never had any ambition – not much anyhow – and as well be there as any place else. . . . And now I'm so used to it that I couldn't leave even if I wanted to. I live so quietly that even coming here has been too much of an adventure for me. All the time I've been saying "Tomorrow I shall be back at work, tomorrow I shall be back at work." I'll be glad to get home.'

'Yes, I can understand that.'

'Can you? You used to be different.'

'Yes, but things *are* different here. One works. One doesn't think. One doesn't want to think. I used to lie abed until ten at one time, now I'm up at half-past five every morning and I'm not a bit more tired. I'm kept busy all day. I sleep sound. I don't dream. And I hate anything that comes to disturb the routine.'

'Like me?'

'No, not like you. I hate being ill, lying in bed listening to the others and not working myself.'

'And you don't get into panics any longer?'

'No, no more panics.'

'You don't weep? You're not ambitious any longer? – that's so strange! . . . Yes, it *is* good to have one's life settled, to fear nothing and hope for nothing.'

She cast a quick, puzzled look at him.

'Do you still go to early Mass?' she asked.

'Yes, just as before.'

They fell into silence again. A little mist was rising from the town; one side of the bay was flanked with a wall of gold; a cool wind from the sea blew up to them, stirring the thick foliage and tossing her light, black veil. A bell rang out suddenly and she rose.

'What are your lodgings like?' she asked, her cheeks reddening. 'I hope you look after yourself and that they feed you properly. You used to be so careless.'

'Oh, yes, yes. They're very decent. And you – how do you find the place agreeing with you? Better than the city?'

'Oh, of course,' she said wearily, 'it is milder here.'

They went silently up the path towards the convent and parted as they had met, awkwardly, almost without looking at one another.

'No,' he thought, as he passed through the convent gate, 'that's over!' But he knew that for days, perhaps for months, birds and dogs, flowers, his early-morning walks through the country, the trees in summer, all those things that had given him pleasure would give him nothing but pain. The farmers coming from the fair, shouting to one another forward and back from their lumbering carts brought to mind his dreams of yesterday, and he grieved that God had created men without the innocence of natural things, had created them subtle and capricious, with memories in which the past existed like a statue, perfect and unapproachable.

And as the train carried him back to the city the clangour of its wheels that said 'ruthutta ruthutta ruthutta' dissolved into a bright mist of conversation through which he distinctly heard a woman's voice, but the voice said nothing; it was like memory, perfect and unapproachable; and his mind was weighed down by an infinite melancholy that merged with the melancholy of the dark countryside through which he passed – a countryside of lonely, steelbright pools that were islanded among the silhouettes of hills and trees. Ironically he heard himself say again, 'Yes, it *is* good to have one's life settled, to fear nothing and hope for nothing.'

And the train took him ever farther and farther away and replied with its petulant metallic voice –

'Ruthutta ruthutta ruthutta!'

Peasants

When Michael John Cronin stole the funds of the Carricknabreena Hurling, Football and Temperance Association, commonly called the Club, everyone said: 'Devil's cure to him!' ' 'Tis the price of him!' 'Kind father for him!' 'What did I tell you?' and the rest of the things people say when an acquaintance has got what is coming to him.

And not only Michael John but the whole Cronin family, seed, breed, and generation, came in for it; there wasn't one of them for twenty miles round or a hundred years back but his deeds and sayings were remembered and examined by the light of this fresh scandal. Michael John's father (the heavens be his bed!) was a drunkard who beat his wife, and his father before him a landgrabber. Then there was an uncle or grand-uncle who had been a policeman and taken a hand in the bloody work at Mitchelstown long ago, and an unmarried sister of the same whose good name it would by all accounts have needed a regiment of husbands to restore. It was a grand shaking-up the Cronins got altogether, and anyone who had a grudge in for them, even if it was no more than a thirty-third cousin, had rare sport, dropping a friendly word about it and saying how sorry he was for the poor mother till he had the blood lighting in the Cronin eyes.

There was only one thing for them to do with Michael John; that was to send him to America and let the thing blow over, and that, no doubt, is what they would have done but for a certain unpleasant and extraordinary incident.

Father Crowley, the parish priest, was chairman of the committee. He was a remarkable man, even in appearance; tall, powerfully built, but very stooped, with shrewd, loveless eyes that rarely softened to anyone except two or three old people. He was a strange man, well on in years, noted for his strong political views, which never happened to coincide with those

213

of any party, and as obstinate as the devil himself. Now what should Father Crowley do but try to force the committee to prosecute Michael John?

The committee were all religious men who up to this had never as much as dared to question the judgements of a man of God: yes, faith, and if the priest had been a bully, which to give him his due he wasn't, he might have danced a jig on their backs and they wouldn't have complained. But a man has principles, and the like of this had never been heard of in the parish before. What? Put the police on a boy and he in trouble?

One by one the committee spoke up and said so. 'But he did wrong,' said Father Crowley, thumping the table. 'He did wrong and he should be punished.'

'Maybe so, father,' said Con Norton, the vice-chairman, who acted as spokesman. 'Maybe you're right, but you wouldn't say his poor mother should be punished too and she a widow-woman?'

'True for you!' chorused the others.

'Serve his mother right!' said the priest shortly. 'There's none of you but knows better than I do the way that young man was brought up. He's a rogue and his mother is a fool. Why didn't she beat Christian principles into him when she had him on her knee?'

'That might be, too,' Norton agreed mildly. 'I wouldn't say but you're right, but is that any reason his Uncle Peter should be punished?'

'Or his Uncle Dan?' asked another.

'Or his Uncle James?' asked a third.

'Or his cousins, the Dwyers, that keep the little shop in Lissnacarriga, as decent a living family as there is in County Cork?' asked a fourth.

'No, father,' said Norton, 'the argument is against you.'

'Is it indeed?' exclaimed the priest, growing cross. 'Is it so? What the devil has it to do with his Uncle Dan or his Uncle James? What are ye talking about? What punishment is it to them, will ye tell me that? Ye'll be telling me next 'tis a punishment to me and I a child of Adam like himself.'

'Wisha now, father,' asked Norton incredulously, 'do you mean 'tis no punishment to them having one of their own blood made a public show? Is it mad you think we are? Maybe 'tis a thing you'd like done to yourself?'

'There was none of my family ever a thief,' replied Father Crowley shortly.

'Begor, we don't know whether there was or not,' snapped a little man called Daly, a hot-tempered character from the hills.

'Easy, now! Easy, Phil!' said Norton warningly.

'What do you mean by that?' asked Father Crowley, rising and grabbing his hat and stick.

'What I mean,' said Daly, blazing up, 'is that I won't sit here and listen to insinuations about my native place from any foreigner. There are as many rogues and thieves and vagabonds and liars in Cullough as ever there were in Carricknabreena – ay, begod, and more, and bigger! That's what I mean.'

'No, no, no, no,' Norton said soothingly. 'That's not what he means at all, father. We don't want any bad blood between Cullough and Carricknabreena. What he means is that the Crowleys may be a fine substantial family in their own country, but that's fifteen long miles away, and this isn't their country, and the Cronins are neighbours of ours since the dawn of history and time, and 'twould be a very queer thing if at this hour we handed one of them over to the police. . . . And now, listen to me, father,' he went on, forgetting his role of pacificator and hitting the table as hard as the rest, 'if a cow of mine got sick in the morning, 'tisn't a Cremin or a Crowley I'd be asking for help, and damn the bit of use 'twould be to me if I did. And everyone knows I'm no enemy of the Church but a respectable farmer that pays his dues and goes to his duties regularly.'

'True for you! True for you!' agreed the committee.

'I don't give a snap of my finger what you are,' retorted the priest. 'And now listen to me, Con Norton. I bear young Cronin no grudge, which is more than some of you can say, but I know my duty and I'll do it in spite of the lot of you.'

He stood at the door and looked back. They were gazing blankly at one another, not knowing what to say to such an impossible man. He shook his fist at them.

'Ye all know me,' he said. 'Ye know that all my life I'm fighting the long-tailed families. Now, with the help of God, I'll shorten the tail of one of them.'

Father Crowley's threat frightened them. They knew he was an obstinate man and had spent his time attacking what he called the 'corruption' of councils and committees, which was all very well as long as it happened outside your own parish. They dared not oppose him openly because he knew too much about all of them and, in public at least, had a lacerating tongue. The solution they favoured was a tactful one. They formed themselves into a Michael John Cronin Fund Committee and canvassed the parishioners for subscriptions to pay off what Michael John had stolen. Regretfully they decided that Father Crowley would hardly countenance a football match for the purpose.

Then with the defaulting treasurer, who wore a suitably contrite air, they marched up to the presbytery. Father Crowley was at his dinner but he told the housekeeper to show them in. He looked up in astonishment as his dining-room filled with the seven committeemen, pushing before them the cowed Michael John.

'Who the blazes are ye?' he asked, glaring at them over the lamp.

'We're the Club Committee, father,' replied Norton.

'Oh, are ye?'

'And this is the treasurer – the ex-treasurer, I should say.'

'I won't pretend I'm glad to see him,' said Father Crowley grimly.

'He came to say he's sorry, father,' went on Norton. 'He is sorry, and that's as true as God, and I'll tell you no lie. . . .' Norton made two steps forward and in a dramatic silence laid a heap of notes and silver on the table.

'What's that?' asked Father Crowley.

'The money, father. 'Tis all paid back now and there's nothing more between us. Any little crossness there was, we'll say no more about it, in the name of God.'

The priest looked at the money and then at Norton.

'Con,' he said, 'you'd better keep the soft word for the judge. Maybe he'll think more of it than I do.'

'The judge, father?'

'Ay, Con, the judge.'

There was a long silence. The committee stood with open mouths, unable to believe it.

'And is that what you're doing to us, father?' asked Norton in a trembling voice. 'After all the years, and all we done for you, is it you're going to show us up before the whole country as a lot of robbers?'

'Ah, ye idiots, I'm not showing ye up.'

'You are then, father, and you're showing up every man, woman, and child in the parish,' said Norton. 'And mark my words, 'twon't be forgotten for you.'

The following Sunday Father Crowley spoke of the matter from the altar. He spoke for a full half-hour without a trace of emotion on his grim old face, but his sermon was one long, venomous denunciation of the 'long-tailed families' who, according to him, were the ruination of the country and made a mockery of truth, justice, and charity. He was, as his congregation agreed, a shockingly obstinate old man who never knew when he was in the wrong.

After Mass he was visited in his sacristy by the committee. He gave Norton a terrible look from under his shaggy eyebrows, which made that respectable farmer flinch.

'Father,' Norton said appealingly, 'we only want one word with you. One word and then we'll go. You're a hard character, and you said some bitter things to us this morning; things we never deserved from you. But we're quiet, peaceable poor men and we don't want to cross you.'

Father Crowley made a sound like a snort.

'We came to make a bargain with you, father,' said Norton, beginning to smile.

'A bargain?'

'We'll say no more about the whole business if you'll do one little thing – just one little thing – to oblige us.'

'The bargain!' the priest said impatiently. 'What's the bargain?'

'We'll leave the matter drop for good and all if you'll give the boy a character.'

'Yes, father,' cried the committee in chorus. 'Give him a character! Give him a character!'

'Give him a what?' cried the priest.

'Give him a character, father, for the love of God,' said Norton emotionally. 'If you speak up for him, the judge will leave him off and there'll be no stain on the parish.'

'Is it out of your minds you are, you halfwitted angashores?' asked Father Crowley, his face suffused with blood, his head trembling. 'Here am I all these years preaching to ye about decency and justice and truth and ye no more understand me than that wall there. Is it the way ye want me to perjure myself? Is it the way ye want me to tell a damned lie with the name of Almighty God on my lips? Answer me, is it?'

'Ah, what perjure!' Norton replied wearily. 'Sure, can't you say a few words for the boy? No one is asking you to say much. What harm will it do you to tell the judge he's an honest, good-living, upright lad, and that he took the money without meaning any harm?'

'My God!' muttered the priest, running his hands distractedly through his grey hair. 'There's no talking to ye, no talking to ye, ye lot of sheep.'

When he was gone the committeemen turned and looked at one another in bewilderment.

'That man is a terrible trial,' said one.

'He's a tyrant,' said Daly vindictively.

'He is, indeed,' sighed Norton, scratching his head. 'But in God's holy name, boys, before we do anything, we'll give him one more chance.'

That evening when he was at his tea the committeemen called again. This time they looked very spruce, businesslike, and independent. Father Crowley glared at them.

'Are ye back?' he asked bitterly. 'I was thinking ye would be. I declare to my goodness, I'm sick of ye and yeer old committee.'

'Oh, we're not the committee, father,' said Norton stiffly.

'Ye're not?'

'We're not.'

'All I can say is, ye look mighty like it. And, if I'm not being impertinent, who the deuce are ye?'

'We're a deputation, father.'

'Oh, a deputation! Fancy that, now. And a deputation from what?'

'A deputation from the parish, father. Now, maybe you'll listen to us.'

'Oh, go on! I'm listening, I'm listening.'

'Well, now, 'tis like this, father,' said Norton, dropping his airs and graces and leaning against the table. ' 'Tis about that little business this morning. Now, father, maybe you don't understand us and we don't understand you. There's a lot of misunderstanding in the world today, father. But we're quiet simple poor men that want to do the best we can for everybody, and a few words or a few pounds wouldn't stand in our way. Now, do you follow me?'

'I declare,' said Father Crowley, resting his elbows on the table, 'I don't know whether I do or not.'

'Well, 'tis like this, father. We don't want any blame on the parish or on the Cronins, and you're the one man that can save us. Now all we ask of you is to give the boy a character –'

'Yes, father,' interrupted the chorus, 'give him a character! Give him a character!'

'Give him a character, father, and you won't be troubled by him again. Don't say no to me now till you hear what I have to say. We won't ask you to go next, nigh or near the court. You have pen and ink beside you and one couple of lines is all you need write. When 'tis over you can hand Michael John his ticket to America and tell him not to show his face in Carricknabreena again. There's the price of his ticket, father,' he added, clapping a bundle of notes on the table. 'The Cronins themselves made it up, and we have his mother's word and his own word that he'll clear out the minute 'tis all over.'

'He can go to pot!' retorted the priest. 'What is it to me where he goes?'

'Now, father, can't you be patient?' Norton asked reproachfully. 'Can't you let me finish what I'm saying? We know 'tis no advantage to you, and that's the very thing we came to talk about. Now, supposing – just supposing for the sake of argument – that you do what we say, there's a few of us here, and between us, we'd raise whatever little contribution to the parish fund you'd think would be reasonable to cover the expense and trouble to yourself. Now do you follow me?'

'Con Norton,' said Father Crowley, rising and holding the edge of the table, 'I follow you. This morning it was perjury, and now 'tis bribery, and the Lord knows what 'twill be next. I see I've been wasting my breath. . . . And I see too,' he added savagely, leaning across the table towards them, 'a pedigree bull would be more use to ye than a priest.'

'What do you mean by that, father?' asked Norton in a low voice.

'What I say.'

'And that's a saying that will be remembered for you the longest day you live,' hissed Norton, leaning towards him till they were glaring at one another over the table.

'A bull,' gasped Father Crowley. 'Not a priest.'

' 'Twill be remembered.'

'Will it? Then remember this too. I'm an old man now. I'm forty years a priest, and I'm not a priest for the money or power or glory of it, like others I know. I gave the best that was in me – maybe 'twasn't much but 'twas more than many a better man would give, and at the end of my days . . .' lowering his voice to a whisper he searched them with his terrible eyes, '. . . at the end of my days, if I did a wrong thing, or a bad thing, or an unjust thing, there isn't man or woman in this parish that would brave me to my face and call me a villain. And isn't that a poor story for an old man that tried to be a good priest?' His voice changed again and he raised his head defiantly. 'Now get out before I kick you out!'

And true to his word and character not one word did he say in Michael John's favour the day of the trial, no more than if he was a black. Three months Michael John got and by all accounts he got off light.

He was a changed man when he came out of jail, downcast and dark in himself. Everyone was sorry for him, and people who had never spoken to him before spoke to him then. To all of them he said modestly: 'I'm very grateful to you, friend, for overlooking my misfortune.' As he wouldn't go to America, the committee made another whip-round and between what they had collected before and what the Cronins had made up to send him to America, he found himself with enough to open a small shop. Then he got a job in the County Council, and an agency for some shipping company, till at last he was able to buy a public-house.

As for Father Crowley, till he was shifted twelve months later, he never did a day's good in the parish. The dues went down and the presents went down, and people with money to spend on Masses took it fifty miles away sooner than leave it to him. They said it broke his heart.

He has left unpleasant memories behind him. Only for him, people say, Michael John would be in America now. Only for him he would never have married a girl with money, or had it to lend to poor people in the hard times, or ever sucked the blood of Christians. For, as an old man said to me of him: 'A robber he is and was, and a grabber like his grandfather before him, and an enemy of the people like his uncle, the policeman; and though some say he'll dip his hand where he dipped it before, for myself I have no hope unless the mercy of God would send us another Moses or Brian Boru to cast him down and hammer him in the dust.'

The Bridal Night

It was sunset, and the two great humps of rock made a twilight in the cove where the boats were lying high up the strand. There was one light only in a little whitewashed cottage. Around the headland came a boat and the heavy dipping of its oars was like a heron's flight. The old woman was sitting on the low stone wall outside her cottage.

'Tis a lonesome place,' said I.

'Tis so,' she agreed, 'a lonesome place, but any place is lonesome without one you'd care for.'

'Your own flock are gone from you, I suppose?' I asked.

'I never had but the one,' she replied, 'the one son only,' and I knew because she did not add a prayer for his soul that he was still alive.

'Is it in America he is?' I asked. (It is to America all the boys of the locality go when they leave home.)

'No, then,' she replied simply. 'It is in the asylum in Cork he is on me these twelve years.'

I had no fear of trespassing on her emotions. These lonesome people in wild places, it is their nature to speak; they must cry out their sorrows like the wild birds.

'God help us!' I said. 'Far enough!'

'Far enough,' she sighed. 'Too far for an old woman. There was a nice priest here one time brought me up in his car to see him. All the ways to this wild place he brought it, and he drove me into the city. It is a place I was never used to, but it eased my mind to see poor Denis well-cared-for and well-liked. It was a trouble to me before that, not knowing would they see what a good boy he was before his madness came on him. He knew me; he saluted me, but he said nothing until the superintendent came to tell me the tea was ready for me. Then poor Denis raised his head and says: "Leave ye not forget the toast. She was ever a great one for her bit of toast." It seemed to give him ease and he cried after. A good boy he was and is. It was like him after seven long years to think of his old mother and her little bit of toast.'

'God help us,' I said for her voice was like the birds', hurrying high, immensely high, in the coloured light, out to sea to the last islands where their nests were.

'Blessed be His holy will,' the old woman added, 'there is no turning aside what is in store. It was a teacher that was here at the time. Miss Regan her name was. She was a fine big jolly girl from the town. Her father had a shop there. They said she had three hundred pounds to her own cheek the day she set foot in the school, and – 'tis hard to believe but 'tis what they all said: I will not belie her – 'twasn't banished she was at all but she came here of her own choice, for the great liking she had for the sea and the mountains. Now, that is the story, and with my own eyes I saw her, day in day out, coming down the little pathway you came yourself from the road and sitting beyond there in a hollow you can hardly see, out of the wind. The neighbours could make nothing of it, and she being a stranger, and with only the book Irish, they left her alone. It never seemed to take a peg out of her, only sitting in that hole in the rocks, as happy as the day is long, reading her little book or writing her letters. Of an odd time she might bring one of the little scholars along with her to be picking posies.

'That was where my Denis saw her. He'd go up to her of an evening and sit on the grass beside her, and off and on he might take her out in the boat with him. And she'd say with that big laugh of hers: "Denis is my beau." Those now were her words and she meant no more harm by it than the child unborn, and I knew it and Denis knew it, and it was a little joke we had, the three of us. It was the same way she used to joke about her little hollow. "Mrs Sullivan," she'd say, "leave no one near it. It is my nest and my cell and my little prayer-house, and maybe I would be like the birds and catch the smell of the stranger and then fly away from ye all." It did me good to hear her laugh, and whenever I saw Denis moping or idle I would say it to him myself: "Denis, why wouldn't you go out and pay your attentions to Miss Regan and all saying you are her intended?" It was only a joke. I would say the same thing to her face, for Denis was such a quiet boy, no way rough or accustomed to the girls at all – and how would he in this lonesome place?

'I will not belie her; it was she saw first that poor Denis was after more than company, and it was not to this cove she came at all then but to the little cove beyond the headland, and 'tis hardly she would go there itself without a little scholar along with her. "Ah," I says, for I missed her company, "isn't it the great stranger Miss Regan is becoming?" and Denis would put on his coat and go hunting in the dusk till he came to whatever spot she was. Little ease that was to him, poor boy, for he lost his tongue entirely, and lying on his belly before her, chewing an old bit of grass, is all he would do till she got up and left him. He could not help himself, poor boy. The madness was on him, even then, and it was only when I saw the plunder done that I knew there was no cure for him only to put her out of his mind entirely. For 'twas madness in him and he knew it, and that was what made him lose his tongue – he that was maybe without the price of an ounce of 'baccy – I will not deny it: often enough he had to do without it when the hens would not be laying, and often enough stirabout and praties was all we had for days. And there was she with money to her name in the bank! And that wasn't all, for he was a good boy; a quiet, good-natured boy, and another would take pity on him, knowing he would make her a fine steady husband, but she was not the sort, and well I knew it from the first day I laid eyes on her, that her hand would never rock the cradle. There was the madness out and out.

'So here was I, pulling and hauling, coaxing him to stop at home, and hiding whatever little thing was to be done till evening the way his hands would not be idle. But he had no heart in the work, only listening, always listening, or climbing the cnuceen to see would he catch a glimpse of her coming or going. And, oh, Mary, the heavy sigh he'd give when his bit of supper was over and I bolting the house for the night, and he with the long hours of darkness forninst him – my heart was broken thinking of it. It was the madness, you see. It was on him. He could hardly sleep or eat, and at night I would hear him, turning and groaning as loud as the sea on the rocks.

'It was then when the sleep was a fever to him that he took to walking in the night. I remember well the first night I heard him lift the latch. I put on my few things and went out after him. It was standing here I heard his feet on the stile. I went back and latched the door and hurried after him. What else could I do, and this place terrible after the fall of night with rocks and hills and water and streams, and he, poor soul, blinded with the dint of sleep. He travelled the road a piece, and then took to the hills and I followed him with my legs all torn with briars and furze. It was over beyond by the new house that he gave up. He turned to me then the way a little child that is running away turns and clings to your knees; he turned to me and said: "Mother, we'll go home now. It was the bad day for you ever you brought me into the world." And as the day was breaking I got him back to bed and covered him up to sleep.

'I was hoping that in time he'd wear himself out, but it was worse he was getting. I was a strong woman then, a mayen-strong woman. I could cart a load of seaweed or dig a field with any man, but the night-walking broke me. I knelt one night before the Blessed Virgin and prayed whatever was to happen, it would happen while the light of life was in me, the way I would not be leaving him lonesome like that in a wild place.

'And it happened the way I prayed. Blessed be God, he woke that night or the next night on me and he roaring. I went in to him but I couldn't hold him. He had the strength of five men. So I went out and locked the door behind me. It was down the hill I faced in the starlight to the little house above the cove. The Donoghues came with me: I will not belie them; they were fine powerful men and good neighbours. The father and the two sons came with me and brought the rope from the boats. It was a hard struggle they had of it and a long time before they got him on the floor, and a longer time before they got the ropes on him. And when they had him tied they put him back into bed for me, and I covered him up, nice and decent, and put a hot stone to his feet to take the chill of the cold floor off him.

'Sean Donoghue spent the night sitting beside the fire with me, and in the morning he sent one of the boys off for the doctor. Then Denis called me in his own voice and I went into him. "Mother," says Denis, "will you leave me this way against the time they come for me?" I hadn't the heart. God knows I hadn't. "Don't do it, Peg," says Sean. "If 'twas a hard job trussing him before, it will be harder the next time, and I won't answer for it."

' "You're a kind neighbour, Sean," says I, "and I would never make little of you, but he is the only son I ever reared and I'd sooner he'd kill me now than shame him at the last."

'So I loosened the ropes on him and he lay there very quiet all day without breaking his fast. Coming on to evening he asked me for the sup of tea and he drank it, and soon after the doctor and another man came in the car. They said a few words to Denis but he made them no answer and the doctor gave me the bit of writing. "It will be tomorrow before they come for him," says he, "and 'tisn't right for you to be alone in the house with the man." But I said I would stop with him and Sean Donoghue said the same.

'When darkness came on there was a little bit of a wind blew up from the sea and Denis began to rave to himself, and it was her name he was calling all the time. "Winnie," that was her name, and it was the first time I heard it spoken. "Who is that he is calling?" says Sean. "It is the schoolmistress," says I, "for though I do not recognize the name, I know 'tis no one else he'd be asking for." "That is a bad sign," says Sean. "He'll get worse as the night goes on and the wind rises. 'Twould be better for me go down and get the boys to put the ropes on him again while he's quiet." And it was then something struck me, and I said: "May be if she came to him herself for a minute he would be quiet after." "We can try it anyway," says Sean, "and if the girl has a kind heart she will come."

'It was Sean that went up for her. I would not have the courage to ask her. Her little house is there on the edge of the hill; you can see it as you go back the road with the bit of garden before it the new teacher left grow wild. And it was a true word Sean said for 'twas worse Denis was getting, shouting out against the wind for us to get Winnie for him. Sean was a long time away or maybe I felt it long, and I thought it might be the way she was afeared to come. There are many like that, small blame to them. Then I heard her step that I knew so well on the boreen beside the house and I ran to the door, meaning to say I was sorry for the trouble we were giving her, but when I opened the door Denis called out her name in a loud voice, and the crying fit came on me, thinking how light-hearted we used to be together.

'I couldn't help it, and she pushed in apast me into the bedroom with her face as white as that wall. The candle was lighting on the dresser. He turned to her roaring with the mad look in his eyes, and then went quiet all of a sudden, seeing her like that overright him with her hair all rumbled in the wind. I was coming behind her. I heard it. He put up his two poor hands and the red mark of the ropes on his wrists and whispered to her: "Winnie, asthore, isn't it the long time you were away from me?"

' "It is, Denis, it is indeed," says she, "but you know I couldn't help it."

' "Don't leave me any more now, Winnie," says he, and then he said no more, only the two eyes lighting out on her as she sat by the bed. And Sean Donoghue brought in the little stooleen for me, and there we were, the three of us, talking, and Denis paying us no attention, only staring at her.

'"Winnie," says he, "lie down here beside me."

'"Oye," says Sean, humouring him, "don't you know the poor girl is played out after her days' work? She must go home to bed."

'"No, no, no," says Denis and the terrible mad light in his eyes. "There is a high wind blowing and 'tis no night for one like her to be out. Leave her sleep here beside me. Leave her creep in under the clothes to me the way I'll keep her warm."

'"Oh, oh, oh, oh," says I, "indeed and indeed, Miss Regan, 'tis I'm sorry for bringing you here. 'Tisn't my son is talking at all but the madness in him. I'll go now," says I, "and bring Sean's boys to put the ropes on him again."

'"No, Mrs Sullivan," says she in a quiet voice. "Don't do that at all. I'll stop here with him and he'll go fast asleep. Won't you, Denis?"

'"I will, I will," says he, "but come under the clothes to me. There does a terrible draught blow under that door."

'"I will indeed, Denis," says she, "if you'll promise me to go to sleep."

'"Oye, whisht, girl," says I. '"'Tis you that's mad. While you're here you're in my charge, and how would I answer to your father if you stopped in here by yourself?"

'"Never mind about me, Mrs Sullivan," she said. "I'm not a bit in dread of Denis. I promise you there will no harm come to me. You and Mr Donoghue can sit outside in the kitchen and I'll be all right here."

'She had a worried look but there was something about her there was no mistaking. I wouldn't take it on myself to cross the girl. We went out to the kitchen, Sean and myself, and we heard every whisper that passed between them. She got into the bed beside him: I heard her. He was whispering into her ear the sort of foolish things boys do be saying at that age, and then we heard no more only the pair of them breathing. I went to the room door and looked in. He was lying with his arm about her and his head on her bosom, sleeping like a child, sleeping like he slept in his good days with no worry at all on his poor face. She did not look at me and I did not speak to her. My heart was too full. God help us, it was an old song of my father's that was going through my head: "Lonely Rock is the one wife my children will know."

'Later on, the candle went out and I did not light another. I wasn't a bit afraid for her then. The storm blew up and he slept through it all, breathing nice and even. When it was light I made a cup of tea for her and beckoned her from the room door. She loosened his hold and slipped out of bed. Then he stirred and opened his eyes.

' "Winnie," says he, "where are you going?"

' "I'm going to work, Denis," says she. "Don't you know I must be at school early?"

' "But you'll come back to me tonight, Winnie?" says he.

' "I will, Denis," says she. "I'll come back, never fear."

'And he turned on his side and went fast asleep again.

'When she walked into the kitchen I went on my two knees before her and kissed her hands. I did so. There would no words come to me, and we sat there, the three of us, over our tea, and I declare for the time being I felt 'twas worth it all, all the troubles of his birth and rearing and all the lonesome years ahead.

'It was a great ease to us. Poor Denis never stirred, and when the police came he went along with them without commotion or handcuffs or anything that would shame him, and all the words he said to me was: "Mother, tell Winnie I'll be expecting her."

'And isn't it a strange and wonderful thing? From that day to the day she left us there did no one speak a bad word about what she did, and the people couldn't do enough for her. Isn't it a strange thing and the world as wicked as it is, that no one would say the bad word about her?'

Darkness had fallen over the Atlantic, blank grey to its farthest reaches.

A Thing of Nothing

1

Ned Lynch was a decent poor slob of a man with a fat purple face, a big black moustache like the villain in a melodrama, and a paunch. He had a brassy voice that took an effort of his whole being to reduce it by a puff, sleepy bloodshot eyes, and a big head. Katty, who was a well-mannered, convent-educated girl, thought him very old-fashioned. He said the country was going to the dogs and the land being starved to put young fellows into professions, 'educating them out of their knowledge', he said. 'What do they want professions for?' he asked. 'Haven't they the hills and the fields – God's great, wonderful book of Nature?' He courted her in the same stiff sentimental way, full of poetic nonsense about 'your holy delicate white hands' and 'the weaker sex'.

The weaker sex indeed! You should see him if he had a headache. She havered for years about marrying him at all. Her family thought he was a very good catch, but Katty would have preferred a professional man. At last she suggested that they should separate for a year to see whether they couldn't do better for themselves. He put on a sour puss at that, but Katty went off to business in Dublin just the same. Except for one drunken medical who borrowed money from her, she didn't meet any professional men, and after lending the medico more money than she could afford, she was glad enough to come back and marry Ned. She didn't look twenty-five, but she was thirty-nine. The day of the marriage he handed her three anonymous letters about herself and the medico.

Katty thought a lot about the anonymous letters. She thought she knew the quarter they had come from. Ned had a brother called Jerry who was a different class of man entirely. He was tall and dark and lean as a rake, with a high colour and a pair of bright-blue eyes. Twenty years before, himself and Ned had had some disagreement about politics and he had opened Ned with a poker. They hadn't spoken since, but as Jerry had two sons and only one farm, Katty saw just why it mightn't suit him that Ned and herself would marry.

She was a good wife and a good manager; a great woman to send to an auction. She was pretty and well behaved; she dressed younger than her years in short coloured frocks and wide hats that she had to hold the brim of on a windy morning. She managed to double the business inside two years. But before the first year was well out she began to see rocks ahead. First there was Ned's health. He looked a giant of a man, but his sister had died of blood pressure, and he had a childish craze for meat and pastries. You could see him outside the baker's, looking in with mournful, bloodshot eyes. He would saunter in and stroll out with a little bag of cakes behind his back, hide them under the counter, and eat them when she wasn't looking. Sometimes she came into the shop and found him with his whole face red and one cheek stuffed. She never said anything then; she was much too much a lady, but afterwards she might reproach him gently with it.

And then to crown her troubles one day Father Ring called and Ned and himself went connyshuring in the parlour. A few days later – oh, dear, she thought bitterly, the subtlety of them! – two country boys walked in. One was Con Lynch, Jerry's second son. He was tall and gawkish, with a big, pale, bony face; he walked with a pronounced stoop as if his sole amusement was watching his feet, his hands behind his back, his soft hat down the back of his neck, and the ragged ends of his trousers trailing round the big boots.

He looked at Katty and then looked away; then looked at her again and said: 'Good morra.' Katty put her hands on the counter and said with a smile: 'How d'ye do?' 'Oh, all right,' said Con, as if he thought she was presuming. Ned didn't say anything. He was behind the counter of the bar in his shirt-sleeves.

'Two bottles of stout, i' ye plaze,' said Con with a take-it-or-leave-it air, planking down the two-shilling piece he had squeezed in the palm of one hand. Ned looked at the money and then at Con. Finally he turned to the shelves and poured out three stiff glasses of Irish.

'Porter is a cold drink between relations,' he said in his kind, lazy way.

'Begor, 'tis true for you,' said Con, resting his two elbows on the counter while his whole face lit up with a roguish smile. ' 'Tis a thin, cold, unneighbourly Protestant sort of drink.'

After that Con and his brother Tom dropped in regularly. Tom was secretary of some political organization and, though very uncouth, able to hold his own by sheer dint of brass, but Con was uncouth without any qualification. He sat with one knee in the air and his hands locked about it as if he had sprained his ankle, or crouched forward with his hands joined between his legs in a manner that Katty would have been too ladylike to describe, and he jumped from one position to another as if a flea had bitten him. When she gave him salad for tea he handed it back to her. 'Take that away and gi' me a bit o' mate, i' ye plaze,' he said with no shyness at all. And the funny thing was that Ned, who in his old-fashioned way knew so much better, only smiled. When he was going, Ned always slipped a packet of cigarettes into his pocket, but Con always pulled them out again. 'What are thim? Faga? Chrisht! Ah, the blessings of God on you!' And then he smiled his rogue's smile, rubbed his hands vigorously, lowered his head as if he were going to butt the first man he met, and plunged out into the street.

It was easy to see how the plot was developing. She was a year married and no child!

2

One day a few weeks later Katty heard a scuffle. She looked out the shop window and saw Jerry with the two boys holding him by the arms while he let on to be trying to break free of them.

'Come on, come on, and don't be making a show of us!' said Tom angrily.

'I don't give a Christ in hell,' cried his father in a shrill tremolo, his wild blue eyes sweeping the sunlit street in every direction except the shop. 'I'll go where I'm asked.'

'You'll go where you're told,' said Con with great glee – clearly he thought his father was a great card. 'Come on, you ould whore you, come on!'

Ned heard the scuffle and leaned over the counter to see what it was. He gave no sign of being moved by it. There was a sort of monumental dignity about Ned, about the slowness of his thoughts, the depth of his sentiment, and the sheer volume of his voice, which enabled him to time a scene with the certainty of an old stage hand. He lifted the flap of the counter and moved slowly out into the centre of the shop and then stopped and held out his hand. That, by the way, did it. Jerry gave a whinny like a young colt and sprang to take the proffered hand. They stood like that for a full minute, moryah they were too overcome to speak! Katty watched them with a bitter little smile.

'You know the fair lady of my choice,' said Ned at last.

'I'm very glad to meet you, ma'am,' said Jerry, turning his knife-blue eyes on her, his dropped chin and his high, small perfect teeth making it sound like the greeting of a well-bred weasel to a rabbit. They all retired to the back parlour, where Katty brought the drinks. The atmosphere was maudlin. After arranging for Katty and himself to spend the next Sunday at the farm, Ned escorted them down the street. When he came back there were tears in his eyes – a foolish man!

'Well,' he said, standing in the middle of the shop with his hands behind his back and his bowler hat well down over his eyes, ''twas nice being all under the one roof again.'

'It must have been grand,' said Katty, affecting to be very busy. 'I suppose 'twas Father Ring did it,' she added over her shoulder with subtle mockery.

'Ah,' said Ned, looking stolidly out at the sunlit street with swimming eyes, 'we're getting older and wiser. What fools people are to embitter their lives about nothing! There won't be much politics where we're going.'

'I wonder if 'tis that,' said Katty, as if she were talking to herself while inwardly she fumed at the stupidity of the man.

'Ah, what else could it be?' asked Ned, wrapped up in whatever sentimental fantasies he was weaving.

'I suppose 'twould never be policy?' she asked archly, looking up from under her brows with a knowing smile.

'How could it be policy, woman?' asked Ned, his voice harsh with indignation. 'What has he to gain by policy?'

'Ah, how would I know?' she said, reaching towards a high shelf. 'He might be thinking of the shop for Con.'

'He'd be thinking a very long way ahead,' said Ned after a pause, but she saw it had gone home.

'Maybe he's hoping 'twouldn't be so long,' she said smoothly.

'How's that?' said Ned.

'Julia, God rest her, went very suddenly,' said Katty.

'He'd be a very foolish man to count on me doing the same,' boomed Ned, but his face grew purple from shame and anger – shame that he had no children of his own, anger that she had pricked the sentimental bubble he had blown about Jerry and the boys.

It was a warning to Katty. Twice in the next year she satisfied herself that she was having a baby, and each time put the whole house into confusion. She lay upstairs on the sofa with a handbell at her side, made baby clothes, ordered the cradle, even got an option on a pram. To secure herself against accidents she slept in the spare room. And then it passed off and with a look like murder she returned to the big bedroom. Ned stared at her over the bedclothes with an incredulous, long-suffering air and then heaved a heavy sigh and turned in.

She knew he blamed her. After being taken in like that it would be weeks before he started again. Weaker sex, indeed! One would think it was he that was trying to start the baby. But Katty blamed herself as well. It was the final year in Dublin and the goings-on with the drunken medico that had finished her. For days on end she sat over the range in the kitchen with a little shawl over her shoulders, shivering and tight-lipped, taking little tots of brandy when Ned's back was turned and complaining of him to the servant girl. To make it worse, the daughter of another shopkeeper came home on holidays from England; a nurse with fast, flighty ways that appealed to Ned. He was always in and out there, full of old-fashioned gallantries. He kissed her hand and even called her 'a rose'. It reached Katty's ears and she clamped her lips. She was far too well bred to make vulgar scenes. Instead, with her feet on the fender, hands joined in her lap, she asked in the most casual friendly way:

'Ned, do you think that was a proper remark to make to the Dunne girl?'

'What remark?' asked Ned, growing crimson – it showed his guilty conscience.

'Well, Ned, you can hardly pretend you don't know, considering that the whole town is talking about it.'

'Are you mad, woman?' he shouted, his voice brassy with rage.

'I only asked a simple question, Ned,' she said with resignation, fixing him with her clear blue eyes. 'Of course, if you prefer not to answer there's no more to be said.'

'You have me driven distracted!' cried Ned. 'I can't be polite to a neighbour's daughter but you sulk for days on me.'

'Polite!' said Katty to the range. 'However,' she added, 'I suppose I have no cause to complain. The man that would do worse to me wouldn't be put out by a little thing like that.'

'Do worse to you?' shouted Ned, going purple as if he was in danger of congestion. 'What did I ever do to you?'

'Aren't you planning to leave me in my old age without a roof over my head?' she asked suddenly, turning on him.

'I'm not planning to leave anything to anyone yet,' roared Ned. 'With the help of the Almighty God, when I do 'twill be to a child of my own.'

'Indeed, I hope so,' said Katty, 'but after all, if the worst came to the worst –'

'If the worst came to the worst,' he interrupted solemnly, 'we don't know which of us the Lord – glory and praise to His holy name – might take first.'

'Amen, O Lord,' breathed Katty piously, and then went on in her original tone. 'I'm not saying you'll be the first to go, and the way I am, Ned,' she added bitterly, 'I wouldn't wish it. But 'tis only common prudence to be prepared for the worst. You know yourself how Julia went.'

'My God,' he said mournfully, addressing his remarks out the empty hall, 'the foolishness of it! We have only a few short years on the earth; we come and go like the leaves of the trees, and instead of enjoying ourselves, we wear our hearts out with planning and contriving.'

'Ah, Ned,' she said, goaded to fury, as she always was by his philosophizing and poetry talk, ''tis easy it comes to you. I only wish the money would come as easy. I didn't work myself to the bone in the shop to be left a beggar in my old age.'

'A beggar?' he cried. 'Do you think I wouldn't provide for you?'

'Provide for me?' she gibed. 'Con Lynch in the shop and me in the back room! Fine provisions I'd get!'

'I never said I'd leave it to Con Lynch,' said Ned chokingly.

'Then what is he coming here for?' she shrieked, suddenly bounding into the middle of the kitchen and spreading out her arms. 'What is he doing in my home? Can't you do what any other man would do and let them know you're leaving the shop to me?'

'I can't,' he shouted back, 'and you know I can't.'

'Why not?' she said, stamping.

'Because 'tis an old custom. The property goes with the name.'

'Not with the people I was brought up with,' she said proudly.

'Well, 'twas with those I was brought up with,' said Ned. 'Women as good as you were satisfied. Ay, and better than you! Better than you,' he added with a backward glance as he went out.

She dropped back beaten into her chair. She was afraid to cross him further. He looked like a man that might drop dead at any moment. She was only a stranger, a foreigner, with no link at all between herself and him. Con Lynch was more to him now than she was. It was only then she realized it was time to stop looking after the shop and look after herself instead.

In the autumn she said she was going to Dublin to see a specialist. Ned didn't say anything to dissuade her, but it was clear he had no faith in it. She didn't see a specialist. Instead she saw a nurse she had known in Dublin, another old flame of the medico's. Nurse O'Mara kept a maternity home on the canal. She was a tall, handsome woman with a fine figure and a long face that was growing just the least shade hard. She listened to Katty with screwed-up eyes and a good-natured smile. She was tickled by the situation. After all, if she hadn't got much out of the medico, Katty hadn't got much more.

'And you don't think that 'tis any use?' asked Katty doubtfully.

'I wouldn't say so,' said the nurse.

'And I suppose there's nothing else I can do?' asked Katty in a low voice and an almost playful tone, never taking her blue eyes from the nurse's face.

'Unless you'd borrow one,' said the nurse mockingly.

'That's what I mean,' said Katty slyly.

'You're not serious?' said the nurse, her smile withering.

'Haven't I reason?' asked Katty, her smile growing broader.

'You'd never get away with it.'

'Why not, girl?' asked Katty almost inaudibly. 'Who's to know? If there was someone that was willing?'

'Oh, hundreds of them,' said the nurse, with the bitterness of the childless woman.

'You'd know where to find one I could ask,' murmured Katty, still with her eyes steadily fixed.

'I suppose so,' said the nurse doubtfully. 'There's nothing illegal about it. I'm not supposed to know what you're up to.'

'And to have my letters addressed to your place,' continued Katty.

'Why not?' asked Nurse O'Mara with a shrug. 'For that matter, you can come and stay any time you like.'

'That's all I want,' said Katty with blazing eyes. 'I have a hundred or so put on one side. I'll give it to you, and you can make whatever arrangements you like.'

She returned to town triumphant with two new hats, wider and more girlish than those she usually wore. Then she set about a reorganization of the house, running up and down stairs and chattering with the maid.

'Well?' said Ned lazily, interpreting her behaviour with a touch of anxiety. 'He gave you some hope?'

'I don't know if you'd call it hope,' said Katty, furrowing her brow. 'He thought I mightn't come out of it. Of course, I'll have to go back to him if anything happens.'

'But he thought it might?' asked Ned.

'Wisha,' said Katty, 'like the rest of them he wouldn't like to give an opinion.'

That, she saw, impressed Ned more than any more favourable verdict could have done. Almost from that on, he looked at her every morning with a solicitous, questioning air. Katty kept her mouth shut and went on with the housework. One night she said with her nunlike air: 'I think I'll sleep in the spare room for the present.' Even then she could see he only half believed her, but as the weeks passed, he started coming up to her in the evenings, settling the fire, and retailing whatever gobbets of gossip he had picked up in the bar. He started to tell her about his own boyhood, a thing he had never done before.

Jerry called once with Con and was brought upstairs with appropriate solemnity. She knew he had only come to see for himself, and she watched while the electric-blue eyes roved distractedly about the room till they alighted like a bluebottle on her stomach. That settled it so far as Jerry was concerned. He was crafty but not long-sighted. When the game looked like going against him he threw in his hand. He didn't come back, nor did

Tom, though Con dropped in once or twice out of pure good nature. To Katty's surprise, Ned noticed and resented it.

'Ah,' she said charitably, 'I wouldn't mind that. They're probably busy on the farm this weather.'

'They weren't so busy they couldn't go to Hartnett's,' said Ned, who made it his business to know all they did.

'Ah, well, Hartnett's is near enough to them,' said Katty, protesting against his unreasonableness.

'This place was near enough to them too when they thought they had a chance of the money,' said Ned resentfully.

She looked at him archly from under her brows. She felt the time was ripe to say what she had to say.

'They didn't send you any more anonymous letters?' she asked lightly.

'They can say what they like now,' said Ned, growing red.

Her smile faded as she watched him go out of the room. She knew now she had made herself secure against any suspicions the Lynches might have of her, but the change in Ned himself was something she hadn't allowed for and it upset her.

It even frightened her the day she was setting out for Dublin. She saw him in the bedroom packing a little case.

'What do you want that for?' she asked, going cold.

'You don't think I'm going to let you go to Dublin alone?' he replied.

'But I may be there for weeks,' she said despairingly.

'Ah, well,' he said as he continued to pack, 'I'm due a little holiday. I have it fixed up with Bridie.'

Katty sat on the bed and bit her lip. Somehow or other the Lynches had succeeded in instilling their suspicions into him and he was coming to see for himself. What could she do? Nothing. She knew O'Mara wouldn't be a party to any deception; it would be too much of a risk. 'Mother of God, direct me!' she prayed, joining her hands in her lap.

'You're not afraid I'll run off with a soldier?' she asked lightly.

'That's the very thing I am afraid of,' said Ned, turning round on her. Suddenly his eyes clouded with emotion. 'It won't be wishing to anyone that tries to get you,' he added, with a feeble attempt to keep up the joke.

'Wisha, Ned,' she cried, rushing across the room to him, her heart suddenly lightened of a load, ''tisn't the way you think anything will happen to me?'

'No, little girl,' he said, putting his arm about her. 'Nor I wouldn't wish it for a thousand pounds.'

'Ah, is it a fine strong woman like me?' she cried skittishly, almost insane with relief. 'What fear there is of me! Maybe I'll let you come up when the next one is arriving.'

3

From Kingsbridge she took a taxi to the maternity home and got rid of some of her padding on the way. O'Mara opened the door for her herself. Katty sat on the edge of a sofa by the window, her hands joined in her lap, and looked expectantly up at the nurse.

'Well,' she asked in a low voice, 'any luck?'

'You'd better not try this game on too often,' said O'Mara with amusement. 'You'd never get past me with that complexion.'

'I'm not likely to try, am I?' asked Katty complacently. 'That girl you wrote about,' she added in the same conspiratorial tone, 'is she still here?'

'She is. You can see her now.'

'I suppose you don't know anything about her?' Katty asked wistfully.

'She's a school-teacher,' replied the nurse cautiously.

'Oh, Law!' said Katty in surprise. She hadn't expected anyone of her own class; it sounded too good to be true; and as plain as if it were written there, her pinched little face registered the doubt whether there wasn't a catch in it somewhere. 'I don't know her by any chance, do I?' she added innocently.

'I hope not,' replied the nurse smoothly. 'What you don't know won't harm you.'

'Oh, I'm not asking for information,' protested Katty a shade too eagerly. 'But you think she'll agree?' she said, dropping her voice again.

'She'll be a fool if she doesn't.'

'Of course, I'll pay her well,' said Katty. 'I wouldn't ask anyone to do a thing like that for nothing.'

'I wouldn't mention that, if I was you,' said O'Mara dryly. 'She's not trying to make a profit on it.'

'Oh,' said Katty, suddenly beginning to shiver all over, 'I'd give all I ever had in the world to be out of it.'

'But why?' asked O'Mara in surprise. 'You're over the worst of it now.'

'It's Ned,' said Katty with a haggard look. 'He'd murder me.'

'Ah, well,' said O'Mara with gruff kindness, 'it's a bit late in the day to be thinking of that,' and she led Katty up the stairs past a big Venetian window that lit the well and overlooked the canal bank. The lights were already lit outside. Through the trees she saw brown-red houses with flights of steps leading to hall doors, and a hump-backed limestone bridge.

There was a girl in bed in the room they entered; a young woman of twenty-eight or thirty with a plump pale face and a helmet of limp brown hair. Her face at any rate was innocent enough.

'This is the lady I was speaking about, Monica,' said the nurse with a crooked smile. (Obviously she took a certain malicious pleasure in the whole business.) 'I'll leave ye to discuss it for a while.'

She went out, switching on the electric light as she did. Katty shook hands with the girl and then glanced shyly at the cot.

'Oh, isn't he lovely?' she cried with genuine admiration.

'He's sweet,' said the girl called Monica, in a curiously common voice, and then reached out for a cigarette.

'I never smoke, thanks,' said Katty, and then hastily drew a chair over to the bed, resting her hands on her lap and smiling under her big hat in a guilty, schoolgirl way that was curiously attractive.

'I suppose,' she said, throwing back her head, 'you must think I'm simply terrible?'

It wasn't intended to be a good opening but it turned out that way. The girl smiled, and her broad face crinkled.

'And what about me?' she asked, putting them both at once on a common level. 'Will you get away with it though?'

'Oh, I'll have to get away with it, girl,' said Katty flatly. 'My livelihood depends on it. Did nurse tell you?'

'She did, but I still don't understand what you did to your husband to make him do that to you.'

'Oh, that's an old custom,' said Katty eagerly, seeing at once the doubt in the girl's mind. 'Now, I know what you're thinking,' she added with a smile, raising her finger in warning, 'but 'tisn't that at all. Ned isn't a bit like that. I won't wrong him. He is a country boy, and he hasn't the education, but apart from that he's the best poor slob that ever lived.' She was surprised herself at the warmth that crept into her voice when she spoke of him. 'So you see,' she added, dropping her voice and smiling discreetly, 'you needn't be a bit afraid of us. We'd both be mad about him.'

'Strange as it may seem,' said Monica, her voice growing sullen and resentful, 'I'm a bit mad about him myself.'

'Oh, you are, to be sure,' said Katty warmly. 'What other way would you be?' At the same time she was bitterly disappointed. She began to realize that it wasn't going to be so easy after all. Worse than that, she had taken a real fancy to the baby. The mother, whatever her faults, was beautiful; she was an educated woman; you could see she wasn't common. 'Of course,' she added, shaking her head, 'the idea would never have crossed my mind only that nurse thought you might be willing. And then, I felt it was like God's doing. . . . You are one of us, I suppose?' she asked, raising her brows discreetly.

'God alone knows what I am,' said the girl, taking a deep pull of the cigarette. 'A bloody atheist or something.'

'Oh, how could you?' asked Katty in a shocked tone. 'You're convent-educated, aren't you?'

'Mm.'

'I'd know a convent girl anywhere,' said Katty, shaking her head with an admiring smile. 'You can always tell. I went to the Ursulines myself. But you see what I mean? There was I looking for a child to adopt, and you looking for a home for yours, and Nurse O'Mara bringing us together. It seemed like God's doing.'

'I don't know what you want bringing God into it for,' said Monica impatiently. 'The devil would do as well.'

'Ah,' said Katty with a knowing smile, 'that's only because you're feeling weak. . . . But tell me,' she added, still wondering whether there wasn't a catch in it, 'I'm not being curious or anything – but isn't it a wonder the priest wouldn't make him marry you?'

'Who told you he wouldn't marry me?' asked Monica quietly.

'Oh, Law!' cried Katty, feeling that this was probably the catch. 'Was it the way he was beneath you?' she asked with the least shade of disappointment.

'Not that I know of,' said Monica brassily. Then she turned her eyes to the ceiling and blew out another cloud of smoke. 'He asked me was I sure he was the father,' she added lightly, almost as if it amused her.

'Fancy that!' said Katty in bewilderment. 'But what made him say that, I wonder.'

'It seems,' said Monica in the same tone, 'he thought I was going with another fellow at the same time.'

'And you weren't?' said Katty knowingly.

'Not exactly,' said Monica dryly, giving Katty a queer look that she didn't quite understand.

'And you wouldn't marry him?' said Katty, knowing perfectly well that the girl was only trying to take advantage of her simplicity. Katty wasn't as big a fool as that though. 'Hadn't you great courage?' she added.

'Oh, great,' said Monica in the same ironic tone.

'The dear knows,' said Katty regretfully, thinking of her own troubles with the medico, 'they're a handful, the best of them! But are you sure you're not being hasty?' she added with girlish coyness, cocking her little head. 'Don't you think when you meet him again and he sees the baby, ye might make it up?'

'If I thought that,' said the girl deliberately, 'I'd walk out of this into the canal, and the kid along with me.'

'Oh, Law!' said Katty, feeling rather out of her depth and the least bit frightened. At the same time she now wanted the baby with something like passion. It was the same sort of thing she sometimes felt at auctions for little gewgaws from women's dressing-tables or bits of old china; as if she couldn't live without it. No other child would ever satisfy her. She'd bid up to the last farthing for it – if only she knew what to bid.

Then Nurse O'Mara came back and leaned on the end of the bed, her knees bent and her hands clasped.

'Well,' she asked, looking from one to the other with a mocking smile, 'how did ye get on?'

'Oh, grand, nurse,' said Katty with sudden gaiety. 'We were only waiting for yourself to advise us.'

'Why?' asked the nurse. 'What is there between ye?'

'Only that I don't want to part with him,' said Monica steadily.

'Aren't you tired of him yet?' asked the nurse ironically.

'Jesus, woman, be a bit human!' said Monica with exasperation. 'He's all I have and I had trouble enough having him.'

'That's nothing to the trouble you'll have keeping him,' said the nurse.

'I know that well enough,' said Monica in a more reasonable tone, 'but

I want to be able to see him. I want to know that he's well and happy.'

'Oh, if that's all that's troubling you,' said Katty eagerly, 'you can see him as much as you like at our place.'

'She could not,' said the nurse angrily. 'The less the pair of you see of one another, the better for both. . . . Listen, Mon,' she said pleadingly, 'I don't care what you do. I'm only speaking for your good.'

'I know that, Peggy,' said Monica.

'I know you think you're going to do marvels for that kid, but you're not. I know the sort of places they're brought up in and the sort that bring them up – the ones that live. I tell you, after the first time, you wouldn't be so keen on seeing him again.'

Monica was staring at the window, which had faded in the pale glare of the electric light. There was silence for a few moments. Katty heard the night wind whistling across the rooftops from the bay. The trees along the canal heard it too and sighed. Something about it impressed her; the wind, and the women's voices, and the sleeping baby, and the heart contracted inside her as she thought of Ned, waiting at home. She pulled herself together with fictitious brightness.

'Now, nurse,' she said firmly, 'it isn't fair to push the young lady too hard. We'll give her till tomorrow night, and I'll say a prayer to Our Lady of Good Counsel to direct her.'

'I'll give her all the good counsel she wants,' said the nurse coarsely. 'If you're thinking of yourself, Monica, you might as well say no now. We won't have to look far for someone else. If you're thinking of the kid and want to give him a fair chance in life after bringing him into it, you'd better say yes while you have the chance.'

Monica suddenly turned her face away, her eyes filling with tears.

'She can have him,' she said in a dull voice.

'Oh, thank you, thank you,' said Katty eagerly. 'And I give you my word you'll never have cause to regret it.'

'But for Christ's sake don't leave him in the room with me tonight,' cried the girl, leaping up in bed and turning her wild eyes on Nurse O'Mara. 'I'm warning ye now, don't leave him where I can lay my hands on him. I tell ye I won't be responsible.'

Katty bit her lip and her face went white.

'There's supper waiting for you downstairs,' said the nurse, beckoning her to go.

'You're sure I couldn't be of any assistance?' whispered Katty.

'Certain,' said the nurse dryly.

As Katty turned to look back, the girl threw herself down again, holding her head in her hands. The nurse from the end of the bed looked at her with a half-mocking, half-pitying smile, the smile of a childless woman. The baby was still asleep.

Michael's Wife

The station – it is really only a siding with a shed – was empty but for the station-master and himself. When he saw the station-master change his cap he rose. From far away along the water's edge came the shrill whistle of the train before it puffed into view with its leisurely air that suggested a trot.

Half a dozen people alighted and quickly dispersed. In a young woman wearing a dark-blue coat who lingered and looked up and down the platform he recognized Michael's wife. At the same moment she saw him but her face bore no smile of greeting. It was the face of a sick woman.

'Welcome, child,' he said, and held out his hand. Instead of taking it, she threw her arms about him and kissed him. His first impulse was to discover if anyone had noticed, but almost immediately he felt ashamed of the thought. He was a warm-hearted man and the kiss silenced an initial doubt. He lurched out before her with the trunk while she carried the two smaller bags.

' 'Tis a long walk,' he said with embarrassment.

'Why?' she asked wearily. 'Can't I drive with you?'

'You'd rather have McCarthy's car but 'tisn't back from Cork yet.'

'I would not. I'd rather drive with you.'

' 'Tis no conveyance,' he said angrily, referring to the old cart. Nevertheless he was pleased. She mounted from behind and sat on her black trunk. He lifted himself in after her, and they jolted down the village with the bay on their left. Beyond the village the road climbed a steep hill. Through a hedge of trees the bay grew upon the sight with a wonderful brightness because of the dark canopy of leaves. On and up, now to right, now to left, till the trees ceased, the bay disappeared over the brow of a hill, and they drove along a sunlit upland road with sunken fences. Hills like mattresses rose to their right, a brilliant green except where they were broken by cultivated patches or clumps of golden furze; a bog, all brown with bright pools and tall grey reeds, flanked the road.

'Ye were in about eight, I'd say,' he commented, breaking the silence.

'Oh yes. About that.'

'I seen ye.'

'You did?'

'I was on the look out. When she rounded the head I ran in and told the wife "Your daughter-in-law's coming." She nearly had me life when she seen 'twas only the ould liner.'

The girl smiled.

'Ah, now,' he added proudly, a moment later, 'there's a sight for you!'

She half raised herself on the edge of the cart and looked in the direction his head indicated. The land dropped suddenly away from beneath their feet, and the open sea, speckled white with waves and seagulls' wings, stretched out before them. The hills, their smooth flanks patterned with the varying colours of the fields, flowed down to it in great unbroken curves, and the rocks looked very dark between their wind-flawed brightness and the brightness of the water. In little hollows nestled houses and cottages, diminutive and quaint and mostly of a cold, startling whiteness that was keyed up here and there by the spring-like colour of fresh thatch. In the clear air the sea was spread out like a great hall with all its folding doors thrown wide; a dancing floor, room beyond room, each narrower and paler than the last, till on the farthest reaches steamers that were scarcely more than dots jerked to and fro as on a wire.

Something in the fixity of the girl's pose made Tom Shea shout the mare to a standstill.

' 'Tis the house beyond,' he said, brandishing his stick. 'The one with the slate roof on the hill.'

With sudden tenderness he looked quizzically down at her from under his black hat. This stranger girl with her American clothes and faintly American accent was his son's wife and would some day be the mother of his grandchildren. Her hands were gripping the front of the cart. She was weeping. She made no effort to restrain herself or conceal her tears, nor did she turn her eyes from the sea. He remembered a far-away evening when he had returned like this, having seen off his son.

'Yes,' he said after a moment's silence. ' 'Tis so, 'tis so.'

A woman with a stern and handsome face stood in the doorway. As everything in Tom seemed to revolve about a fixed point of softness; his huge frame, his comfortable paunch, his stride, his round face with the shrewd, brown, twinkling eyes and the big grey moustache, so everything in her seemed to obey a central reserve. Hers was a nature refined to the point of hardness, and while her husband took colour from everything about him, circumstances or acquaintance would, you felt, leave no trace on her.

One glance was enough to show her that he had already surrendered. She, her look said, would not give in so easily. But sooner than he she recognized the signals of fatigue.

'You're tired out, girl!' she exclaimed.

'I am,' replied the younger woman, resting her forehead in her hands as though to counteract a sudden giddiness. In the kitchen she removed her hat and coat and sat at the head of the table where the westering light caught her. She wore a pale-blue frock with a darker collar. She was very dark, but the pallor of illness had bleached the dusk from her skin. Her cheekbones were high so that they formed transparencies beneath her eyes. It was a very Irish face, long and spiritual, with an inherent melancholy that might dissolve into sudden anger or equally sudden gaiety.

'You were a long time sick,' said Maire Shea, tossing a handful of brosna on the fire.

'I was.'

'Maybe 'twas too soon for you to travel?'

'If I didn't, I'd have missed the summer at home.'

'So Michael said, so Michael said.'

'Ah,' declared Tom with burning optimism, 'you won't be long pulling round now, with God's help. There's great air here, powerful air.'

'You'll be finding us rough, simple poor people,' added his wife with dignity, taking from him a parcel that contained a cheap glass sugar-bowl to replace the flowered mug without a handle that had served them till now. 'We're not used to your ways nor you to ours but we have a great will to please you.'

'We have,' agreed Tom heartily. 'We have indeed.'

The young woman ate nothing, only sipped her tea that smelled of burnt wood, and it was clear, as when she tried to pour milk from the large jug, that she was completely astray in her new surroundings. And that acute sense of her discomfort put a strain on the two old people, on Tom especially, whose desire to make a good impression was general and strong.

After tea she went upstairs to rest. Maire came with her.

' 'Tis Michael's room,' she said. 'And that's Michael's bed.'

It was a bare, green-washed room with a low window looking on to the front of the house, an iron bed and an oleograph of the Holy Family. For a moment an old familiar feeling of wild jealousy stole over Maire Shea, but when the girl, in undressing, exposed the scar across her stomach, she felt guilty.

'You'll sleep now,' she said softly.

'I ought to.'

Maire stole down the straight stair. Tom was standing in the doorway, his black hat over his eyes, his hands clasped behind his back.

'Well?' he asked in a whisper.

'Whist!' she replied irritably. 'She shouldn't be travelling at all. I don't know what come over Michael, and to leave her and he knowing well we have no facility. The cut in her stomach – 'tis the length of your arm.'

'Would I run up and tell Kate not to come? Herself and Joan will be in soon.'

' 'Twould be no use. All the neighbours will be in.'

'So they will, so they will,' he admitted in a depressed tone.

He was very restless. After a while he stole upstairs and down again on tiptoe.

'She's asleep. But whisper, Moll, she must have been crying.'

' 'Tis weakness.'

'Maybe she'd be lonely.'

' 'Tis weakness, 'tis weakness. She should never be travelling.'

Later Kate and Joan arrived and after them three or four other women. Twilight fell within the long whitewashed kitchen; and still they talked in subdued voices. Suddenly the door on the stair opened and Michael's wife appeared. She seemed to have grown calmer, though she still retained something of the air of a sleepwalker, and in the half-light with her jet-black eyes and hair, her long pale face had a curious ethereal beauty.

The sense of strain was very noticeable. Tom fussed about her in a helpless fidgety way till the women, made nervous by it, began to mock and scold him. Even then a question put at random caused him to fret.

'Can't ye leave her alone now, can't ye? Can't ye see she's tired? Go on with yeer ould talk, leave ye, and don't be bothering her any more.'

'No, no,' she said. 'I'm not so tired now.' Her voice retained a memory of her native Donegal in a certain dry sweetness.

'Have a sup of this,' urged Tom. 'A weeshy sup – 'twill do you no harm.'

She refused the drink, but two of the other women took it, and Tom, having first toasted 'her lovely black eyes', drank a glass without pausing for breath. He gave a deep sigh of content.

> 'The curate was drunk and the midwife was tipsy
> And I was baptized in a basin of whiskey,'

he hummed. He refilled his glass before sitting down beside the open door. The sky turned deep and deeper blue above the crown of a tree that looked in the low doorway and a star winked at the window-pane. Maire rose and lit the wall-lamp with its tin reflector. From far away in a lag between two headlands a voice was calling and calling on a falling cadence 'Taaaamie! Taaaamie!' and in the distance the call had a remote and penetrating sweetness. When it ceased there came to their ears the noise of the sea, and suddenly it was night. The young woman drew herself up. All were silent. One of the women sighed. The girl looked up, throwing back her head.

'I'm sorry, neighbours,' she said. 'I was only a child when I left Ireland and it's all strange to me now.'

' 'Tis surely,' replied Kate heartily. ' 'Tis lonely for you. You're every bit as strange as we'd be in the heart of New York.'

'Just so, just so,' exclaimed Tom with approval.

'Never mind,' continued Kate. 'You have me to take your part.'

'You be damned!' retorted Tom in mock indignation. 'No one is going to look after that girl but meself.'

'A deal she have to expect from either of ye!' added Maire coldly. 'It wouldn't occur to ye she should be in bed.'

She dipped a candle in the fire and held it above her head. The girl followed her. The others sat on and talked; then all took their leave together. Maire, busy about the house and yard for a long time, heard voices and footsteps coming back to her on the light land wind.

She was thinking in her dispassionate way of Michael's wife. She had thought of her often before, but now she found herself at sea. It wasn't only that the girl was a stranger and a sick one at that, but – and this Maire had never allowed for – she was the child of a strange world, the atmosphere of which had come with her, disturbing judgement. Less clearly than Kate or Tom, yet clearly enough, she realized that the girl was as strange amongst them as they would be in New York. In the bright starlight a cluster of whitewashed cottages stood out against the hillside like a frame of snow about its orange window-squares. For the first time Maire looked at it, and with a strange feeling of alienation wondered what it was like to one unused to it.

A heavy step startled her. She turned in to see that Tom had disappeared. Heated with drink and emotion he had tiptoed up the stairs and opened the girl's door. He was surprised to find her sitting on the low window-ledge in her dressing-gown. From the darkness she was looking out with strange eyes on the same scene Maire had been watching with eyes grown too familiar, hills, whitewashed cottages and sea.

'Are 'oo awake?' he asked – a stupid question.

'Wisha, for goodness' sake will you come down and leave the girl sleep?' came Maire's voice in irritation from the foot of the stairs.

'No, no, no,' he whispered nervously.

'What is it?' asked the girl.

'Are 'oo all right?'

'Quite, thanks.'

'We didn't disturb 'oo?'

'Not at all.'

'Come down out of that, you ould fool!' cried Maire in an exasperated tone.

'I'm coming, I'm coming – Jasus, can't you give us a chance?' he added angrily. 'Tell me,' this in a whisper, 'the ould operation, 'twon't come again you?'

He bent over her, hot and excited, his breath smelling of whiskey.

'I don't understand you.'

'Ah,' he said in the same low tone, 'wouldn't it be a terrible misfortune? A terrible misfortune entirely! 'Tis great life in a house, a child is.'

'Oh, no,' she answered hastily, nervously, as though she were growing afraid.

'Are 'oo sure? What did the doctors say?'

'It won't, it won't.'

'Ah, glory be to the hand of God!' he said turning away, ''tis a great ease to my mind to know that. A great ease! A great ease! I'm destroyed thinking of it.'

He stumbled downstairs to face his wife's anger that continued long after he had shut up the house for the night. She had a bitter tongue when she chose to use it, and she chose now. For weeks they had been screwing themselves up, to make a good impression on Michael's wife, and now it was spoiled by a drunken fool of a man.

He turned and tossed, unable to sleep at the injustice of it. As though a man wouldn't want to know a thing like that, as though he mightn't ask his own daughter-in-law a civil question, without being told he was worse than a black, a heathen savage from Africa, without niceness or consideration except for his own dirty gut!

He, Tom Shea, who tried to leave a good impression on every hog, dog and devil that came the road!

2

In the morning Michael's wife was somewhat better. The sun appeared only at intervals, but for the greater part of the day she was able to sit by the gable where she had a view of the sea in shelter from the wind. A stream ran just beneath her, and a hedge of fuchsia beside it bordered a narrow stony laneway leading to the strand. The chickens raced about her with a noise like distant piping and from the back of the house came the complaining voice of a hen saying without pause, 'Oh, God! God! God! God!'

Occasionally Maire came and sat beside her on a low stool. Maire asked no questions – her pride again – and the conversation was strained, almost hostile, until the girl became aware of what ailed her: curiosity for the minute trifles of their life in America, hers and Michael's; the details that had become so much part of her that she found it difficult to remember them. How much the maid was paid, how the milk was delivered, the apartment house with its central heating, the negro lift-hop, the street-cars and the rest of it. At last her mind seemed to embrace the old woman's vivid and unlettered mind trying to construct a picture of the world in which her son lived, and she continued to talk for the sake of talking, as though the impersonality of it was a relief.

It was different when at dinner-time Tom came in from the strand in a dirty old shirt and pants, his black hat well forward on his eyes.

'Listen, girleen,' he said in a gruff voice, very different from that of the previous night, as with legs crossed and hands joined behind his back he leaned against the wall. 'Tell that husband of yours he should write oftener to his mother. Women are like that. If 'twas your own son now, you'd understand.'

'I know, I know,' she said hastily.

'Of course you do. You're a fine big-hearted girl, and don't think we're not thankful to you. The wife now, she's a fine decent woman but she have queer ways. She wouldn't thank God Almighty if she thought He was listening, and she'll never say it to you but she said it to others, how good you are to us.'

'Don't blame Michael,' she replied in a low voice. 'It isn't his fault.'

'I know, sure, I know.'

'He never has time.'

'Mention it to him though, you! Mention it to him. The letter to say you were coming, 'twas the first we had from himself for months. Tell him 'tis his mother, not me at all.'

'If you only knew how he wanted to come!' she exclaimed with a troubled glance.

'Yes, yes, yes; but 'twill be two years more before he can. Two years to one at his hour of life 'tis only like tomorrow, but for old people that never know the time or the place . . . ! And that same, it may be the last he'll see of one or the other of us. And we've no one but him, girleen, more's the pity.'

It was certainly different with Tom, who had but one approach to any situation.

In a few days she had regained something of her strength. Tom cut her a stout ashplant and she went for short walks, to the strand, to the little harbour or to the post office which was kept by Tom's sisters. Mostly she went alone. To his delight the weather turned showery, but it never completely broke.

All day long the horizon was peopled by a million copper-coloured cloudlets, rounded and tiny and packed back to the very limits of the sky like cherubs in a picture of the Madonna. Then they began to swell, bubble on bubble, expanding, changing colour; one broke away from the mass and then another; it grew into a race; they gathered, sending out dark streamers that blackened the day and broke the patina of the water with dark-green stormy paths; lastly, a shrill whistle of wind and wild driving rain enveloped everything in mist. She took shelter under a rock or at the lee-side of a fence, and watched the shower dissolve in golden points of light that grew into a sunlit landscape beyond, as the clouds like children in frolic terror scampered back pell-mell to the horizon, the blue strip of sky they left broadening, the rain thinning, the fields and sea stripping off their scum of shadow till everything was sparkling and steaming again.

What it meant to her they could only guess when she returned. Whenever she remained too long in the house the shadow came on her again. Kate bade them take no notice.

She seemed to be very drawn towards Kate. Her walks often took her to the post office, and there she sat for hours with the two sisters, frequently sharing their meals, and listening to Kate's tales of old times in the parish, about her parents and her brother Tom, but most frequently about Michael's youth.

Kate was tall and bony with a long nose, long protruding chin and wire spectacles. Her teeth, like her sister's, were all rotten. She was the sort country people describe as having a great heart, a masterful woman, always busy, noisy and good-humoured. Tom, who was very proud of her, told how she had gone off for a major operation carrying a basket of eggs to sell so that she wouldn't have her journey for nothing. Her sister Joan was a nun-like creature who had spent some time in an asylum. She had a wonderfully soft, round, gentle face with traces of a girlish complexion, a voice that seldom rose above a whisper and the most lovely eyes; but when the cloud came on her she was perverse and obstinate. On the wall of the living-room, cluttered thick with pictures, was a framed sampler in ungainly lettering, 'Eleanor Joan Shea, March 1881.' She was nominally postmistress but it was Kate who did the work.

As much as Michael's wife took to them, they took to her. Joan would have wept her eyes out for a homeless dog, but Kate's sympathy was marked by a certain shrewdness.

'You had small luck in your marriage,' she said once.

'How?' The young woman looked at her blankly.

'For all you're only married a year you had your share of trouble. No honeymoon, then the sickness and now the separation.'

'You're right. It's nothing but separations.'

'Ye had only seven months together?'

'Only seven.'

'Ah, God help you, I never saw a lonelier creature than you were the night you came. But that's how we grow.'

'Is it, I wonder?'

' 'Tis, 'tis. Don't I know it?'

'That's what Father Coveney says,' wailed Joan, 'but I could never understand it myself. All the good people having all the misfortunes that don't deserve them, and the bad ones getting off.'

'You'll be happier for it in the latter end, and you've a good boy in Michael. . . . Musha, listen to me talking about Michael again. One'd think I was his mother.'

'You might be.'

'How so?'

'He has a lot of your ways.'

'Ah, now, I always said it! Didn't I, Joan? And why wouldn't he? When his mother leathered him 'twas up to me he came for comfort.'

'He often said it – you made a man of him.'

'I did,' said Kate proudly. 'I did so. Musha, he was a wild boy and there was no one to understand him when he was wild. His mother – not judging her – was born heavy with the weight of sense.'

Kate rarely lost the chance of a jeer at Maire.

'You're getting to like us, I think?' she said at last.

'I am,' admitted the girl. 'When I came first I was afraid.'

'You won't be so glad to get back to the States.'

'I wish I never saw the States again.'

'Och, aye!'

'It's true.'

'Ah, well. Two years more and ye'll be back together. And what's a couple of years to one of your age?'

'More than you think.'

'True, true, years are only as you feel them.'

'And I'll never come back here again.'

'Ach, bad cess to you, you're giving into it again! And now, listen to me. 'Tis a thing I often said to Tom Shea, why wouldn't ye come back? What's stopping ye? Never mind that ould fool telling you Michael wouldn't get a job! Why wouldn't he? And only Tom was such a gligin he'd never have left the boy go away.'

To Tom's disgust the weather cleared without heavy rain, though there was little sun, and that wandering, bursting out here and there on the hills or in mirror-like patches on the water and then fading into the same grey sultry light. Now, early and late, Michael's wife was out, sitting on the rocks or striding off to the village. She became a familiar figure on the roads in her blue dress with her ashplant. At first she stood far off, watching the men at the nets or sitting at the crossroads; as time went on she drew nearer, and one day a fisherman hailed her and spoke to her.

After that she went everywhere, into their houses, on to the quay and out in the boats when they went fishing. Maire Shea didn't like it, but all the men had known Michael as a boy and had tales of him and his knowledge of boats and fishing, and after a few days it was as though she too had grown up with them. It may be also that she gathered something from those hours on the water, in silent coves on grey days when the wind shook out a shoal of lights, or in the bay when the thunderous light moved swiftly, starting sudden hares of brightness from every hollow, blue from the hills, violet from the rocks, primrose from the fields, and here and there a mysterious milky glow that might be rock or field or tree. It may be these things deepened her knowledge so that she no longer felt a stranger when she walked in the morning along the strand, listening to the tide expand the great nets of weed with a crisp, gentle, pervasive sound like rain, or from her window saw the moon plunge its silver drill into the water.

But there was a decided change in her appearance and in her manner. She had filled out, her face had tanned and the gloomy, distraught air had left it.

'There,' said Tom, 'didn't I tell ye we'd make a new woman of her? Would anyone know her for the girl she was the night she came? Would they? I declare to me God, the time she opened the door and walked down the stairs I thought her own were calling.'

Kate and Joan, too, were pleased. They liked her for her own sake and Michael's sake, but they had come to love her for the sake of her youth and freshness. Only Maire held her peace. Nothing had ever quite bridged the gap between the two women; in every word and glance of hers there was an implicit question. It was some time before she succeeded in infecting Tom. But one day he came for comfort to Kate. He was downcast, and his shrewd brown eyes had a troubled look.

'Kate,' he said, going to the heart of things as his way was, ' 'tis about Michael's wife.'

'Och, aye! What about her?' asked Kate, pulling a wry face. ' 'Tisn't complaining you are?'

'No, but tell me what you think of her.'

'What I think?'

' 'Tis Maire.'

'Well?'

'She's uneasy.'

'Uneasy about what, aru?'

'She thinks the girl have something on her mind.'

'Tom Shea, I tell you now as I told you many a time before your wife is a suspicious woman.'

'Wisha, wisha, can't you forget all that? I never seen such a tribe for spite. We know ye never got on. But now, Kate, you can't deny she's a clever woman.'

'And what do the clever woman think?'

'She thinks the pair of them had a row; that's what she thinks now plain and straight, and I won't put a tooth in it.'

'I doubt it.'

'Well now, it might be some little thing a few words would put right.'

'And I'm to say the few words?'

'Now Kate, 'twas my suggestion, my suggestion entirely. The way 'tis with Moll, she'd say too much or say too little.'

'She would,' agreed Kate with grim amusement. Maire Shea had the reputation for doing both.

Next day she reported that the idea was absurd. He had to be content, for Kate too was no fool. But the question in Maire's manner never ceased to be a drag on him, and for this he did not know whether to blame her or the girl. Three weeks had passed and he began to find it intolerable. As usual he came to Kate.

'The worst of it is,' he said gloomily, 'she's making me as bad as herself. You know the sort I am. If I like a man, I don't want to be picking at what he says like an ould hen, asking "What did he mean by this?" or "What's he trying to get out of me now?" And 'tisn't that Moll says anything, but she have me so bothered I can hardly talk to the girl. Bad luck to it, I can't even sleep. . . . And last night – '

'What happened last night?'

He looked at her gloomily from under his brows.

'Are you making fun of me again?'

'I am not. What happened last night?'

'I heard her talking in her sleep.'

'Michael's wife?'

'Yes.'

'And what harm if she do in itself?'

'No harm at all!' howled Tom in a sudden rage, stamping up and down the kitchen and shaking his arms. 'No harm in the bloody world, but, Chrisht, woman, I tell you it upsot me.'

Kate looked at him over her wire spectacles with scorn and pity.

'Me mother's hood cloak that wasn't worn since the day she died, I must get it out for you. You'll never be a proper ould woman without it.'

'Moll,' said Tom that night as they were going to bed, 'you're dreaming.'

'How so?'

'About Michael's wife.'

'Maybe I am,' she admitted grudgingly, yet surprising him by any admission at all.

'You are,' he said to clinch it.

'I had my reasons. But this while past she's different. Likely Kate said something to her.'

'She did.'

'That explains it so,' said Maire complacently.

Two nights later he was wakened suddenly. It happened now that he did waken like that at any strange noise. He heard Michael's wife again speaking in her sleep. She spoke in a low tone that dwindled drowsily away into long silences. With these intervals the voice went on and on, very low, sometimes expressing – or so it seemed to him – a great joy, sometimes as it were pleading. But the impression it left most upon him was one of intimacy and tenderness. Next morning she came down late, her eyes red. That same day a letter came from Donegal. When she had read it she announced in a halting way that her aunt was expecting her.

'You won't be sorry to go,' said Maire, searching her with her eyes.

'I will,' replied the girl simply.

'If a letter comes for you!'

' 'Tisn't likely. Any letters there are will be at home. I never expected to stay so long.'

Maire gave her another long look. For the first time the girl gave it back, and for a moment they looked into one another's eyes, mother and wife.

'At first,' said Maire, turning her gaze to the fire, 'I didn't trust you. I'm a straight woman and I'll tell you that. I didn't trust you.'

'And now?'

'Right or wrong, whatever anyone may say, I think my son chose well for himself.'

'I hope you'll always think it,' replied the girl in the same serious tone. She looked at Maire, but the older woman's air repelled sentiment. Then she rose and went to the door. She stood there for a long time. The day was black and heavy, and at intervals a squall swept its shining net over the surface of the water.

And now the positions of Tom and his wife were reversed as frequently happens with two such extremes of temperament. Before dusk rain began to fall in torrents. He went out late to the post office and sat between his two sisters, arguing.

'There's a woman all out,' he said bitterly. 'She upsets me and then sits down on me troubles. What's on the girl's mind? There's something queer about her, something I can't make out. I've a good mind to send word to Michael.'

'And what would you say?' asked Kate. 'Disturbing him without cause! Can't you be sensible!'

'I can't be sensible,' he replied angrily. 'She's here in my charge and if anything happened her – '

'Nothing will happen her.'

'But if it did?'

'She's all right. She got back her health that none of us thought she would. Besides, she's going away.'

'That's what's worrying me,' he confessed. 'She'll leave me with the trouble on me, and I haven't the words to walk back and have it out with her.'

He returned late through the driving rain. The women had gone to bed. He turned in but could not sleep. The wind rose gradually from the squalls that shook the house and set the window-panes rattling.

All at once he caught it again, the damned talking. He lay perfectly still in order not to wake Maire. Long intervals of silence and then the voice again. In a sudden agony of fear he determined to get up and ask what was on her mind. Anything was better than the fear that was beginning to take hold of him. He lifted himself in the bed, hoping to crawl out over Maire's feet without waking her. She stirred, and he crouched there listening to the wind and the voice above his head, waiting till his wife should settle out again. And then, suddenly in a moment when wind and sea seemed to have died down to a murmur, the voice above him rose in three anguished mounting breaths that ended in a suppressed scream. 'Michael! Michael! Michael!'

With a groan he sank back and covered his eyes with his hands. He felt another hand coldly touching his forehead and his heart. For one wild, bewildering moment it was as though Michael had really entered the room above his head, had passed in his living body across all those hundreds of miles of waves and storm and blackness; as though all the inexpressible longing of his young wife had incarnated him beside her. He made the sign of the cross as if against some evil power. And after that there was silence but for the thunder of the rising storm.

Next morning he would have avoided her eyes, but there was something about her that made him look and look in spite of himself. A nervous exaltation had crystallized in her, making her seem ethereal, remote and lovely. Because of the rain that still continued to pour Maire would have had her remain, but she insisted.

She went out in heavy boots and raincoat to say good-bye to Kate and Joan. Joan wept. 'Two years,' said Kate in her hearty way, ' 'twill be no time passing, no time at all.' When she left it was as if a light had gone out in the childless house.

Maire's good-bye was sober but generous too.

'I know Michael is in good hands,' she said.

'Yes,' replied the girl with a radiant smile, 'he is.'

And they drove off through the rain. The sea on which she looked back was blinded by it, all but a leaden strip beside the rocks. She crouched over her black trunk with averted head. Tom, an old potato bag over his shoulders, drove into it, head down. The fear had not left him. He looked down at her once or twice, but her face was hidden in the collar of her raincoat.

They left the seemingly endless, wind-swept upland road and plunged down among the trees that creaked and roared above their heads, spilling great handfuls of water into the cart. His fear became a terror.

When he stood before the carriage door he looked at her appealingly. He could not frame the question he looked; it was a folly he felt must pass from him unspoken; so he asked it only with his eyes, and with her eyes she answered him – a look of ecstatic fulfilment.

The whistle went. She leaned out of the carriage window as the train lurched forward, but he was no longer looking. He raised his hands to his eyes and swayed to and fro, moaning softly to himself. For a long time he remained like that, a ridiculous figure with the old potato bag and the little pool of water that gradually gathered on the platform about his feet.

A Bachelor's Story

Every old bachelor has a love story in him if only you can get at it. This is usually not very easy because a bachelor is a man who does not lightly trust his neighbour, and by the time you can identify him as what he is, the cause of it all has been elevated into a morality, almost a divinity, something the old bachelor himself is afraid to look at for fear it might turn out to be stuffed. And woe betide you if he does confide in you, and you, by word or look, suggest that you do think it is stuffed, for that is how my own friendship with Archie Boland ended.

Archie was a senior Civil Servant, a big man with a broad red face and hot blue eyes and a crust of worldliness and bad temper overlaying a nature that had a lot of sweetness and fun in it. He was a man who affected to believe the worst of everyone, but he saw that I appreciated his true character, and suppressed his bad temper most of the time, except when I trespassed on his taboos, religious and political. For years the two of us walked home together. We both loved walking, and we both liked to drop in at a certain pub by the canal bridge where they kept good draught stout. Whenever we encountered some woman we knew, Archie was very polite and even effusive in an old-fashioned way, raising his hat with a great sweeping gesture and bowing low over the hand he held as if he were about to kiss it, which I swear he would have done on the least encouragement. But afterwards he would look at me under his eyebrows with a knowing smile and tell me things about their home life which the ladies would have been very distressed to hear, and this, in turn, would give place to a sly look that implied that I was drawing my own conclusions from what he said, which I wasn't, not usually.

'I know what you think, Delaney,' he said one evening, carefully putting down the two pints and lowering himself heavily into his seat. 'You think I'm a bad case of sour grapes.'

'I wasn't thinking anything at all,' I said.

'Well, maybe you mightn't be too far wrong at that,' he conceded, more to his own view of me than to anything else. 'But it's not only that, Delaney. There are other things involved. You see, when I was your age I had an experience that upset me a lot. It upset me so much that I felt I could never go through the same sort of thing again. Maybe I was too idealistic.'

I never heard a bachelor yet who didn't take a modest pride in his own idealism. And there in the far corner of that pub by the canal bank on a rainy autumn evening, Archie took the plunge and told me the story of the experience that had turned him against women, and I put my foot in it and turned him against me as well. Ah, well, I was younger then!

You see, in his earlier days Archie had been a great cyclist. Twice he had cycled round Ireland, and had made any amount of long trips to see various historic spots, battlefields, castles, and cathedrals. He was no scholar, but he liked to know what he was talking about and had no objection to showing other people that they didn't. 'I suppose you know that place you were talking about, James?' he would purr when someone in the office stuck his neck out. 'Because if you don't, I do.' No wonder he wasn't too popular with the staff.

One evening Archie arrived in a remote Connemara village where four women teachers were staying, studying Irish, and after supper he got to chatting with them, and they all went for a walk along the strand. One was a young woman called Madge Hale, a slight girl with blue-grey eyes, a long clear-skinned face, and a rather breathless manner, and Archie did not take long to see that she was altogether more intelligent than the others, and that whenever he said something interesting her whole face lit up like a child's.

The teachers were going on a trip to the Aran Islands next day, and Archie offered to join them. They visited the tiny oratories, and, as none of the teachers knew anything about these, Archie in his well-informed way described the origin of the island monasteries and the life of the hermit monks in the early mediaeval period. Madge was fascinated and kept asking questions about what the churches had looked like, and Archie, flattered into doing the dog, suggested that she should accompany him on a bicycle trip the following day, and see some of the later monasteries. She agreed at once enthusiastically. The other women laughed, and Madge laughed, too, though it was clear that she didn't really know what they were laughing about.

Now, this was one sure way to Archie's heart. He disliked women because they were always going to parties or the pictures, painting their faces, and taking aspirin in cartloads. There was altogether too much nonsense about them for a man of his grave taste, but at last he had met a girl who seemed absolutely devoid of nonsense and was serious through and through.

Their trip next day was a great success, and he was able to point out to her the development of the monastery church through the mediaeval abbey to the preaching church. That evening when they returned, he suggested, half in jest, that she should borrow the bicycle and come back to Dublin with him. This time she hesitated, but it was only for a few moments as she considered the practical end of it, and then her face lit up in the same eager way, and she said in her piping voice: 'If you think I won't be in your way, Archie.'

Now, she was in Archie's way, and very much in his way, for he was a man of old-fashioned ideas, who had never in his life allowed a woman he was accompanying to pay for as much as a cup of tea for herself, who felt that to have to excuse himself on the road was little short of obscene, and who endured the agonies of the damned when he had to go to a country hotel with a pretty girl at the end of the day. When he went to the reception desk he felt sure that everyone believed unmentionable things about him and he had an overwhelming compulsion to lecture them on the subject of their evil imaginations. But for this, too, he admired her – by this time any other girl would have been wondering what her parents and friends would say if they knew she was spending the night in a country hotel with a man, but the very idea of scandal never seemed to enter Madge's head. And it was not, as he shrewdly divined, that she was either fast or flighty. It was merely that it had never occurred to her that anything she and Archie might do could involve any culpability.

That settled Archie's business. He knew she was the only woman in the world for him, though to tell her this when she was more or less at the mercy of his solicitations was something that did not even cross his mind. He had a sort of old-fashioned chivalry that set him above the commoner temptations. They cycled south through Clare to Limerick, and stood on the cliffs overlooking the Atlantic; the weather held fine, and they drifted through the flat apple country to Cashel and drank beer and lemonade in country pubs, and finally pushed over the hills to Kilkenny, where they spent their last evening wandering in the dusk under the ruins of mediaeval abbeys and inns, studying effigies and blazons; and never once did Archie as much as hold her hand or speak to her of love. He scowled as he told me this, as though I might mock him from the depths of my own small experience, but I had no inclination to do so, for I knew the enchantment of the senses that people of chaste and lonely character feel in one another's company and that haunts the memory more than all the passionate embraces of lovers.

When they separated outside Madge's lodgings in Rathmines late one summer evening, Archie felt that he was at last free to speak. He held her hand as he said good-bye.

'I think we had quite good fun, don't you?' he asked.

'Oh, yes, Archie,' she cried, laughing in her delight. 'It was wonderful. It was the happiest holiday I ever spent.'

He was so encouraged by this that he deliberately retained hold of her hand.

'That's the way I feel,' he said, beginning to blush. 'I didn't want to say it before because I thought it might embarrass you. I never met a woman like you before, and if you ever felt you wanted to marry me I'd be honoured.'

For a moment, while her face darkened as though all the delight had drained from it, he thought that he had embarrassed her even now.

'Are you sure, Archie?' she asked nervously. 'Because you don't know me very long, remember. A few days like that is not enough to know a person.'

'That's a thing that soon rights itself,' Archie said oracularly.

'And, besides, we'd have to wait a long while,' she added. 'My people aren't very well off; I have two brothers younger than me, and I have to help them.'

'And I have a long way to go before I get anywhere in the Civil Service,' he replied good-humouredly, 'so it may be quite a while before I can do what I like, as well. But those are things that also right themselves, and they right themselves all the sooner if you do them with an object in mind.

I know my own character pretty well,' he added thoughtfully, 'and I know it would be a help to me. And I'm not a man to change his mind.'

She still seemed to hesitate; for a second or two he had a strong impression that she was about to refuse him, but then she thought better of it. Her face cleared in the old way, and she gave her nervous laugh.

'Very well, Archie,' she said. 'If you really want me, you'll find me willing.'

'I want you, Madge,' he replied gravely, and then he raised his hat and pushed his bicycle away while she stood outside her gate in the shadow of the trees and waved. I admired that gesture even as he described it. It was so like Archie, and I could see that such a plighting of his word would haunt him as no passionate love-making would ever do. It was magnificent, but it was not love. People should be jolted out of themselves at times like those, and when they are not so jolted it frequently means, as it did with Archie, that the experience is only deferred till a less propitious time.

However, he was too innocent to know anything of that. To him the whole fantastic business of walking out with a girl was miracle enough in itself, like being dumped down in the middle of some ancient complex civilization whose language and customs he was unfamiliar with. He might have introduced her to history, but she introduced him to operas and concerts, and in no time he was developing prejudices about music as though it was something that had fired him from boyhood, for Archie was by nature a gospel-maker. Even when I knew him, he shook his head over my weakness for Wagner. Bach was the man, and somehow Bach at once ceased to be a pleasure and became a responsibility. It was part of the process of what he called 'knowing his own mind'.

On fine Sundays in autumn they took their lunch and walked over the mountains to Enniskerry, or cycled down the Boyne Valley to Drogheda. Madge was a girl of very sweet disposition, so that they rarely had a falling-out, and even at the best of times this must have been an event in Archie's life, for he had an irascible, quarrelsome, gospel-making streak. It was true that there were certain evenings and week-ends that she kept to herself to visit her old friends and an ailing aunt in Miltown, but these did not worry Archie, who believed that this was how a conscientious girl should be. As a man who knew his own mind, he liked to feel that the girl he was going to marry was the same.

Oh, of course it was too perfect! Of course, an older hand would have waited to see what price he was expected to pay for all those perfections, but Archie was an idealist, which meant that he thought Nature was in the job solely for his benefit. Then one day Nature gave him a rap on the knuckles just to show him that the boot was on the other foot.

In town he happened to run into one of the group of teachers he had met in Connemara during the holidays and invited her politely to join him in a cup of tea. Archie favoured one of those long mahogany teahouses in Grafton Street where daylight never enters; he was a creature of habit, and this was where he had eaten his first lunch in Dublin, and there he would continue to go till some minor cataclysm like marriage changed the current of his life.

'I hear you're seeing a lot of Madge,' said the teacher gaily as if this were a guilty secret between herself and Archie.

'Oh, yes,' said Archie as if it weren't. 'And with God's help I expect to be doing the same for the rest of my life.'

'So I heard,' she said joyously. 'I'm delighted for Madge, of course. But I wonder whatever happened that other fellow she was engaged to?'

'Why?' asked Archie, who knew well that she was only pecking at him and refused to let her see how sick he felt. 'Was she engaged to another fellow?'

'Ah, surely she must have told you that!' the teacher cried with mock consternation. 'I hope I'm not saying anything wrong,' she added piously. 'Maybe she wasn't engaged to him after all. He was a teacher, too, I believe – somewhere on the South Side. What was his name?'

'I'll ask her and let you know,' replied Archie blandly. He was giving nothing away till he had had more time to think of it.

All the same he was in a very ugly temper. Archie was one of those people who believe in being candid with everybody, even at the risk of unpleasantness, which might be another reason that he had so few friends when I knew him. He might, for instance, hear from somebody called Mahony that another man called Devins had said he was inclined to be offensive in argument, which was a reasonable enough point of view, but Archie would feel it his duty to go straight to Devins and ask him to repeat the remark, which, of course, would leave Devins wondering who it was that had been trying to make mischief for him, so he would ask a third man whether Mahony was the tell-tale, and a fourth would repeat the question to Mahony, till eventually, I declare to God, Archie's inquisition would have the whole office by the ears.

Archie, of course, had felt compelled to confess to Madge every sin of his past life, which, from the point of view of this narrative, was quite without importance, and he naturally assumed when Madge did not do the same that it could only be because she had nothing to confess. He realized now that this was a grave mistake since everyone has something to confess, particularly women.

He could have done with her what he would have done with someone in the office and asked her what she meant, but this did not seem sufficient punishment to him. Though he didn't recognize it, Archie's pride was deeply hurt. He regarded Madge's silence as equivalent to an insult, and in the matter of insults he felt it was his duty to give as good as he got. So, instead of having it out with her as another man might have done, he proceeded to make her life a misery. He continued to walk out with her as though nothing had happened, and then brought the conversation gently round to various domestic disasters which had or had not occurred in his own experience and all of which had been caused solely by someone's deceit. This was intended to scare the wits out of Madge, as no doubt it did. Then he called up a friend of his in the Department of Education and asked him out for a drink.

'The Hale girl?' his friend said thoughtfully. 'Isn't she engaged to that assistant in St Joseph's? Wheeler, a chap with a lame leg? I think I heard that. Why? You're not keen on her yourself by any chance?'

'Ah, you know me,' Archie replied with a fat smile.

'Why then, indeed, I do not,' said his friend. 'But if you mean business you'd want to hurry up. Now you mention it, they were only supposed to be waiting till he got a headship somewhere. He's a nice fellow, I believe.'

'So I'm told,' said Archie, and went away with a smile on his lips and murder in his heart. Those forthright men of the world are the very devil once they get a bee in their bonnets. Othello had nothing on a Civil Servant of twelve years' standing and a blameless reputation. So he still continued to see Madge, though now his method of tormenting her was to press her about those odd evenings she was supposed to spend with her aunt or those old friends she spoke of. He realized that some of those evenings were probably really spent as innocently as she described them, since she showed neither embarrassment nor distress at his probing and gibing. It was the others that caused her to wince, and those were the ones he concentrated on.

'I could meet you when you came out, you know,' he said in a benign tone that almost glowed.

'But I don't know when I'll be out, Archie,' she replied, blushing and stammering.

'Ah, well, even if you didn't get out until half-past ten – and that would be late for a lady her age – it would still give us time for a little walk. That's if the night was fine, of course. It's all very well, doing your duty by old friends, but you don't want to deny yourself every little pleasure.'

'I couldn't promise anything, Archie, really I couldn't,' she said almost angrily, and Archie smiled to himself, the smug smile of the old inquisitor whose helpless victim has begun to give himself away.

The road where Madge lived was one of those broad Victorian roads you find scattered all over the hills at the south side of Dublin, with trees along the pavement and deep gardens leading to pairs of merchants' houses, semi-detached and solidly built, with tall basements and high flights of steps. Next night, Archie was waiting at the corner of a side-street in the shadow, feeling like a detective as he watched her house. He had been there only about ten minutes when she came out and tripped down the steps. When she emerged from the garden, she turned right up the hill, and Archie followed, guided more by the distinctive clack of her heels than by the glimpses he caught of her passing swiftly under a street lamp.

She reached the bus stop at the top of the road, and a man came up and spoke to her. He was a youngish man in a bright tweed coat, hatless and thin, dragging a lame leg. He took her arm, and they went off together in the direction of the Dodder bank. As they did, Archie heard her happy, eager, foolish laugh, and it sounded exactly as though she were laughing at him.

He was beside himself with misery. He had got what he had been seeking, which was full confirmation of the woman's guilt, and now he had no idea what to do with it. To follow them and have it out on the river bank in the darkness was one possibility, but he realized that Wheeler – if this was Wheeler – probably knew as little of him as he had known of Wheeler, and that it would result only in general confusion. No, it was that abominable woman he would have to have it out with. He returned slowly to his post, turned into a public-house just round the corner, and sat swallowing whiskey in silence until another customer unwittingly touched on one of his pet political taboos. Then he sprang to his feet, and, though no one had invited his opinion, he thundered for several minutes against people with slave minds, and stalked out with a virtuous feeling that his wrath had been entirely disinterested.

This time he had to wait for over half an hour in the damp and cold, and this did not improve his temper. Then he heard her footsteps, and guessed that the young man had left her at the same spot where they had met. It could, of course, have been the most innocent thing in the world, intended merely to deceive inquisitive people in her lodging house, but to Archie it seemed all guile and treachery. He crossed the road and stood under a tree beside the gate, so well concealed that she failed altogether to see him till he stepped out to meet her. Then she started back.

'Who's that?' she asked in a startled whisper, and then, after a look, added with what sounded like joy and was probably merely relief: 'Oh, Archie, it's you!' Then, as he stood there glowering at her, her tone changed again and he could detect the consternation as she asked:

'What are you doing here, Archie?'

'Waiting,' Archie replied in a voice as hollow as his heart felt.

'Waiting? But for what, Archie?'

'An explanation.'

'Oh, Archie!' she exclaimed with childish petulance. 'Don't talk to me that way!'

'And what way would you like me to talk to you?' he retorted, letting fly with his anger. 'I suppose you're going to tell me now you were at your aunt's?'

'No, Archie,' she replied meekly. 'I wasn't. I was out with a friend.'

'A friend?' repeated Archie.

'Not a friend exactly either, Archie,' she added in distress.

'Not exactly,' Archie repeated with grim satisfaction. 'With your fiancé, in fact?'

'That's true, Archie,' she admitted. 'I don't deny that. You must let me explain.'

'The time for explanations is past,' Archie thundered magnificently, though the moment before he had been demanding one. 'The time for explanations was three months ago. For three months and more, your whole life has been a living lie.'

This was a phrase Archie had thought up, entirely without assistance, drinking whiskey in the pub. He may have failed to notice that it was not entirely original. It was intended to draw blood, and it did.

'I wish you wouldn't say things like that, Archie,' Madge said in an unsteady voice. 'I know I didn't tell you the whole truth, but I wasn't trying to deceive you.'

'No, of course you weren't trying,' said Archie. 'You don't need to try. What you ought to try some time is to tell the truth.'

'But I am telling the truth,' she said indignantly. 'I'm not a liar, Archie, and I won't have you saying it. I couldn't help getting engaged to Pat. He asked me, and I couldn't refuse him.'

'You couldn't refuse him?'

'No. I told you you should let me explain. It happened before, and I won't have it happen again.'

'What happened?'

'Oh, it's a long story, Archie. I once refused a boy at home in our own place and – he died.'

'He died?' Archie said incredulously.

'Well, he committed suicide. It was an awful thing to happen, but it wasn't my fault. I was young and silly, and I didn't know how dangerous it was. I thought it was just all a game, and I led him on and made fun of him. How could I know the way a boy would feel about things like that?'

'Hah!' Archie grunted uncertainly, feeling that as usual she had thought too quickly for him, and that all his beautiful anger accumulated over weeks would be wasted on some pointless argument. 'And I suppose you felt you couldn't refuse me either?'

'Well, as a matter of fact, Archie,' she said apologetically, 'that was the way I felt.'

'Good God!' exploded Archie.

'It's true, Archie,' she said in a rush. 'It wasn't until weeks after that I got to like you really, the way I do now. I was hoping all that time we were together that you didn't like me that way at all, and it came as a terrible blow to me, Archie. Because, as you see, I was sort of engaged already, and it's not a situation you'd like to be in yourself, being engaged to two girls at the one time.'

'And I suppose you thought *I*'d commit suicide?' Archie asked incredulously.

'But I didn't know, Archie. It wasn't until afterwards that I really got to know you.'

'You didn't know!' he said, choking with anger at the suggestion that he was a man of such weak and commonplace stuff. 'You didn't *know!* Good God, the vanity and madness of it! And all this time you couldn't tell me about the fellow you say committed suicide on account of you.'

'But how could I, Archie?' she asked despairingly. 'It's not the sort a thing a girl likes to think of, much less to talk about.'

'No,' he said, breathing deeply, 'and so you'll go through life, tricking and deceiving every honourable man that comes your way – all out of pure kindness of heart. That be damned for a yarn!'

'It's not a yarn, Archie,' she cried hotly. 'It's true, and it never happened with anyone, only Pat and you, and one young fellow at home, but the last I heard of him he was walking out with another girl, and I dare say he's over it by now. And Pat would have got over it the same if only you'd had patience.'

The picture of yet a third man engaged to his own fiancée was really too much for Archie, and he knew that he could never stand up to this little liar in argument.

'Madge,' he said broodingly, 'I do not like to insult any woman to her face, least of all a woman I once respected, but I do not believe you. I can't believe anything you say. You have behaved to me in a deceitful and dishonourable manner, and I can't trust you any longer.'

Then he turned on his heel and walked heavily away, remembering how on this very spot, a few months before, he had turned away with his heart full of hope, and he realized that everything people said about women was true down to the last bitter gibe, and that never again would he trust one of them.

'That was the end of my attempts at getting married,' he finished grimly. 'Of course, she wrote and gave me the names of two witnesses I could refer to if I didn't believe her, but I couldn't even be bothered replying.'

'Archie,' I asked in consternation, 'you don't mean that you really dropped her?'

'Dropped her?' he repeated, beginning to scowl. 'I never spoke to the woman again, only to raise my hat to her whenever I met her on the street. I don't even know what happened to her after, whether she married or not. I have some pride.'

'But, Archie,' I said despairingly, 'suppose she was simply telling the truth?'

'And suppose she was?' he asked in a murderous tone.

Then I began to laugh. I couldn't help it, though I saw it was making him mad. It was raining outside on the canal bank, and I wasn't laughing at Archie so much as at myself. Because, for the first time, I found myself falling in love with a woman from the mere description of her, as they do in the old romances, and it was an extraordinary feeling, as though there existed somewhere some pure essence of womanhood that one could savour outside the body.

'But damn it, Archie,' I cried, 'you said yourself she was a serious girl. All you're telling me now is that she was a sweet one as well. It must have been hell for her, being engaged to two men in the same town and trying to keep both of them happy till the other fellow got tired of her and left her free to marry you.'

'Or free for a third man to come along and put her in the same position again,' said Archie with a sneer.

I must say I had not expected that one, and for a moment it stopped me dead. But there is no stopping a man who is in love with a shadow as I was then, and I was determined on finding justification for myself.

'But after all, Archie,' I said, 'isn't that precisely why you marry a woman like that? Can you imagine marrying one of them if the danger wasn't there? Come, Archie, don't you see that the whole business of the suicide is irrelevant? Every nice girl behaves exactly as though she had a real suicide in her past. That's what makes her a nice girl. It's not easy to defend it rationally, but that's the way it is. Archie, I think you made a fool of yourself.'

'It's not possible to defend it rationally or any other way,' Archie said with finality. 'A woman like that is a woman without character. You might as well stick your head in a gas-oven and be done with it as marry a girl like that.'

And from that evening on, Archie dropped me. He even told his friends that I had no moral sense and would be bound to end up bad. Perhaps he was right, perhaps I shall end up as badly as he believed; but, on the other hand, perhaps I was only saying to him all the things he had been saying to himself for years in the bad hours coming on to morning, and he only wanted reassurance from me, not his own sentence on himself pronounced by another man's lips. But, as I say, I was very young and didn't understand. Nowadays I should sympathize and congratulate him on his narrow escape, and leave it to him to proclaim what an imbecile he was.

Fish for Friday

Ned McCarthy, the teacher in a village called Abbeyduff, was wakened one morning by his sister-in-law. She was standing over him with a cynical smile and saying in a harsh voice:

'Wake up! 'Tis started.'

'What's started, Sue?' Ned asked wildly, jumping up in bed with an anguished air.

'Why?' she asked dryly. 'Are you after forgetting already? There's no immediate hurry, but you'd better get the doctor.'

'Oh, the doctor!' sighed Ned, remembering all at once why he was sleeping alone in the little back room and why that unpleasant female was in the house. She only came when Kitty was having a baby, and she went round like a Redemptorist missioner on an annual retreat.

He dressed in a hurry, said a few words of encouragement to Kitty, talked to the kids while swallowing a cup of tea, and got out the car. He was a well-built man in his early forties with fair hair and pale grey eyes, nervous and excitable under his placid manner. He had plenty to be excited about. The house, for instance. It was a fine house, an old shooting lodge, set back at a distance of two fields from the main road, with a lawn leading to the river and steep gardens climbing the wooded hill behind. It was an ideal house, in fact, the sort he had always dreamed of, where Kitty could keep a few hens and he could garden and get in a bit of shooting. But scarcely had he settled in than he realized it was a mistake. The loneliness of the long evenings when dusk settled on the valley was something he had never even imagined.

He had lamented it to Kitty, and it was she who had suggested the car, but even this had drawbacks because it needed as much attention as a baby. When Ned was alone in it he chatted to it encouragingly; when it stopped he kicked it viciously, and the villagers swore he had actually been seen stoning it. This and the fact that he sometimes talked to himself when he hadn't the car to talk to had given rise to the legend that he had a slate loose.

He drove down the lane and across the footbridge to the main road. Then he stopped before the public-house at the corner which his friend, Tom Hurley, owned.

'Anything you want in town, Tom?' he shouted.

'What's that, Ned?' said a voice from within, and Tom himself, a small, round, russet-faced man, came out with his wrinkled grin.

'I have to go to town. Is there anything you want?'

'No, no, Ned, I think not, thanks,' Tom said in his hasty way, all the words trying to come out together. 'All we wanted was fish for the dinner, and the Jordans are bringing that.'

'I'd sooner them than me,' Ned said, making a face.

'Och, isn't it the devil, Ned?' Tom said with a look of real anguish. 'The damn smell hangs round the shop the whole day. But what the hell else can you do on a Friday? Is it a spin you're going for?'

'No, for the doctor,' said Ned.

'Och, I see,' said Tom, beginning to beam. His expression exaggerated almost to caricature whatever emotion his interlocutor might be expected to feel. 'Ah, please God, it'll go off all right. There's no hurry, is there? Come in and have a drop.'

'No, thanks, Tom,' Ned said with resignation. 'I'd better not start so early.'

'Ah, hell to your soul, you will,' fussed Tom. 'It won't take you two minutes. Hard enough it was for me to keep you sober the time the first fellow arrived.'

Ned got out of the car and followed Tom inside.

'That's right, Tom,' he said in surprise. 'I'd forgotten about that. Who was it was here?'

'Och, God, you had half the countryside in,' Tom said, shaking his head. 'It was a terrible night, a terrible night. You had Jack Martin, the teacher, and Owen Hennessey, and that publican friend of yours from town – what's that his name is? – Cronin. That's right, Larry Cronin. Ye must have dropped just where ye stood, glasses and all. The milkman found ye next morning littering the floor, and ye never even locked the doors after ye. Ye could have had my licence taken from me.'

'Do you know, I'd forgotten about that completely,' said Ned with a pleased smile. 'My memory isn't what it was. I suppose we're getting old.'

'Och, well, 'tis never the same after the first,' said Tom, and he poured a large drink for Ned and a few spoonfuls for himself. 'God, isn't it astonishing what the first one does for you, Ned?' he added in his eager way, bending across the counter. 'You feel you're getting a new lease of life. And by the time the second comes you're beginning to wonder will the damn thing ever stop. God forgive me for talking,' he said, lowering his voice. 'Herself would have my life if she heard me.'

'Still, there's a lot of truth in it, Tom,' said Ned, relieved to feel that the gloom in his mind was nothing unusual. 'It's not the same thing at all. And I suppose that even that is only an illusion. Like when you fall in love and think you're getting first prize in the lottery, while all the time it's only Nature's little way of putting you on the spot.'

'Ah, well, they say it all comes back when you're a grandfather,' said Tom with a chuckle.

'But who wants to be a grandfather?' asked Ned, already feeling sorry for himself with his home upset, that unpleasant woman bossing the house and more money to be found somewhere.

He drove off but his mood had darkened. It was a grand bit of road between his house and the town, with the river below him on the left, and the hills at either side with the first faint wash of green on them like an unfinished water-colour. Walking or driving, it was a real pleasure to him because of the prospect of civilization at the other end. The town was only a little rundown port, but it had shops and pubs and villas with electric light, and a water supply that did not give out in May, and there were all sorts of interesting people to be met there. But the prospect didn't cheer him now. He realized that the rapture of being a father doesn't go on repeating itself and it gave him no pleasure at all to look forward to being a grandfather. He felt decrepit enough the way he was.

At the same time he was haunted by some memory of days when he was not decrepit but careless and gay. He had been a Volunteer and roamed the hills for months with a column, wondering where he would spend the night. Then it had all seemed uncomfortable and dangerous enough, but at least he had felt free. Maybe, like an illusion of re-birth at finding himself a father, it was only an illusion of freedom, but it was terrible to think he wouldn't be able to feel it any more. It was associated in his mind with high hills and wide views, but now his life had descended into a valley like the one he was driving along. He had descended into it by the quiet path of duty – a steady man, a sucker for responsibilities, treasurer of the Hurling Club, treasurer of the Republican Party, secretary of three other organizations. He talked to the car as he did whenever something was too much on his mind.

'It's all Nature, old girl,' he said despondently. 'It gives you a set of illusions, but all the time it's only bending you to its own purposes as if you were a cow or a tree. You'd be better off with no illusions at all. No illusions about anything! That way, Nature wouldn't get you quite so soon.'

Being nervous, he did not like to drive through the town. He did it when he had to, but it made him flustered and fidgety so that he missed seeing who was on the streets, and a town was nothing without people. He usually parked his car outside Cronin's pub on the way in and walked the rest of the way. Larry Cronin was an old comrade of revolutionary days who had married into the pub.

He went in to tell Larry. This was quite unnecessary as Larry knew every car for miles around and was well aware of Ned's little weakness, but it was a habit and Ned was a man of more habits than he realized himself.

'I'm leaving the old bus for half an hour, Larry,' he called through the door in a plaintive tone that expressed regret for the inconvenience he was causing Larry and grief for the burden that was being put on himself.

'Ah, come in, man, come in!' cried Larry, a tall, engaging man with a handsome face and a sunny smile that was quite sincere if Larry liked you and damnably hypocritical if he didn't. His mouth was like a showcase with the array of false teeth in it. 'What has you out at this hour of the morning?'

'Oh, Nature, Nature,' Ned said with a laugh, digging his hands into his trouser pockets.

'How do you mean, Nature?' asked Larry, who did not understand the allusive ways of intellectuals but admired them none the less.

'Kitty, I mean. I'm going for the doctor.'

'Ah, the blessings of God on you!' Larry said jovially. 'Is this the third or the fourth? You lose count after a while, don't you? You might as well have a resiner as you're in. Ah, you will, you will, God blast you! 'Tis hard on the nerves. That was a great night we had the time the boy was born.'

'Wasn't it?' said Ned, beaming at the way people remembered it. 'I was only talking to Tom Hurley about it.'

'Ah, what the hell does Hurley know about it?' Larry asked contemptuously, pouring out a half tumbler of whiskey with the air of a lord. 'The bloody man went to bed at two. That fellow is too cautious to be good. But Jack Martin gave a great account of himself. Do you remember? The whole first act of *Tosca*, orchestra and all. "The southern sunlight" he called it. You didn't see Jack since he came back?'

'Was Jack away?' Ned asked in surprise. He felt easier now, being on the doctor's doorstep, and anyhow he knew the doctor would only be waiting.

'Ah, God he was,' said Larry, throwing his whole weight on the counter. 'In Paris, would you believe it? He's on the batter again, of course. Wait till you hear him on Paris! 'Tis only the mercy of God if Father Clery doesn't get to hear of it.'

'That's where you're wrong, Larry,' Ned said with a smile. 'Martin doesn't have to mind himself at all. Father Clery will do all that for him. If an inspector comes round while Martin is on it, Father Clery will take him out to look at the antiquities.'

'Begod, you might be right, Ned,' said Larry. 'But you or I couldn't do it. God Almighty, man, we'd be slaughtered alive. 'Tisn't worried you are about Kitty?' he asked gently.

'Ah, no, Larry,' said Ned. 'It's only that at times like this a man feels himself of no importance. A messenger boy would do as well. We're all dragged down to the same level.'

'And damn queer we'd be if we weren't,' said Larry with his lazy, sunny smile, the smile Ned remembered from the day Larry threw a Mills bomb into a lorry of soldiers. 'Unless you'd want to have the bloody baby yourself.'

'Ah, it's not only that, Larry,' Ned said gloomily. 'It's not that at all. But you can't help wondering what it's all about.'

'Why, then indeed, that's true for you,' said Larry, who, as a result of his own experience in the pub had developed a gloomy and philosophic view of human existence. After all, a man can't be looking at schizophrenia for ten hours a day without wondering if it's all strictly necessary. 'And 'tis at times like this you notice it – men coming and going like the leaves on the trees. Ah, God, 'tis a great mystery.'

But that wasn't what Ned was thinking about either. He was thinking of his own lost youth and what had happened to him.

'That's not what I mean, Larry,' he said, drawing neat figures on the counter with the bottom of his glass. 'What I mean is you can't help wondering what happened yourself. We knew one another when we were young, and look at us now, forty odd and our lives are over and we have nothing to show for them. It's as if when you married some good went out of you.'

'Small loss as the fool said when he lost Mass,' retorted Larry, who had found himself a comfortable berth in the pub and lost his thirst for adventure.

'That's the bait, of course,' Ned said with a grim smile. 'That's where Nature gets us every time. A small contribution; you'll never miss it, and before you know where you are, you're bankrupt.'

'Ah, how bad Nature is!' exclaimed Larry, not relaxing his grin. 'When your first was born you were walking mad round the town, looking for people to celebrate it with, and there you are now, looking for sympathy! God, man, isn't it a great thing to have someone to share your troubles with and give a slap on the ass to, even if she does let the crockery fly once in a while? What the hell about an old bit of china?'

'That's all very well, Larry, *if* that's all it costs,' said Ned darkly.

'And what the hell else does it cost?' asked Larry. 'Twenty-one meals a week and a couple of pounds of tea. Sure, 'tis for nothing!'

'And what about your freedom?' Ned asked. 'What about the old days on the column?'

'Ah, that was different, Ned,' Larry said with a sigh, and all at once his smile went out and his eyes took on a dreamy, far-away look. 'But sure, everything was different then. I don't know what the hell is after coming over the country at all.'

'The same thing that's come over you and me,' Ned said with finality. 'Nature kidded us, the way it kidded us when we got married, and the way it kidded us when the first child was born. There's nothing worse than illusions for getting you into the rut. We had our freedom and we didn't value it. Now our lives are run for us by women the way they were when we were kids. This is Friday and what do I find? Hurley waiting for someone to bring home the fish. You waiting for the fish. I'll go home to a nice plate of fish, and I'll guarantee to you, Larry, not one man in that flying column is having meat for his dinner today. One few words in front of the altar and it's fish for Friday the rest of your life. And they call this a man's country!'

'Still, Ned, there's nothing nicer than a good bit of fish,' Larry said wistfully. 'If 'tis well done, mind you. *If* 'tis well done. And I grant you 'tisn't often you get it well done. God, I had some fried plaice in Kilkenny last week that had me turned inside out. I declare to God if I stopped that car once I stopped it six times, and by the time I got home I was after caving in like a sandpit.'

'And yet I can remember you in Tramore, letting on to be a Protestant to get bacon and eggs on Friday,' Ned said accusingly.

'Oh, that's the God's truth,' Larry said joyously. 'I was a divil for meat, God forgive me. I used to go mad seeing the Protestants lowering it, and me there with nothing only a boiled egg. And the waitress, Ned – do you remember the waitress that wouldn't believe I was a Protestant till I said the "Our Father" the wrong way for her? She said I had too open a face for a Protestant. How well she'd know a thing like that about the "Our Father", Ned!'

'A woman would know anything she had to know to make you eat fish,' Ned said, finishing his drink and turning away. 'And you may be reconciled to it, Larry,' he added with a mournful smile, 'but I'm not. I'll eat it because I'm damned with a sense of duty, and I don't want to get Kitty into trouble with the neighbours, but please God, I'll see one more revolution before I die, even if I have to swing for it.'

'Ah, well,' sighed Larry, 'youth is a great thing, sure enough. . . . Coming, Hanna, coming!' he boomed as a woman's voice yelled from the room upstairs. He gave Ned a nod and a wink to suggest that he enjoyed it, but Ned knew that that scared little rabbit of a wife of his would be wanting to know about the Protestant prayers, and would then go to Confession and ask the priest was it a reserved sin and should Larry be sent to the Bishop. And then he remembered Larry during the Dunkeen ambush when they had to run for it, pleading with that broad smile of his, 'Ah, Christ, Ned, let me have one more crack at them!' 'No life, no life,' Ned said aloud to himself as he sauntered down the hill past the church. And it was a great mistake taking a drink whenever he felt badly about the country because it always made the country seem worse.

Someone clapped him suddenly on the shoulder. It was Jack Martin, the vocational-school teacher, a small, plump, nervous man with a baby complexion, a neat greying moustache and big, blue, innocent eyes. Ned's face lit up. Of all his friends Martin was the one he warmed to most. He was a talented man and a good baritone. His wife had died a few years before and left him with the two children, but he had not married again and had been a devoted if over-anxious father. Yet two or three times a year, and always coming on to his wife's anniversary, he went on a tearing drunk that left some legend behind. There was the time he tried to teach Verdi to the tramp who played the penny whistle and the time his housekeeper hid his trousers and he got out of the window in his pyjamas and had to be brought home by the parish priest.

'McCarthy, you scoundrel, you were hoping to give me the slip,' he said delightedly in his shrill nasal voice. 'Come in here one minute till I tell you something. God, you'll die!'

'If you wait there ten minutes, Jack, I'll be back to you,' said Ned. 'There's only one little job I have to do, and then I'll be able to give you my full attention.'

'All right, all right, but have one little drink before you go,' Martin said irritably. 'One drink and I'll release you on your own recognizances. You'll never guess where I was, Ned. I woke up there, as true as God!'

Martin was like that. Ned decided good-humouredly that five minutes' explanation in the bar was easier than ten minutes' argument in the street. It was quite clear that Martin was 'on it'. He was full of clock-work vitality, rushing to the counter for fresh drinks, fumbling over money, trying to carry glasses without spilling them, and talking thirteen to the dozen. Ned beamed at him. Drunk or sober, he liked the man.

'Ned, I'll give you three guesses where I was.'

'Let me see,' said Ned in mock meditation. 'I suppose 'twould never be Paris?' and then laughed boyishly at Martin's hurt air.

'You can't do anything in this town,' said Martin. 'Next, I suppose you'll be telling me what I did there.'

'No,' said Ned gravely. 'It's Father Clery who'll be telling about that – from the pulpit.'

'Ah, to hell with Father Clery!' said Martin. 'No, Ned, this is se-e-e-rious. This is vital. It only came to me in the last week. We're only wasting our time in this misfortunate country.'

'You're probably right,' Ned said urbanely. 'The question is, what else can you do with Time?'

'Ah, this isn't philosophy, man,' Martin said testily. 'This is se-e-e-rious, I tell you.'

'I know how serious it is all right,' Ned said complacently. 'Only five minutes ago I was asking Larry Cronin where our youth was gone.'

'Youth?' said Martin. 'But you can't call that youth, what we have in this country. Drinking bad porter in public-houses after closing time and listening to someone singing "The Rose of Tralee". Sure, that's not life, man.'

'But isn't that the question?' asked Ned. 'What is Life?' Ned couldn't help promoting words like 'time' and 'life' to the dignity of capital letters.

'How the hell would I know?' asked Martin. 'I suppose you have to go out and look for the bloody thing. You're not going to find it round here. You have to go south, where they have sunlight and wine and good cooking and women with a bit of go.'

'And you don't think it would be the same thing there?' Ned asked quietly.

'Oh, God, dust and ashes! Dust and ashes!' wailed Martin. 'Don't go on with that! Don't we get enough of it every Sunday in the chapel?'

Now, Ned was very fond of Martin, and admired the vitality with which in his forties he still pursued a fancy, but he could not let him get away with the notion that Life was merely a matter of geography.

'But that's a way Life has,' he said oracularly. 'You think you're seeing it, and it turns out it was somewhere else all the time. Like women; the girl you lose is the one that could have made you happy. Or revolutions; you always fought the wrong battle. I dare say there are people in the south wishing they could be in some wild place like this. I admit it's rather difficult to imagine, but I suppose it could happen. No, Jack, we might as well resign ourselves to the fact that wherever Life was, it wasn't where we were looking for it.'

'For God's sake!' cried Martin. 'You're talking like an old man of ninety-five.'

'I'm forty-two,' Ned said with quiet emphasis, 'and I have no illusions left. You still have a few. Mind, I admire you for it. You were never a fighting man like Cronin or myself. Maybe that's what saved you. You kept your youthfulness longer. You escaped the big disillusionments. But Nature has her eye on you as well. You're light and airy now, but what way will you be next week? We pay for our illusions, Jack. They're only sent to drag us deeper into the mud.'

'Ah, 'tisn't that with me at all, Ned,' said Martin. 'It's my stomach. I can't keep it up.'

'No, Jack, it's not your stomach. It's the illusion. I saw other men with the same illusion and I know the way you'll end up. You'll be in and out of the chapel ten times a day for fear once wasn't enough, with your head down for fear you'd catch a friend's eye and be led astray, beating your breast, lighting candles and counting indulgences. And that, Jack, may be the last illusion of all.'

'I don't know what the hell is after coming over you,' Martin said in bewilderment. 'You're – you're being positively personal. And Father Clery knows perfectly well the sort of man I am. I have all Shaw's plays on my shelf, and I never tried to hide them from anybody.'

'I know that, Jack, I know that,' Ned said sadly, overcome by the force of his own oratory. 'And I'm not being personal, because it isn't a personal matter. It's only Nature working through you. It works through me as well only it gets me in a different way. My illusion was a different sort, and look at me now. I turn every damn thing into a duty, and in the end I'm good for nothing. I know the way I'll die too. I'll disintegrate into a husband, a father, a schoolteacher, a local librarian, and fifteen different sorts of committee men, and none of them with enough energy to survive. Unless, with God's help, I die on a barricade.'

'What barricade?' asked Martin, who found all this hard to follow.

'Any barricade,' Ned said with a wild sweep of his arms. 'I don't care what it's for so long as it means a fight. I don't want to die of disseminated conscientiousness. I don't want to be one of Nature's errand boys. I'm not even a good one. Here I am arguing with you in a pub instead of doing what I was sent to do.' He paused for a moment to think and then broke into his boyish laugh, because he realized that for the moment he had forgotten what it was. 'Whatever the hell it was,' he added. 'Well, that beats everything! That's what duty does for you!'

'Ah, that's only because it wasn't important,' said Martin.

'That's where you're wrong again, Jack,' said Ned, beginning to enjoy the situation thoroughly. 'Maybe it was of no importance to us but it was probably of great importance to Nature. What *was* the damn thing? My memory's gone to hell.'

He closed his eyes and lay back limply in his chair, though even through his self-induced trance he smiled at the absurdity of it.

'No good,' he said briskly, starting up. 'It's an extraordinary thing, the way it disappears as if the ground opened and swallowed it. And there's nothing you can do about it. It'll come back of its own accord, and there won't be any reason for that either. I was reading an article about a German doctor who says you forget because it's too unpleasant to think about.'

'It's not a haircut?' Martin asked helpfully, and Ned, a tidy man, shook his head.

'Or clothes?' Martin went on. 'Women are great on clothes.'

'No,' said Ned, frowning. 'I'm sure it wasn't anything for myself.'

'Or for the kids? Shoes or the like?'

'It could be, I suppose,' said Ned. 'Something flashed across my mind just then.'

'If it's not that it must be groceries.'

'I don't see how it could be. Williams deliver them every week, and they're nearly always the same.'

'In that case it's bound to be something to eat,' said Martin. 'They're always forgetting things – bread or butter or milk.'

'I suppose so, but I'm damned if I know what,' said Ned. 'Jim,' he said to the barman, 'I'm after forgetting the message I was sent on. What do you think of that?'

'Ah, I suppose 'twas fish, Mr Mac,' said the barman.

'Fish!' said Martin. 'The very thing.'

'Fish?' repeated Ned, stroking his forehead. 'I suppose it could be, now you mention it. I know I offered to bring it for Tom Hurley and I had a bit of an argument with Larry Cronin about it. He seems to like it.'

'I can't stand the damn stuff,' said Martin, 'only the housekeeper has to have it for the kids.'

'Ah, 'tis fish all right, Mr Mac,' the barman said. 'In an hour's time you wouldn't forget it, not with the stink of it all round the town. I never could stand it myself since the last war and all the poor unfortunates getting drowned. You'd feel you were making a cannibal out of yourself.'

'Well, obviously, it has something to do with fish,' said Ned with a laugh. 'It may not exactly be fish, but it's something very like it. Anyway, if that's the case, there's no particular hurry. We'll have another of these, Jim.'

'Whether it is or not, she'll take it as kindly meant,' said Martin. 'The same as flowers. Women in this country don't seem to be able to distinguish between them.'

Two hours later, the two friends, more talkative than ever, drove up to Ned's house for lunch.

'Mustn't forget the fish,' Ned said with a knowing smile as he reached back for it. 'The spirit of the revolution, Jack – that's what it's come to.'

At that moment they both heard the wail of a new-born infant from the front bedroom. Ned grew very white.

'What's that, Ned?' asked Martin, and Ned gave a deep sigh.

'That's the fish, Jack, I'm afraid,' said Ned.

'Oh, God, I'm not going in so,' Martin said hastily, getting out of the car. 'Tom Hurley will give me a bit of bread and cheese.'

'Nonsense, man!' Ned said boldly, knowing perfectly well what his welcome would be if he went in alone. 'I'll get you something. That's not what's worrying me at all. What's worrying me is why I thought it could be fish. That's what I can't understand.'

A Story by Maupassant

People who have not grown up in a provincial town won't know what I mean when I say what Terry Coughlan meant to me. People who have won't need to know.

As kids we lived a few doors from each other on the same terrace, and his sister, Tess, was a friend of my sister, Nan. There was a time when I was rather keen on Tess myself. She was a small, plump, gay little thing, with rosy cheeks like apples, and she played the piano very well. In those days I sang a bit, though I hadn't much of a voice. When I sang Mozart, Beethoven, or even Wagner, Terry would listen with brooding approval. When I sang commonplace stuff, Terry would make a face and walk out. He was a good-looking lad with a big brow and curly black hair, a long, pale face and a pair of intent dark eyes. He was always well spoken and smart in his appearance. There was nothing sloppy about him.

When he could not learn something by night he got up at five in the morning to do it, and whatever he took up, he mastered. Even as a boy he was always looking forward to the day when he'd have money enough to travel, and he taught himself French and German in the time it took me to find out I could not learn Irish. He was cross with me for wanting to learn it; according to him it had 'no cultural significance', but he was crosser still with me because I couldn't learn it. 'The first thing you should learn to do is to work,' he would say gloomily. 'What's going to become of you if you don't?' He had read somewhere that when Keats was depressed, he had a wash and brush up. Keats was his god. Poetry was never much in my line, except Shelley, and Terry didn't think much of him.

We argued about it on our evening walks. Maybe you don't remember the sort of arguments you had when you were young. Lots of people prefer not to remember, but I like thinking of them. A man is never more himself than when he talks nonsense about God, Eternity, prostitution, and the necessity for having mistresses. I argued with Terry that the day of poetry was over, and that the big boys of modern literature were the fiction writers – the ones we'd heard of in Cork at that time, I mean – the Russians and Maupassant.

'The Russians are all right,' he said to me once. 'Maupassant you can forget.'

'But why, Terry?' I asked.

'Because whatever you say about the Russians, they're noble,' he said. 'Noble' was a great word of his at the time: Shakespeare was 'noble', Turgenev was 'noble', Beethoven was 'noble'. 'They are a religious people, like the Greeks, or the English of Shakespeare's time. But Maupassant is slick and coarse and commonplace. Are his stories literature?'

'Ah, to hell with literature!' I said. 'It's life.'

'Life in this country?'

'Life in his own country, then.'

'But how do you know?' Terry asked, stopping and staring at me. 'Humanity is the same here as anywhere else. If he's not true of the life we know, he's not true of any sort of life.'

Then he got the job in the monks' school and I got the job in Carmody's and we began to drift apart. There was no quarrel. It was just that I liked company and Terry didn't. I got in with a wild group – Marshall and Redmond and Donnelan, the solicitor – and we sat up until morning, drinking and settling the future of humanity. Terry came with us once, but he didn't talk, and when Donnelan began to hold forth on Shaw and the Life Force I could see his face getting dark. You know Donnelan's line – 'But what I mean – what I want to say – Jasus, will somebody let me talk? I have something important to say.' We all knew that Donnelan was a bit of a joke, but when I said good-night to Terry in the hall he turned on me with an angry look.

'Do those friends of yours do anything but talk?' he asked.

'Never mind, Terry,' I said. 'The Revolution is coming.'

'Not if they have anything to say to it,' Terry said, and walked away from me. I stood there for a while, feeling sorry for myself, as you do when you know that the end of a friendship is in sight. It didn't make me happier when I went back to the room and Donnelan looked at me as if he didn't believe his eyes.

'Magner,' he asked, 'am I dreaming or was there someone with you?'

Suddenly, for no particular reason, I lost my temper.

'Yes, Donnelan,' I said. 'But somebody I wouldn't expect you to recognize.'

That, I suppose, was the last flash of the old love, and after that it was bogged down in argument. Donnelan said that Terry lacked flexibility – flexibility!

Occasionally I met Tess with her little shopping basket and her round rosy cheeks, and she would say reproachfully, 'Ah, Ted, aren't you becoming a great stranger? What did we do to you at all?' And a couple of times I dropped round to sing a song and borrow a book, and Terry told me about his work as a teacher. He was a bit disillusioned with his job, and you wouldn't wonder. Some of the monks kept a mackintosh and muffler handy so that they could drop out to the pictures after dark with some doll. And then there was a thundering row when Terry discovered that a couple of his brightest boys were being sent up for public examinations under the names of notorious ignoramuses, so as to bolster up the record. When Brother Dunphy, the headmaster, argued with Terry that it was only a simple act of charity, Terry replied sourly that it seemed to him more like a criminal offence. After that he got the reputation of being impossible and was not consulted when Patrick Dempsey, the boy he really liked, was put up for examination as Mike MacNamara, the County Councillor's son – Mike the Moke, as Terry called him.

Now, Donnelan is a gas-bag, and, speaking charitably, a bit of a fool, but there were certain things he learned in his Barrack Street slum. One night he said to me, 'Ted, does that fellow Coughlan drink?' 'Drink?' I said, laughing outright at him. 'Himself and a sparrow would have about the same consumption of liquor.' Nothing ever embarrassed Donnelan, who had the hide of a rhinoceros.

'Well, you might be right,' he said reasonably, 'but, begor, I never saw a sparrow that couldn't hold it.'

I thought myself that Donnelan was dreaming, but next time I met Tess I sounded her. 'How's that brother of yours keeping?' I asked. 'Ah, fine, Ted, why?' she asked, as though she was really surprised. 'Oh, nothing,' I said. 'Somebody was telling me that he wasn't looking well.'

'Ah, he's that way this long time, Ted,' she replied, 'and 'tis nothing only the want of sleep. He studies too hard at night, and then he goes wandering all over the country, trying to work off the excitement. Sure, I'm always at him!'

That satisfied me. I knew Tess couldn't tell me a lie. But then, one moonlight night about six months later, three or four of us were standing outside the hotel – the night porter had kicked us out in the middle of an argument, and we were finishing it there. Two was striking from Shandon when I saw Terry coming up the pavement towards us. I never knew whether he recognized me or not, but all at once he crossed the street, and even I could see that the man was drunk.

'Tell me,' said Donnelan, peering across at him, 'is that a sparrow I see at this hour of night?' All at once he spun round on his heels, splitting his sides with laughing. 'Magner's sparrow!' he said. 'Magner's sparrow!' I hope in comparing Donnelan with a rhinoceros I haven't done injustice to either party.

I saw then what was happening. Terry was drinking all right, but he was drinking unknown to his mother and sister. You might almost say he was drinking unknown to himself. Other people could be drunkards, but not he. So he sat at home reading, or pretending to read, until late at night, and then slunk off to some low pub on the quays where he hoped people wouldn't recognize him, and came home only when he knew his family was in bed.

For a long time I debated with myself about whether I shouldn't talk to him. If I made up my mind to do it once, I did it twenty times. But when I ran into him in town, striding slowly along, and saw the dark, handsome face with the slightly ironic smile, I lost courage. His mind was as keen as ever – it may even have been a shade too keen. He was becoming slightly irritable and arrogant. The manners were as careful and the voice was as pleasant as ever – a little too much so. The way he raised his hat high in the air to some woman who passed and whipped the big handkerchief from his breast pocket reminded me of an old actor going down in the world. The farther down he went the worse the acting got. He wouldn't join me for a drink; no, he had this job that simply must be finished tonight. How could I say to him, 'Terry, for God's sake, give up trying to pretend you have work to do. I know you're an impostor and you're drinking yourself to death.' You couldn't talk like that to a man of his kind. People like him are all of a piece; they have to stand or fall by something inside themselves.

He was forty when his mother died, and by that time it looked as though he'd have Tess on his hands for life as well. I went back to the house with him after the funeral. He was cruelly broken up. I discovered that he had spent his first few weeks abroad that summer and he was full of it. He had stayed in Paris and visited the cathedrals round, and they had made a deep impression on him. He had never seen real architecture before. I had a vague hope that it might have jolted him out of the rut he had been getting into, but I was wrong. It was worse he was getting.

Then, a couple of years later, I was at home one evening, finishing up some work, when a knock came to the door. I opened it myself and saw old Pa Hourigan, the policeman, outside. Pa had a schoolgirl complexion and a white moustache, China-blue eyes and a sour elderly mouth, like a baby who has learned the facts of life too soon. It surprised me because we never did more than pass the time of day.

'May I speak to you for a moment, Mr Magner?' he asked modestly. ' 'Tis on a rather private matter.'

'You can to be sure, Sergeant,' I said, joking him. 'I'm not a bit afraid. 'Tis years since I played ball on the public street. Have a drink.'

'I never touch it, going on night duty,' he said, coming into the front room. 'I hope you will pardon my calling, but you know I am not a man to interfere in anyone else's private affairs.'

By this time he had me puzzled and a bit anxious. I knew him for an exceptionally retiring man, and he was clearly upset.

'Ah, of course you're not,' I said. 'No one would accuse you of it. Sit down and tell me what the trouble is.'

'Aren't you a friend of Mr Coughlan, the teacher?' he asked.

'I am,' I said.

'Mr Magner,' he said, exploding on me, 'can you do nothing with the man?'

I looked at him for a moment and had a premonition of disaster.

'Is it as bad as that?' I asked.

'It cannot go on, Mr Magner,' he said, shaking his head. 'It cannot go on. I saved him before. Not because he was anything to me, because I hardly knew the man. Not even because of his poor decent sister, though I pity her with my whole heart and soul. It was for the respect I have for education. And you know that, Mr Magner,' he added earnestly, meaning (which was true enough) that I owed it to him that I had never paid a fine for drinking during prohibited hours.

'We all know it, Sergeant,' I said. 'And I assure you, we appreciate it.'

'No one knows, Mr Magner,' he went on, 'what sacrifices Mrs Hourigan and myself made to put that boy of ours through college, and I would not give it to say to him that an educated man could sink so low. But there are others at the barracks who don't think the way I do. I name no names, Mr Magner, but there are those who would be glad to see an educated man humiliated.'

'What is it, Sergeant?' I asked. 'Drink?'

'Mr Magner,' he said indignantly, 'when did I ever interfere with an educated man for drinking? I know when a man has a lot on his mind he cannot always do without stimulants.'

'You don't mean drugs?' I asked. The idea had crossed my mind once or twice.

'No, Mr Magner, I do not,' he said, quivering with indignation. 'I mean those low, loose, abandoned women that I would have whipped and transported.'

If he had told me that Terry had turned into a common thief, I couldn't have been more astonished and horrified. Horrified is the word.

'You don't mind my saying that I find that very hard to believe, Sergeant?' I asked.

'Mr Magner,' he said with great dignity, 'in my calling a man does not use words lightly.'

'I know Terry Coughlan since we were boys together, and I never as much as heard an unseemly word from him,' I said.

'Then all I can say, Mr Magner, is that I'm glad, very glad that you've never seen him as I have, in a condition I would not compare to the beasts.' There were real tears in the old man's eyes. 'I spoke to him myself about it. At four o'clock this morning I separated him from two of those vile creatures that I knew well were robbing him. I pleaded with him as if he was my own brother. "Mr Coughlan," I said, "what will your soul do at the Judgement?" And Mr Magner, in decent society I would not repeat the disgusting reply he made me.'

'*Corruptio optimi pessima*,' I said to myself.

'That is Latin, Mr Magner,' the old policeman said with real pleasure.

'And it means "Lilies that fester smell far worse than weeds", Sergeant,'
I said. 'I don't know if I can do anything. I suppose I'll have to try. If he
goes on like this he'll destroy himself, body and soul.'

'Do what you can for his soul, Mr Magner,' whispered the old man,
making for the door. 'As for his body, I wouldn't like to answer.' At the
door he turned with a mad stare in his blue eyes. 'I would not like to
answer,' he repeated, shaking his grey pate again.

It gave me a nasty turn. Pa Hourigan was happy. He had done his duty
but mine still remained to be done. I sat for an hour, thinking about it, and
the more I thought, the more hopeless it seemed. Then I put on my hat
and went out.

Terry lived at that time in a nice little house on College Road; a little
red-brick villa with a bow window. He answered the door himself, a slow,
brooding, black-haired man with a long pale face. He didn't let on to be
either surprised or pleased.

'Come in,' he said with a crooked smile. 'You're a great stranger, aren't
you?'

'You're a bit of a stranger yourself, Terry,' I said jokingly. Then Tess
came out, drying her hands in her apron. Her little cheeks were as rosy as
ever, but the gloss was gone. I had the feeling that now there was nothing
much she didn't know about her brother. Even the nervous smile suggested
that she knew what I had come for – of course, old Hourigan must have
brought him home.

'Ah, Ted, 'tis a cure for sore eyes to see you,' she said. 'You'll have a
cup? You will, to be sure.'

'You'll have a drink,' Terry said.

'Do you know, I think I will, Terry,' I said, seeing a nice natural opening
for the sort of talk I had in mind.

'Ah, you may as well have both,' said Tess, and a few minutes later she
brought in the tea and cake. It was like old times until she left us, and then
it wasn't. Terry poured out the whiskey for me and the tea for himself,
though his hand was shaking so badly that he could scarcely lift his cup. It
was not all pretence; he didn't want to give me an opening, that was all.
There was a fine print over his head – I think it was a Constable of Salisbury
Cathedral. He talked about the monastery school, the usual clever, bitter,
contemptuous stuff about monks, inspectors, and pupils. The whole thing
was too carefully staged, the lifting of the cup and the wiping of the

moustache, but it hypnotized me. There was something there you couldn't do violence to. I finished my drink and got up to go.

'What hurry is on you?' he asked irritably.

I mumbled something about it's getting late.

'Nonsense!' he said. 'You're not a boy any longer.'

Was he just showing off his strength of will or hoping to put off the evil hour when he would go slinking down the quays again?

'Ah, they'll be expecting me,' I said, and then, as I used to do when we were younger, I turned to the bookcase. 'I see you have a lot of Maupassant at last,' I said.

'I bought them last time I was in Paris,' he said, standing beside me and looking at the books as though he were seeing them for the first time.

'A death-bed repentance?' I asked lightly, but he ignored me.

'I met another great admirer of his there,' he said sourly. 'A lady you should meet some time.'

'I'd love to if I ever get there,' I said.

'Her address is the Rue de Grenelle,' he said, and then with a wild burst of mockery, 'the left-hand pavement.'

At last his guard was down, and it was Maupassant's name that had done it. And still I couldn't say anything. An angry flush mounted his pale dark face and made it sinister in its violence.

'I suppose you didn't know I indulged in that hideous vice?' he snarled.

'I heard something,' I said. 'I'm sorry, Terry.'

The angry flush died out of his face and the old brooding look came back.

'A funny thing about those books,' he said. 'This woman I was speaking about, I thought she was bringing me to a hotel. I suppose I was a bit muddled with drink, but after dark one of these places is much like another. "This isn't a hotel," I said when we got upstairs. "No," she said, "it's my room."'

As he told it, I could see that he was living it all over again, something he could tell nobody but myself.

'There was a screen in the corner. I suppose it's the result of reading too much romantic fiction, but I thought there might be somebody hidden behind it. There was. You'd never guess what?'

'No.'

'A baby,' he said, his eyes boring through me. 'A child of maybe eighteen months. I wouldn't know. While I was looking, she changed him. He didn't wake.'

'What was it?' I asked, searching for the message that he obviously thought the incident contained. 'A dodge?'

'No,' he said almost grudgingly. 'A country girl in trouble, trying to support her child, that's all. We went to bed and she fell asleep. I couldn't. It's many years now since I've been able to sleep like that. So I put on the light and began to read one of the books that I carried round in my pocket. The light woke her and she wanted to see what I had. "Oh, Maupassant," she said. "He's a great writer." "Is he?" I said. I thought she might be repeating something she'd picked up from one of her customers. She wasn't. She began to talk about *Boule de Suif*. It reminded me of the arguments we used to have in our young days.' Suddenly he gave me a curious boyish smile. 'You remember, when we used to walk up the river together.'

'Oh, I remember,' I said with a sigh.

'We were terrible young idiots, the pair of us,' he said sadly. 'Then she began to talk about *The Tellier Household*. I said it had poetry. "Oh, if it's poetry you want, you don't go to Maupassant. You go to Vigny, you go to Musset, but Maupassant is life, and life isn't poetry. It's only when you see what life can do to you that you realize what a great writer Maupassant is." . . . Wasn't that an extraordinary thing to happen?' he asked fiercely, and again the angry colour mounted his cheeks.

'Extraordinary,' I said, wondering if Terry himself knew how extraordinary it was. But it was exactly as if he were reading the thoughts as they crossed my mind.

'A prostitute from some French village, a drunken old waster from an Irish provincial town, lying awake in the dawn in Paris, discussing Maupassant. And the baby, of course. Maupassant would have made a lot of the baby.'

'I declare to God, I think if I'd been in your shoes, I'd have brought them back with me,' I said. I knew when I said it that I was talking nonsense, but it was a sort of release for all the bitterness inside me.

'What?' he asked, mocking me. 'A prostitute and her baby? My dear Mr Magner, you're becoming positively romantic in your old age.'

'A man like you should have a wife and children,' I said.

'Ah, but that's a different story,' he said malevolently. 'Maupassant would never have ended a story like that.'

And he looked at me almost triumphantly with those mad, dark eyes. I knew how Maupassant would have ended that story all right. Maupassant, as the girl said, was life, and life was pretty nearly through with Terry Coughlan.

In the Train

1

'There!' said the sergeant's wife. 'You would hurry me.'

'I always like being in time for a train,' replied the sergeant, with the equability of one who has many times before explained the guiding principle of his existence.

'I'd have had heaps of time to buy the hat,' added his wife.

The sergeant sighed and opened his evening paper. His wife looked out on the dark platform, pitted with pale lights under which faces and faces passed, lit up and dimmed again. A uniformed lad strode up and down with a tray of periodicals and chocolates. Farther up the platform a drunken man was being seen off by his friends.

'I'm very fond of Michael O'Leary,' he shouted. 'He is the most sincere man I know.'

'I have no life,' sighed the sergeant's wife. 'No life at all. There isn't a soul to speak to; nothing to look at all day but bogs and mountains and rain – always rain! And the people! Well, we've had a fine sample of them, haven't we?'

The sergeant continued to read.

'Just for the few days it's been like heaven. Such interesting people! Oh, I thought Mr Boyle had a glorious face! And his voice – it went through me.'

The sergeant lowered his paper, took off his peaked cap, laid it on the seat beside him, and lit his pipe. He lit it in the old-fashioned way, ceremoniously, his eyes blinking pleasurably like a sleepy cat's in the match-flare. His wife scrutinized each face that passed and it was plain that for her life meant faces and people and things and nothing more.

'Oh, dear!' she said again. 'I simply have no existence. I was educated in a convent and play the piano; my father was a literary man, and yet I am compelled to associate with the lowest types of humanity. If it was even a decent town, but a village!'

'Ah,' said the sergeant, gapping his reply with anxious puffs, 'maybe with God's help we'll get a shift one of these days.' But he said it without conviction, and it was also plain that he was well-pleased with himself, with the prospect of returning home with his pipe and his paper.

'Here are Magner and the others,' said his wife as four other policemen passed the barrier. 'I hope they'll have sense enough to let us alone. . . . How do you do? How do you do? Had a nice time, boys?' she called with sudden animation, and her pale, sullen face became warm and vivacious. The policemen smiled and touched their caps but did not halt.

'They might have stopped to say good evening,' she added sharply, and her face sank into its old expression of boredom and dissatisfaction. 'I don't think I'll ask Delancey to tea again. The others make an attempt but, really, Delancey is hopeless. When I smile and say: "Guard Delancey, wouldn't you like to use the butter-knife?" he just scowls at me from under his shaggy brows and says without a moment's hesitation: "I would not."'

'Ah, Delancey is a poor slob,' the sergeant said affectionately.

'Oh, yes, but that's not enough, Jonathan. Slob or no slob, he should make an attempt. He's a young man; he should have a dinner jacket at least. What sort of wife will he get if he won't even wear a dinner jacket?'

'He's easy, I'd say. He's after a farm in Waterford.'

'Oh, a farm! A farm! The wife is only an incidental, I suppose?'

'Well, now, from all I hear she's a damn nice little incidental.'

'Yes, I suppose many a nice little incidental came from a farm,' answered his wife, raising her pale brows. But the irony was lost on him.

'Indeed yes, indeed yes,' he said fervently.

'And here,' she added in biting tones, 'come our charming neighbours.'

Into the pale lamplight stepped a group of peasants. Not such as one sees near a capital but in the mountains and along the coasts. Gnarled, wild, with turbulent faces, their ill-cut clothes full of character, the women in pale brown shawls, the men wearing black sombreros and carrying big sticks, they swept in, ill at ease, laughing and shouting defiantly. And so much part of their natural environment were they that for a moment they seemed to create about themselves rocks and bushes, tarns, turf-ricks, and sea.

With a prim smile the sergeant's wife bowed to them through the open window.

'How do you do? How do you do?' she called. 'Had a nice time?'

At the same moment the train gave a jolt and there was a rush in which the excited peasants were carried away. Some minutes passed; the influx of passengers almost ceased, and a porter began to slam the doors. The drunken man's voice rose in a cry of exultation.

'You can't possibly beat O'Leary,' he declared. 'I'd lay down my life for Michael O'Leary.'

Then, just as the train was about to start, a young woman in a brown shawl rushed through the barrier. The shawl, which came low enough to hide her eyes, she held firmly across her mouth, leaving visible only a long thin nose with a hint of pale flesh at either side. Beneath the shawl she was carrying a large parcel.

She looked hastily around; a porter shouted to her and pushed her towards the nearest compartment, which happened to be that occupied by the sergeant and his wife. He had actually seized the handle of the door when the sergeant's wife sat up and screamed.

'Quick! Quick!' she cried. 'Look who it is! She's coming in. Jonathan! Jonathan!'

The sergeant rose with a look of alarm on his broad red face. The porter threw open the door, with his free hand grasping the woman's elbow. But when she laid eyes on the sergeant's startled face she stepped back, tore herself free, and ran crazily up the platform. The engine shrieked; the porter slammed the door with a curse; somewhere another door opened and shut, and the row of watchers, frozen into effigies of farewell, now dark now bright, began to glide gently past the window, and the stale, smoky air was charged with the breath of open fields.

2

The four policemen spread themselves out in a separate compartment and lit cigarettes.

'Poor old Delancey!' Magner said with his reckless laugh. 'He's cracked on her all right.'

'Cracked on her,' agreed Fox. 'Did ye see the eye he gave her?'

Delancey smiled sheepishly. He was a tall, handsome, black-haired young man with the thick eyebrows described by the sergeant's wife. He was new to the force and suffered from a mixture of natural gentleness and country awkwardness.

'I am,' he said in his husky voice. 'The devil admire me, I never hated anyone yet, but I think I hate the living sight of her.'

'Oh now, oh now!' protested Magner.

'I do. I think the Almighty God must have put that one into the world with the one main object of persecuting me.'

'Well indeed,' said Foley, ' 'tis a mystery to me how the sergeant puts up with her. If any woman up and called me by an outlandish name like Jonathan when everyone knew my name was plain John I'd do fourteen days for her – by God, I would, and a calendar month.'

The four men were now launched on a favourite topic that held them for more than an hour. None of them liked the sergeant's wife and all had stories to tell against her. From these there emerged the fact that she was an incurable scandalmonger and mischiefmaker who couldn't keep quiet about her own business, much less about that of her neighbours. And while they talked the train dragged across a dark plain, the heart of Ireland, and in the moonless night tiny cottage-windows blew past like sparks from a fire, and a pale simulacrum of the lighted carriages leaped and frolicked over hedges and fields. Magner shut the window and the compartment began to fill with smoke.

'She'll never rest till she's out of Farranchreesht,' he said.

'That she mightn't!' groaned Delancey.

'How would you like the city yourself, Dan?' asked Magner.

'Man dear,' exclaimed Delancey with sudden brightness, 'I'd like it fine. There's great life in a city.'

'You're welcome to it,' said Foley, folding his hands across his paunch.

'Why so? What's wrong with it?'

'I'm better off where I am.'

'But the life!'

'Life be damned! What sort of life is it when you're always under someone's eye? Look at the poor devils in court.'

'True enough, true enough,' agreed Fox.

'Ah, yes, yes,' said Delancey, 'but the adventures they have!'

'What adventures?'

'There was a sergeant in court only yesterday telling me one thing that happened himself. 'Twas an old maid without a soul in the world that died in an old loft on the quays. The sergeant put a new man on duty outside the door while he went back to report, and all he had to do was kick the door and frighten off the rats.'

'That's enough, that's enough!' cried Foley.

'Yes, yes, but listen now, listen can't you?' cried Delancey. 'He was there ten minutes with a bit of candle when the door at the foot of the stairs began to open. "Who's there?" says he, getting a bit nervous. "Who's there I say?" No answer, and still the door kept opening. Then he gave a laugh. What was it only an old cat? "Puss, puss," says he, "come on up, puss." Then he gave another look and the hair stood up on his head. There was another bloody cat coming in. "Get out!" says he to scare them, and then another cat came in and then another, and in his fright he dropped the candle. The cats began to hiss and bawl and that robbed him of the last stitch of sense. He made down the stairs, and if he did he trod on a cat, and went down head over heels, and when he tried to grip something 'twas a cat he gripped, and he felt the claws tearing his face. He was out for three weeks after.'

'That's a bloody fine adventure,' said Foley with bitter restraint.

'Isn't it thought?' Delancey said eagerly. 'You'd be a long time in Farranchreesht before anything like that would happen you.'

'That's the thing about Farranchreesht, lad,' said Magner. ' 'Tis a great ease to be able to put on your cap and go for a drink any hour of the day or night.'

'Yes,' added Foley, 'and to know the worst case you're likely to have in ten years is a bit of a scrap about politics.'

'I don't know,' Delancey sighed dreamily. 'Chrisht, there's great charm about the Criminal Courts.'

'Damn the much they had for you when you were in the box,' growled Foley.

'I know, sure, I know,' admitted Delancey crestfallen. 'I was sweating.'

'Shutting your eyes you were,' said Magner, 'like a kid afraid he was going to get a box on the ear.'

'Still,' said Delancey, 'this sergeant I'm talking about, he said after a while you wouldn't mind that no more than if 'twas a card party. He said you'd talk back to the judge as man to man.'

'I dare say that's true,' agreed Magner.

There was silence in the smoky compartment that jolted and rocked on its way across Ireland, and the four occupants, each touched with that morning wit which afflicts no one so much as state witnesses, thought of how they'd speak to the judge now if only they had him before them as man to man. They looked up to see a fat red face behind the door, and a moment later it was dragged back.

'Is this my carriage, gentlemen?' asked a meek and boozy voice.

'No, 'tisn't. Go on with you!' snapped Magner.

'I had as nice a carriage as ever was put on a railway train,' said the drunk, leaning in, 'a handsome carriage, and 'tis lost.'

'Try farther on,' suggested Delancey.

'Ye'll excuse me interrupting yeer conversation, gentlemen.'

'That's all right, that's all right.'

'I'm very melancholic. My best friend, I parted him this very night, and 'tis unknown to anyone, only the Almighty and Merciful God [here the drunk reverently raised his bowler hat and let it slide down the back of his neck to the floor] if I'll ever lay eyes on him again in this world. Good-night, gentlemen, and thanks, thanks for all yeer kindness.'

As the drunk slithered away up the corridor Delancey laughed. Fox, who had remained thoughtful, resumed the conversation where it had left off.

'Delancey wasn't the only one that was sweating,' he said.

'He was not,' agreed Foley. 'Even the sergeant was a bit shook.'

'He was very shook. When he caught up the poison mug to identify it he was shaking, and before he could put it down it danced a jig on the table.'

'Ah, dear God, dear God,' sighed Delancey, 'what killed me most entirely was the bloody old model of the house. I didn't mind anything else only the house. There it was, a living likeness, with the bit of grass in front and the shutter hanging loose, and every time I looked at it I was in the back lane in Farranchreesht, and then I'd look up and see the lean fellow in the wig pointing his finger at me.'

'Well, thank God,' said Foley with simple devotion, 'this time tomorrow I'll be in Ned Ivers's back with a pint in my fist.'

Delancey shook his head, a dreamy smile playing upon his dark face.

'I don't know,' he said. ''Tis a small place, Farranchreesht; a small, mangy old place with no interest or advancement in it.' His face lit up as the sergeant appeared in the corridor.

'Here's the sergeant now,' he said.

'He wasn't long getting tired of Julietta,' whispered Magner maliciously.

The door was pushed back and the sergeant entered, loosening the collar of his tunic. He fell into a corner seat, crossed his legs, and accepted the cigarette which Delancey proffered.

'Well, lads,' he exclaimed. 'What about a jorum?'

'Isn't it remarkable?' said Foley. 'I was only just talking about it.'

'I have noted before now, Peter,' said the sergeant, 'that you and me have what might be called a simultaneous thirst.'

3

The country folk were silent and exhausted. Kendillon drowsed now and then, but he suffered from blood-pressure, and after a while his breathing grew thicker and stronger till at last it exploded in a snort and he started up, broad awake and angry. In the silence rain spluttered and tapped along the roof and the dark window-panes streamed with shining runnels of water that trickled to the floor. Moll Mhor scowled, her lower lip thrust out. She was a great flop of a woman with a big, coarse, powerful face. The other two women whose eyes were closed had their brown shawls drawn tight about their heads, but Moll's was round her shoulders and the gap above her breasts was filled with a blaze of scarlet.

'Aren't we home yet?' Kendillon asked crossly, starting awake after one of his drowsing fits.

Moll glowered at him.

'No, nor won't be. What scour is on you?'

'My little house,' moaned Kendillon.

'My little house,' mimicked Moll. ' 'Twasn't enough for you to board the windows and put barbed wire on the gate.'

' 'Tis all very well for you that have someone to mind yours for you,' he snarled.

One of the women laughed softly and turned a haggard virginal face within the cowl of her shawl.

' 'Tis that have me laughing,' she explained apologetically. 'Tim Dwyer this week past at the stirabout pot.'

'And making the beds,' chimed in the third woman.

'And washing the children's faces! Glory be to God, he'll be mad.'

'Ay,' said Moll, 'and his chickens running off with Thade Kendillon's roof.'

'My roof is it?' he asked.

'Yes.'

' 'Tis a good roof,' he said roughly. ' 'Tis a better roof than ever was seen over your head since the day you married.'

'Oh, Mary my mother!' sighed Moll, ' 'tis a great pity of me this three hours and I looking at the likes of you instead of my own fine bouncing man.'

' 'Tis a new thing to hear you praising Sean then,' said a woman.

'I wronged him,' Moll said contritely. 'I did so. I wronged him before God and the world.'

At this moment the drunken man pulled back the door of the compartment and looked from face to face with an expression of deepening melancholy.

'She's not here,' he said in disappointment.

'Who's not here, mister?' asked Moll with a wink at the others.

'I'm looking for my own carriage, ma'am,' said the drunk with melancholy dignity, 'and whatever the bloody hell they done with it, 'tis lost. The railways in this country are gone to hell.'

'Wisha, if that's all that's worrying you, wouldn't you sit here with me?' asked Moll. 'I'm here so long I'm forgetting what a real man looks like.'

'I would with great pleasure,' replied the drunk politely, 'but 'tisn't only the carriage. 'Tis my travelling-companion. I'm a lonely man; I parted my best friend this very night; I found one to console me, and then when I turned my back – God took her!'

And with a dramatic gesture he closed the door and continued on his way. The country folk sat up, blinking. The smoke of the men's pipes filled the compartment and the heavy air was laden with the smell of homespun and turf-smoke, the sweet pungent odour of which had penetrated every fibre of their clothes.

'Listen to the rain!' said one of the women. 'We'll have a wet walk home.'

' 'Twill be midnight before we're in,' said another.

'Ah, what matter sure when the whole country will be up? There'll be a lot of talking done in Farranchreesht tonight.'

'A lot of talking and no sleep.'

'Oh, Farranchreesht! Farranchreesht!' cried the young woman with the haggard face, the ravaged lineaments of which were suddenly transfigured. 'Farranchreesht and the sky over you, I wouldn't change places with the Queen of England tonight!'

And suddenly Farranchreesht, the bare bogland with the hump-backed mountain behind, the little white houses and the dark fortifications of turf that made it seem like the flame-blackened ruin of some mighty city, all was lit up in their minds. An old man sitting in a corner, smoking a broken clay pipe, thumped his stick on the floor.

'Well now,' said Kendillon darkly, 'wasn't it great impudence in her to come back?'

'Wasn't it indeed?' echoed one of the women.

'I'd say she won't be there long,' he went on knowingly.

'You'll give her the hunt, I suppose?' asked Moll politely, too politely.

'If no one else do, I'll give her the hunt myself. What right have she in a decent place?'

'Oh, the hunt, the hunt,' agreed a woman. 'Sure, no one could ever darken her door again.'

'And what the hell did we tell all the lies for?' asked Moll with her teeth on edge to be at Kendillon. 'Thade Kendillon there swore black was white.'

'What else would I do, woman? There was never an informer in my family.'

'I'm surprised to hear it,' said Moll vindictively, but the old man thumped his stick three or four times for silence.

'We all told our story,' he said, 'and we told it well. And no one told it better than Moll. You'd think to hear her she believed it herself.'

'I declare to God I very nearly did,' she said with a wild laugh.

'I seen great changes in my time, great changes,' the old man said, shaking his head, 'and now I see a greater change still.'

A silence followed his words. There was profound respect in all their eyes. The old man coughed and spat.

'What change is that, Colm?' asked Moll.

'Did any of ye ever think the day would come when a woman in our parish would do the like of that?'

'Never, never.'

'But she might do it for land?'

'She might.'

'Or for money?'

'She might so.'

'She might indeed. When the hunger is money people kill for the money; when the hunger is land people kill for the land. But what are they killing for now? I tell ye, there's a great change coming. In the ease of the world people are asking more. When I was a boy in the barony if you killed a beast you made six pieces of it, one for yourself and the rest for the neighbours. The same if you made a catch of fish. And that's how it was with us from the beginning of time. But now look at the change! The people aren't as poor or as good or as generous or as strong.'

'Or as wild,' added Moll with a vicious glance at Kendillon. ' 'Tis in the men you'd mostly notice the change.'

The door opened and Magner, Delancey, and the sergeant entered. Magner was already drunk.

'I was lonely without you, Moll,' he said. 'You're the biggest and brazenest and cleverest liar of the lot and you lost me my sergeant's stripes, but I'll forgive you everything if you'll give us one bar of the "Colleen Dhas Roo".'

4

'I'm a lonely man,' said the drunk. 'And I'm going back to a lonely habitation.'

'My best friend,' he continued, 'I left behind me – Michael O'Leary, the most sincere man I know. 'Tis a great pity you don't know Michael and a great pity Michael don't know you. But look at the misfortunate way things happen! I was looking for someone to console me, and the moment I turned my back you were gone.'

He placed his hand solemnly under the woman's chin and raised her face to the light. With the other hand he stroked her cheeks.

'You have a beautiful face,' he said reverently, 'a beautiful face. But what's more important, you have a beautiful soul. I look into your eyes and I see the beauty of your nature. Allow me one favour. Only one favour before we part.'

He bent and kissed her. Then he picked up his bowler which had fallen once more, put it on back to front, took his dispatch case, and got out.

The woman sat on alone. Her shawl was thrown open and beneath it she wore a bright-blue blouse. The carriage was cold, the night outside black and cheerless, and within her something had begun to contract that threatened to crush the very spark of life in her. She could no longer fight it off even when for the hundredth time she went over the scenes of the previous day; the endless hours in the dock, the wearisome questions and speeches she could not understand, and the long wait in the cells till the jury returned. She felt again the shiver of mortal anguish that went through her when the chief warder beckoned angrily from the stairs and the wardress, glancing hastily in a hand-mirror, pushed her forward. She saw the jury with their expressionless faces. She was standing there alone, in nervous twitches jerking back the shawl from her face to give herself air. She was trying to say a prayer but the words were being drowned in her mind by the thunder of nerves, crashing and bursting. She could feel one which had escaped dancing madly at the side of her mouth, but was powerless to recapture it.

'The verdict of the jury is that Helena Maguire is not guilty.' Which was it? Death or life? She could not say. 'Silence! Silence!' shouted the usher though no one had tried to say anything. 'Any other charge?' asked a weary voice. 'Release the prisoner.' 'Silence!' shouted the usher again. The chief warder opened the door of the dock and she began to run. When she reached the steps she stopped and looked back to see if she was being followed. A policeman held open a door and she found herself in an ill-lit, draughty stone corridor. She stood there, the old shawl about her face. The crowd began to emerge. The first was a tall girl with a rapt expression as though she were walking on air. When she saw the woman she halted, her hands went up in an instinctive gesture, as though to feel her, to caress her. It was that look of hers, that gait as of a sleepwalker that brought the woman to her senses. . . .

But now the memory had no warmth in her mind, and the something within her continued to contract, smothering her with loneliness, shame, and fear. She began to mutter crazily to herself. The train, now almost empty, was stopping at every little wayside station. Now and again a blast from the Atlantic pushed at it as though trying to capsize it.

She looked up as the door slammed open and Moll came in, swinging her shawl behind her.

'They're all up the train. Wouldn't you come?'

'No, no, I couldn't.'

'Why couldn't you? Who are you minding? Is it Thade Kendillon?'

'No, no, I'll stop as I am.'

'Here, take a sup of this.' Moll fumbled in her shawl and produced a bottle of liquor as pale as water. 'Wait till I tell you what Magner said! That fellow is a limb of the devil. "Have you e'er a drop, Moll?" says he. "Maybe I have," says I. "What is it?" says he. "For God's sake, baptize it quick and call it whiskey."'

The woman took the bottle and put it to her lips. She shivered as she drank.

' 'Tis a good drop,' said Moll approvingly.

Next moment there were loud voices in the corridor. Moll grabbed the bottle and hid it under her shawl. But it was only Magner, the sergeant, and Delancey. After them came the two countrywomen, giggling. Magner held out his hand.

'Helena,' he said, 'accept my congratulations.'

She took his hand, smiling awkwardly.

'We'll get you the next time though,' he added.

'Musha, what are you saying, mister?'

'Not a word. You're a clever woman, a remarkable woman, and I give you full credit for it. You threw dust in all our eyes.'

'Poison is supposed to be an easy thing to trace but it beat me to trace it,' said the sergeant, barely concealing his curiosity.

'Well, well, there's things they're saying about me!' she said with a nervous laugh.

'Tell him,' advised Magner. 'There's nothing he can do to you now. You're as safe as the judge himself. Last night when the jury came in with the verdict you could have stood there in the dock and said: "Ye're wrong. I did it. I got the stuff in such and such a place. I gave it to him because he was old and dirty and cantankerous and a miser. I did it and I'm proud of it." You could have said every word of that and they couldn't have laid a finger on you.'

'Indeed, what a thing I'd say!'

'Well, you could.'

'The law is truly a remarkable phenomenon,' said the sergeant, who was also rather squiffy. 'Here you are, sitting at your ease at the expense of the state, and for one simple word of a couple of letters you could be up in Mountjoy, waiting for the rope and the morning jaunt.'

The woman shuddered. The young woman with the ravaged face looked up.

' 'Twas the holy will of God,' she said.

' 'Twas all the bloody lies Moll Mhor told,' replied Magner.

' 'Twas the will of God.'

'There was many hanged in the wrong,' said the sergeant.

'Even so, even so, 'twas God's will.'

'You have a new blouse, Helena,' said the other woman in an envious tone.

'I seen it last night in a shop on the quays.'

'How much was it?'

'Honour of God!' exclaimed Magner, looking at the woman in stupefaction. 'Is that all you had to think of? You should have been on your bended knees before the altar.'

'And sure I was,' she answered indignantly.

'Women!' exclaimed Magner with a gesture of despair. He winked at Moll and they retired to the next compartment. But the interior was reflected clearly in the corridor window, and the others could see the pale quivering image of the policeman lift the bottle to his lips and blow a long silent blast on it. The young woman who had spoken of the blouse laughed.

'There'll be one good day's work done on the head of the trial,' she said.

'How so?' asked the sergeant.

'Dan Canty will make a great brew of poteen while ye have all yeer backs turned.'

'I'll get Dan Canty yet,' replied the sergeant stiffly.

'You will, the way you got Helena.'

'I'll get him yet,' he said as he consulted his watch. 'We'll be in in another quarter of an hour. 'Tis time we were all getting back to our respective compartments.'

Magner entered and the other policemen rose. The sergeant fastened his collar and buckled his belt. Magner swayed, holding the doorframe, a mawkish smile on his thin, handsome, dissipated face.

'Well, good-night to you now, ma'am,' said the sergeant primly. 'I'm as glad for all our sakes things ended as they did.'

'Good night, Helena,' said Magner, bowing low and promptly tottering. 'There'll be one happy man in Farranchreesht tonight.'

'Come on, Joe,' protested the sergeant.

'One happy man,' Magner repeated obstinately. ' 'Tis his turn now.'

'You're drunk, man,' said Delancey.

'You wanted him,' Magner said heavily. 'Your people wouldn't let you have him but you have him now in spite of them all.'

'Do you mean Cady Driscoll?' hissed the woman with sudden anger, leaning towards Magner, the shawl tight about her head.

'Never mind who I mean. You have him.'

'He's no more to me now than the salt sea.'

The policemen went out first, the women followed, Moll Mhor laughing boisterously. The woman was left alone. Through the window she could see little cottages stepping down over wet and naked rocks to the water's edge. The flame of life had narrowed in her to a pinpoint, and she could only wonder at the force that had caught her up, mastered her and then thrown her aside.

'No more to me,' she repeated dully to her own image in the glass, 'no more to me than the salt sea.'

The Corkerys

May MacMahon was a good-looking girl, the only child of Jack MacMahon, the accountant, and his wife, Margaret. They lived in Cork, on Summerhill, the steep street that led from the flat of the city to the heights of Montenotte. She had always lived the life of a girl of good family, with piano lessons, dancing class, and crushes on her schoolfriends' brothers. Only occasionally did she wonder what it was all about, and then she invariably forgot to ask her father, who would certainly know. Her father knew everything, or almost everything. He was a tall, shy, good-looking man, who seemed to have been expecting martyrdom from his earliest years and drinking Irish whiskey to endure it. May's mother was small and pretty and very opinionated, though her opinions varied, and anyway did not last long. Her father's opinions never varied, and lasted for ever.

When May became friendly with the Corkery family, it turned out that he had always had strong opinions about them as well. Mr Corkery, a mild, inarticulate solicitor, whom May remembered going for lonely walks for the good of his health, had died and left his family with very limited means, but his widow had good connections and managed to provide an education (mostly free) for all six children. Of the boys, the eldest, Tom, was now a Dominican, and Joe, who came next in line, was also going in for the priesthood. The Church was in the family's blood, because Mrs Corkery's brother was the Dean and her sister was Mother Superior of the convent of an enclosed order outside the city. Mrs Corkery's nickname among the children was 'Reverend Mother', and they accused her of imitating her sister, but Mrs Corkery only sniffed and said if everybody became priests and nuns there would soon be no Church left. Mrs Corkery seemed to believe quite seriously that the needs of the Church were the only possible excuse for sex.

From knowing the Corkerys May began to realize at last what life was about. It was no longer necessary to ask her father. Anyway he wouldn't know. He and her mother were nice but commonplace. Everything they said and did was dull and predictable, and even when they went to Mass on Sunday they did so only because everyone else did it. The Corkerys were rarely dull and never predictable. Though their whole life seemed to centre on the Church, they were not in the least pietistic. The Dean fought with Mrs Corkery; Father Tim fought with Joe; the sisters fought with their brothers, who, they said, were getting all the attention, and fought one another when their brothers were not available. Tessie, the eldest girl, known as 'The Limb of the Devil', or just 'The Limb', was keeping company with a young stockbroker who told her a lot of dirty stories, which she repeated with great gusto to her brothers, particularly to Father Tim. This, however, was for family reasons, because they all agreed that Tim was inclined to put on airs.

And then The Limb astonished everybody by entering the convent where her aunt was Mother Superior. May attended the Reception in the little convent chapel, which struck her to the heart by its combination of poverty and gentility. She felt that the ceremony might have been tolerable in a great cathedral with a choir and thundering organ, but not in that converted drawing-room, where the nuns knelt along the side walls and squeaked like mourners. The Limb was laid out on the altar and first covered with roses as though she were dead; then an old nun clipped her long black hair with a shears. It fell and lay at her head as though it too had died. May drew a quick breath and glanced at Joe, who was kneeling beside her. Though he had his hands over his face, she knew from the way his shoulders moved that he was crying. Then she cried, too.

For a full week the ceremony gave her the horrors every time she remembered it, and she felt she should have nothing more to do with such an extraordinary family. All the same, a week with her parents was enough to make her realize the attraction of the Corkerys even more than before.

'Did it scare you, May?' Rosie, the second girl, asked with a wicked grin. 'Cripes, it put the fear of God into me. I'm not having any of that *de profundis* stuff; I'm joining a decent missionary order.' This was the first May had heard of Rosie's vocation. Inside a year, she, too, was in a convent, but in Rome, and 'having a gas time', as she casually reported home.

They really were an extraordinary family, and the Dean was as queer as any of them. The Sunday following the ceremony May was at dinner there, and he put his hand firmly on her shoulder as though he were about to yank off her dress, and gave her a crooked smile that would have convinced any reasonable observer that he was a sex maniac, and yet May knew that almost every waking moment his thoughts were concentrated on outwitting the Bishop, who seemed to be the greatest enemy of the Church since Nero. The Bishop was a Dominican, and the Dean felt that a monk's place was in the cloister.

'The man is a bully!' he said, with an astonishment and grief that would have moved any audience but his own family.

'Oh, now, Mick!' said Mrs Corkery placidly. She was accustomed to hearing the Bishop denounced.

'I'm sorry, Josephine,' the Dean said with a formal regret that rang equally untrue. 'The man is a bully. An infernal bully, what's more. I'm not criticizing you or the Order, Tim,' he said, looking at his nephew over his spectacles, 'but monks simply have no place in ecclesiastical affairs. Let them stick to their prayers is what I say.'

'And a queer way the world would be only for them,' Joe said. Joe was going for the secular priesthood himself, but he didn't like to see his overwhelming uncle get away with too much.

'Their influence on Church history has been disastrous!' the Dean bellowed, reaching for his cigarette case. 'Always, or almost always, disastrous. That man thinks he knows everything.'

'Maybe he does,' said Joe.

'Maybe,' said the Dean, like an old bull who cannot ignore a dart from any quarter. 'But as well as that, he interferes in everything, and always publicly, always with the greatest possible amount of scandal. "I don't like the model of that church"; "Take away that statue"; "That painting is irreverent". Begob, Joe, I don't think even you know as much as that. I declare to God, Josephine, I believe if anyone suggested it to him that man would start inspecting the cut of the schoolgirls' panties.' And when everyone roared with laughter, the Dean raised his head sternly and said, 'I mean it.'

Peter, the youngest boy, never got involved in these family arguments about the Bishop, the Orders, or the future of the Church. He was the odd man out. He was apprenticed in his father's old firm and would grow up to be owner or partner. In every Irish family there is a boy like Peter whose task it is to take on the family responsibilities. It was merely an accident that he was the youngest. What counted was that he was his mother's favourite. Even before he had a mind to make up, he knew it was not for him to become too involved, because someone would have to look after his mother in her old age. He might marry, but it would have to be a wife who suited her. He was the ugliest of the children, though with a monkey ugliness that was almost as attractive as Father Tim's film-star looks and Joe's ascetic masculine fire. He was slow, watchful, and good-humoured, with high cheekbones that grew tiny bushes of hair, and he had a lazy malice that could often be as effective as the uproarious indignation of his brothers and sisters.

May, who saw the part he had been cast for, wondered whether she couldn't woo Mrs Corkery as well as another girl.

After Rosie there was Joe, who was ordained the following year, and then Sheela did what seemed – in that family, at least – the conventional thing and went into the same convent as Tessie.

It was an extraordinary family, and May was never quite able to understand the fascination it had for her. Partly, of course – and this she felt rather than understood – it was the attraction of the large family for the only child, the sheer relief of never having to wonder what you were going to play next. But beside this there was an attraction rather like that of a large theatrical family – the feeling that everything was related to a larger imaginative world. In a sense, the Corkerys always seemed to be playing.

She knew that her own being in love with Peter was part of her love affair with the family as a whole, the longing to be connected with them, and the teasing she got about Peter from his brothers and sisters suggested that they, too, recognized it and were willing to accept her as one of themselves. But she also saw that her chance of ever marrying Peter was extremely slight, because Peter was not attracted by her. When he could have been out walking with her he was out walking with his friend Mick MacDonald, and when the pair of them came in while she was in the house, Peter behaved to her as though she were nothing more than a welcome stranger. He was always polite, always deferential – unlike Tim and Joe, who treated her as though she were an extra sister, to be slapped on the bottom or pushed out of the way as the mood struck them.

May was a serious girl; she had read books on modern psychology, and she knew that the very quality that made Peter settle for a life in the world made him unsuitable as a husband. It was strange how right the books were about that. He was dominated by his mother, and he could flirt with her as he never flirted with May. Clearly, no other woman would ever entirely replace his mother in his heart. In fact (May was too serious a girl not to give things their proper names), Peter was the very type of the homosexual – the latent homosexual, as she learned to call it.

Other boys *wanted* to go out with her, and she resented Peter's unfailing courtesy, though in more philosophic spells she realized that he probably couldn't help it, and that when he showed his almost boyish hero-worship of Mick MacDonald before her it was not his fault but Nature's. All the same, she thought it very uncalled-for on the part of Nature, because it left her no particular interest in a world in which the only eligible young man was a queer. After a year or two of this, her thoughts turned more and more to the quiet convent where the Corkery girls contentedly carried on their simple lives of meditation and prayer. Once or twice she dropped a dark hint that she was thinking of becoming a nun herself, but each time it led to a scene with her father.

'You're a fool, girl!' he said harshly, getting up to pour himself an extra drink. May knew he didn't altogether resent being provoked, because it made him feel entitled to drink more.

'Now, Jack, you must not say things like that,' her mother said anxiously.

'Of course I have to say it. Look at her! At her age! And she doesn't even have a boy!'

'But if there isn't a boy who interests her!'

'There are plenty of boys who'd interest her if only she behaved like a natural girl,' he said gloomily. 'What do you think a boy wants to do with a girl? Say the rosary? She hasn't behaved naturally ever since she got friendly with that family – what's their name?'

'Corkery,' Mrs MacMahon said, having failed to perceive that not remembering the Corkerys' name was the one way the poor man had of getting back at them.

'Whatever their name is, they've turned her into an idiot. That's no great surprise. They never had any brains to distribute, themselves.'

'But still, Jack, you will admit they've got on very well.'

'They've got on very well!' he echoed scornfully. 'In the Church! Except that young fellow, the solicitor's clerk, and I suppose he hadn't brains enough even for the Church. They should have put him in the friars.'

'But after all, their uncle is the Dean.'

'Wonderful Dean, too,' grumbled Jack MacMahon. 'He drove me out of twelve o'clock Mass, so as not to listen to his drivel. He can hardly speak decent English, not to mind preaching a sermon. "A bunch of baloney!"' he quoted angrily. 'If we had a proper bishop, instead of the one we have, he'd make that fellow speak correctly in the pulpit at least.'

'But it's only so that his congregation will understand him, Jack.'

'Oh, his congregation understands him only too well. Himself and his tall hat and his puffed-up airs! Common, that's what he is, and that's what all the family are, on both sides. If your daughter wants to be a nun, you and the Corkerys can arrange it between you. But not one penny of my money goes into their pockets, believe me!'

May was sorry to upset him, but for herself she did not mind his loathing of the whole Corkery family. She knew that it was only because he was fond of her and dreaded being left without her in his old age. He had spoiled her so long as she was not of an age to answer him back, and she guessed he was looking forward to spoiling his grandchildren even worse because he would not live long enough to hear them answer him back. But this, she realized, was what the Corkerys had done for her – made all that side of life seem unimportant.

She had a long talk with Mother Agatha, Mrs Corkery's sister, about her vocation, which confirmed her in her resolution. Mother Agatha was very unlike her sister, who was loud-voiced and humorous. The Mother Superior was pale, thin, cool, and with the slightest trace of an ironic wit that might have passed unnoticed by a stupider girl. But May noticed it, and realized that she was being observed very closely indeed.

She and her mother did the shopping for the trousseau, but the bills and parcels were kept carefully out of her father's sight. Drunk or sober, he refused to discuss the matter at all. 'It would only upset him just now, poor man,' her mother said philosophically. He was drinking heavily, and when he was in liquor he quarrelled a lot with her mother about little things. With May he avoided quarrels, or even arguments, and it struck her that he was training himself for a life in which he would no longer have her to quarrel with. On the day of the Reception he did not drink at all, which pleased her, and was icily polite to everybody, but when, later, she appeared behind the parlour grille, all in white, and the sun caught her, she saw his face in the darkness of the parlour, with all the life drained out of it, and suddenly he turned and left without a word. It was only then that a real feeling of guilt sprang up in her at the thought of the miserable old age that awaited him – a man like him, who loved young creatures who could not answer him back, and who would explain to them unweariedly about the sun and moon and geography and figures. She had answered him back in a way that left him with nothing to look forward to.

All the same, there was something very comforting about the life of an enclosed Order. It had been organized a long, long time before, by people who knew more about the intrusions of the outside world than May did. The panics that had seized her about her ability to sustain the life diminished and finally ceased. The round of duties, services, and mortifications was exactly what she had needed, and little by little she felt the last traces of worldliness slip from her – even the very human worry about the old age of her father and mother. The convent was poor, and not altogether from choice. Everything in the house was mean and clean and cheerful, and May grew to love the old drawing-room that had been turned into a chapel, where she knelt, in her own place, through the black winter mornings when at home she would still be tucked up comfortably in bed. She liked the rough feeling of her clothes and the cold of the floor through her sandals, though mostly she liked the proximity of Tessie and Sheela.

There were times when, reading the lives of the saints, she wished she had lived in more heroic times, and she secretly invented minor mortifications for herself to make sure she could endure them. It was not until she had been in the convent for close on a year that she noticed that the minor mortifications were liable to be followed by major depressions. Though she was a clever woman, she did not try to analyse this. She merely lay awake at night and realized that the nuns she lived with – even Tessie and Sheela – were not the stuff of saints and martyrs, but ordinary women who behaved in religion very much as they would have behaved in marriage, and who followed the rule in the spirit in which her father went to Mass on Sundays. There was nothing whatever to be said against them, and any man who had got one of them for a wife would probably have considered himself fortunate, but all the same there was something about them that was not quite grown-up. It was very peculiar and caused her great concern. The things that had really frightened her about the Order when she was in the world – the loneliness, the austerity, the ruthless discipline – now seemed to her meaningless and harmless. After that she saw with horror that the great days of the Church were over, and that they were merely a lot of perfectly commonplace women play-acting austerity and meditation.

'But my dear child,' Mother Agatha said when May wept out her story to her, 'of course we're only children. Of course we're only play-acting. How else does a child learn obedience and discipline?'

And when May talked to her about what the Order had been in earlier days, that vague, ironic note crept into Mother Superior's voice, as though she had heard it all many times before. 'I know, Sister,' she said, with a nod. 'Believe me, I do know that the Order was stricter in earlier times. But you must remember that it was not founded in a semi-arctic climate like ours, so there was less chance of the sisters dying of double pneumonia. I have talked to half the plumbers in town, but it seems that central heating is not understood here. . . . Everything is relative. I'm sure we suffer just as much in our very comfortable sandals as the early sisters suffered in their bare feet, and probably at times rather more, but at any rate we are not here for the sole purpose of suffering mortification, whatever pleasures it may hold for us.'

Every word Mother Agatha said made perfect sense to May while she was saying it, and May knew she was being ungrateful and hysterical, but when the interview was over and the sound of her sobs had died away, she was left with the impression that Mother Agatha was only another commonplace woman, with a cool manner and a sarcastic tongue, who was also acting the part of a nun. She was alone in a world of bad actors and actresses, and the Catholicism she had known and believed in was dead.

A few weeks later she was taken to a private nursing home. 'Just for a short rest, Sister,' as Mother Agatha said. 'It's a very pleasant place, and you will find a lot of other Religious there who need a rest as well.'

There followed an endless but timeless phase of weeping and confusion, when all May's ordinary life was broken up and strange men burst into her room and examined her and asked questions she did not understand and replied to questions of hers in a way that showed they had not understood them either. Nobody seemed to realize that she was the last Catholic in the world; nobody understood her tears about it. Above all, nobody seemed to be able to hear the gramophone record that played continuously in her head, and that stopped only when they gave her an injection.

Then, one spring day, she went into the garden for a walk and a young nurse saw her back to her room. Far ahead of them, at the other end of a long, white corridor, she saw an old man with his back to her, and remembered that she had seen his face many times before and had perceived, without paying attention to, his long, gloomy, ironic face. She knew she must have remembered him, because now she could see nothing but his back, and suddenly the words 'Who is that queer old man?' broke through the sound of the gramophone record, surprising her as much as they seemed to surprise the young nurse.

'Oh, him!' the nurse said, with a smile. 'Don't you know him? He's been here for years.'

'But why, Nurse?'

'Oh, he doesn't think he's a priest, and he is one really, that's the trouble.'

'But how extraordinary!'

'Isn't it?' the nurse said, biting her lower lip in a smile. 'Cripes, you'd think 'twas something you wouldn't forget. He's nice, really, though,' she added gravely, as though she felt she had been criticizing him.

When they reached May's room, the young nurse grinned again, in a guilty way, and May noticed that she was extravagantly pretty, with small gleaming front teeth.

'*You're* getting all right, anyway,' she said.

'Oh, really?' May said vaguely, because she knew she was not getting all right. 'Why do you think that, Nurse?'

'Oh, you get to spot things,' the nurse said with a shrug, and left May uncomforted, because she didn't know if she really did get well how she could face the convent and the other nuns again. All of them, she felt, would be laughing at her. Instead of worrying about the nuns, she went into a mournful daydream about the old priest who did not think he was a priest, and next day, when her father called, she said intensely, 'Daddy, there's a priest in here who doesn't believe he's a priest – isn't that extraordinary?' She did not hear the tone of her own voice or know how reasonable it sounded, and so she was surprised when her father looked away and started fumbling mechanically in his jacket pocket for a cigarette.

'Well, you don't have to think you're a nun either,' he said, with an unsteady voice. 'Your mother has your own room ready for you when you come home.'

'Oh, but Daddy, I have to go back to the convent.'

'Oh, no you don't. No more convents for you, young lady! That's fixed up already with Mother Superior. It was all a mistake from the beginning. You're coming straight home to your mother and me.'

Then May knew she was really going to get well, and she wanted to go home with him at once, not to go back up the stairs behind the big iron door where there was always an attendant on duty. She knew that going back home meant defeat, humiliation, and despair, but she no longer cared even about that. She just wanted to take up her life again at the point where it had gone wrong, when she had first met the Corkerys.

Her father brought her home and acted as though he had rescued her from a dragon's den. Each evening, when he came home from work, he sat with her, sipping at his drink and talking quietly and comfortably. She felt he was making great efforts to assure that she felt protected and relaxed. Most of the time she did, but there were spells when she wanted her mother to put her back in the nursing home.

'Oh, I couldn't do that,' her mother said characteristically. 'It would upset your poor father too much.'

But she did discuss it with the doctor – a young man, thin and rather unhealthy-looking, who looked as though he, too, was living on his nerves – and he argued with May about it.

'But what am I to do, Doctor, when I feel like this?' she asked plaintively.

'Go out and get jarred,' he said briskly.

'Get what, Doctor?' she asked feebly.

'Jarred,' he repeated without embarrassment. 'Stoned. Polluted. Drunk. I don't mean alone, of course. You need a young fellow along with you.'

'Oh, not that again, Doctor!' she said, and for some reason her voice came out exactly like Mother Agatha's – which was not how she intended it to sound.

'And some sort of a job,' he went on remorselessly. 'There isn't a damn thing wrong with you except that you think you're a failure. You're not, of course, but as a result of thinking you are you've scratched the surface of your mind all over, and when you sit here like this, looking out at the rain, you keep rubbing it so that it doesn't heal. Booze, lovemaking, and hard work – they keep your hands away from the sore surface, and then it heals of its own accord.'

She did her best, but it didn't seem to heal as easily as all that. Her father got her a job in the office of a friend, and she listened, in fascination, to the chatter of the other secretaries. She even went out in the evening with a couple of them and listened to their common little love stories. She knew if she had to wait until she talked like that about fellows in order to be well, her case was hopeless. Instead, she got drunk and told them how she had been for years in love with a homosexual, and, as she told it, the story became so hopeless and dreadful that she sobbed over it herself. After that she went home and wept for hours, because she knew that she had been telling lies, and betrayed the only people in the world whom she had really cared for.

Her father made a point of never referring at all to the Corkerys, the convent, or the nursing home. She knew that for him this represented a real triumph of character, because he loathed the Corkerys more than ever for what he believed they had done to her. But even he could not very well ignore the latest development in the saga. It seemed that Mrs Corkery herself had decided to become a nun. She announced placidly to everyone that she had done her duty by her family, who were now all comfortably settled, and that she felt free to do what she had always wanted to do anyhow. She discussed it with the Dean, who practically excommunicated her on the spot. He said the family would never live down the scandal, and Mrs Corkery told him it wasn't the scandal that worried him at all but the loss of the one house where he could get a decent meal. If he had a spark of manliness, she said, he would get rid of his housekeeper, who couldn't cook, was a miserable sloven, and ordered him about as if he were a schoolboy. The Dean said she would have to get permission in writing from every one of her children, and Mrs Corkery replied calmly that there was no difficulty whatever about that.

May's father didn't really want to crow, but he could not resist pointing out that he had always said the Corkerys had a slate loose.

'I don't see anything very queer about it,' May said stubbornly.

'A woman with six children entering a convent at her age!' her father said, not even troubling to grow angry with her. 'Even the Dean realizes it's mad.'

'It *is* a little bit extreme, all right,' her mother said, with a frown, but May knew she was thinking of her.

May had the feeling that Mrs Corkery would make a very good nun, if for no other reason than to put her brother and Mother Agatha in their place. And of course, there were other reasons. As a girl she had wanted to be a nun, but for family reasons it was impossible, so she had become a good wife and mother, instead. Now, after thirty years of pinching and scraping, her family had grown away from her and she could return to her early dream. There was nothing unbalanced about that, May thought bitterly. *She* was the one who had proved unbalanced.

For a while it plunged her back into gloomy moods, and they were made worse by the scraps of gossip that people passed on to her, not knowing how they hurt. Mrs Corkery had collected her six letters of freedom and taken them herself to the Bishop, who had immediately given in. 'Spite!' the Dean pronounced gloomily. 'Nothing but spite – all because I don't support his mad dream of turning a modern city into a mediaeval monastery.'

On the day of Mrs Corkery's Reception, May did not leave the house at all. It rained, and she sat by the sitting-room window, looking across the city to where the hills were almost invisible. She was living Mrs Corkery's day through – the last day in the human world of an old woman who had assumed the burden she herself had been too weak to accept. She could see it all as though she were back in that mean, bright little chapel, with the old woman lying out on the altar, covered with roses like a corpse, and an old nun shearing off her thin grey locks. It was all so intolerably vivid that May kept bursting into sudden fits of tears and whimpering like a child.

One evening a few weeks later, she came out of the office in the rain and saw Peter Corkery at the other side of the street. She obeyed her first instinct and bowed her head so as not to look at him. Her heart sank as he crossed the road to accost her.

'Aren't you a great stranger, May?' he asked, with his cheerful grin.

'We're very busy in the office these days, Peter,' she replied, with false brightness.

'It was only the other night Joe was talking about you. You know Joe is up in the seminary now?'

'No. What's he doing?'

'Teaching. He finds it a great relief after the mountains. And, of course, you know about the mother.' This was it!

'I heard about it. I suppose ye're all delighted?'

'*I* wasn't very delighted,' he said, and his lips twisted in pain. ' 'Twas the most awful day I ever spent. When they cut off her hair –'

'You don't have to remind me.'

'I disgraced myself, May. I had to run out of the chapel. And here I had two nuns after me, trying to steer me to the lavatory. Why do nuns always think a man is looking for a lavatory?'

'I wouldn't know. I wasn't a very good one.'

'There are different opinions about that,' he said gently, but he only hurt her more.

'And I suppose you'll be next?'

'How next?'

'I was sure you had a vocation, too.'

'I don't know,' he said thoughtfully. 'I never really asked myself. I suppose, in a way, it depends on you.'

'And what have I to say to it?' she asked in a ladylike tone, though her heart suddenly began to pant.

'Only whether you're going to marry me or not. Now I have the house to myself and only Mrs Maher looking after me. You remember Mrs Maher?'

'And you think I'd make a cheap substitute for Mrs Maher, I suppose?' she asked, and suddenly all the pent-up anger and frustration of years seemed to explode inside her. She realized that it was entirely because of him that she had become a nun, because of him she had been locked up in a nursing home and lived the life of an emotional cripple. 'Don't you think that's an extraordinary sort of proposal – if it's intended to be a proposal.'

'Why the hell should I be any good at proposing? How many girls do you think I've proposed to?'

'Not many, since they didn't teach you better manners. And it would never occur to yourself to say you loved me. Do you?' she almost shouted. 'Do you love me?'

'Sure, of course I do,' he said, almost in astonishment. 'I wouldn't be asking you to marry me otherwise. But all the same –'

'All the same, all the same, you have reservations!' And suddenly language that would have appalled her to hear a few months before broke from her, before she burst into uncontrollable tears and went running homeward through the rain. 'God damn you to Hell, Peter Corkery! I wasted my life on you, and now in the heel of the hunt all you can say to me is "All the same". You'd better go back to your damn pansy pals, and say it to them.'

She was hysterical by the time she reached Summerhill. Her father's behaviour was completely characteristic. He was the born martyr and this was only another of the ordeals for which he had been preparing himself all his life. He got up and poured himself a drink.

'Well, there is one thing I'd better tell you now, daughter,' he said quietly but firmly. 'That man will never enter this house in my lifetime.'

'Oh, nonsense, Jack MacMahon!' his wife said in a rage, and she went and poured herself a drink, a thing she did under her husband's eye only when she was prepared to fling it at him. 'You haven't a scrap of sense. Don't you see now that the boy's mother only entered the convent because she knew he'd never feel free while she was in the world?'

'Oh, Mother!' May cried, startled out of her hysterics.

'Well, am I right?' her mother said, drawing herself up.

'Oh, you're right, you're right,' May said, beginning to sob again. 'Only I was such a fool it never occurred to me. Of course, she was doing it for me.'

'And for her son,' said her mother. 'And if he's anything like his mother, I'll be very proud to claim him for a son-in-law.'

She looked at her husband, but saw that she had made her effect and could now enjoy her drink in peace. 'Of course, in some ways it's going to be very embarrassing,' she went on peaceably. 'We can't very well say "Mr Peter Corkery, son of Sister Rosina of the Little Flower" or whatever the dear lady's name is. In fact, it's very difficult to see how we're going to get it into the Press at all. However, as I always say, if the worst comes to the worst, there's a lot to be said for a quiet wedding. . . . I do hope you were nice to him, May?' she asked.

It was only then that May remembered that she hadn't been in the least nice and, in fact, had used language that would have horrified her mother. Not that it would make much difference. She and Peter had travelled so far together, and by such extraordinary ways.

Old-Age Pensioners

On Friday evening as I went up the sea road for my evening walk I heard the row blowing up at the other side of the big ash tree, near the jetty. I was sorry for the sergeant, a decent poor man. When a foreign government imposed a cruel law, providing for the upkeep of all old people over seventy, it never gave a thought to the policeman who would have to deal with the consequences. You see, our post office was the only one within miles. That meant that each week we had to endure a procession of old-age pensioners from Caheragh, the lonely, rocky promontory to the west of us, inhabited – so I am told – by a strange race of people, alleged to be descendants of a Portuguese crew who were driven ashore there in days gone by. That I couldn't swear to; in fact, I never could see trace or tidings of any foreign blood in Caheragh, but I was never one for contradicting the wisdom of my ancestors. But government departments have no wisdom, ancestral or any other kind, so the Caheraghs drew their pensions with us, and the contact with what we considered civilization being an event in their lonesome lives, they usually brought their families to help in drinking them. That was what upset us. To see a foreigner drunk in our village on what we rightly considered our money was more than some of us could stand.

So Friday, as I say, was the sergeant's busy day. He had a young guard called Coleman to assist him, but Coleman had troubles of his own. He was a poet, poor fellow, and desperately in love with a publican's daughter in Coole. The girl was incapable of making up her mind about him, though her father wanted her to settle down; he told her all young men had a tendency to write poetry up to a certain age, and that even himself had done it a few times until her mother knocked it out of him. But her view was that poetry, like drink, was a thing you couldn't have knocked out of you, and that the holy all of it would be that Coleman would ruin the business on her. Every week we used to study the *Coole Times*, looking for another poem, either a heart-broken 'Lines to D—', saying that Coleman would never see her more, or a 'Song'. 'Song' always meant they were after making it up. The sergeant had them all cut out and pasted in an album; he thought young Coleman was lost in the police.

When I was coming home the row was still on, and I went inside the wall to have a look. There were two Caheraghs: Mike Mountain and his son, Patch. Mike was as lean as a rake, a gaunt old man with mad blue eyes. Patch was an upstanding fellow but drunk to God and the world. The man who was standing up for the honour of the village was Flurry Riordan, another old-age pensioner. Flurry, as you'd expect from a bachelor of that great age, was quarrelsome and scurrilous. Fifteen years before, when he was sick and thought himself dying, the only thing troubling his mind was that a brother he had quarrelled with would profit by his death, and a neighbour had come to his cottage one morning to find Flurry fast asleep with his will written in burnt stick on the whitewashed wall over his bed.

The sergeant, a big, powerful man with a pasty face and deep pouches under his eyes, gave me a nod as I came in.

'Where's Guard Coleman from you?' I asked.

'Over in Coole with the damsel,' he replied.

Apparently the row was about a Caheragh boat that had beaten one of our boats in the previous year's regatta. You'd think a thing like that would have been forgotten, but a bachelor of seventy-six has a long memory for grievances. Sitting on the wall overlooking the jetty, shadowed by the boughs of the ash, Flurry asked with a sneer, with such wonderful sailors in Caheragh wasn't it a marvel that they couldn't sail past the Head – an unmistakable reference to the supposed Portuguese origin of the clan. Patch replied that whatever the Caheragh people sailed it wasn't bum-boats, meaning, I suppose, the pleasure boat in which Flurry took summer visitors about the bay.

'What sailors were there ever in Caheragh?' snarled Flurry. 'If they had men against them instead of who they had they wouldn't get off so easy.'

'Begor, 'tis a pity you weren't rowing yourself, Flurry,' said the sergeant gravely. 'I'd say you could still show them a few things.'

'Ten years ago I might,' said Flurry bitterly, because the sergeant had touched on another very sore subject; his being dropped from the regatta crews, a thing he put down entirely to the brother's intrigues.

'Why then, indeed,' said the sergeant, 'I'd back you still against a man half your age. Why don't you and Patch have a race now and settle it?'

'I'll race him,' shouted Patch with the greatest enthusiasm, rushing for his own boat. 'I'll show him.'

'My boat is being mended,' said Flurry shortly.

'You could borrow Sullivan's,' said the sergeant.

Flurry only looked at the ground and spat. Either he wasn't feeling energetic or the responsibility was too much for him. It would darken his last days to be beaten by a Caheragh. Patch sat in his shirt-sleeves in the boat, resting his reeling head on his oars. For a few minutes it looked as if he was out for the evening. Then he suddenly raised his face to the sky and let out the wild Caheragh war-whoop, which sounded like all the seagulls in Ireland practising unison-shrieking. The effect on Flurry was magical. At that insulting sound he leaped from the wall with an oath, pulled off his coat, and rushed to the slip to another boat. The sergeant, clumsy and heavy-footed, followed, and the pair of them sculled away to where Sullivan's boat was moored. Patch followed them with his eyes.

'What's wrong with you, you old coward?' he yelled. 'Row your own boat, you old sod, you!'

'Never mind,' said Mike Mountain from the top of the slip. 'You'll beat him, boat or no boat. . . . He'll beat him, ladies and gentlemen,' he said confidently to the little crowd that had gathered. 'Ah, Jase, he's a great man in a boat.'

'I'm a good man on a long course,' Patch shouted modestly, his eyes searching each of us in turn. 'I'm slow getting into my stroke.'

'At his age I was the same,' confided his father. 'A great bleddy man in a boat. Of course, I can't do it now – eighty-one; drawing on for it. I haven't the same energy.'

'Are you ready, you old coward?' shrieked Patch to Flurry who was fumbling savagely in the bottom of Sullivan's boat for the rowlocks.

'Shut up, you foreign importation!' snarled Flurry.

He found the rowlocks and pulled the boat round in a couple of neat strokes; then hung on his oars till the sergeant got out. For seventy-six he was still a lively man.

'Ye know the race now?' said the sergeant. 'To the island and back.'

'Round the island, sergeant,' said Mike Mountain plaintively. 'Patch is like me; he's slow to start.'

'Very good, very good,' said the sergeant. 'Round the island it is, Flurry. Are ye ready now, both of ye?'

'Ready,' grunted Flurry.

'Yahee!' shrieked Patch again, brandishing an oar over his head like a drumstick.

'Mind yourself now, Patch!' said the sergeant who seemed to be torn between his duty as an officer of the peace and his duty as umpire. 'Go! – ye whoors,' he added under his breath so that only a few of us heard him.

They did their best. It is hard enough for a man with a drop in to go straight even when he's facing his object, but it is too much altogether to expect him to do it backwards. Flurry made for the *Red Devil*, the doctor's sailing boat, and Patch, who seemed to be fascinated by the very appearance of Flurry, made for him, and the two of them got there almost simultaneously. At one moment it looked as if it would be a case of drowning, at the next of manslaughter. There was a splash, a thud, and a shout, and I saw Flurry raise his oar as if to lay out Patch. But the presence of the sergeant probably made him selfconscious, for instead he used it to push off Patch's boat.

'God Almighty!' cried Mike Mountain with an air of desperation, 'did ye ever see such a pair of misfortunate bosthoons? Round the island, God blast ye!'

But Patch, who seemed to have an absolute fixation on Flurry, interpreted this as a command to go round him, and, seeing that Flurry wasn't at all sure what direction he was going in, this wasn't as easy as it looked. He put up one really grand spurt, and had just established himself successfully across Flurry's bow when it hit him and sent him spinning like a top, knocking one oar clean out of his hand. Sullivan's old boat was no good for racing, but it was grand for anything in the nature of tank warfare, and as Flurry had by this time got into his stroke, it would have taken an Atlantic liner to stop him. Patch screamed with rage, and then managed to retrieve his oar and follow. The shock seemed to have given him new energy.

Only gradually was the sergeant's strategy beginning to reveal itself to me. The problem was to get the Caheraghs out of the village without a fight, and Flurry and Patch were spoiling for one. Anything that would exhaust the pair of them would make his job easier. It is not a method recommended in Police Regulations, but it has the distinct advantage of leaving no unseemly aftermath of summonses and cross-summonses which, if neglected, may in time turn into a regular vendetta. As a spectacle it really wasn't much. Darkness had breathed on the mirror of the water. A bonfire on the island set a pendulum reflection swinging lazily to and fro, darkening the bay at either side of it. There was a milky light over the hill of Croghan; the moon was rising.

The sergeant came up to me with his hand over his mouth and his big head a little on one side, a way he had of indicating to the world that he was speaking aside.

'I see by the paper how they're after making it up again,' he whispered anxiously. 'Isn't she a changeable little divil?'

It took me a moment or two to realize that he was referring to Coleman and the publican's daughter; I always forget that he looks on me as a fellow-artist of Coleman's.

'Poets prefer them like that,' I said.

'Is that so?' he exclaimed in surprise. 'Well, everyone to his own taste.' Then he scanned the bay thoughtfully and started suddenly. 'Who the hell is that?' he asked.

Into the pillar of smoky light from the bonfire a boat had come, and it took us a little while to identify it. It was Patch's, and there was Patch himself pulling leisurely to shore. He had given up the impossible task of going round Flurry. Some of the crowd began to shout derisively at him but he ignored them. Then Mike Mountain took off his bowler hat and addressed us in heart-broken tones.

'Stone him!' he besought us. 'For Christ's sake, ladies and gentlemen, stone him! He's no son of mine, only a walking mockery of man.'

He began to dance on the edge of the slip and shout insults at Patch who had slowed up and showed no inclination to meet him.

'What the hell do you mean by it?' shouted Mike. 'You said you'd race the man and you didn't. You shamed me before everyone. What sort of misfortunate old furniture are you?'

'But he fouled me,' Patch yelled indignantly. 'He fouled me twice.'

'He couldn't foul what was foul before,' said his father. 'I'm eighty-one, but I'm a better man than you. By God, I am.'

A few moments later Flurry's boat hove into view.

'Mike Mountain,' he shouted over his shoulder in a sobbing voice, 'have you any grandsons you'd send out against me now? Where are the great Caheragh sailors now, I'd like to know?'

'Here's one of them,' roared Mike, tearing at the lapels of his coat. 'Here's a sailor if you want one. I'm only a feeble old man, but I'm a better man in a boat than either of ye. Will you race me, Flurry? Will you race me now, I say?'

'I'll race you to hell and back,' panted Flurry contemptuously.

Mike excitedly peeled off his coat and tossed it to me. Then he took off his vest and hurled it at the sergeant. Finally he opened his braces, and, grabbing his bowler hat, he made a flying leap into his own boat and tried to seize the oars from Patch.

''Tisn't fair,' shouted Patch, wrestling with him. 'He fouled me twice.'

'Gimme them oars and less of your talk,' snarled his father.

'I don't care,' screamed Patch. 'I'll leave no man lower my spirit.'

'Get out of that boat or I'll have to deal with you officially,' said the sergeant sternly. 'Flurry,' he added, 'wouldn't you take a rest?'

'Is it to beat a Caheragh?' snarled Flurry viciously as he brought Sullivan's boat round again.

Again the sergeant gave the word and the two boats set off. This time there were no mistakes. The two old men were rowing magnificently, but it was almost impossible to see what happened them. A party of small boys jumped into another boat and set out after them.

'A pity we can't see it,' I said to the sergeant.

'It might be as well,' he grunted gloomily. 'The less witnesses the better. The end of it will be a coroner's inquest, and I'll lose my bleddy job.'

Beneath us on the slip, Patch, leaning against the slimy wall, seemed to have fallen asleep. The sergeant looked down at him greedily.

'And 'tis only dawning on me that the whole bleddy lot of them ought to be in the lock-up,' he muttered.

'Sergeant,' I said, 'you ought to be in the diplomatic service.'

He brought his right hand up to shield his mouth, and with his left elbow he gave me an agonizing dig in the ribs that nearly knocked me.

'Whisht, you divil you! Whisht, whisht, whisht!' he said.

The pendulum of firelight, growing a deeper red, swayed with the gentle motion of an old clock, and from the bay we could hear the excited voices of the boatful of boys, cheering on the two old men.

' 'Tis Mike,' said someone, staring out into the darkness.

' 'Tisn't,' said a child's voice. ' 'Tis Flurry. I sees his blue smock.'

It was Flurry. We were all a little disappointed. I will say for our people that whatever quarrel they may have with the Portuguese, in sport they have a really international outlook. When old Mike pulled in a few moments later he got a rousing cheer. The first to congratulate him was Flurry.

'Mike,' he shouted as he tied up Sullivan's boat, 'you're a better man than your son.'

'You fouled me,' shouted Patch.

In response to the cheer Mike rose in the rocking boat. He stood in the bow and then, recollecting his manners, took off his hat. As he removed his hand from his trousers, they fell about his scraggy knees, but he failed to perceive that.

'Ladies and gentlemen,' he said pantingly, ' 'twasn't a bad race. An old man didn't wet the blade of an oar these twelve months, 'twasn't a bad race at all.'

'Begod, Mike,' said Flurry, holding out his hand from the slip, 'you were a good man in your day.'

'I was, Flurry,' said Mike, taking his hand and staring up affectionately at him. 'I was a powerful man in my day, my old friend, and you were a powerful man yourself.'

It was obvious that there was going to be no fight. The crowd began to disperse in an outburst of chatter and laughter. Mike turned to us again, but only the sergeant and myself were listening to him. His voice had lost its carrying power.

'Ladies and gentlemen,' he cried, 'for an old man that saw such hard days, 'tis no small thing. If ye knew what me and my like endured ye'd say the same. Ye never knew them, and with the help of the Almighty God ye never will. Cruel times they were, but they're all forgotten. No one remembers them, no one tells ye, the troubles of the poor man in the days gone by. Many's the wet day I rowed from dawn to dark, ladies and gentlemen; many's the bitter winter night I spent, ditching and draining, dragging down the sharp stones for my little cabin by starlight and moonlight. If ye knew it all, ye'd say I was a great man. But 'tis all forgotten, all, all, forgotten!'

Old Mike's voice had risen into a wail of the utmost poignancy. The excitement and applause had worked him up, and all the past was rising in him as in a dying man. But there was no one to hear him. The crowd drifted away up the road. Patch tossed the old man's clothes into the boat, and, sober enough now, stepped in and pushed off in silence, but his father still stood in the bow, his bowler hat in his hand, his white shirt flapping about his naked legs.

We watched him till he was out of sight, but even then I could hear his voice bursting out in sharp cries of self-pity like a voice from the dead. All the loneliness of the world was in it. A flashlight glow outlined a crest of rock at the left-hand side of the bay, and the moonlight, stealing through a barrier of cloud, let a window of brightness into the burnished water. The peace was safe for another week. I handed the sergeant a cigarette and he fell into step beside me.

'He's in the wrong job altogether,' he whispered, and again I had to pull myself together to realize the way his mind had gone on, working quietly along its own lines. ' 'Tis in Dublin he ought to be. There's nothing for a fellow like that in our old job. Sure, you can see for yourself.'

The Long Road to Ummera

Stay for me there. I will not fail
To meet thee in that hollow vale.

Always in the evenings you saw her shuffle up the road to Miss O.'s for her little jug of porter, a shapeless lump of an old woman in a plaid shawl, faded to the colour of snuff, that dragged her head down on to her bosom where she clutched its folds in one hand; a canvas apron and a pair of men's boots without laces. Her eyes were puffy and screwed up in tight little buds of flesh and her rosy old face that might have been carved out of a turnip was all crumpled with blindness. The old heart was failing her, and several times she would have to rest, put down the jug, lean against the wall, and lift the weight of the shawl off her head. People passed; she stared at them humbly; they saluted her; she turned her head and peered after them for minutes on end. The rhythm of life had slowed down in her till you could scarcely detect its faint and sluggish beat. Sometimes from some queer instinct of shyness she turned to the wall, took a snuffbox from her bosom, and shook out a pinch on the back of her swollen hand. When she sniffed it it smeared her nose and upper lip and spilled all over her old black blouse. She raised the hand to her eyes and looked at it closely and reproachfully, as though astonished that it no longer served her properly. Then she dusted herself, picked up the old jug again, scratched herself against her clothes, and shuffled along close by the wall, groaning aloud.

When she reached her own house, which was a little cottage in a terrace, she took off her boots, and herself and the old cobbler who lodged with her turned out a pot of potatoes on the table, stripping them with their fingers and dipping them in the little mound of salt while they took turn and turn about with the porter jug. He was a lively and philosophic old man called Johnny Thornton.

After their supper they sat in the firelight, talking about old times in the country and long-dead neighbours, ghosts, fairies, spells, and charms. It always depressed her son, finding them together like that when he called with her monthly allowance. He was a well-to-do businessman with a little grocery shop in the South Main Street and a little house in Sunday's Well, and nothing would have pleased him better than that his mother should share all the grandeur with him, the carpets and the china and the chiming clocks. He sat moodily between them, stroking his long jaw, and wondering why they talked so much about death in the old-fashioned way, as if it was something that made no difference at all.

'Wisha, what pleasure do ye get out of old talk like that?' he asked one night.

'Like what, Pat?' his mother asked with her timid smile.

'My goodness,' he said, 'ye're always at it. Corpses and graves and people that are dead and gone.'

'Arrah, why wouldn't we?' she replied, looking down stiffly as she tried to button the open-necked blouse that revealed her old breast. 'Isn't there more of us there than here?'

'Much difference 'twill make to you when you won't know them or see them!' he exclaimed.

'Oye, why wouldn't I know them?' she cried angrily. 'Is it the Twomeys of Lackroe and the Driscolls of Ummera?'

'How sure you are we'll take you to Ummera!' he said mockingly.

'Och aye, Pat,' she asked, shaking herself against her clothes with her humble stupid wondering smile, 'and where else would you take me?'

'Isn't our own plot good enough for you?' he asked. 'Your own son and your grandchildren?'

'Musha, indeed, is it in the town you want to bury me?' She shrugged herself and blinked into the fire, her face growing sour and obstinate. 'I'll go back to Ummera, the place I came from.'

'Back to the hunger and misery we came from,' Pat said scornfully.

'Back to your father, boy.'

'Ay, to be sure, where else? But my father or grandfather never did for you what I did. Often and often I scoured the streets of Cork for a few ha-pence for you.'

'You did, amossa, you did, you did,' she admitted, looking into the fire and shaking herself. 'You were a good son to me.'

'And often I did it and the belly falling out of me with hunger,' Pat went on, full of self-pity.

' ''Tis true for you,' she mumbled, ' 'tis, 'tis, 'tis true. 'Twas often and often you had to go without it. What else could you do and the way we were left?'

'And now our grave isn't good enough for you,' he complained. There was real bitterness in his tone. He was an insignificant little man and jealous of the power the dead had over her.

She looked at him with the same abject, half-imbecile smile, the wrinkled old eyes almost shut above the Mongolian cheekbones, while with a swollen old hand, like a pot-stick, it had so little life in it, she smoothed a few locks of yellow-white hair across her temples – a trick she had when troubled.

'Musha, take me back to Ummera, Pat,' she whined. 'Take me back to my own. I'd never rest among strangers. I'd be rising and drifting.'

'Ah, foolishness, woman!' he said with an indignant look. 'That sort of thing is gone out of fashion.'

'I won't stop here for you,' she shouted hoarsely in sudden, impotent fury, and she rose and grasped the mantelpiece for support.

'You won't be asked,' he said shortly.

'I'll haunt you,' she whispered tensely, holding on to the mantelpiece and bending down over him with a horrible grin.

'And that's only more of the foolishness,' he said with a nod of contempt. 'Haunts and fairies and spells.'

She took one step towards him and stood, plastering down the two little locks of yellowing hair, the half-dead eyes twitching and blinking in the candlelight, and the swollen crumpled face with the cheeks like cracked enamel.

'Pat,' she said, 'the day we left Ummera you promised to bring me back. You were only a little gorsoon that time. The neighbours gathered round me and the last word I said to them and I going down the road was: "Neighbours, my son Pat is after giving me his word and he'll bring me back to ye when my time comes." . . . That's as true as the Almighty God is over me this night. I have everything ready.' She went to the shelf under the stairs and took out two parcels. She seemed to be speaking to herself as she opened them gloatingly, bending down her head in the feeble light of the candle. 'There's the two brass candlesticks and the blessed candles alongside them. And there's my shroud aired regular on the line.'

'Ah, you're mad, woman,' he said angrily. 'Forty miles! Forty miles into the heart of the mountains!'

She suddenly shuffled towards him on her bare feet, her hand raised clawing the air, her body like her face blind with age. Her harsh croaking old voice rose to a shout.

'I brought you from it, boy, and you must bring me back. If 'twas the last shilling you had and you and your children to go to the poorhouse after, you must bring me back to Ummera. And not by the short road either! Mind what I say now! The long road! The long road to Ummera round the lake, the way I brought you from it. I lay a heavy curse on you this night if you bring me the short road over the hill. And ye must stop by the ash tree at the foot of the boreen where ye can see my little house and say a prayer for all that were ever old in it and all that played on the floor. And then – Pat! Pat Driscoll! Are you listening? Are you listening to me, I say?'

She shook him by the shoulder, peering down into his long miserable face to see how was he taking it.

'I'm listening,' he said with a shrug.

'Then' – her voice dropped to a whisper – 'you must stand up overright the neighbours and say – remember now what I'm telling you! – "Neighbours, this is Abby, Batty Heige's daughter, that kept her promise to ye at the end of all."'

She said it lovingly, smiling to herself, as if it were a bit of an old song, something she went over and over in the long night. All West Cork was in it: the bleak road over the moors to Ummera, the smooth grey pelts of the hills with the long spider's-web of the fences ridging them, drawing the scarecrow fields awry, and the whitewashed cottages, poker-faced between their little scraps of holly bushes, looking this way and that out of the wind.

'Well, I'll make a fair bargain with you,' said Pat as he rose. Without seeming to listen she screwed up her eyes and studied his weak melancholy face. 'This house is a great expense to me. Do what I'm always asking you. Live with me and I'll promise I'll take you back to Ummera.'

'Oye, I will not,' she replied sullenly, shrugging her shoulders helplessly, an old sack of a woman with all the life gone out of her.

'All right,' said Pat. ' 'Tis your own choice. That's my last word; take it or leave it. Live with me and Ummera for your grave, or stop here and a plot in the Botanics.'

She watched him out the door with shoulders hunched about her ears. Then she shrugged herself, took out her snuffbox and took a pinch.

'Arrah, I wouldn't mind what he'd say,' said Johnny. 'A fellow like that would change his mind tomorrow.'

'He might and he mightn't,' she said heavily, and opened the back door to go out to the yard. It was a starry night and they could hear the noise of the city below them in the valley. She raised her eyes to the bright sky over the back wall and suddenly broke into a cry of loneliness and helplessness.

'Oh, oh, oh, 'tis far away from me Ummera is tonight above any other night, and I'll die and be buried here, far from all I ever knew and the long roads between us.'

Of course old Johnny should have known damn well what she was up to the night she made her way down to the cross, creeping along beside the railings. By the blank wall opposite the lighted pub Dan Regan, the jarvey, was standing by his old box of a covered car with his pipe in his gob. He was the jarvey all the old neighbours went to. Abby beckoned to him and he followed her into the shadow of a gateway overhung with ivy. He listened gravely to what she had to say, sniffing and nodding, wiping his nose in his sleeve, or crossing the pavement to hawk his nose and spit in the channel, while his face with its drooping moustaches never relaxed its discreet and doleful expression.

Johnny should have known what that meant and why old Abby, who had always been so open-handed, sat before an empty grate sooner than light a fire, and came after him on Fridays for the rent, whether he had it or not, and even begrudged him the little drop of porter which had always been give and take between them. He knew himself it was a change before death and that it all went into the wallet in her bosom. At night in her attic she counted it by the light of her candle and when the coins dropped from her lifeless fingers he heard her roaring like an old cow as she crawled along the naked boards, sweeping them blindly with her palms. Then he heard the bed creak as she tossed about in it, and the rosary being taken from the bedhead, and the old voice rising and falling in prayer; and sometimes when a high wind blowing up the river roused him before dawn he could hear her muttering: a mutter and then a yawn; the scrape of a match as she peered at the alarm clock – the endless nights of the old – and then the mutter of prayer again.

But Johnny in some ways was very dense, and he guessed nothing till the night she called him and, going to the foot of the stairs with a candle in his hand, he saw her on the landing in her flour-bag shift, one hand clutching the jamb of the door while the other clawed wildly at her few straggly hairs.

'Johnny!' she screeched down at him, beside herself with excitement. 'He was here.'

'Who was there?' he snarled back, still cross with sleep.

'Michael Driscoll, Pat's father.'

'Ah, you were dreaming, woman,' he said in disgust. 'Go back to your bed in God's holy name.'

'I was not dreaming,' she cried. 'I was lying broad awake, saying my beads, when he come in the door, beckoning me. Go down to Dan Regan's for me, Johnny.'

'I will not indeed, go down to Dan Regan's for you. Do you know what hour of night it is?'

' 'Tis morning.'

' 'Tis. Four o'clock! What a thing I'd do! . . . Is it the way you're feeling bad?' he added with more consideration as he mounted the stairs. 'Do you want him to take you to hospital?'

'Oye, I'm going to no hospital,' she replied sullenly, turning her back on him and thumping into the room again. She opened an old chest of drawers and began fumbling in it for her best clothes, her bonnet and cloak.

'Then what the blazes do you want Dan Regan for?' he snarled in exasperation.

'What matter to you what I want him for?' she retorted with senile suspicion. 'I have a journey to go, never you mind where.'

'Ach, you old oinseach, your mind is wandering,' he cried. 'There's a devil of a wind blowing up the river. The whole house is shaking. That's what you heard. Make your mind easy now and go back to bed.'

'My mind is not wandering,' she shouted. 'Thanks be to the Almighty

God I have my senses as good as you. My plans are made. I'm going back now where I came from. Back to Ummera.'

'Back to where?' Johnny asked in stupefaction.

'Back to Ummera.'

'You're madder than I thought. And do you think or imagine Dan Regan will drive you?'

'He will drive me then,' she said, shrugging herself as she held an old petticoat to the light. 'He's booked for it any hour of the day or night.'

'Then Dan Regan is madder still.'

'Leave me alone now,' she muttered stubbornly, blinking and shrugging. 'I'm going back to Ummera and that was why my old comrade came for me. All night and every night I have my beads wore out, praying the Almighty God and his Blessed Mother not to leave me die among strangers. And now I'll leave my old bones on a high hilltop in Ummera.'

Johnny was easily persuaded. It promised to be a fine day's outing and a story that would delight a pub, so he made tea for her and after that went down to Dan Regan's little cottage, and before smoke showed from any chimney on the road they were away. Johnny was hopping about the car in his excitement, leaning out, shouting through the window of the car to Dan and identifying big estates that he hadn't seen for years. When they were well outside the town, himself and Dan went in for a drink, and while they were inside the old woman dozed. Dan Regan roused her to ask if she wouldn't take a drop of something and at first she didn't know who he was and then she asked where they were and peered out at the public-house and the old dog sprawled asleep in the sunlight before the door. But when next they halted she had fallen asleep again, her mouth hanging open and her breath coming in noisy gusts. Dan's face grew gloomier. He looked hard at her and spat. Then he took a few turns about the road, lit his pipe and put on the lid.

'I don't like her looks at all, Johnny,' he said gravely. 'I done wrong. I see that now. I done wrong.'

After that, he halted every couple of miles to see how she was and Johnny, threatened with the loss of his treat, shook her and shouted at her. Each time Dan's face grew graver. He walked gloomily about the road, clearing his nose and spitting in the ditch. 'God direct me!' he said solemnly. ' 'Twon't be wishing to me. Her son is a powerful man. He'll break me yet. A man should never interfere between families. Blood is thicker than water. The Regans were always unlucky.'

When they reached the first town he drove straight to the police barrack and told them the story in his own peculiar way.

'Ye can tell the judge I gave ye every assistance,' he said in a reasonable broken-hearted tone. 'I was always a friend of the law. I'll keep nothing back – a pound was the price agreed. I suppose if she dies 'twill be manslaughter. I never had hand act or part in politics. Sergeant Daly at the Cross knows me well.'

When Abby came to herself she was in a bed in the hospital. She began to fumble for her belongings and her shrieks brought a crowd of unfortunate old women about her.

'Whisht, whisht, whisht!' they said. 'They're all in safe-keeping. You'll get them back.'

'I want them now,' she shouted, struggling to get out of bed while they held her down. 'Leave me go, ye robbers of hell! Ye night-walking rogues, leave me go. Oh, murder, murder! Ye're killing me.'

At last an old Irish-speaking priest came and comforted her. He left her quietly saying her beads, secure in the promise to see that she was buried in Ummera no matter what anyone said. As darkness fell, the beads dropped from her swollen hands and she began to mutter to herself in Irish. Sitting about the fire, the ragged old women whispered and groaned in sympathy. The Angelus rang out from a near-by church. Suddenly Abby's voice rose to a shout and she tried to lift herself on her elbow.

'Ah, Michael Driscoll, my friend, my kind comrade, you didn't forget me after all the long years. I'm a long time away from you but I'm coming at last. They tried to keep me away, to make me stop among foreigners in the town, but where would I be at all without you and all the old friends? Stay for me, my treasure! Stop and show me the way. . . . Neighbours,' she shouted, pointing into the shadows, 'that man there is my own husband, Michael Driscoll. Let ye see he won't leave me to find my way alone. Gather round me with yeer lanterns, neighbours, till I see who I have. I know ye all. 'Tis only the sight that's weak on me. Be easy now, my brightness, my own kind loving comrade. I'm coming. After all the long years I'm on the road to you at last. . . .'

It was a spring day full of wandering sunlight when they brought her the long road to Ummera, the way she had come from it forty years before.

The lake was like a dazzle of midges; the shafts of the sun revolving like a great millwheel poured their cascades of milky sunlight over the hills and the little whitewashed cottages and the little black mountain-cattle among the scarecrow fields. The hearse stopped at the foot of the lane that led to the roofless cabin just as she had pictured it to herself in the long nights, and Pat, looking more melancholy than ever, turned to the waiting neighbours and said:

'Neighbours, this is Abby, Batty Heige's daughter, that kept her promise to ye at the end of all.'

The Wreath

When Father Fogarty read of the death of his friend, Father Devine, in a Dublin nursing home, he was stunned. He was a man who did not understand the irremediable. He took out an old seminary group, put it on the mantelpiece and spent the evening looking at it. Devine's clever, pale, shrunken face stood out from the rest, not very different from what it had been in his later years except for the absence of pinc-nez. He and Fogarty had been boys together in a provincial town where Devine's father had been a schoolmaster and Fogarty's mother had kept a shop. Even then, everybody had known that Devine was marked out by nature for the priesthood. He was clever, docile and beautifully mannered. Fogarty's vocation had come later and proved a surprise, to himself as well as to others.

They had been friends over the years, affectionate when together, critical and sarcastic when apart. They had not seen one another for close on a year. Devine had been unlucky. As long as the old Bishop, Gallogly, lived, he had been fairly well sheltered, but Lanigan, the new one, disliked him. It was partly Devine's own fault. He could not keep his mouth shut. He was witty and waspish and said whatever came into his head about colleagues who had nothing like his gifts. Fogarty remembered the things Devine had said about himself. Devine had affected to believe that Fogarty was a man of many personalities, and asked with mock humility which he was now dealing with – Nero, Napoleon or St Francis of Assisi.

It all came back: the occasional jaunts together, the plans for holidays abroad that never took place; and now the warm and genuine love for Devine which was so natural to Fogarty welled up in him, and, realizing that never again in this world would he be able to express it, he began to weep. He was as simple as a child in his emotions. When he was in high spirits he devised practical jokes of the utmost crudity; when he was depressed he brooded for days on imaginary injuries: he forgot lightly, remembered suddenly and with exaggerated intensity, and blamed himself cruelly and unjustly for his own short-comings. He would have been astonished to learn that, for all the intrusions of Nero and Napoleon, his understanding had continued to develop when that of cleverer men had dried up, and that he was a better and wiser man at forty than he had been twenty years before.

But he did not understand the irremediable. He had to have someone to talk to, and for want of a better, rang up Jackson, a curate who had been Devine's other friend. He did not really like Jackson, who was worldly, cynical and something of a careerist, and he usually called him by the worst name in his vocabulary – a Jesuit. Several times he had asked Devine what he saw in Jackson but Devine's replies had not enlightened him much. 'I wouldn't trust myself too far with the young Loyola if I were you,' Fogarty had told Devine with his worldly swagger. Now, he had no swagger left.

'That's terrible news about Devine, Jim, isn't it?' he said.

'Yes,' Jackson drawled in his usual cautious, cagey way, as though he were afraid to commit himself even about that. 'I suppose it's a happy release for the poor devil.'

That was the sort of tone that maddened Fogarty. It sounded as though Jackson were talking of an old family pet who had been sent to the vet's.

'I hope he appreciates it,' he said gruffly. 'I was thinking of going to town and coming back with the funeral. You wouldn't come, I suppose?'

'I don't very well see how I could, Jerry,' Jackson replied in a tone of mild alarm. 'It's only a week since I was up last.'

'Ah, well, I'll go myself,' said Fogarty. 'You don't know what happened him, do you?'

'Ah, well, he was always anaemic,' Jackson said lightly. 'He should have looked after himself, but he didn't get much chance with old O'Leary.'

'He wasn't intended to,' Fogarty said darkly, indiscreet as usual.

'What?' Jackson asked in surprise. 'Oh no,' he added, resuming his worldly tone. 'It wasn't a sinecure, of course. He was fainting all over the shop. Last time was in the middle of Mass. By then, of course, it was too late. When I saw him last week I knew he was dying.'

'You saw him last week?' Fogarty repeated.

'Oh, just for a few minutes. He couldn't talk much.'

And again, the feeling of his own inadequacy descended on Fogarty. He realized that Jackson, who seemed to have as much feeling as a mowing machine, had kept in touch with Devine, and gone out of his way to see him at the end, while he, the devoted, warm-hearted friend, had let him slip from sight into eternity and was now wallowing in the sense of his own loss.

'I'll never forgive myself, Jim,' he said humbly. 'I never even knew he was sick.'

'I'd like to go to the funeral myself if I could,' said Jackson. 'I'll ring you up later if I can manage it.'

He did manage it, and that evening they set off in Fogarty's car for the city. They stayed in an old hotel in a side-street where porters and waiters all knew them. Jackson brought Fogarty to a very pleasant restaurant for dinner. The very sight of Jackson had been enough to renew Fogarty's doubts. He was a tall, thin man with a prim, watchful, clerical air, and he knew his way around. He spent at least ten minutes over the menu and the wine list, and the head waiter danced attendance on him as head waiters do only when they are either hopeful or intimidated.

'You needn't bother about me,' Fogarty said to cut short the rigmarole. 'I'm having steak.'

'Father Fogarty is having steak, Paddy,' Jackson said suavely, looking at the head waiter over his spectacles with what Fogarty called his 'Jesuit' air. 'Make it rare. And stout, I fancy. It's a favourite beverage of the natives.'

'I'll spare you the stout,' Fogarty said, enjoying the banter. 'Red wine will do me fine.'

'Mind, Paddy,' Jackson said in the same tone, 'Father Fogarty said *red* wine. You're in Ireland now, remember.'

Next morning they went to the parish church where the coffin was resting on trestles before the altar. Beside it, to Fogarty's surprise, was a large wreath of roses. When they got up from their knees, Devine's uncle, Ned, had arrived with his son. Ned was a broad-faced, dark-haired, nervous man, with the anaemic complexion of the family.

'I'm sorry for your trouble, Ned,' said Fogarty.

'I know that, father,' said Ned.

'I don't know if you know Father Jackson. He was a great friend of Father Willie's.'

'I heard him speak of him,' said Ned. 'He talked a lot about the pair of ye. Ye were his great friends. Poor Father Willie!' he added with a sigh. 'He had few enough.'

Just then the parish priest came in and spoke to Ned Devine. His name was Martin. He was a tall man with a stern, unlined, wooden face and candid blue eyes like a baby's. He stood for a few minutes by the coffin, then studied the breastplate and wreath, looking closely at the tag. It was only then that he beckoned the two younger priests towards the door.

'Tell me, what are we going to do about that thing?' he asked with a professional air.

'What thing?' Fogarty asked in surprise.

'That wreath,' Martin replied with a nod over his shoulder.

'What's wrong with it?'

' 'Tis against the rubrics,' replied the parish priest in the complacent tone of a policeman who has looked up the law on the subject.

'For heaven's sake, what have the rubrics to do with it?' Fogarty asked impatiently.

'The rubrics have a whole lot to do with it,' Martin replied with a stern glance. 'And, apart from that, 'tis a bad custom.'

'You mean Masses bring in more money?' Fogarty asked with amused insolence.

'I do not mean Masses bring in more money,' replied Martin who tended to answer every remark verbatim, like a solicitor's letter. It added to the impression of woodenness he gave. 'I mean that flowers are a Pagan survival.' He looked at the two young priests with the same anxious, innocent, wooden air. 'And here am I, week in, week out, preaching against flowers, and a blooming big wreath of them in my own church. And on a priest's coffin, what's more! What am I to say about that?'

'Who asked you to say anything?' Fogarty asked angrily. 'The man wasn't from your diocese.'

'Now, that's all very well,' said Martin. 'That's bad enough by itself, but it isn't the whole story.'

'You mean because it's from a woman?' Jackson broke in lightly in a tone that would have punctured any pose less substantial than Martin's.

'I mean, because it's from a woman, exactly.'

'A woman!' said Fogarty in astonishment. 'Does it say so?'

'It does not say so.'

'Then how do you know?'

'Because it's red roses.'

'And does that mean it's from a woman?'

'What else could it mean?'

'I suppose it could mean it's from somebody who didn't study the language of flowers the way you seem to have done,' Fogarty snapped.

He could feel Jackson's disapproval of him weighing on the air, but when Jackson spoke it was at the parish priest that his coldness and nonchalance were directed.

'Oh, well,' he said with a shrug. 'I'm afraid we know nothing about it, father. You'll have to make up your own mind.'

'I don't like doing anything when I wasn't acquainted with the man,' Martin grumbled, but he made no further attempt to interfere, and one of the undertaker's men took the wreath and put it on the hearse. Fogarty controlled himself with difficulty. As he banged open the door of his car and started the engine his face was flushed. He drove with his head bowed and his brows jutting down like rocks over his eyes. It was what Devine had called his Nero look. As they cleared the main streets he burst out.

'That's the sort of thing that makes me ashamed of myself, Jim. Flowers are a Pagan survival! And they take it from him, what's worse. They take it from him. They listen to that sort of stuff instead of telling him to shut his big ignorant gob.'

'Oh, well,' Jackson said tolerantly, taking out his pipe, 'we're hardly being fair to him. After all, he didn't know Devine.'

'But that only makes it worse,' Fogarty said hotly. 'Only for our being there he'd have thrown out that wreath. And for what? His own dirty, mean, suspicious mind!'

'Ah, I wouldn't go as far as that,' Jackson said, frowning. 'I think in his position I'd have asked somebody to take it away.'

'You would?'

'Wouldn't you?'

'But why, in God's name?'

'Oh, I suppose I'd be afraid of the scandal – I'm not a very courageous type.'

'Scandal?'

'Whatever you like to call it. After all, some woman sent it.'

'Yes. One of Devine's old maids.'

'Have you ever heard of an old maid sending a wreath of red roses to a funeral?' Jackson asked, raising his brows, his head cocked.

'To tell you the God's truth, I might have done it myself,' Fogarty confessed with boyish candour. 'It would never have struck me that there was anything wrong with it.'

'It would have struck the old maid all right, though.'

Fogarty turned his eyes for a moment to stare at Jackson. Jackson was staring back. Then he missed a turning and reversed with a muttered curse. To the left of them the Wicklow mountains stretched away southwards, and between the grey walls the fields were a ragged brilliant green under the tattered sky.

'You're not serious, Jim?' he said after a few minutes.

'Oh, I'm not suggesting that there was anything wrong,' Jackson said, gesturing widely with his pipe. 'Women get ideas. We all know that.'

'These things can happen in very innocent ways,' Fogarty said with ingenuous solemnity. Then he scowled again and a blush spread over his handsome craggy face. Like all those who live mainly in their imaginations, he was always astonished and shocked at the suggestions that reached him from the outside world: he could live with his fantasies only by assuming that they were nothing more. Jackson, whose own imagination was curbed and even timid, who never went at things like a thoroughbred at a gate, watched him with amusement and a certain envy. Just occasionally he felt that he himself would have liked to welcome a new idea with that boyish wonder and panic.

'I can't believe it,' Fogarty said angrily, tossing his head.

'You don't have to,' Jackson replied, nursing his pipe and swinging round in the seat with his arm close to Fogarty's shoulder. 'As I say, women get these queer ideas. There's usually nothing in them. At the same time, I must say *I* wouldn't be very scandalized if I found out that there was something in it. If ever a man needed someone to care for him, Devine did in the last year or two.'

'But not Devine, Jim,' Fogarty said, raising his voice. 'Not Devine! You could believe a thing like that about me. I suppose I could believe it about you. But I knew Devine since we were kids, and he wouldn't be capable of it.'

'I never knew him in that way,' Jackson admitted. 'In fact, I scarcely knew him at all, really. But I'd have said he was as capable of it as the rest of us. He was lonelier than the rest of us.'

'God, don't I know it?' Fogarty said in sudden self-reproach. 'I could understand if it was drink.'

'Oh, not drink!' Jackson said with distaste. 'He was too fastidious. Can you imagine him in the D.T.s like some old parish priest, trying to strangle the nurses?'

'But that's what I say, Jim. He wasn't the type.'

'Oh, you must make distinctions,' said Jackson. 'I could imagine him attracted by some intelligent woman. You know yourself how he'd appeal to her, the same way he appealed to us, a cultured man in a country town. I don't have to tell you the sort of life an intelligent woman leads, married to some lout of a shopkeeper or a gentleman farmer. Poor devils, it's a mercy that most of them aren't educated.'

'He didn't give you any hint who she was?' Fogarty asked incredulously. Jackson had spoken with such conviction that it impressed him as true.

'Oh, I don't even know if there was such a woman,' Jackson said hastily, and then he blushed too. Fogarty remained silent. He knew now that Jackson had been talking about himself, not Devine.

As the country grew wilder and furze bushes and ruined keeps took the place of pastures and old abbeys, Fogarty found his eyes attracted more and more to the wreath that swayed lightly with the hearse, the only spot of pure colour in the whole landscape with its watery greens and blues and greys. It seemed an image of the essential mystery of a priest's life. What, after all, did he really know of Devine? Only what his own temperament suggested, and mostly – when he wasn't being St Francis of Assisi – he had seen himself as the worldly one of the pair; the practical, coarse-grained man who cut corners, and Devine as the saint, racked by the fastidiousness and asceticism that exploded in his bitter little jests. Now his mind boggled at the idea of the agony that alone could have driven Devine into an entanglement with a woman; yet the measure of his incredulity was that of the conviction he would presently begin to feel. When once an unusual idea broke through his imagination, he hugged it, brooded on it, promoted it to the dignity of a revelation.

'God, don't we lead terrible lives?' he burst out at last. 'Here we are, probably the two people in the world who knew Devine best, and even we have no notion what that thing in front of us means.'

'Which might be as well for our peace of mind,' said Jackson.

'I'll engage it did damn little for Devine's,' Fogarty said grimly. It was peculiar; he did not believe yet in the reality of the woman behind the wreath, but already he hated her.

'Oh, I don't know,' Jackson said in some surprise. 'Isn't that what we all really want from life?'

'Is it?' Fogarty asked in wonder. He had always thought of Jackson as a cold fish, and suddenly found himself wondering about that as well. After all, there must have been something in him that attracted Devine. He had the feeling that Jackson, who was, as he recognized, by far the subtler man, was probing him, and for the same reason. Each was looking in the other for the quality that had attracted Devine, and, which, having made him their friend might make them friends also. Each was trying to see how far he could go with the other. Fogarty, as usual, was the first with a confession.

'I couldn't do it, Jim,' he said earnestly. 'I was never even tempted, except once, and then it was the wife of one of the men who was in the seminary with me. I was crazy about her. But when I saw what her marriage to the other fellow was like, I changed my mind. She hated him like poison, Jim. I soon saw she might have hated me in the same way. It's only when you see what marriage is really like, as we do, that you realize how lucky we are.'

'Lucky?' Jackson repeated mockingly.

'Aren't we?'

'Did you ever know a seminary that wasn't full of men who thought they were lucky? They might be drinking themselves to death, but they never doubted their luck? Nonsense, man! Anyway, why do you think she'd have hated you?'

'I don't,' Fogarty replied with a boyish laugh. 'Naturally, I think I'd have been the perfect husband for her. That's the way Nature kids you.'

'Well, why shouldn't you have made her a perfect husband?' Jackson asked quizzically. 'There's nothing much wrong with you that I can see. Though I admit I can see you better as a devoted father.'

'God knows you might be right,' Fogarty said, his face clouding again. It was as changeable as an Irish sky, Jackson thought with amusement. 'You could get on well enough without the woman, but the kids are hell. She had two. "Father Fogey" they used to call me. And my mother was as bad,' he burst out. 'She was wrapped up in the pair of us. She always wanted us to be better than everybody else, and when we weren't she used to cry. She said it was the Fogarty blood breaking out in us – the Fogartys were all horse dealers.' His handsome, happy face was black with all the old remorse and guilt. 'I'm afraid she died under the impression that I was a Fogarty after all.'

'If the Fogartys are any relation to the Martins, I'd say it was most unlikely,' Jackson said, half-amused, half-touched.

'I never knew till she was dead how much she meant to me,' Fogarty said broodingly. 'Hennessey warned me not to take the Burial Service myself, but I thought it was the last thing I could do for her. He knew what he was talking about, of course. I disgraced myself, bawling like a blooming kid, and he pushed me aside and finished it for me. My God, the way we gallop through that till it comes to our own turn! Every time I've read it since, I've read it as if it were for my mother.'

Jackson shook his head uncomprehendingly.

'You feel these things more than I do,' he said. 'I'm a cold fish.'

It struck Fogarty with some force that this was precisely what he had always believed himself and that now he could believe it no longer.

'Until then, I used to be a bit flighty,' he confessed. 'After that I knew it wasn't in me to care for another woman.'

'That's only more of your nonsense,' said Jackson impatiently. 'Love is just one thing, not half a dozen. If I were a young fellow looking for a wife I'd go after some girl who felt like that about her father. You probably have too much of it. I haven't enough. When I was in Manister there was a shopkeeper's wife I used to see. I talked to her and lent her books. She was half-crazy with loneliness. Then one morning I got home and found her standing outside my door in the pouring rain. She'd been there half the night. She wanted me to take her away, to "save" her, as she said. You can imagine what happened her after.'

'Went off with someone else, I suppose?'

'No such luck. She took to drinking and sleeping with racing men. Sometimes I blame myself for it. I feel I should have kidded her along. But I haven't enough love to go round. You have too much. With your enthusiastic nature you'd probably have run off with her.'

'I often wondered what I would do,' Fogarty said shyly.

He felt very close to tears. It was partly the wreath, brilliant in the sunlight, that had drawn him out of his habitual reserve and made him talk in that way with a man of even greater reserve. Partly, it was the emotion of returning to the little town where he had grown up. He hated and avoided it; it seemed to him to represent all the narrowness and meanness that he tried to banish from his thoughts, but at the same time it contained all the nostalgia and violence he had felt there; and when he drew near it again a tumult of emotions rose in him that half-strangled him. He was watching for it already like a lover.

'There it is!' he said triumphantly, pointing to a valley where a tapering Franciscan tower rose on the edge of a clutter of low Georgian houses and thatched cabins. 'They'll be waiting for us at the bridge. That's how they'll be waiting for me when my turn comes, Jim.'

A considerable crowd had gathered at the farther side of the bridge to escort the hearse to the cemetery. Four men shouldered the shiny coffin over the bridge past the ruined castle and up the hilly Main Street. Shutters were up on the shop fronts, blinds were drawn, everything was at a standstill except where a curtain was lifted and an old woman peered out.

'Counting the mourners,' Fogarty said with a bitter laugh. 'They'll say I had nothing like as many as Devine. That place,' he added, lowering his voice, 'the second shop from the corner, that was ours.'

Jackson took it in at a glance. He was puzzled and touched by Fogarty's emotion because there was nothing to distinguish the little market town from a hundred others. A laneway led off the hilly road and they came to the abbey, a ruined tower and a few walls, with tombstones sown thickly in quire and nave. The hearse was already drawn up outside and people had gathered in a semi-circle about it. Ned Devine came hastily up to the car where the two priests were donning their vestments. Fogarty knew at once that there was trouble brewing.

'Whisper, Father Jerry,' Ned muttered in a strained excited voice. 'People are talking about that wreath. I wonder would you know who sent it?'

'I don't know the first thing about it, Ned,' Fogarty replied, and suddenly his heart began to beat violently.

'Come here a minute, Sheela,' Ned called, and a tall, pale girl with the stain of tears on her long bony face left the little group of mourners and joined them. Fogarty nodded to her. She was Devine's sister, a school-teacher who had never married. 'This is Father Jackson, Father Willie's other friend. They don't know anything about it either.'

'Then I'd let them take it back,' she said doggedly.

'What would you say, father?' Ned asked, appealing to Fogarty, and suddenly Fogarty felt his courage desert him. In disputing with Martin he had felt himself an equal on neutral ground, but now the passion and prejudice of the little town seemed to rise up and oppose him, and he felt himself again a boy, rebellious and terrified. You had to know the place to realize the hysteria that could be provoked by something like a funeral.

'I can only tell you what I told Father Martin already,' he said, growing red and angry.

'Did he talk about it too?' Ned asked sharply.

'There!' Sheela said vindictively. 'What did I tell you?'

'Well, the pair of you are cleverer than I am,' Fogarty said. 'I saw nothing wrong with it.'

'It was no proper thing to send to a priest's funeral,' she hissed with prim fury. 'And whoever sent it was no friend of my brother.'

'You saw nothing wrong with it, father?' Ned prompted appealingly.

'But I tell you, Uncle Ned, if that wreath goes into the graveyard we'll be the laughing stock of the town,' she said in an old-maidish frenzy. 'I'll throw it out myself if you won't.'

'Whisht, girl, whisht, and let Father Jerry talk!' Ned said furiously.

'It's entirely a matter for yourselves, Ned,' Fogarty said excitedly. He was really scared now. He knew he was in danger of behaving imprudently in public, and sooner or later, the story would get back to the Bishop, and it would be suggested that he knew more than he pretended.

'If you'll excuse me interrupting, father,' Jackson said suavely, giving Fogarty a warning glance over his spectacles. 'I know this is none of my business.'

'Not at all, father, not at all,' Ned said passionately. 'You were the boy's friend. All we want is for you to tell us what to do.'

'Oh, well, Mr Devine, that would be too great a responsibility for me to take,' Jackson replied with a cagey smile, though Fogarty saw that his face was very flushed. 'Only someone who really knows the town could advise you about that. I only know what things are like in my own place. Of course, I entirely agree with Miss Devine,' he said, giving her a smile that suggested that this, like crucifixion, was something he preferred to avoid. 'Naturally, Father Fogarty and I have discussed it already. I think personally that it was entirely improper to send a wreath.' Then his mild, clerical voice suddenly grew menacing and he shrugged his shoulders with an air of contempt. 'But, speaking as an outsider, I'd say if you were to send that wreath back from the graveyard, you'd make yourself something far worse than a laughing stock. You'd throw mud on a dead man's name that would never be forgotten for you the longest day you lived. . . . Of course, that's only an outsider's opinion,' he added urbanely, drawing in his breath in a positive hiss.

'Of course, of course, of course,' Ned Devine said, clicking his fingers and snapping into action. 'We should have thought of it ourselves, father. 'Twould be giving tongues to the stones.'

Then he lifted the wreath himself and carried it to the graveside. Several of the men by the gate looked at him with a questioning eye and fell in behind him. Some hysteria had gone out of the air. Fogarty gently squeezed Jackson's hand.

'Good man, Jim!' he said in a whisper. 'Good man you are!'

He stood with Jackson at the head of the open grave beside the local priests. As their voices rose in the psalms for the dead and their vestments billowed about them, Fogarty's brooding eyes swept the crowd of faces he had known since his childhood and which were now caricatured by age and pain. Each time they came to rest on the wreath which stood at one side of the open grave. It would lie there now above Devine when all the living had gone, his secret. And each time it came over him in a wave of emotion that what he and Jackson had protected was something more than a sentimental token. It was the thing that had linked them to Devine, and for the future would link them to one another – love. Not half a dozen things, but one thing, between son and mother, man and sweetheart, friend and friend.

The Mass Island

When Father Jackson drove up to the curates' house, it was already drawing on to dusk, the early dusk of late December. The curates' house was a red-brick building on a terrace at one side of the ugly church in Asragh. Father Hamilton seemed to have been waiting for him and opened the front door himself, looking white and strained. He was a tall young man with a long, melancholy face that you would have taken for weak till you noticed the cut of the jaw.

'Oh, come in, Jim,' he said with his mournful smile. ' 'Tisn't much of a welcome we have for you, God knows. I suppose you'd like to see poor Jerry before the undertaker comes.'

'I might as well,' Father Jackson replied briskly. There was nothing melancholy about Jackson, but he affected an air of surprise and shock. ' 'Twas very sudden, wasn't it?'

'Well, it was and it wasn't, Jim,' Father Hamilton said, closing the front door behind him. 'He was going downhill since he got the first heart attack, and he wouldn't look after himself. Sure, you know yourself what he was like.'

Jackson knew. Father Fogarty and himself had been friends, of a sort, for years. An impractical man, excitable and vehement, Fogarty could have lived for twenty years with his ailment, but instead of that, he allowed himself to become depressed and indifferent. If he couldn't live as he had always lived, he would prefer not to live at all.

They went upstairs and into the bedroom where he was. The character was still plain on the stern, dead face, though, drained of vitality, it had the look of a studio portrait. That bone structure was something you'd have picked out of a thousand faces as Irish, with its odd impression of bluntness and asymmetry, its jutting brows and craggy chin, and the snub

351

nose that looked as though it had probably been broken twenty years before in a public-house row.

When they came downstairs again, Father Hamilton produced half a bottle of whiskey.

'Not for me, thanks,' Jackson said hastily. 'Unless you have a drop of sherry there?'

'Well, there is some Burgundy,' Father Hamilton said. 'I don't know is it any good, though.'

' 'Twill do me fine,' Jackson replied cheerfully, reflecting that Ireland was the country where nobody knew whether Burgundy was good or not. 'You're coming with us tomorrow, I suppose?'

'Well, the way it is, Jim,' Father Hamilton replied, 'I'm afraid neither of us is going. You see, they're burying poor Jerry here.'

'They're what?' Jackson asked incredulously.

'Now, I didn't know for sure when I rang you, Jim, but that's what the brother decided, and that's what Father Hanafey decided as well.'

'But he told you he wanted to be buried on the Mass Island, didn't he?'

'He told everybody, Jim,' Father Hamilton replied with growing excitement and emotion. 'That was the sort he was. If he told one, he told five hundred. Only a half an hour ago I had a girl on the telephone from the Island, asking when they could expect us. You see, the old parish priest of the place let Jerry mark out the grave for himself, and they want to know should they open it. But now the old parish priest is dead as well, and, of course, Jerry left nothing in writing.'

'Didn't he leave a will, even?' Jackson asked in surprise.

'Well, he did and he didn't, Jim,' Father Hamilton said, looking as if he were on the point of tears. 'Actually, he did make a will about five or six years ago, and he gave it to Clancy, the other curate, but Clancy went off on the Foreign Mission and God alone knows where he is now. After that, Jerry never bothered his head about it. I mean, you have to admit the man had nothing to leave. Every damn thing he had he gave away – even the old car, after he got the first attack. If there was any loose cash around, I suppose the brother has that.'

Jackson sipped his Burgundy, which was even more Australian than he had feared, and wondered at his own irritation. He had been irritated enough before that, with the prospect of two days' motoring in the middle of winter, and a night in a godforsaken pub in the mountains, a hundred and fifty miles away at the other side of Ireland. There, in one of the lakes, was an island where in Cromwell's time, before the causeway and the little oratory were built, Mass was said in secret, and it was here that Father Fogarty had wanted to be buried. It struck Jackson as sheer sentimentality; it wasn't even as if it was Fogarty's native place. Jackson had once allowed Fogarty to lure him there, and had hated every moment of it. It wasn't only the discomfort of the public-house, where meals erupted at any hour of the day or night as the spirit took the proprietor, or the rain that kept them confined to the cold dining-and-sitting-room that looked out on the gloomy mountainside, with its couple of whitewashed cabins on the shore of the lake. It was the over-intimacy of it all, and this was the thing that Father Fogarty apparently loved. He liked to stand in his shirt-sleeves behind the bar, taking turns with the proprietor, who was one of his many friends, serving big pints of porter to rough mountainy men, or to sit in their cottages, shaking in all his fat whenever they told broad stories or sang risky folk songs. 'God, Jim, isn't it grand?' he would say in his deep voice, and Jackson would look at him over his spectacles with what Fogarty called his 'jesuitical look', and say, 'Well, I suppose it all depends on what you really like, Jerry.' He wasn't even certain that the locals cared for Father Fogarty's intimacy; on the contrary, he had a strong impression that they much preferred their own reserved old parish priest, whom they never saw except twice a year, when he came up the valley to collect his dues. That had made Jackson twice as stiff. And yet now when he found out that the plans that had meant so much inconvenience to him had fallen through, he was as disappointed as though they had been his own.

'Oh, well,' he said with a shrug that was intended to conceal his perturbation, 'I suppose it doesn't make much difference where they chuck us when our time comes.'

'The point is, it mattered to Jerry, Jim,' Father Hamilton said with his curious shy obstinacy. 'God knows, it's not anything that will ever worry me, but it haunted him, and somehow, you know, I don't feel it's right to flout a dead man's wishes.'

'Oh, I know, I know,' Jackson said lightly. 'I suppose I'd better talk to old Hanafey about it. Knowing I'm a friend of the Bishop's he might pay more attention to me.'

'He might, Jim,' Father Hamilton replied sadly, looking away over Jackson's head. 'As you say, knowing you're a friend of the Bishop's, he might. But I wouldn't depend too much on it. I talked to him till I was black in the face, and all I got out of him was the law and the rubrics. It's the brother Hanafey is afraid of. You'll see him this evening, and, between ourselves, he's a tough customer. Of course, himself and Jerry never had much to say to one another, and he'd be the last man in the world that Jerry would talk to about his funeral, so now he doesn't want the expense and inconvenience. You wouldn't blame him, of course. I'd probably be the same myself. By the way,' Father Hamilton added, lowering his voice, 'before he does come, I'd like you to take a look round Jerry's room and see is there any little memento you'd care to have – a photo or a book or anything.'

They went into Father Fogarty's sitting-room, and Jackson looked at it with a new interest. He knew of old the rather handsome library – Fogarty had been a man of many enthusiasms, though none of long duration – the picture of the Virgin and Child in Irish country costume over the mantelpiece, which some of his colleagues had thought irreverent, and the couple of fine old prints. There was a newer picture that Jackson had not seen – a charcoal drawing of the Crucifixion from a fifteenth-century Irish tomb, which was brutal but impressive.

'Good Lord!' Jackson exclaimed with a sudden feeling of loss. 'He really had taste, hadn't he?'

'He had, Jim,' Father Hamilton said, sticking his long nose into the picture. 'This goes to a young couple called Keneally, outside the town, that he was fond of. I think they were very kind to him. Since he had the attack, he was pretty lonely, I'd say.'

'Oh, aren't we all, attack or no attack,' Jackson said almost irritably.

Father Hanafey, the parish priest of Asragh, was a round, red, cherubic-looking old man with a bald head and big round glasses. His house was on the same terrace as the curates'. He, too, insisted on producing the whiskey Jackson so heartily detested, when the two priests came in to consult him, but Jackson had decided that this time diplomacy required he should show proper appreciation of the dreadful stuff. He felt sure he was going to be very sick next day. He affected great astonishment at the quality of Father Hanafey's whiskey, and first the old parish priest grew shy, like a schoolgirl whose good looks are being praised, then he looked self-satisfied, and finally he became almost emotional. It was a great pleasure, he said, to meet a young priest with a proper understanding of whiskey. Priests no longer seemed to have the same taste, and as far as most of them were concerned, they might as well be drinking poteen. It was only when it was seven years old that Irish began to be interesting, and that was when you had to catch it and store it in sherry casks to draw off what remained of crude alcohol in it, and give it that beautiful roundness that Father Jackson had spotted. But it shouldn't be kept too long, for somewhere along the line the spirit of a whiskey was broken. At ten, or maybe twelve, years old it was just right. But people were losing their palates. He solemnly assured the two priests that of every dozen clerics who came to his house not more than one would realize what he was drinking. Poor Hamilton grew red and began to stutter, but the parish priest's reproofs were not directed at him.

'It isn't you I'm talking about, Father Hamilton, but elderly priests, parish priests, and even canons, that you would think would know better, and I give you my word, I put the two whiskeys side by side in front of them, the shop stuff and my own, and they could not tell the difference.'

But though the priest was mollified by Father Jackson's maturity of judgement, he was not prepared to interfere in the arrangements for the funeral of his curate. 'It is the wish of the next of kin, Father,' he said stubbornly, 'and that is something I have no control over. Now that you tell me the same thing as Father Hamilton, I accept it that this was Father Fogarty's wish, and a man's wishes regarding his own interment are always to be respected. I assure you, if I had even one line in Father Fogarty's writing to go on, I would wait for no man's advice. I would take the responsibility on myself. Something on paper, Father, is all I want.'

'On the other hand, Father,' Jackson said mildly, drawing on his pipe, 'if Father Fogarty was the sort to leave written instructions, he'd hardly be the sort to leave such unusual ones. I mean, after all, it isn't even the family burying ground, is it?'

'Well, now, that is true, Father,' replied the parish priest, and it was clear that he had been deeply impressed by this rather doubtful logic. 'You have a very good point there, and it is one I did not think of myself, and I have given the matter a great deal of thought. You might mention it to his brother. Father Fogarty, God rest him, was *not* a usual type of man. I think you might even go so far as to say that he was a rather *unusual* type of man, and not orderly, as you say – not by any means orderly. I would certainly mention that to the brother and see what he says.'

But the brother was not at all impressed by Father Jackson's argument when he turned up at the church in Asragh that evening. He was a good-looking man with a weak and pleasant face and a cold shrewdness in his eyes that had been lacking in his brother's.

'But why, Father?' he asked, turning to Father Hanafey. 'I'm a busy man, and I'm being asked to leave my business for a couple of days in the middle of winter, and for what? That is all I ask. What use is it?'

'It is only out of respect for the wishes of the deceased, Mr Fogarty,' said Father Hanafey, who clearly was a little bit afraid of him.

'And where did he express those wishes?' the brother asked. 'I'm his only living relative, and it is queer he would not mention a thing like that to me.'

'He mentioned it to Father Jackson and Father Hamilton.'

'But when, Father?' Mr Fogarty asked. 'You knew Father Jerry, and he was always expressing wishes about something. He was an excitable sort of man, God rest him, and the thing he'd say today might not be the thing he'd say tomorrow. After all, after close on forty years, I think I have the right to say I knew him,' he added with a triumphant air that left the two young priests without a leg to stand on.

Over bacon and eggs in the curates' house, Father Hamilton was very despondent. 'Well, I suppose we did what we could, Jim,' he said.

'I'm not too sure of that,' Jackson said with his 'jesuitical air', looking at Father Hamilton sidewise over his spectacles. 'I'm wondering if we couldn't do something with that family you say he intended the drawing for.'

'The Keneallys,' said Father Hamilton in a worried voice. 'Actually, I saw the wife in the church this evening. You might have noticed her crying.'

'Don't you think we should see if they have anything in writing?'

'Well, if they have, it would be about the picture,' said Father Hamilton. 'How I know about it is she came to me at the time to ask if I couldn't do something for him. Poor man, he was crying himself that day, according to what she told me.'

'Oh dear!' Jackson said politely, but his mind was elsewhere. 'I'm not really interested in knowing what would be in a letter like that. It's none of my business. But I would like to make sure that they haven't something in writing. What did Hanafey call it – "something on paper"?'

'I dare say we should inquire, anyway,' said Father Hamilton, and after supper they drove out to the Keneallys', a typical small red-brick villa with a decent garden in front. The family also was eating bacon and eggs, and Jackson shuddered when they asked him to join them. Keneally himself, a tall, gaunt, cadaverous man, poured out more whiskey for them, and again Jackson felt he must make a formal attempt to drink it. At the same time, he thought he saw what attraction the house had for Father Fogarty. Keneally was tough and with no suggestion of lay servility towards the priesthood, and his wife was beautiful and scatterbrained, and talked to herself, the cat, and the children simultaneously. 'Rosaleen!' she cried determinedly. 'Out! Out I say! I told you if you didn't stop meowing you'd have to go out. . . . Angela Keneally, the stick! . . . You do not want to go to the bathroom, Angela. It's only five minutes since you were there before. I will not let Father Hamilton come up to you at all unless you go to bed at once.'

In the children's bedroom, Jackson gave a finger to a stolid-looking infant, who instantly stuffed it into his mouth and began to chew it, apparently under the impression that he would be bound to reach sugar at last.

Later, they sat over their drinks in the sitting-room, only interrupted by Angela Keneally, in a fever of curiosity, dropping in every five minutes to ask for a biscuit or a glass of water.

'You see, Father Fogarty left no will,' Jackson explained to Keneally. 'Consequently, he'll be buried here tomorrow unless something turns up. I suppose he told you where he wanted to be buried?'

'On the Island? Twenty times, if he told us once. I thought he took it too far. Didn't you, Father?'

'And me not to be able to go!' Mrs Keneally said, beginning to cry. 'Isn't it awful, Father?'

'He didn't leave anything in writing with you?' He saw in Keneally's eyes that the letter was really only about the picture, and raised a warning hand. 'Mind, if he did, I don't want to know what's in it! In fact, it would be highly improper for anyone to be told before the parish priest and the next of kin were consulted. All I do want to know is whether' – he waited a moment to see that Keneally was following him – 'he did leave any written instructions, of any kind, with you.'

Mrs Keneally, drying her tears, suddenly broke into rapid speech. 'Sure, that was the day poor Father Jerry was so down in himself because we were his friends and he had nothing to leave us, and – '

'Shut up, woman!' her husband shouted with a glare at her, and then Jackson saw him purse his lips in quiet amusement. He was a man after Jackson's heart. 'As you say, Father, we have a letter from him.'

'Addressed to anybody in particular?'

'Yes, to the parish priest, to be delivered after his death.'

'Did he use those words?' Jackson asked, touched in spite of himself.

'Those very words.'

'God help us!' said Father Hamilton.

'But you had not time to deliver it?'

'I only heard of Father Fogarty's death when I got in. Esther was at the church, of course.'

'And you're a bit tired, so you wouldn't want to walk all the way over to the presbytery with it. I take it that, in the normal way, you'd post it.'

'But the post would be gone,' Keneally said with a secret smile. 'So that Father Hanafey wouldn't get it until maybe the day after tomorrow. That's what you were afraid of, Father, isn't it?'

'I see we understand one another, Mr Keneally,' Jackson said politely.

'You wouldn't, of course, wish to say anything that wasn't strictly true,' said Keneally, who was clearly enjoying himself enormously, though his wife had not the faintest idea of what was afoot. 'So perhaps it would be better if the letter was posted now, and not after you leave the house.'

'Fine!' said Jackson, and Keneally nodded and went out. When he returned, a few minutes later, the priests rose to go.

'I'll see you at the Mass tomorrow,' Keneally said. 'Good luck, now.'

Jackson felt they'd probably need it. But when Father Hanafey met them in the hall, with the wet snow falling outside, and they explained about the letter, his mood had clearly changed. Jackson's logic might have worked some sort of spell on him, or perhaps it was just that he felt they were three clergymen opposed to a layman.

'It was very unforeseen of Mr Keneally not to have brought that letter to me at once,' he grumbled, 'but I must say I was expecting something of the sort. It would have been very peculiar if Father Fogarty had left no instructions at all for me, and I see that we can't just sit round and wait to find out what they were, since the burial is tomorrow. Under the circumstances, Father, I think we'd be justified in arranging for the funeral according to Father Fogarty's known wishes.'

'Thanks be to God,' Father Hamilton murmured as he and Father Jackson returned to the curates' house. 'I never thought we'd get away with that.'

'We haven't got away with it yet,' said Jackson. 'And even if we do get away with it, the real trouble will be later.'

All the arrangements had still to be made. When Mr Fogarty was informed, he slammed down the receiver without comment. Then a phone call had to be made to a police station twelve miles from the Island, and the police sergeant promised to send a man out on a bicycle to have the grave opened. Then the local parish priest and several old friends had to be informed, and a notice inserted in the nearest daily. As Jackson said wearily, romantic men always left their more worldly friends to carry out their romantic intentions.

The scene at the curates' house next morning after Mass scared even Jackson. While the hearse and the funeral car waited in front of the door, Mr Fogarty sat, white with anger, and let the priests talk. To Jackson's surprise, Father Hanafey put up a stern fight for Father Fogarty's wishes.

'You have to realize, Mr Fogarty, that to a priest like your brother the Mass is a very solemn thing indeed, and a place where the poor people had to fly in the Penal Days to hear Mass would be one of particular sanctity.'

'Father Hanafey,' said Mr Fogarty in a cold, even tone. 'I am a simple businessman, and I have no time for sentiment.'

'I would not go so far as to call the veneration for sanctified ground mere sentiment, Mr Fogarty,' the old priest said severely. 'At any rate, it is now clear that Father Fogarty left instructions to be delivered to me after his death, and if those instructions are what we think them, I would have a serious responsibility for not having paid attention to them.'

'I do not think that letter is anything of the kind, Father Hanafey,' said Mr Fogarty. 'That's a matter I'm going to inquire into when I get back, and if it turns out to be a hoax, I am going to take it further.'

'Oh, Mr Fogarty, I'm sure it's not a hoax,' said the parish priest, with a shocked air, but Mr Fogarty was not convinced.

'For everybody's sake, we'll hope not,' he said grimly.

The funeral procession set off. Mr Fogarty sat in the front of the car by the driver, sulking. Jackson and Hamilton sat behind and opened their breviaries. When they stopped at a hotel for lunch, Mr Fogarty said he was not hungry and stayed outside in the cold. And when he did get hungry and came into the dining-room, the priests drifted into the lounge to wait for him. They both realized that he might prove a dangerous enemy.

Then, as they drove on in the dusk, they saw the mountain country ahead of them in a cold, watery light, a light that seemed to fall dead from the ragged edge of a cloud. The towns and villages they passed through were dirtier and more derelict. They drew up at a crossroads, behind the hearse, and heard someone talking to the driver of the hearse. Then a car fell into line behind them. 'Someone joining us,' Father Hamilton said, but Mr Fogarty, lost in his own dream of martyrdom, did not reply. Half a dozen times within the next twenty minutes, the same thing happened, though sometimes the cars were waiting in lanes and by-roads with their lights on, and each time Jackson saw a heavily coated figure standing in the roadway shouting to the hearse driver: 'Is it Father Fogarty ye have there?' At last they came to a village where the local parish priest's car was waiting outside the church, with a little group about it. Their headlights caught a public-house, isolated at the other side of the street, glaring with whitewash, while about it was the vague space of a distant mountainside.

Suddenly Mr Fogarty spoke. 'He seems to have been fairly well known,' he said with something approaching politeness.

The road went on, with a noisy stream at the right-hand side of it falling from group to group of rocks. They left it for a by-road, which bent to the right, heading towards the stream, and then began to mount, broken by ledges of naked rock, over which hearse and cars seemed to heave themselves like animals. On the left-hand side of the road was a little white-washed cottage, all lit up, with a big turf fire burning in the open hearth and an oil lamp with an orange glow on the wall above it. There was a man standing by the door, and as they approached he began to pick his way over the rocks towards them, carrying a lantern. Only then did Jackson notice the other lanterns and flashlights, coming down the mountain or crossing the stream, and realize that they represented people, young men and girls and an occasional sturdy old man, all moving in the direction of the Mass Island. Suddenly it hit him, almost like a blow. He told himself not to be a fool, that this was no more than the desire for novelty one should expect to find in out-of-the-way places, mixed perhaps with vanity. It was all that, of course, and he knew it, but he knew, too, it was something more. He had thought when he was here with Fogarty that those people had not respected Fogarty as they respected him and the local parish priest, but he knew that for him, or even for their own parish priest, they would never turn out in midwinter, across the treacherous mountain bogs and wicked rocks. He and the parish priest would never earn more from the people of the mountains than respect; what they gave to the fat, unclerical young man who had served them with pints in the bar and egged them on to tell their old stories and bullied and ragged and even fought them was something infinitely greater.

The funeral procession stopped in a lane that ran along the edge of a lake. The surface of the lake was rough, and they could hear the splash of the water upon the stones. The two priests got out of the car and began to vest themselves, and then Mr Fogarty got out, too. He was very nervous and hesitant.

'It's very inconvenient, and all the rest of it,' he said, 'but I don't want you gentlemen to think that I didn't know you were acting from the best motives.'

'That's very kind of you, Mr Fogarty,' Jackson said. 'Maybe we made mistakes as well.'

'Thank you, Father Jackson,' Mr Fogarty said, and held out his hand. The two priests shook hands with him and he went off, raising his hat.

'Well, that's one trouble over,' Father Hamilton said wryly as an old man plunged through the mud towards the car.

'Lights is what we're looking for!' he shouted. 'Let ye turn her sidewise and throw the headlights on the causeway the way we'll see what we're doing.'

Their driver swore, but he reversed and turned the front of the car till it almost faced the lake. Then he turned on his headlights. Somewhere farther up the road the parish priest's car did the same. One by one, the ranked headlights blazed up, and at every moment the scene before them grew more vivid – the gateway and the stile, and beyond it the causeway that ran towards the little brown stone oratory with its mock Romanesque doorway. As the lights strengthened and steadied, the whole island became like a vast piece of theatre scenery cut out against the gloomy wall of the mountain with the tiny whitewashed cottages at its base. Far above, caught in a stray flash of moonlight, Jackson saw the snow on its summit. 'I'll be after you,' he said to Father Hamilton, and watched him, a little perturbed and looking behind him, join the parish priest by the gate. Jackson resented being seen by them because he was weeping, and he was a man who despised tears – his own and others'. It was like a miracle, and Father Jackson didn't really believe in miracles. Standing back by the fence to let the last of the mourners pass, he saw the coffin, like gold in the brilliant light, and heard the steadying voices of the four huge mountainy men who carried it. He saw it sway above the heads, shawled and bare, glittering between the little stunted holly bushes and hazels.

READ MORE IN PENGUIN

In every corner of the world, on every subject under the sun, Penguin represents quality and variety – the very best in publishing today.

For complete information about books available from Penguin – including Puffins, Penguin Classics and Arkana – and how to order them, write to us at the appropriate address below. Please note that for copyright reasons the selection of books varies from country to country.

In the United Kingdom: Please write to *Dept. EP, Penguin Books Ltd, Bath Road, Harmondsworth, West Drayton, Middlesex UB7 0DA*

In the United States: Please write to *Consumer Services, Penguin Putnam Inc., 405 Murray Hill Parkway, East Rutherford, New Jersey 07073-2136.* VISA and MasterCard holders call 1-800-631-8571 to order Penguin titles

In Canada: Please write to *Penguin Books Canada Ltd, 10 Alcorn Avenue, Suite 300, Toronto, Ontario M4V 3B2*

In Australia: Please write to *Penguin Books Australia Ltd, 487 Maroondah Highway, Ringwood, Victoria 3134*

In New Zealand: Please write to *Penguin Books (NZ) Ltd, Private Bag 102902, North Shore Mail Centre, Auckland 10*

In India: Please write to *Penguin Books India Pvt Ltd, 11 Community Centre, Panchsheel Park, New Delhi 110017*

In the Netherlands: Please write to *Penguin Books Netherlands bv, Postbus 3507, NL-1001 AH Amsterdam*

In Germany: Please write to *Penguin Books Deutschland GmbH, Metzlerstrasse 26, 60594 Frankfurt am Main*

In Spain: Please write to *Penguin Books S. A., Bravo Murillo 19, 1°B, 28015 Madrid*

In Italy: Please write to *Penguin Italia s.r.l., Via Vittorio Emanuele 45Ia, 20094 Corsico, Milano*

In France: Please write to *Penguin France, 12, Rue Prosper Ferradou, 31700 Blagnac*

In Japan: Please write to *Penguin Books Japan Ltd, Iidabashi KM-Bldg, 2-23-9 Koraku, Bunkyo-Ku, Tokyo 112-0004*

In South Africa: Please write to *Penguin Books South Africa (Pty) Ltd, P.O. Box 751093, Gardenview, 2047 Johannesburg*

PENGUIN MODERN CLASSICS

THE GREEN FOOL
PATRICK KAVANAGH

'Mystic vision ... fantastic humour ... one of the few authentic accounts of life in twentieth-century Ireland' *Irish Press*

Time hardly mattered in the village of Mucker, the birthplace of poet and writer Patrick Kavanagh. Full of wry humour, Kavanagh's unsentimental and evocative account of his Irish rural upbringing describes a patriarchal society surviving on the edge of poverty, sustained by the land and an insatiable love of gossip. There are tales of schoolboy skirmishes, blackberrying and night-time salmon-poaching; of country weddings and fairs, of political banditry and religious pilgrimages; and of farm-work in the fields and kicking mares.

Kavanagh's experiences inspired him to write poetry which immortalized a fast-disappearing way of life and brought him recognition as one of Ireland's great poets.

PENGUIN MODERN CLASSICS

FALCONER
JOHN CHEEVER

'As dynamic and simmering as the atmosphere in prison before a riot'
Sunday Times

Ezekiel Farragut, a college professor and heroin addict hooked on methadone, is sent to Falconer Correctional Facility after murdering his brother. Enclosed in a filthy cell, witness to the day-to-day savagery of the guards and his fellow prisoners – murderers, conmen and thieves – Farragut believes he is one of the living dead.

But although he lives behind bars, no one can imprison his mind. As memories of his traumatic childhood and troubled marriage come flooding back, Farragut must struggle to survive and remain human amid the relentless brutality of Falconer.

'It is rough, it is elegant, it is pure. It is also indispensable if you earnestly desire to know what is happening to the human soul in the USA' Saul Bellow

PENGUIN MODERN CLASSICS

FIRST LOVE AND OTHER NOVELLAS
THE END/ THE EXPELLED/ THE CALMATIVE/ FIRST LOVE

SAMUEL BECKETT

'He is the most courageous, remorseless writer going. He brings forth a body of beauty …' Harold Pinter

Written in 1946, in what he later called 'a frenzy of writing', these four novellas are among the finest substantial works resulting from Beckett's decision to use French as his language of literary composition. Richly humorous, they offer a fascinating insight into preoccupations which remained constant throughout the work of a writer who transformed the art of the novel and contemporary theatre.

The aim of this new edition is to provide, as far as possible, the most accurate texts in English of the novellas.

Edited with an Introduction and Notes by Gerry Dukes

PENGUIN MODERN CLASSICS

DUBLINERS
JAMES JOYCE

'Joyce's early short stories remain undimmed in their brilliance' *Sunday Times*

Joyce's first major work, written when he was only twenty-five, brought his city to the world for the first time. His stories are rooted in the rich detail of Dublin life, portraying ordinary, often defeated lives with unflinching realism. He writes of social decline, sexual desire and exploitation, corruption and personal failure, yet creates a brilliantly compelling, unique vision of the world and of human experience.

'Joyce redeems his Dubliners, assures their identity, and makes their social existence appear permanent and immortal, like the streets they walk' Tom Paulin

With an Introduction and Notes by Terence Brown